Dani Atkins was born in Loth
London. She moved to rural as

'A heart-warming story of love and loss that will stay with you long after the last page' *My Weekly*

'A beautiful romance with a twist' *Woman*

'If you like Jodi Picoult then you'll love *This Love*' *Lovereading*

'Such a beautiful book' *Brewandbooksreview*

'A true celebration of life, family and relationships' *culturefly*

'What a stunningly beautiful love story, I'm bereft that it's over' *RatherTooFondofBooks*

'Heart-breakingly beautiful. A must-read' *blogsbybooksby*

'Flawless' *reabookreview*

'I wholeheartedly recommend this to anyone' *rachelsrandomreads*

'Poignant and heartfelt' *vivavoce*

'A heartbreaker of a book' *handwrittengirl*

While I Was Sleeping

DANI ATKINS

**SIMON &
SCHUSTER**

London · New York · Sydney · Toronto · New Delhi

A CBS COMPANY

First published in Great Britain by Simon & Schuster UK Ltd, 2018
A CBS COMPANY

1 3 5 7 9 10 8 6 4 2

Simon & Schuster UK Ltd
1st Floor
222 Gray's Inn Road
London WC1X 8HB

Simon & Schuster Australia, Sydney
Simon & Schuster India, New Delhi

www.simonandschuster.co.uk
www.simonandschuster.com.au
www.simonandschuster.co.in

A CIP catalogue record for this book
is available from the British Library

Paperback ISBN: 978-1-4711-6593-1
eBook ISBN: 978-1-4711-6594-8

Typeset in the UK by M Rules
Printed and bound by CPI Group (UK) Ltd, Croydon, CR0 4YY

While I Was Sleeping

For Bev,
Whose story inspired this book
And whose courage inspires everyone who meets her

PART ONE

Chapter 1

Maddie

Thirty-eight likes. Not bad for the middle of the day when everyone is supposed to be at work and not browsing on Facebook. I sat back in my chair and took another mouthful of butterscotch latte, no longer worrying about the calories, which was probably unusual for a bride who was only four days away from her wedding.

I scrolled back up to the photograph I had posted earlier. It made me smile. I was sitting in the hair salon, about to go through the final trial run for my big day. Halfway through backcombing my hair the stylist had been called away to take an emergency telephone call, leaving me sitting in a chair beside the window, looking like Wurzel Gummidge on a bad hair day. I couldn't resist. I'd leant down and slid the phone from my bag and taken a quick photo of my reflection in the mirror. *Trying out a new look for the wedding. What do you think?* was the caption I'd added to the photograph. I stared at the image and pincered my fingers to enlarge it, and frowned. I should have taken the time to crop the photo, I realised. I could have cut out the trainee walking towards me with a cup of coffee in hand, and also the burly-looking bald guy in the black leather jacket, staring through the salon's plate-glass window from the pavement. Never mind. It was still amusing.

'You do realise you're a little obsessed, don't you?' Ryan had asked, a few months after we had started dating.

'With you?' I'd asked, looking up at him through long black lashes.

'I hope, with me,' he'd said warmly, threading his fingers through mine. 'But actually I meant with the constant posting of every single moment of your life.'

I had looked at him carefully, making sure that he wasn't genuinely annoyed, but all I could see was the same tender expression that he reserved just for me.

'Not *every* moment,' I said, meaningfully. Ryan's eyes had twinkled mischievously. 'But I *do* work in media,' I'd continued, 'so it could be argued that *not* being active on social media would border on career suicide.'

He'd laughed then and gently removed the phone from my hand. 'Some things are definitely best kept private,' he'd said, pulling me towards him.

Sitting in the coffee house, I smiled at the memory. It was growing uncomfortably warm beside the window, which was bathed in June sunshine, and for a moment I regretted my choice of table, but it had been the only one free. The early lunch crowd had taken all the booths, and the place was busy, as evidenced by the long snaking queue at the counter waiting for take-outs.

I swallowed down my last mouthful of panini, and just for a moment felt a sudden cresting wave of queasiness trying to interrupt my day. I wouldn't let it. I had a list of chores that I was determined to get through and, despite his offer of help, most of them couldn't be shared with my fiancé.

'It's sweet of you to volunteer, but these are down to me. And besides, there's no way you're going to see me in my wedding dress before Saturday. That's assuming they've managed to let out the seams, of course,' I'd added, a tiny frown puckering my brow. 'Otherwise I'm getting married in jeans and T-shirt.'

'You'd still be the most beautiful bride, ever,' he had said loyally as his hand strayed down from my waist to the small, but now visible bump. It hadn't been there when I'd ordered my wedding dress, and I could only hope the team of seamstresses at Fleurs Bridal Gowns were miracle workers and could give me a few more inches of fabric for Saturday. Most of my family were still unaware of our news, and we really didn't want to go public with it until after the wedding.

I glanced at my watch. Fleurs was over on the other side of town, and the tube station was close by. There was no real need to catch a cab, despite my assurances to Ryan that morning that I would do so. A vaguely troubled expression had been etched on the planes and contours of the face I'd grown to love, as he kissed me goodbye at the door. If it hadn't been for a business meeting he couldn't cancel, I doubt he'd have left me that morning. His concern was easy to read as he did a silent appraisal of my colour, which was always pale, but today was only one shade up from alabaster. So much for that bloom of pregnancy that everyone likes to talk about. For the past fourteen weeks I'd looked more like an extra in a vampire movie.

'Perhaps you should take things easy this morning, and go back to bed for a while?' he suggested gently.

That was the moment, the *only* moment, when perhaps I could have rewritten my own future. But I'd felt nothing, no lurking feeling of foreboding, no presentiment of danger, no inkling that events in the next few hours were going to spiral so dramatically out of my control.

'Too much to do,' I replied, winding my arms around his waist for one last hug. 'There's time enough to sleep when you're dead.' I'd said those exact words. I really had.

Although I still had my own flat, I spent practically every night at Ryan's, and as soon as we returned from our honeymoon we planned to start looking for a place to buy. Somewhere with a garden, I mused, lost in an image of the two of us sitting on a lawn, with a tiny version of us gurgling up from a chequered blanket, chubby little legs riding an invisible bicycle in the air. That one would *definitely* be going on Facebook.

That morning had begun no differently than any other.

I'd woken in Ryan's bed, his arms locked tightly around me, as though he was afraid I might inadvertently wander away during the night. My eyes had fluttered open to a room bathed in early morning sunbeams with dancing dust motes, but I had no time to appreciate their warmth, for I was already on my feet and racing for the bathroom. My thoughts were only on that early-morning sprint, which I'd taken to timing. Today I achieved an impressive eight seconds. A 'PB'. I would have congratulated myself, if I hadn't been too busy throwing up at the time.

Ryan's hand had been there moments later, cool against the back of my neck as he held back a thick handful of my long black hair. In his other hand he held a glass of iced water which I gratefully reached for when I was done. Swill, spit, swallow, my new morning mantra. I looked up from my kneeling position and saw his deep blue eyes once again clouded with concern.

'I'm so sorry, Maddie.'

I took the hand he offered, and got to my feet, already feeling loads better. 'Why? *You* didn't make me sick.'

'But I *did* make you pregnant.'

My eyes softened as I inched closer towards him. 'I think we *both* did that.'

Ryan's smile was like a beacon, drawing me in. It was the first thing I'd ever noticed about him. It had lasered across a crowded room at the boring industry event where we'd met. He'd been looking directly at me, this stranger who seemed so inexplicably familiar that I'd almost waved. Instead, I'd glanced awkwardly over my shoulder, certain that the person he was *actually* smiling at would be standing right behind me. But no one was there, and so I'd smiled back. That had been eighteen months ago, and I'd pretty much been smiling every single day since then.

Ryan had joined me beneath the refreshing jets of the shower. My eyes were shut beneath the cascade, which rained on my head like a miniature waterfall, but I'd felt the sudden cool draught of air on my soapy limbs as the door of the cubicle opened and then closed. My vision was blurred by the water, but when it cleared all I could see was him; tall and broad-shouldered, still tanned from the holiday we'd taken in Spain. The holiday from which we'd returned with a far-from-expected souvenir. My hands had slid unconsciously to the small bump that could no longer be disguised beneath my clothes, and was the reason for the last-minute wedding dress alterations. Ryan's fingers tangled with mine, all slippery with soap bubbles as they glided over my belly.

His blond hair had darkened to brown beneath the water. 'Is there room in your busy schedule to add one more item to your agenda?' he'd asked, pulling me gently towards him.

You always remember the *first* time you make love with the person you want to spend the rest of your life with. But the *last* time can somehow just trickle through your fingers, unremarked and without ceremony, like water circling a drain.

*

Off to Fleurs wedding dress shop. Let's hope it fits! I tweeted rapidly as I got to my feet and gathered up my cardigan and the collection of carrier bags I'd accumulated so far that day. Perhaps that's why I failed to notice that I hadn't picked up the most important bag of all, my handbag, which was still hanging over the back of my chair. I'd only gone a hundred metres down the road when I discovered my mistake, and the realisation made my stomach lurch more violently than even the worst bout of morning sickness.

Inside the bag was an envelope containing more cash than I'd ever withdrawn from the bank in my entire life. Even before the cashier's concerned enquiry, I was apprehensive about carrying around so much money. Too late I realised that this was one job that I should definitely have passed to Ryan. This much money should never be entrusted to a woman who was clearly suffering from a prenatal case of 'baby brain'.

I turned and ran back towards the coffee shop, fearfully anticipating the worst-case scenario. How would we pay the caterer, the venue, and the balance on my dress if the money I'd withdrawn from the bank that morning had been stolen? The pavements, which I swear had been empty only moments before, were now strewn with buggy-pushing mothers, meandering tourists stopping to take photographs, and idle window-shoppers. I ran with my head down, like an American footballer in a tackle, and in my panic crashed into a man who was hurriedly emerging from a doorway. My shoulder collided with his, and for a second I teetered on the edge of falling. Suddenly all thoughts of the thousands of pounds dangling temptingly on the back of that chair were swept away by a much larger concern. The baby. If I fell, would I hurt the baby? Luckily after a second or two when it could so easily have gone either way, I regained my balance. I glanced back at the man who'd barged into me – or had I barged into him? Either way, he hadn't bothered to hang around to apologise or see whether or not I'd ended up in a crumpled heap on the pavement. All I could see of him was a broad black-jacketed shape, disappearing down a side street.

The bag was exactly where I'd left it. And although the young couple who were about to occupy the table looked somewhat startled as I charged towards them, all red-faced and out of breath, they smiled benignly and handed over my handbag. They looked quite embarrassed as I thanked them repeatedly between wheezy gasps.

I walked towards the tube station on legs that were still tingling from the unexpected sprint, and kept my handbag securely clamped under one arm as I descended the escalator.

It was only eight stops on the underground, and it was one of the best times of day to be travelling on the tube in the summer. With the trains half empty there was less chance of finding your nose pressed up against the armpit of the one passenger in the carriage who'd forgotten to apply their deodorant that morning.

If the train had been any busier, I would never have noticed him. If I'd brought a book to read, or even my kindle, I would never have been glancing idly up and down the carriage as the train rumbled slowly past the stations. He was sitting on the very end seat by the door, about as far away from me in the carriage as it was possible to get. My eyes went past him the first time, but then some silent trigger woke up in the depths of my brain and a metaphorical light began to flash. *I knew that man, didn't I?*

He was in his forties, heavy-set and stocky, in a way that made it difficult to tell if he'd got like that from hours spent in the gym or the pub. He was wearing heavy Doc Martens boots, but he didn't look like a labourer, because they were immaculately clean. As were his blue jeans and white T-shirt. There were tattoos on both his forearms, but from this distance I couldn't make out their design. *Where did I know him from?*

As though rifling through a file index, I began to flip through the possibilities. Was it through work? I met a lot of people and attended many events, yet somehow he didn't seem to slot comfortably into that category. His appearance seemed more 'raw' than the types I usually met in those circles. For a moment I wondered if I knew him off the TV; there was a definite look of Grant Mitchell from *EastEnders* about him. Almost as if he could sense my eyes on him, the man suddenly straightened in his seat and glanced up. He looked right past the dozen or so people sitting in between us, as his eyes fixed on me. A smile hovered uncertainly on my lips. If I *did* know him from somewhere, and had forgotten him, it was going to be really embarrassing if he recognised me now. But he didn't say anything, or nod, or wave in acknowledgement. His eyes were dark and flat, like a shark's, which I'm sure was just a trick of the weird lighting they have on the tube. Those eyes flickered over me, in that unpleasant assessing way some men do quite unconsciously, and then he looked away, clearly disinterested. He picked up a discarded newspaper from a nearby seat and flicked it open.

I didn't look his way again, because the last thing I wanted to do was engage in another unfortunate locking of our eyes. The first time had felt uncomfortable enough. I pulled the cloak of invisibility, the one that commuters so frequently shroud themselves in, a little more tightly around my shoulders, and dismissed him from my thoughts.

I saw him again as I was exiting the station. He was halfway up the escalator ahead of me. It was a popular destination, and not a huge coincidence that we'd both got off there. As I continued to watch him, he shifted position and then, like a matador with a cape, swept a black leather jacket over one shoulder, dangling it on one finger by its loop. And that's when the penny dropped – well, it felt like lots of pennies actually, as though I'd scored a jackpot on a one-armed bandit. He was the man I'd accidentally photographed and put up on Facebook in my post from the hair salon. I gave myself a small mental pat on the back for finally placing him. *In your face, baby brain*. I was still firing on almost all my cylinders.

I was halfway across the zebra crossing, and could see

the entrance to Fleurs a short distance up ahead, when it occurred to me that in a city as large as London, how weird was it to randomly bump into the same stranger in two different locations?

Thirty anxious minutes later, after breathing in as much as I could possibly do without passing out, my wedding dress successfully zipped up. There was a definite spring in my step as I left Fleurs, despite parting with a sizeable chunk of money to pay the balance. Beneath the soles of my sandals I could feel the heat of the pavement, and the day was now bright enough to make sunglasses a necessity, and not merely a fashion statement. I was in no particular hurry to repeat my underground journey, so decided to walk for a while and then perhaps hop on a bus.

Buying an ice cream cone, complete with a crumbly chocolate flake, seemed like a decadent indulgence, but I did it anyway, taking the quickly dripping cone to a bench tucked away from the main thoroughfare.

I pulled out my phone for another peek at the last photograph I'd taken. It was impossible not to smile as I studied the image I'd captured in the wedding shop changing room. The dress had looked even better on than I'd remembered, and the champagne-coloured silk suited my pale complexion and long dark hair far better than white would have done. As I enlarged the photo, my eyes widened accordingly. Pregnancy had been kind, because I'd never had that kind of cleavage before. I looked down at the scooped neckline of my T-shirt and smiled. 'You can both stay,' I said, then laughed as a passer-by glanced my way enquiringly. I guess sitting on a bench talking to your boobs was a bit eccentric, but what the hell, everything was finally falling into place. It was one of those rare moments of pure unadulterated happiness that flood through you. If my blood was tested right this minute, I bet the endorphin level would be right off the chart.

A group of excitable Japanese tourists walked past, exclaiming delightedly at absolutely nothing at all, as far as I could see, and I smiled at them, because I felt exactly the same. But that smile faltered a moment later as I noticed a figure on the far side of the crowd. He was largely obscured by the rest of the group; there was no way to see anything of him, except a shiny bald pate. There was no reason at all to assume it was the same man whose path had crossed mine twice before that day. For God's sake, there were *thousands* of bald men in the city; it was highly unlikely to be him. Yet all at once some of the joy I'd been feeling began to seep away. The ice cream suddenly seemed too sweet, too sticky, and the chocolate flake was melting unappealingly over the edge of the cone. I threw it into an adjacent waste bin, my appetite abruptly gone.

The phone rang in the palm of my hand, so unexpectedly that I almost dropped it. I checked the number before answering, giving myself a moment or two to smile, because he was a master at hearing even the tiniest nuance of distress in my voice.

'Hi, Dad. How are you?'

'I'm fine, sweetheart. I thought I'd give you a call while I had a free moment. Your mum's just having a quick nap.'

I swallowed the tiny lump in my throat, because he'd hear it otherwise, he always did. Watching Mum, while pretending that he wasn't watching her at all, was an all-consuming pastime. It was practically all he did. And the fact that he only felt able to relax enough to make a telephone call while she slept told me the answer to my next question, but I asked it anyway.

'How is she?'

'Doing much better, I think.' I bit my lip and studied a blue-grey pigeon, which was scratching hopefully by my feet at someone's dropped sandwich crumbs. Dip, peck, swallow. The pigeon's movements were mesmerising and exhausting, as though he neither knew nor cared how long it would take to fill his stomach on crumbs. He just kept on pecking. Much like my father was doing; taking small sharp jabs at the truth, because the whole of it was simply too enormous to stomach.

'That new medication is going to make all the difference. I feel it in my bones,' he declared with confidence.

'I hope so, Dad,' I said quietly. They *were* making astonishing advances with early-onset dementia all the time, although my father's continued positivity was often as exhausting to watch as the pigeon.

'So, how are the wedding preparations going? Are you nearly there yet?'

'Almost,' I said with a smile, thinking of the remaining items on my list, which I really ought to be tackling, instead of sitting in the sun scoffing ice cream.

'If there's anything you want me or your mum to do, you just let us know, okay, Maddie?'

I nodded and cleared my throat, although my eyes were still a little blurred by tears. Mum and I had always loved watching those reality wedding shows on TV. We'd dissect them afterwards, as though critiquing an art-house film. We would ponder on the questionable bridal gowns, the unflattering bridesmaids' outfits, and argue about how many tiers it took to make a wedding cake look tacky. We used to tell ourselves that when it came to *my* wedding, we'd know every potential pitfall to avoid. We'd had years of valuable research, courtesy of those TV shows. Except when the time came to make all those decisions about my big day, Mum wasn't up to doing it any more. A little bit of absentmindedness – the kind of forgetfulness you initially laugh at and make jokes about, grew to the type of condition that suddenly wasn't funny at all. Certainly not after a doctor has put a label on it.

'The only thing you both have to do is check in to the hotel and relax. Then on the day, Mum can sit there and have a good cry while you walk your wobbly-legged daughter up the aisle,' I said.

'You won't have wobbly legs,' my dad said confidently. 'I've never known you more certain about anything than you are about Ryan.'

I smiled, remembering all the scathing comments some of my earlier boyfriends had earned in the past. I'd done my fair share of frog-kissing over the years, before finally finding a prince smiling at me across a crowded room. That my parents loved Ryan almost as much as I did was just the icing on the cake. A three-tiered cake, the perfect number, which Mum would approve of – or at least she would have done.

Dad's call had left me in a reflective mood, which I tried to outpace as I got up from my bench and resumed walking down the street. Today was not about brooding on the things in my life I wished I could change. It was about celebrating the life I was about to live . . . as Mrs Ryan Turner. And even the wait of four days seemed like an annoying and unnecessary delay. I was more than ready for the rest of my life to begin right now.

In an effort to recoup some lost time, I quickened my pace when I heard a familiar rumbling sound down the road behind me. At the bus stop up ahead, I could see people picking up bags, reaching for purses and passes, and shuffling impatiently from foot to foot. I ran the last few metres to the stop, to the accompaniment of the hiss of air brakes. I dropped into a vacant seat by a window, my mind on nothing other than the printer's where I was heading next to collect the table place settings. As the bus progressed in stop-start staccato bursts along its route, I wondered if I'd chosen wisely. For so early in the afternoon there did seem to be an awful lot of traffic on the road. Everywhere

I looked were red buses, black cabs, and intrepid cyclists weaving dangerously between them. I winced as one cut in front of a taxi, hearing the squeal of hastily applied brakes. I saw an angrily waved arm protrude from the cab's window and the muted rumble of obscenities, which was answered by a single-digit response from the cyclist. No harm, but plenty of foul.

I was still watching the traffic when I glanced up and noticed we were once again by the underground station. There was a young ginger-haired man standing beside a newspaper stand, thrusting copies of a freebie paper into commuters' hands, and a small market stall with overpriced apples on a bed of biliously green artificial grass. And beside them, in the shadows, was an indistinct shape. He was standing to one side, careful not to block the entrance, and over one tattooed arm was slung his black leather jacket.

I felt my throat tighten, and swallowing was suddenly something that I had to consciously instruct my muscles to do. *He was waiting for me.* Even as the thought came into my head, I was already dismissing it. Of course he wasn't. I didn't know him, and he didn't know me. It was just one of those weird freaky one-in-a-million coincidences that happen every now and then. So what if we'd both travelled to the same station? That meant nothing. *Do you know how many people must use this station every day?* The sane part of my brain asked the other half; the half that was doing a very poor job at not overreacting. Hundreds, that's how many. Possibly thousands. And yes, it stood to reason if he alighted at that station earlier, then he was going to return to it whenever he was finished doing whatever it was he had to do.

The traffic was still crawling agonisingly slowly. And before I could turn away from the window or switch seats, the bus ground to a temporary halt, directly opposite the station entrance. The man was studying his phone, but at the hiss of the brakes he looked up, and as though he knew *exactly* in which window to find me, his eyes went to mine. This time, I fancied there was a glimmer of recognition in his. He levered himself away from the tiled station wall, and my eyes widened in alarm, as though he'd drawn out a weapon. Frantically I glanced up ahead at the congested traffic as the man began to walk away from the station, and head towards a bus stop, a few hundred metres along the road. There was no one waiting beside it, and I could see that it was a request stop. If none of the passengers wanted to get off, we'd sail straight past it, leaving the menacing man with the leather jacket far behind. But if he got there first, he'd put out his arm and flag us down.

I sat tensely in my seat, too irrationally panicked to look back down the street to see if the bald man was still walking this way. Keep driving, keep going, keep going, I silently urged the bus. Then a young woman with a child's buggy got to her feet and made her way unsteadily towards the exit. I saw the driver look up and notice her in his mirror. The woman seemed anxious and unsure, and when I heard her speak in a heavily accented voice, I realised she was foreign.

She asked something of an elderly man, who shrugged. She turned to a teenage boy, with trailing white headphones plugged into his ears, who either didn't hear, or couldn't be bothered to answer her.

I saw the driver check his rear-view mirror and flick on his indicator, making preparations to pull over. I glanced over my shoulder. A small crowd of people had just emerged from a pub, choking the stream of pedestrians. Was the man among them, pushing his way past to reach the bus stop?

'Eez this hospital stop?' asked the young foreign woman, addressing the bus in general. The driver was slowing down now. We were going to stop; the doors were going to open; and the man who'd been lurking in the shadows waiting for me was going to get on the bus.

'St Margaret's?' queried the driver.

The woman nodded thankfully.

'No love, that's the next stop. Sit back down and I'll tell you when we get there.'

The driver spun the overlarge steering wheel and we moved back into the flow of traffic, which miraculously had suddenly parted, like a biblical sea. We lurched forward, travelling at a speed that was far more coursing hare than sluggish tortoise and when the bus stop approached, we whistled right past it. Only then did I feel confident enough to look back. The man was running, but he'd left it too late. His face looked thunderous as he realised he wasn't going to be able to reach the stop in time. He had missed the bus. He had missed me.

I thought twice before sending the text. It sounded so stupid that I actually deleted it to begin with, only to pull my phone back out several moments later and compose something far less sensational.

Are you still in your meetings?

I knew his phone would be on silent, and that it might take a while before he was able to discreetly check his messages. But only a minute or so passed before my phone vibrated in my sweat-slick hand.

'Fraid so. God, I'm bored. How's your day going? Is it too late to suggest eloping?

I smiled at that one, marvelling at his ability to calm me, even long-distance. This was all down to those pregnancy hormones, it had to be. I wasn't usually a fanciful person. I was used to London; I'd lived here for years. I travelled alone at night and never thought twice about it. I was not nervous or given to exaggeration. So this – admittedly stupid – overreaction had to be down to a combination of pregnancy hormones and pre-wedding jitters. A dangerous alchemy, that was turning a normal, sane, twenty-eight-year-old into a crazy person.

I knew 'lunatic me' was still at the helm, as my fingers flew over my phone's keypad, sending the message the sane part of me had just deleted.

I'm being followed.

There was an agonising pause of two minutes and forty-nine seconds. I timed them. Then his reply flashed up on my screen.

I know, by one thousand, seven hundred and seventy-five people, I believe, at the last count.

I hit several wrong keys as my fingers pounded out my reply.

Not on Twitter. I mean for real. In real life. There's a man who is following me.

Again there was an uncomfortably long wait. Did he think I was joking? Was this something that sounded even remotely funny? I was teetering on the edge of getting angry when my phone didn't blink with a message, it rang.

'Who's following you?' He didn't bother with hello. From his voice I could tell there was no way he wasn't taking this seriously. Strangely, hearing him sound so worried defused some of my anxiety.

'Are you in your meeting?' I had a sudden vision of a roomful of people – many of whom were going to be at our wedding on Saturday – listening in while Ryan's fiancée slowly lost a few of her marbles.

'No, I stepped out. Where exactly are you?'

'On a number 73 bus. We've just turned down Lincoln Street.'

'Is the man on the bus? Has he approached you in any way? What's he done exactly?'

What *had* he done exactly, I thought, already feeling 'crazy me' curling up in a little ball, as though she wanted to hide. This is how you feel when you smash the button on the fire alarm, and then realise nothing was burning after all.

'He's just been in town, that's all,' I began, hearing how lame my answer sounded. I was good with words, but trying to explain a vague and irrational feeling was a lot harder to convey than concrete facts. And what had the man actually done anyway? He'd photo-bombed my hairdresser selfie – probably without realising it. He'd been on the same underground train as me, got out at my stop, and then hung around for something or someone (not necessarily me) at the station. There was no way of knowing he was the man who'd collided with me as I ran back to the coffee shop, or had been among the Japanese tourists. In my head the threat had seemed very real, but coming out of my mouth it was all starting to sound ridiculous.

'So he didn't do or say anything to you at all?'

'No. Nothing.'

'Didn't threaten you, or do anything intimidating?'

I felt about as stupid as it was possible to feel, without curling up and dying of embarrassment. 'No, he did nothing. I'm sorry, hon, I'm just being daft. Ignore me and go back to your meeting,' I said into the phone, aware that our conversation was being listened to by several of my fellow passengers.

'Where are you heading to next?'

'To the printer's, but—'

'I'll meet you there.'

'No, Ryan. It's okay. I was being silly. There's no need to walk out of work. You said these meetings were important.'

'*You're* important,' he corrected, and I knew from his voice that there was no way I would be able to talk him out of this. And just like that, I fell in love with him all over again.

'Go straight to the printer's and wait for me there,' he said, breaking the connection before I could say thank you, or more importantly 'I love you'. But I was pretty sure he knew that anyway.

Despite knowing that Ryan was on his way, I kept fidgeting anxiously in my seat as the bus meandered through the early-afternoon traffic. I twisted around frequently, trying to catch a glimpse of the road behind us, but my view was blocked by a bus travelling so closely behind ours, the bumpers must have practically been touching. It was right behind us; travelling the same route.

All at once the fear came back as I saw that it too was a number 73, which meant that if the man *was* following me, he could be just metres behind us. I squinted into the shadowy depths of the second bus, but it was impossible to see anything in the darkened interior. Fresh concern was painted all over my features like tribal markings as I swivelled back to face the front. The man had missed *this* bus, but there was no doubt in my mind that he'd caught the one that had followed only moments later. The bald man with the leather jacket was *still* right behind me, and when I got off the bus in ten minutes' time, he would too. I just knew he would.

I was up and waiting by the doors long before the bus had slowed down. I wasn't exactly sure how far the printer's was from the bus stop, as I'd only been there once before. But, if I moved quickly, I could get a head start before the second bus had even come to a stop. I hopped down onto the pavement, and began to weave purposefully through the oncoming crowds. I lost count of how many '*Excuse me*'s I muttered as I slalomed between slow-moving pedestrians like a dog on an agility course. I glanced back only once and saw that the second bus had now reached the stop and had spilled out its passengers onto the pavement. My heart began thudding uncomfortably in my chest and I increased my pace. The printer's was only a few shopfronts away, and no marathon runner could have felt more jubilant crossing the finishing line as I did running up to the two plate-glass doors.

I didn't see the note fixed onto the inside of the glass by four fat blobs of Blu-Tack, and wasted valuable seconds repeatedly trying to open a door that was obviously locked. Eventually I looked up and read the scrawled words written in thick black marker pen on a piece of A4 paper: *Back in 5 minutes.*

I pivoted on my heel and saw the man who'd been haunting me all day working his way through the crowds towards me. My hand went to my throat and the speed of my racing pulse beneath my palm concerned me. I'd never had a panic attack in my entire life, but I had a feeling that situation could well be about to change in the next few minutes. I shrank back against the locked double doors. The entrance was flanked on either side by tall conifers in deep terracotta pots. There was a small possibility that the man hadn't seen me yet. Was it better to stay where I was and hope he wouldn't spot me, or should I keep moving?

My decision – the worst decision of my entire life – was ill-thought-out and hurried, which is weird because, when I remember what happened, it all seemed to be playing in slow motion. I elected to keep going. On the opposite side of the road was a restaurant with huge picture windows. I would wait in there until Ryan arrived at the printer's to meet me, I decided.

It wasn't until I stepped back onto the pavement that I realised how badly I had misjudged how fast the man following me was moving. He was now no more than five metres away. I gasped, knowing too late that I had played this all wrong.

'Hey you!' he called out. It was the first time I had heard him speak, and his voice was surprisingly mellifluous and deep. 'Wait,' he added.

Yeah, like that's going to happen, I thought, turning and starting to run.

'Hey!' he called again, but I didn't turn back around. I thought I could hear the sound of footsteps, heavy booted footsteps, on the pavement behind me, but that might just have been my imagination.

I looked across the four lanes of traffic at the restaurant on the other side of the road and blinked for a moment, as though witnessing a mirage in the desert. A black cab had just pulled up at the kerb, and Ryan was emerging from within it. He was busy pulling notes from his wallet to pay the driver, and hadn't yet seen me. The traffic was busy and constant, and I doubt he would have been able to hear me over the width of the road, but I called out his name anyway.

A gust of wind whipped a crumpled ten-pound note from Ryan's outstretched hand and it fluttered down to the gutter at his feet, costing further precious seconds as he bent to retrieve it. Out of the corner of my eye I could see an approaching black shape getting ever closer. I was about to get mugged on a busy London street, right in front of the man I loved, and there wasn't a single thing he'd be able to do to save me.

'Hey!' the man cried out one last time, now sounding seriously pissed-off with me. But I had no intention of hanging around to make things any easier for him. I saw a small gap between the oncoming cars, hesitated for a split second, and then leapt forward as though jumping nimbly into a skipping-rope game. But this was no children's playground. The startled expression on the driver's face darkened as he applied his brakes. A horn blared in a long angry bleat from a car in the adjacent lane, and I jerked rapidly out of its path. It came so close I could feel the heat of its engine against my back, like the breath of a thwarted dragon. Behind me, the man with the bald head was shouting something, but I couldn't make out what he was saying, because all I could hear was Ryan calling out my name from the other side of the road.

'Maddie!' I turned and began to run towards him and everything he represented: home, safety, and sanctuary. 'MADDIE!' This time there was a different note in his voice, which sounded an awful lot like terror. I looked at him and his mouth was open wide and he was screaming something. And weirdly the bald man behind me was doing exactly the same thing. And because he was much closer than Ryan, I could hear him far more easily.

'Watch out! For Christ's sake, watch out!'

I turned towards him. One of his arms was waving madly. He looked quite distraught, I remember thinking, and what was that in his hand? It looked remarkably like my cardigan, which I didn't even know I'd dropped.

It was the man's flat dark eyes I was staring into in those final seconds. If I could rewrite one single moment of that day, I would turn my head so that it was Ryan's I was looking into when it happened. I think that might have made it a little more bearable.

It was over in an instant. One moment I was standing in the middle of the road, and the next I was flying upwards through the air. I saw sky and then pavement and then bizarrely, sky again. I saw a huge wall of white – the bonnet of the van that had hit me – coming up fast as I fell back down upon it. Oddly I felt no pain as I bounced bonelessly onto the metal, as limp as a rag doll. Even hitting the windscreen and hearing the crackle of shattering safety glass failed to register. I slithered in a fluid confusion of broken limbs back onto the surface of the road. I saw sky again and a moment later a circle of faces, but their features were covered in blood, so much blood. Someone was screaming my name, but they sounded like they were doing so from the end of a very long tunnel. The world was shrinking as the faces became harder to see. I blinked and more blood fell into my eyes, and then everything went quiet and very, very, dark.

Chapter 2

I was in a tunnel; a long, dark, deep tunnel. A whole underground network of tunnels, in fact. They twisted and turned like a maze. Sometimes I thought I caught a fleeting glimpse of light filtering through the darkness, but for the most part it was a perfectly black, inky void. Sounds pierced the perpetual velvet hum of silence: sometimes voices; sometimes loud clattering noises that I couldn't place. Often I could hear my name. Sometimes it was whispered, at others it came out on a sob. On several occasions it was shouted, almost cruelly. But the delivery of the words made no difference, for I was powerless to reply.

Often I heard my mother. Strangely her voice was the clearest and the most lucid of them all. She told me to hold on; that I wasn't alone, and that she was with me. She urged me to keep walking through the darkness until I could find my way back. Back from where? Where was I? Hands touched me. Sometimes roughly, sometimes in a caress. That

30

surely had to be Ryan? I would recognise the feel of his skin against mine anywhere. Other sensations were far less pleasant. There was pain. So much pain. At times it felt as though I was drowning in it; fighting to kick up to reach a surface that never materialised. Everything hurt until I wasn't sure how much more of it I could take and then – unbelievably – there came even more. It felt as though my stomach had been gripped by an angry giant who was slowly twisting it over and over, like a rag being wrung out. The pain was too much, the tunnels were too tempting, I fled back down into them and didn't come up for a very long time.

I was swimming beneath ice. It should have felt cold, but instead the water was warm, and encompassing, like a cocoon. This must be what it feels like in the womb, I thought, and something about that idea bothered me. I tried to hold onto it, but it kept slipping away, as elusive to grasp as a handful of smoke. I moved on a current of nothingness, looking up through a thick opaque layer which had mysteriously turned from black to grey. Up ahead the grey became lighter. Limbs that had felt no pain for a very long time suddenly began to ache. *Stay away from that place*, warned my brain. '*Go towards it, Maddie*,' urged my mother from somewhere in the dark far below me.

I could see a long snaking fissure fracturing the ice above me. I reached up and touched it with my fingertips. It felt sharp and dangerous, and yet I continued to propel myself forward, following it. I moved in total silence, although from somewhere unseen there came a low rumble of sound, like an invisible avalanche. A single shard of light pierced the grey, pierced everything. Like Excalibur scything through the water, it punctured the unbreakable. Light radiated from it, and suddenly I was scrabbling beneath the ice towards it, afraid it would disappear at any moment.

Staying would be so easy, I knew that. I could sink back down to the place where the ice was thick, or I could push against the crack. Because it would break, I knew that it would, all I had to do was push. Push. Push. The instruction filled my head like a long-forgotten memory. My hands were on the ice, my back was arched and I pushed through the frozen barrier.

'Mum!'

Someone shrieked. It wasn't me. I didn't have the strength, breaking through had drained me.

Something fell, or was dropped. I heard a crash and then the sound of breaking china or glass.

'Oh dear God, I can't believe it. You're awake! You're awake!' exclaimed a voice I didn't recognise.

'Mum?' this time my voice was hesitant and unsure. My mother was back in the black void, urging me onward. Whoever this stranger was, with her hands suddenly upon my face, it wasn't her. With an effort that almost broke me, I instructed my eyes to open. They did so reluctantly, as though they'd forgotten how. To begin with I saw nothing. Then gradually my retinas began to awaken from their long hibernation. Shadows separated and my brain slowly began to recall how to process the images it was receiving. A figure hovered over me, I couldn't make out who it was, or what she was saying. I knew they were words, but they sounded foreign, garbled, and incredibly excitable. It took several moments for me to realise it was because she was crying.

The hand that had been touching my face dropped to grip mine where it was lying on something scratchy. A blanket? Was I in a bed? If so, it wasn't mine. I had no idea where I was and suddenly I was very afraid. Perhaps she saw something in my eyes, because suddenly my hand was crushed beneath her fingers, so hard it almost hurt.

'Oh no, you don't, Maddie. You stay with us now. You stay with us!' Never releasing her hold, she reached over and pressed something on the wall. My eyes were suddenly fluttering again, the lids were closing. Even as they shut I could hear the woman begin to shout out into the darkened room, clearly too impatient or unwilling to wait for whoever it was she had summoned. 'She's awake! She's awake! Madeline Chambers is awake!'

It was some time later before my eyes opened again. The room I was in was dark, lit only by a single low-wattage lamp. There was a distinct smell in the air, which took me longer than it should have done to place. Antiseptic. I knew then, without asking, that I was in a hospital. What I didn't know, was why.

The soft swish of leather on linoleum alerted me that I wasn't alone. A nurse – different from the one before – hurried over to the bed. My vision was still blurred and unfocused, so when she leant over me, her face was surrounded by a glowing nimbus of light. She looked like an angel on a Christmas card.

'What happened to me?' I asked. My voice sounded hoarse and croaky, as though each word had fought its way out from beneath thick flakes of rust.

Was it my imagination, or did she hesitate before replying? 'You were involved in an accident, Madeline. You're in St Margaret's hospital.'

St Margaret's? Hadn't I'd heard someone asking about that earlier today? The memory was vague and kept twisting out of my grasp every time I reached out for it. I returned to the nurse's bewildering statement, and slowly shook my head, certain she was mistaken. I couldn't remember anything. 'An accident? No, I ... I don't think so,' I said, my voice small and hesitant. From absolutely nowhere an image of a black leather jacket torpedoed through the fog in my head. I had no idea why.

Fragments of memories began floating down, like tantalising balloons released from a netted ceiling. They dangled above my head, just out of reach. One exploded with a loud and startling bang as I grabbed hold of it. 'Ryan?' I gasped, my voice a panicked question. 'Where's Ryan?' My head twisted on the starchy pillow, as though unable to believe he was not here with me. But the room held no one except the nurse and me. The visitor's chair beside the bed was empty. 'My fiancé ... is he here?'

The nurse's face was suddenly a mask, a professional latex

rubber thing, which revealed nothing. She cleared her throat slightly before answering me, I think I'll always remember that. 'He was here, but he had to leave.'

'Why? Where has he gone?' Ryan would *never* leave me alone, scared and injured, unless he'd been hurt in the same accident. Was that the thing the nurse was doing such a poor job of hiding from me? Because it was clear she wasn't telling me everything. Her face was too full of sympathy, and there was something in her eyes that scared me. Why couldn't I remember anything? 'Is he . . . is he hurt?'

The nurse answered none of my questions, but instead turned to the door. 'I'm going to find one of the duty doctors to talk to you,' she explained, clearly anxious to summon reinforcements. What was it they weren't telling me?

She looked back just once, before slipping out into the hospital corridor. She chewed on her lower lip before speaking. 'Your fiancé wasn't involved in the accident. He's fine. But he went home a while ago. I know he's been phoned and told that you're awake. I'm sure he'll be back soon.'

I flopped back on the pillows, temporarily comforted. Ryan was coming back. Everything would soon be all right.

While I waited in the dark for my world to be restored to order, I tried to make sense of the little I'd been told so far. I'd been in an accident, they said. And they must be right, for why else would I be in hospital? But what were my injuries? Very slowly I lifted one arm from the mattress. It felt stiff and heavy, as though the bones within it had been turned to lead. But apart from that, it appeared to work. One by one I conducted an inventory of my limbs. They all ached, and moving them – even the smallest amount – was exhausting. But they weren't bandaged, or encased in plaster. So no bones were broken. Very slowly I lifted one hand and allowed my fingers to explore my face and head. Someone had taken the time to braid my long hair into a plait, which seemed an odd thing to do, but apart from that, everything felt completely normal.

In the quiet of the hospital room, sleep eventually dragged me back under, and with it came dreams; weird dreams that made no sense. I was in a shop, buying something important. A cardigan, I think. And I was worried because no one could find my handbag, and how could I pay for anything if my money was gone? Then everything suddenly shifted, the way it does in dreams, and I was sitting in a hairdresser's chair, but when the stylist instructed me to look in the mirror, the reflection staring back at me was the stuff of nightmares. I had no hair, none at all. I was completely bald.

I gasped myself awake, my hand instinctively going to the plait, even though I could feel it perfectly well behind my neck. Long purple fingers of light were clawing through the dawn sky. I must have been asleep for hours, and if the doctors had come to my room, they had chosen not to wake me.

From the corridor I could hear the sound of approaching footsteps, which slowed and then eventually stopped just outside my door. I could hear a soft murmur of two voices. One was deep and gruff and unfamiliar, but the other was the only one in the world that mattered to me. My head was already turned towards the door as it opened, my heart yearning for him so much it felt like a physical ache. Ryan entered the room behind the doctor and then just rocked on his feet and froze. My tentative smile of greeting faltered before dying on my lips. He looked dreadful. Even in this poor light it was easy to see that my accident had devastated him. His hair was dishevelled, as though he'd run his hands through it a thousand times on his way to my bedside. And his eyes were tormented, as though they knew a pain I couldn't begin to imagine. And then, suddenly, the lock holding back my memories slid open. I saw the street, I saw the bald-headed man holding my cardigan, and at the final moment, when it was too late to avoid the inevitable, I saw the fast-approaching van.

I cried out from my hospital bed, my hand flailing through the air towards my fiancé, and yet for a moment he still hesitated. There was sorrow on his face, and a look of loss and grief. With a sickening lurch I suddenly knew why. My hand flew to my stomach and I ran it hurriedly from one jutting hip bone to the other and back again, following the path the sonographer had taken, gliding across my skin on a slippery coating of gel. My stomach was now flat – no, worse than that – it was concave. The bump was gone. I was crying by the time Ryan finally reached the bedside. I turned to him in heartbroken anguish, the question that needed no answer forcing its way past my trembling lips. 'The baby? Ryan, where's the baby? Did I lose our baby?'

He gathered me into his arms, cradling me against the familiar warmth and smell of him. He held me so tightly that the buttons of his shirt, one which I couldn't ever remember seeing him wear before, made small indents in my cheek. We were both crying, and dimly I was aware of the doctor murmuring something, and then discreetly backing out of the room. I was glad when he went, although Ryan looked considerably less so.

Very gently, as though I was made of spun glass, Ryan lowered me back onto the pillows and perched on the very edge of the visitor's chair. He looked like a runner, waiting on the blocks for the crack of the pistol.

'How are you feeling, Maddie?' he asked, his voice scarcely more than a whisper.

'Like I've been hit by a truck,' I said. I wasn't trying to be funny. Because there was no humour or amusement to be found in this tragedy. The baby we hadn't planned for, but which we had dearly wanted, was gone. And although I knew he would never say it, the weight of guilt fell firmly on my shoulders. I had been negligent. I had been entrusted with something so precious that it could never be replaced, and I had lost it. Me. I had done that.

And yet, my response to Ryan's question was inaccurate, because I *didn't* feel as though I'd been in an accident. I should be in plaster, or traction. I should be bloodied and bruised and in pain. I deserved to be, for I had done this to myself and our baby in one stupid unthinking moment. No wonder Ryan could scarcely bear to continue holding me in his arms.

'I'm not even injured. How is that possible? I remember the van, I remember it hitting me, and then being thrown through the air.'

Ryan groaned, and when I looked at him, tears were streaming down his cheeks. He reached for my hand and the familiarity of his fingers entwined with mine, felt like coming home. 'It was the worst moment of my life. It's in every one of my nightmares. I will never, ever, be able to erase that moment when all I could hear was your scream and then the sound of the van ploughing into you. By the time I got to your side, I was convinced you were dead . . . and I wanted to go with you. I couldn't bear the thought of living for a single minute longer without you.'

Something small in my heart tore away from its moorings at the remembered panic in his voice. 'That you were still alive was a miracle. The paramedics, the doctors, everyone said that it was. I believed it then; and when they called me in the middle of the night to say you had woken up, I believed it again.'

My thumb ran across his hand and knuckles, sweeping backwards and forwards in a caress. There was something about his skin that felt strange; it was hot and dry as though he was coming down with the flu or something. And there was something else, something he'd said that was bothering me. My head was beginning to ache, but I dug deeper, probing to uncover whatever it was that had troubled me.

Beyond, in the corridor, I could hear the rattle of a tea

trolley and the casual sounds of morning greetings and laughter. The sun had crept a little higher, and a few watery rays were slanting through the window. It was going to be another perfect June day. *Or was it?*

'We'll have to cancel the wedding. I don't think we can go ahead now, do you? It wouldn't be right. I think we need to postpone it, to give us time to grieve properly about losing the baby.'

I had lived through many moments with Ryan: happiness; joy; passion; even anger on a few volatile rows, whose only merit was their spectacular reconciliations. But the expression on his face and in his eyes, the pity that oozed out of every single pore in his body as he looked at me, was new and unchartered territory. It was somewhere I had never been, and never wanted to visit.

Ryan's eyes locked on mine, willing me to work out my own truth. I could tell from his face he would rather do anything than say the actual words.

'But we don't have to cancel the wedding, do we?'

Very slowly, as though he was at least three decades older in age, he shook his head.

'Because . . . you've already done it.'

He made a sound, which I took to mean yes. It was hard to tell. The sun was now flooding through the window. The day was promising to be a scorcher, hotter than you'd expect for June.

'What date is it today?'

Ryan shook his head. He didn't speak, although his body

language was positively screaming out for me not to ask him that question.

'Ryan. Look at me. What is today's date?'

He didn't meet my eyes when he answered. Perhaps that was just too much for him to bear. 'It's the tenth of August,' he replied brokenly.

Seven weeks – seven and a half, to be entirely accurate. How was that possible? How could I have lost the last fifty-two days of my life? I could now remember the day of the accident, every last detail, it had all come back. But the weeks I had lost lying in this hospital bed were gone, forever. As completely and totally as the child I'd been carrying.

Panic and confusion raced through me as I stared blindly around the impersonal hospital room, looking for something – anything – to dispute a truth that I could no longer avoid. This, at least, explained Ryan's absence from my bedside, and that of my parents. The vigil he and my family must have lived through immediately following the accident, was now many weeks in the past.

'My parents? Are they okay? Have they been told that I'm awake?'

Ryan nodded, although the grim look still lingered around his eyes, making him appear oddly older. 'They were phoned before I was. I spoke to your dad before I left. He's going to get here as soon as he can.'

The omission was too obvious to go unnoticed. 'He's coming alone?'

Ryan spoke slowly, as though carefully selecting and discarding certain words before formulating his reply. 'Your mum has had a bit of a ... setback ... since your accident,' he eventually supplied, tightening his grip on my hands as though to protect me from the guilt he knew I would feel. But I felt it anyway. As weak and tired as I was, I still recognised a euphemism when I heard one.

'How much of a setback? What happened? Is she all right?'

'I'll let your dad explain it properly,' Ryan said, glancing anxiously towards the door, as though anticipating an interruption. It was only then that I realised he was clearly hoping there would be one. For a man who wanted to spend the rest of his life with me, he seemed suddenly very anxious in my company.

'Is there something else, Ryan? Something you're not telling me? Has it got anything to do with my injuries?'

He shook his head, but he was a poor liar. He always had been.

'No, nothing,' he said, although his jaw looked inexplicably tight. 'You know I should probably let you get some rest now. They warned me I wouldn't be allowed to stay for long. They have tests they need to run now you're ... back.'

He made it sound as though I'd been on a journey. Perhaps the seven-week absence felt that way to him, but to me it was just the next morning.

'I'd rather you stayed with me. Can't you stay?' I sounded like a frightened child on their first day at school.

I tried to tell myself I didn't notice him hesitate, but of

course I did. I knew his face almost as well as the one that stared back at me in the mirror each morning. I had always been able to read him. I'd even known he was going to propose on the night when he did, at least half an hour before he finally managed to get the words out. So I didn't need to ask him how tough the past seven weeks had been for him, the answer was etched on his face, in the small grooves fanning out from his eyes that hadn't been there before.

'For a while,' he said, lifting our joined hands to his lips and gently kissing my knuckles. That was when it first occurred to me that he'd not kissed me, not once, since the moment he had entered my room.

After weeks spent in darkness, the August sun felt uncomfortably bright to my eyes as it streamed through the glass. Ryan had gone to the window, and had his back to me as he worked on untangling the knotted cord of the blinds, with far more concentration than the task probably required. Suddenly he turned back to face me, and I was shocked to see that once again he was close to tears.

'I've missed you so much, Maddie.'

My heart ached, for the pain he'd been through because of me. 'I'm sorry. I'm back now.'

He nodded, but said nothing, and all at once I felt like I was missing something. Something important. He released the blind and it fell with a noisy clatter down to the sill, plunging us both back into the shadows. Ryan crossed back to the bed, walking stiffly in small jerky steps. This time he ignored the visitor's chair, and perched instead on the edge of the mattress. Very gently, he reached out his hand for a tendril of my hair that had escaped from the plait, and wound it around his finger. He'd always loved my long dark hair, teasing me that when I slept with it splayed out on his pillows, I looked like Sleeping Beauty. How ironic those words had turned out to be. He studied the dark strand which he'd wound around his wedding finger like a ring. 'I missed doing this.' Suddenly I was crying too, and I had no idea why. I had a dreadful premonition that he was about to say something I really didn't want to hear.

'You'll never know how much I wish it had been *me* the van had hit, and not you. Because if it had been me, I wouldn't—'

'Madeline,' said a nurse, speaking even before the door to my room was fully open. 'We need to take you up to Neurology now.'

I looked desperately at Ryan, urging him to finish whatever it was he'd been about to say. But his eyes were shuttered more securely than the blinds on the window. He got to his feet and stood back as the nurse and the orderly, who'd been right behind her, released my hospital bed from its bay. Together they performed the NHS equivalent of a three-point turn and positioned the bed in line with the doorway.

'Can my fiancé come with us?' I asked. Ryan was standing behind the bed, out of my field of vision, but I saw the nurse's eyes go to him. No one spoke, but I felt as though there had been a silent conversation between them, which I hadn't been a part of.

'I'm sorry, I'm afraid that's against the regulations. But you can see him later when we bring you back down.'

Ryan leant over the side of the bed, his lips fleeting as they kissed the top of my head.

'You won't leave?' I asked anxiously, reaching for his hand. His fingers squeezed mine reassuringly, and again there was something about the feel of his hand that bothered me.

'I won't leave yet, I promise.'

I would have been so much happier I thought miserably, as the bed was trundled along a wide green corridor towards the waiting lift, if that last sentence hadn't included the word *yet*.

Tests. Scores and scores of tests. Some required my active participation; others required me to do nothing except lie there, completely immobile. They were the easy ones, because I'd had seven weeks of practice at those. Infuriatingly, the medical team carrying out the examinations told me nothing. I had no idea if the readings on their monitors relayed good news or bad.

One of the worst moments had come when the nurse had eased back the bed covers to transfer me into a wheelchair. I'd looked down, genuinely horrified, at the two stick-thin legs protruding from my hospital gown, as though they belonged to someone else. All I could see was the vivid outline of the bones, and so much wasted muscle. Gingerly I'd reached down to touch my thigh, my hand recoiling in horror at how close the bone felt beneath the skin.

'Don't you go worrying about that, now,' comforted the nurse kindly. 'We'll soon have you moaning that you can't fit into your favourite skinny jeans.' Despite the levity in her words, there was a depth of understanding in the way she laid her hand on my shoulder, and squeezed it gently. 'You've been having some pretty full-on physiotherapy while you were ... asleep, to keep everything working properly.' My smile was small and twisted at her euphemism. 'And that's going to continue every day until we have you back on your feet again. *Literally,*' she finished, with an encouraging smile. 'For the time being, you're just going to have to be patient.'

I wondered if that was a little bit of hospital wordplay humour, but realised sadly that it probably wasn't. That was the moment when I first understood I was likely to have to remain in hospital for some time to come. My accident, and the weeks spent in a coma afterwards, were not the kind of thing a person springs back from quickly. The summer wedding Ryan and I had so carefully planned might now very well have to be a winter one, I acknowledged.

'So how did I do?' I asked the nurse, as we descended in the lift back to my own ward. 'Those doctors were like poker players; I couldn't tell if my answers or responses were right or wrong.' The nurse took her hand off the bed frame and squeezed my fingers. My lack of strength as I attempted to return her grip, illustrated how wiped-out the tests had left me. Newborn kittens had more strength than I felt capable of summoning up.

'There are no such things as right or wrong answers here,

Madeline. No one is trying to trick you, or catch you out. All everyone wants is for you to get better as quickly as possible and go home. We're all on the same team.'

I smiled tiredly and looked up into her warm and open, freckled face. 'It's Maddie,' I corrected softly. 'That's what my friends call me.' Oddly, I knew without asking that this woman was deeply invested in me and my care. I wondered if it was possible to bond with someone, even if technically you were lost in the depths of a coma at the time. I certainly felt an inexplicable closeness to someone I'd only just met.

'Have you been my nurse the whole time I've been here?'

'Goodness me no,' she said. 'I've only been on this ward for—' she broke off suddenly, and the cloud of freckles on her cheeks disappeared beneath a deep pink flush. She gave a small frown, as though working out a particularly tricky anagram. When she looked back at me there was a degree of carefulness in her reply. 'I've been helping to look after you for a little while now.'

The lift pinged, announcing we had reached our floor, and there was a definite expression of relief in her eyes as the doors slid open. 'Let's get you back to your room now,' she said, straightening my already perfectly straight blankets, and twitching my pillow into place. 'You need to get some rest.' She was right, I did.

Ryan wasn't in my room when I returned from Neurology, and his absence bothered me far more than I cared to admit. I felt cut off and adrift without him. At my request the friendly nurse obligingly looked for both my bag and phone in the bedside locker, but neither could be found.

'I imagine your parents or your fiancé took them home for safekeeping,' she declared, pushing the door of the cabinet firmly closed.

I flopped back on the starchy pillows, totally exhausted. It was a struggle to keep my eyes open, one which I suspected I would very soon lose.

'I wish Ryan was here. I really need him now.'

'I know you do,' the nurse soothed, and the understanding note in her voice wrapped around me like a warm blanket, which I wore all the way back to unconsciousness.

The blinds had been opened, and the sun was now much lower in the sky. The door to my room was also open, and I could see Ryan standing in the hallway beyond, deep in conversation with a white-coated doctor. I called out his name, and he turned around just a little too quickly to disguise the look of anxiety on his face. He was still rearranging his features as he strode quickly back into my room, the doctor two steps behind him.

'You weren't here,' I said, my voice croaky and more pathetic than I was happy to hear.

'I know. I'm sorry. I was talking to the doctors, and I also spoke to your dad,' he said. I felt like a sheep that had been effectively nudged in the right direction by an experienced border collie. 'He's run into some major delays on the road, but hopes to be here before too much longer.'

And then you're going to want to leave. I had no idea where that thought had come from. But it rang so loudly with the clamour of truth, that for a moment I thought I'd said the words out loud. But Ryan was still looking at me with an expression of tender concern, so I guessed that I hadn't.

'My phone isn't here,' I said, apropos of nothing. It was something I had noticed in the hours since I'd woken up. It was as though my brain had taken too much rest over the last seven weeks, and had forgotten the routes and pathways it should navigate in a conventional conversation.

Surprisingly, Ryan threw back his head and laughed so heartily that the doctor looked on in bemusement. 'I can't believe I'd forgotten your obsession with your mobile phone. What were you planning on doing? Posting a quick tweet from your hospital bed?'

I looked up at him, and for a fleeting moment it was like looking at someone I didn't know. 'I wanted it to phone you,' I said, sounding hurt. 'You weren't here when they brought me back.'

Instantly the humour on his face dried up. 'I'm sorry, Maddie. I wasn't far away.' It wasn't really a satisfactory answer, but apparently it was the only one I was going to get. I was still feeling vaguely unsettled and wrong-footed by his reaction. Was it because he had laughed at me? I honestly didn't think that was the problem. One of the first things that had drawn us together had been our shared sense of humour. Laughter had always featured strongly in our relationship. So what *was it* that was bothering me? The answer came to me in a rush, like a carriage breaking free from a runaway train. It was the comment he'd made about my phone, about how he'd *forgotten* the way it was very much a part of who I was.

'Your phone battery would be dead by now,' Ryan said, his face sober. 'And I think it was probably damaged in the accident anyway.'

'Is it at your place with my other things? There was still quite a lot of cash left in my handbag.'

There was a genuine blank look on his face, as though the thousands of pounds that I'd withdrawn from our joint account on the day of the accident had been forgotten. I could only put his distraction down to the sombre conversation he and the doctor had been having in the hallway. It didn't take a genius to work out that they had surely been discussing my condition.

As if I had prompted an actor who'd forgotten his lines, the doctor began to speak: 'Madeline, I've been going through the initial tests you underwent this morning, and I have to tell you the results are, quite frankly, nothing less than astonishing. To have gone from where you were to this highly responsive and cognitive state is, well . . .' The doctor looked almost embarrassed by his own exuberance. 'Well, to be honest, it's like nothing anyone here has ever seen before. Obviously there's still a very long road ahead to get you back to full strength, and we're going to need to monitor you very closely, but I'm confident that with persistence, hard work, and patience' – there was that word again – 'we should be able to achieve what at one time we had thought would be truly impossible.'

Impossible. The word frightened me. Had my life actually been hanging in the balance after the accident? Ryan was shifting a little uncomfortably from one foot to the other. I'd only ever seen him do that once before, on the night we had gone round to my parents' house, shortly after he had proposed. 'I should have asked him first, you know,' he'd muttered as we stood shoulder-to-shoulder on my parents' porch, waiting for the front door to be opened.

'He's not going to mind. He'll just be glad you're taking me off his hands. He probably thought they'd be lumbered with me for life.'

'I'm sure he did, Miss Austen,' Ryan quipped, giving me a brief kiss, as we heard the sound of approaching footsteps. 'I'm only marrying you for your dowry, you know,' he teased.

'Boy, did *you* back the wrong horse,' I joked, as my father eventually opened the door.

I smiled a little sadly at the old memory, while behind the doctor my fiancé continued to fidget. Something was really bothering him. There was something he and the doctor had been discussing; something that, for reasons known only to them, they had decided I didn't need to be told. Except that I did. Because I already suspected what it was.

'Doctor, the baby I lost—'

Ryan made a small sound, and I knew then how much

losing our unborn child had affected him. Perhaps he felt it even more deeply than me, because initially his excitement at the pregnancy had been so much greater than my own. I felt guilt twist through me. Was this my punishment? To have lost the baby that, to begin with, I hadn't realised how much I wanted? But my reluctance had only been short-lived. I had quickly come around to the idea, and in the end we'd both been equally thrilled at the prospect of becoming parents.

'I understand everything you're saying about having to let my body recover from the accident and the coma. But can you tell us how long we need to wait before we try again?'

'Maddie,' there was an almost pleading note in Ryan's voice.

'Erm . . .'

'Obviously, I know these things take time. But, well, I don't want to wait too long. How long would you recommend that we leave it?'

'Maddie, we really don't need to talk about this right now.'

I turned back to the doctor, who looked like a man desperate for his pager to go off and summon him somewhere else, *right now*.

'A month? Two months?' I persisted. The doctor looked awkwardly at Ryan and then back to me.

'What? What is it that you're not saying here? Everything is okay, isn't it? I *can* still have children?'

The doctor nodded slowly. 'As far as we can tell, yes, you can. That should be perfectly possible.'

The relief swept through me like a tidal wave. 'Thank

God for that. I was getting a little panicky then.' I gave a small laugh, hoping that one of the two men in the room might join in. But neither did.

'I suppose being in a coma for seven weeks must be an unusual complication. Will we need to take that into consideration before trying for another baby?'

'I can't do this,' burst out Ryan. He ran his hand through his hair and looked at the doctor, as though seeking permission for something.

'What?' I cried. 'Ryan, what is it? I don't understand.' But I was talking to his retreating back as he strode swiftly out of the room. 'Where are you going?' I cried out, struggling to sit up so that I could follow him. The doctor's firm hand fell onto my shoulder, pinioning me back to the bed. I struggled beneath it. 'Where has he gone? What were the two of you talking about before I woke up?'

Before the doctor had a chance to answer me – and who knows whether he would have told me the truth – Ryan had returned, with something tucked firmly beneath his arm. He approached the bed, and the closer he got, the less certain he began to look. But he'd gone too far down this particular road to be able to divert from it now.

Carefully, as though he was handling something explosive – which in a way he was – he removed the daily newspaper from beneath his arm, and placed it before me on the bed.

The front cover held a full-page photograph of a man I recognised from the media. He looked a little chubbier than the last photograph I'd seen of him, his colour was ruddy, and his hairline was receding. But that wasn't what was shocking. The thing that made me gasp, and then look up at Ryan with an expression of incredulous humour, was the headline: *President argues his case to Congress.*

'What is this?' I asked, running my finger beneath the bold black letters. 'Is this one of those joke, mock-up newspapers?'

'Don't we all wish that it was!' muttered the doctor, still looking annoyed at whatever road Ryan had decided to take us down.

'That's today's edition,' said Ryan resolutely.

'But . . . but . . . it can't be. That's not the President of the United States. That's——'

'Forget who the damn president is,' interrupted Ryan, sounding almost angry with me. 'That's not why I'm show-ing you the newspaper.'

'Then why?' I began, my voice hesitant and unsure, because suddenly I knew something very important was happening here, and although I had no idea what it was, I already knew I wasn't going to like it.

'Look at the date,' said Ryan, sounding as though he was in pain.

My eyes went up to the top of the newspaper. 'August the tenth,' I said, looking at the words and then back at my fiancé. 'Like you told me earlier.'

His eyes closed, and I believe now that was because he couldn't bear to be looking at me as his words exploded my world to smithereens. 'Not the month, the year,' he commanded.

'Twenty ...' I looked up, my face full of fear. 'Is this a misprint? Or a sick kind of joke?'

'It's neither,' said Ryan, broken.

'But it's not possible. It can't be. It just can't.' I looked back down at the line of black print, and my head was shaking even while a part of me knew that it was all horribly and incredibly true.

'Twenty eighteen? Twenty *eighteen*?'

Both the doctor and Ryan nodded slowly in perfect unison.

'Are you saying that the accident wasn't weeks ago ... it was, it was ...' It was too terrible. It was worse than that; it was a nightmare that I couldn't wake up from.

Ryan's eyes were bright with tears as he looked at me with a sadness I had never seen on his face before.

'It was six years ago, Maddie. You've been in a coma for *six* years.'

Chapter 3

The doctor left. I didn't hear him go, or the closing of the door behind him. There was nothing he could do for me right then. Even Ryan, whose arms had encircled me like two steel bands, was powerless to protect me as the awful truth hit me, then receded, and then hit me again, like a relentless tide.

I felt as if I was tumbling; as though I'd taken a step only to find the final tread on the staircase was no longer there. Crying was beyond me, although I could hear from the catch in his voice that Ryan was struggling to hold back his own emotions.

'How is this possible? Why didn't I wake up for all those years?'

Very gently, Ryan lowered his arms and reached for my hands, which were tightly clenched, imprisoning bunched handfuls of hospital blanket within them. He prised open my fingers with careful persistence, entwining them with his until they formed a complicated origami of digits.

'No one knew,' he explained sadly. 'They tried everything they could. To begin with, the doctors were hopeful; they kept telling us your injuries had been traumatic, so we should expect that it might take time. Then eventually, their voices started to change when they spoke to us. And then the weeks became months, and the months became years, and they didn't sound hopeful any more. In fact, they made it pretty clear that the longer you remained in the coma, the less chance we had of you ever waking up.'

His smile was bittersweet and full of six years of remorse. 'What the doctors are asking themselves today isn't why you were in a coma for so long; it's how come you've woken up at all. They're calling it a miracle, you know.'

Two fat tears formed in readiness at the corners of my eyes. I blinked, and they were set free to run lazily down my cheeks. 'I've lost six years of my life – that doesn't sound miraculous to me. My God, that makes me, what . . . thirty-four now?'

Ryan gave a small sad nod.

'I got old,' I cried forlornly. 'I missed my thirtieth birthday.'

Ryan leant over and wiped the tears from my face with his thumb. 'We had a cake,' he said consolingly, 'with candles.'

'But I wasn't there to blow them out, was I?'

There was more in his eyes than I could cope with at that moment. 'No, Maddie. You weren't there.' And there was something terribly final in those words, almost as though he blamed me for not waking up.

'I must look different now after six years. Can you find me a mirror. I want to see.'

Ryan was clearly reluctant to leave me, and was back so quickly he must surely have mugged the first person who happened to be walking past, carrying a handbag. He held out the small compact to me, and then had to retrieve it again only a minute later, as my fingers were too uncoordinated to open the tiny clasp.

My hand was trembling as I held the mirror up to my face, terrified it would reveal some awful Rip Van Winkle version of how I used to look. But thirty-four doesn't look that much different from twenty-eight apparently, and although my face was gaunt and my cheekbones had never before been so prominent, basically it was still me. It was only as I looked closer that I took in the sallow complexion and the huge panda-like dark circles beneath my eyes, which was the last thing you'd expect to find on someone who'd been asleep for almost seventy-five months.

'You don't look any older,' Ryan said loyally.

'You're only saying that because you love me,' I replied, still looking at my reflection in the two circular disks of glass, which meant I only caught the fleeting tail-end of his troubled expression. I lowered the mirror and looked at him carefully, seeing the passage of years not on my face, but on his. Now that I was looking for it, I wondered how I could possibly have missed it.

'We said we'd grow old together,' I said, with a sad little laugh. 'But then I went and fell asleep and left you to do it alone.' His mouth tightened and twisted slightly, as he once again took my hand. 'It must have been so hard for you. To keep waiting and waiting for me to come back to you.'

'It was even harder for your parents,' Ryan said carefully. 'Especially for your dad. To see your only daughter like that ...' his voice trailed away, and I was surprised by the empathy in his tone.

'I can't wait to see him, and Mum too, of course.'

Ryan looked away for a long minute, and there was something about his posture or the stiffness of his spine that concerned me. Keeping his eyes fixed on absolutely nothing at all beyond my hospital window, he continued in a low confessional tone. 'They never stopped believing, you know. Particularly your dad. When everyone else gave up, when everyone else said you were gone, he never once – not even for a minute – gave up hope.' Very slowly, as though he was a similar age to the man he was speaking of, Ryan turned back to face me. 'He was the only one who still believed.'

There was a pause, a long one. The words that were waiting to fill it hung in the air like stars. Eventually I reached up to pull them down.

'Except you, of course. You still believed.'

If I had slipped a knife between his ribs, I don't think he could have looked in greater pain. 'You *stopped* believing? You didn't think I would ever wake up?'

This was the moment. It was finally here, and suddenly I wanted to run. Except my body was too weak and wouldn't let me. The truth was getting closer, I could hear the roar of its engine, much like the van which had mown me down.

Ryan's hands were still holding mine. The hands that all day had felt odd, and weirdly wrong. My fingers turned under his, my index finger moving slowly down across the palm of his left hand and up his fingers. I felt it straight away, of course I did. Because now I knew what I was looking for. Yet still I checked and checked again, torturing both of us and prolonging the agony. Here it was, beneath the sensitive pad of my fingertip, the reason why his hand had felt strange. On the second finger of his left hand, a shallow but perceptible ridge was grooved into the flesh. It was the place where he wore his wedding ring.

The silence stretched on forever, daring one of us to break it. Ryan eventually got to his feet and walked to the window. I watched him silhouetted against the glass, the man who was mine when I had closed my eyes, and someone else's by the time I opened them again.

'Congratulations,' I said, my voice bitter. 'Who is she?'

Ryan leant his arms against the window frame, as if he was trying to push it out of the wall. His shirt, the one I'd never seen before, was perfectly ironed. Ryan was rubbish at removing the creases whenever he did them, so I guessed she was the one responsible for its immaculate finish. And that small act of intimacy was what started me crying. Because *she* was the one who now picked up the socks that never quite made it into the laundry basket. I'd moaned about that a thousand times; I'd moaned about it only yesterday morning, or so it seemed to me. But I would never get to do so again. Nothing about Ryan or his life was mine any more. And yet all I had done was close my eyes.

He turned his head, and looked at me over his shoulder. 'I loved you. I loved you more than you will ever know.' His voice was hoarse and raw, as though the words were a wound he was ripping open. But the tense he used told me everything I needed to know.

'How long?' I asked, my voice small, yet surprisingly steady, despite the falling tears that I didn't even attempt to wipe away.

'We were married two years ago.' The pronoun he used cut me like a sabre. The thought that he was now a 'we' with someone other than me, seemed like a cruel and sadistic joke. I turned my face into the pillow, it was already damp, but not as much as I suspected it would be by morning. 'But I've actually known her for longer than that.'

My head twisted on the pillow as I turned it towards him. 'While we were together? Did you know her then?' Was this woman, this unknown thief of my future, also part of my past? Had *I* known her? It was small consolation that Ryan looked genuinely horrified by my question.

'No. Of course not. We met after your accident. It was a time when I ... when I really needed someone to lean on.'

Me, I cried silently. *I* was the one you should have leant on. But I could never say those words out loud, and they weren't the right ones anyway, because what I really wanted to say was: *You should have waited for me, because I would have waited for you. Even if it took every day until the end of my life . . . I would have waited for you.*

'What's her name?'

Ryan looked at me for a very long moment. *Why are you doing this?* his eyes asked.

Because I have to know. I have to know it all, mine replied.

'Chloe. Her name is Chloe.' And just like that she became real, not because of her name, but because of the warm sound of it as it fell from his lips. He loved her, I knew that without any shadow of a doubt, because the way he said her name was exactly how he used to say mine.

'They said you'd never wake up,' Ryan said, his voice a whisper. 'The doctors told us it had been too long, that we should say our goodbyes, and to remember you the way you'd been.'

He walked back to my bedside, and my eyes drank him in. Would I ever see him again after today? Would she let him? If I was in her place, I knew I wouldn't.

'For three years I sat at your bedside and wished night and day for a miracle.'

My laugh was bitter and there was no humour in it. 'Well, you know what they say, you should be careful what you wish for—'

'Don't do that,' he begged, reaching for my hand, but I

snatched it away. He had no right holding my hand, when it was hers that wore his ring.

'When the phone went in the middle of the night, when I finally got the call I'd waited six years to receive, all I could feel was indescribable joy that you were back.' His words sounded completely sincere, but when I closed my eyes and imagined that moment, I saw a woman's arm in a darkened room, sleepily laying a hand on his naked shoulder. I saw her kneeling up behind him on their bed, asking him who was calling at this hour. I saw him getting to his feet, grabbing for his clothes, while she sank back upon their mattress. I saw it all as clearly as if I'd been right there beside them.

'I think you should leave now,' I said, my voice trembling with the effort of holding back my need to scream out at the unfairness of it all. Why bring me back into this world? Why wake me up, only to have me realise that everything that was once mine now belonged to someone else?

'Maddie, we still need to talk—'

'No. Not now. There's only so much I can take in one day. I'm done, Ryan. Please just go.' I was going to fall apart, I could feel the seams stretching and beginning to rip open. What happened next would be ugly and noisy, and I wanted no witnesses to it.

But somehow I must have known there was one more bullet left in the chamber, waiting to wound me. I could have said nothing, I could have watched him walk out of my hospital room and left the question unasked, and yet I didn't. One more spin of the barrel, one last round of Russian roulette before he left me and went back home to her.

'What about children, Ryan. Do you have any?'

His hand was already on the doorknob, but it froze at my words. He didn't turn around to answer me, so I never saw the look on his face when he replied. I imagined it might be regret, or even embarrassment. He addressed his words to the wood of the door frame.

'Yes, we do. We have a little girl.' And then, without another word, Ryan left and slipped out into the corridor.

I thought nothing could hurt me more than the pain I was already feeling, I thought I was already at my limit. I thought wrong.

The nurses left me alone for a while, and for that I was thankful, because some types of pain are beyond even the most experienced medical professionals. I needed that time to grieve and mourn – because while everyone else was looking at my awakening as a rebirth, to me it felt like thousands of tiny deaths, one for each day I had lost. Of course I was grateful that my life had been returned to me, but I wanted it *all* back, just the way it had been, not some new and inferior version of it.

'Enough, enough now,' I told myself.

And so, when the freckled-face nurse stuck her head around the edge of my door, I forced my mouth into something that could almost be called a smile, although the sympathy on her face almost set me off again. These people had been in charge of my care for a very long time, and had probably known about all the changes in my life far longer than I had. What else did they know that I didn't, I wondered.

'Is there anything I can get for you, Maddie? Anything you want?'

'Can you make it 2012 again,' I asked. The jaunty reply had sounded more amusing in my head than it did when it came out of my mouth.

'I wish I *could* turn back time for you,' said the nurse, whose name I later learnt was Ellen. 'But you know what it's like, there've been so many NHS cutbacks lately—'

I laughed, and was pleased to discover it felt way better than crying had done. Ellen busied herself with filling my water glass and dropping in a straw, but I could see her watching me carefully from the corner of her eye. I doubted she would be the only healthcare official concerned about my state of mind. As she held the glass while I sipped, I had a sudden flashback of Ryan standing with a drink in hand after every bout of morning sickness. My bottom lip trembled against the plastic straw.

'I can't even begin to imagine how terrible this must all seem right now. But if you're going to get better – and you most definitely *are* going to get better,' she added in a feisty, fighting-talk tone, 'I think you're going to have to learn to forgive the people in your life for moving on.' I looked up at her kind and caring face. 'He never left your side for the longest time,' she said softly.

'And then he did,' I finished sorrowfully.

Perhaps I wasn't being fair on him; after all, I had no idea how much Ryan had suffered, but that didn't stop the swell of anger and jealousy from overwhelming me every time I imagined him with her ... with Chloe. My life had been smashed into pieces, and it seemed to me as though this woman had come across it lying discarded at the edge of the road, had picked it up, and decided to take it for her own.

'My fiancé—' I stopped and drew in a breath before correcting myself. 'My *former* fiancé, told me today that he's a husband and a father now.' Ellen's eyes were steady but held no judgement; she was going to remain resolutely Switzerland. '*We* were pregnant, Ryan and me. I wasn't very far along, but we were going to have a baby.'

Ellen's eyes softened and she laid one hand on my arm in sympathy. 'I know, Maddie. It's in your medical records. I'm so sorry; this is such a lot for you to have to cope with. Would you like something to help you sleep?'

I shook my head, Ryan had said my dad was on his way, and after all this time I should at least be awake when he arrived.

The setting sun was painting my room in an artist's palette of orange and gold when I saw my father for the first time in six years. He looked so much older than I had been expecting. The salt-and-pepper speckling on his hair was now gone – as was most of his hair, come to that. What remained had crept further and further back, and had become the colour of snow recently turned to slush.

He opened the door to my room and then stood in the frame, unmoving, as though what he saw was too incredible to take in. His lips moved soundlessly for a moment before the words came out.

'Hello, Maddie, it's Dad here.'

Did he think he'd changed so much that I wouldn't recognise him? His laugh was raw and sounded embarrassed, and revealed how close he was to tears. 'I'm sorry. Force of habit. They told us to always let you know who we were when we walked in to your room.'

I nodded vigorously, because words would have been impossible. We stared at each other for what seemed like forever. He must have waited for this moment every day since the accident, and yet now it was here, he was like an actor who'd forgotten the lines he'd rehearsed. I imagined no one had told him how to handle this moment, probably because no one had ever expected it would come.

'Daddy?' the childhood name came up from my buried memory banks, and suddenly there was a kaleidoscope of images. He was pushing me on a swing; running behind my bicycle when the trainer wheels came off; beside me in the water when frantic splashing turned into doggy-paddle. His arms were my protection, and he ran across the distance between us and I fell into them like a child. He held me with a fierce strength that belied his years, as we clung together surfing a tidal wave of emotions.

Eventually he drew back, his hands – so much more wrinkled than I recalled – gently cupping my face. 'You came back,' he whispered, his voice no longer steady. 'You came back to us. I always knew that you would.'

He dragged the visitor's chair as close as it could go to my bed, before lowering himself onto it. He did so carefully, and I saw the wince he tried to hide as he settled back against the cracked vinyl upholstery. My family home was many hours' drive away, and I very much doubted that he'd have bothered to stop for a break, or to stretch his legs on the way. It was a long journey for a man his age to drive by himself. And that was something I could no longer avoid asking.

'You came alone?' He nodded slowly, his eyes still firmly fixed on my face, as though he'd never get tired of seeing me awake. 'Ryan mentioned something about Mum ...' My voice trailed away, as I struggled to remember his exact words.

In answer my father reached for my hand, and clasped it firmly in both of his. 'Your mum's not been herself for a while now.' The spectre of something painful flickered behind his watered-down blue eyes, hinting that it was a great deal worse than that. He glanced around the room, as though looking for support. 'Ryan's gone now, has he?'

In every sense of the word, I thought sadly, and nodded.

Something must have shown on my face, for his grip tightened on my hands. 'I'm so sorry, Maddie, about Ryan.'

I shook my head. 'We can talk about that later. Right now I want to know about Mum. You wouldn't have left her alone, so who's at home with her?'

There was an unexpected expression on my dad's face, and it took me a moment to recognise and name it. Guilt. 'She's fine; she's in good hands, but she's not at home any more.' His voice cracked slightly on the admission. 'She needed more care than I was able to give her.' The guilt he so clearly felt jumped from him to me, like a malevolent poltergeist looking for a host.

'Was this because of my accident? Is that what caused it? Did what happened to me make her worse?'

'No, Maddie. Absolutely not.' His voice was suddenly much stronger and more authoritative, using a tone I'd probably not heard since my teenage years. 'You are never, *ever*, to think that, or to blame yourself. Your mum was getting bad for a long time. Don't you remember, even when you were planning your wedding, she couldn't—' He broke off, looking suddenly horrified.

I squeezed his hand, no longer sure who was comforting who any more. 'It's okay, Dad. It's all right to talk about it. I know about Ryan . . . and his wife. I'm going to have to learn to deal with it. For me, time has stood still, but I know things have changed for the rest of you while I've been in here.'

Despite my brave reassurances, my father's voice was still raw with remorse as he haltingly explained that caring for my mother had finally proved too much for him to cope with. The decision to place her in residential care must have broken his heart. 'She seems happy there, more settled. And I go every day, and sit and talk to her – they let me stay as long as I like. Some days are better than others,' he admitted with a revealing sigh. And when he wasn't doing that, he would have been visiting me, I thought sadly. It was little wonder that he appeared to have aged so much in the six years.

'I'm sure the place you found for her is lovely, but doesn't that kind of care cost an absolute fortune?' I asked naively.

He shifted uncomfortably in his seat, and bit his lip. I was slow to understand the expression on his face; the guilt was back, and with it was regret. Slowly the truth dawned on me. 'Oh, Dad. You didn't? You sold the house, didn't you?'

He nodded. 'I'm sorry, Maddie. I didn't have a choice. I know how much you loved that house and how many happy memories we all had there. But it was too big for just me, and I was spending all my time with your mum anyway. Only now I realise I hadn't thought it through properly. I hadn't thought about what would happen when you woke up, and needed somewhere to go back to, somewhere you can get strong and well again.'

I felt like a skittle that keeps getting knocked down every time it was set upright. Where I would go when I eventually left hospital hadn't even occurred to me. Just a few hours earlier I would have said the answer was obvious: I would go wherever Ryan was; or failing that to my family home. Now neither option was open to me.

I looked up at my father's troubled face, and knew the concern upon it was greater than the uncertainty of where I would live. I realised then why the decision to sell might not have been quite as difficult as he had suggested; because despite everything he had said, perhaps he too had never really expected that I would wake up.

Talking had exhausted me, and as much as I fought to stay in the present, in the moment, my eyes kept drifting shut.

'You need to rest now, Maddie. You should try to get some sleep, my love.'

My father got to his feet, pausing only when my hand groped across the blanket until it found his. 'I'm scared, Dad,' I whispered into the twilit room. 'What if I don't wake up again? Or what if I do, and another six years have passed?'

The Adam's apple in the wrinkled skin of his throat bobbed up and down convulsively for a moment, before he brought it under control. 'Well, you're just going to have to, because I've only booked the Travel Lodge for one night.'

I smiled sleepily. 'Always kidding around. Always making a joke.'

My father leaned over and kissed me gently on the forehead. 'Actually, I think that might be the first one I've cracked since they brought you in here.'

I breathed in on a sigh, letting the familiar aroma of his aftershave surround me like a fragrant cloud. 'Will you stay here for a while, just until I go to sleep?' I asked. It was a child's request, the kind you ask when you have a fever, or you wake up from a nightmare and need the comfort of a parent close-by. It wasn't something a woman of my age would ever expect to ask.

My father sat back down on the visitor's chair and there was a battle of emotions on his face. But the one that won through with a landslide victory over the obvious concern, and the relief to have me back, was love. I carried the image with me as I slept. Should I never wake up, it was a good one to take with me, wherever I was going.

But I did wake up. Hospitals are good for a great many things, but getting a peaceful night's rest isn't one of them. I began to realise how unique and astounding my awakening was by the extraordinary number of medical professionals who found a need to visit my room over the next twenty-four hours, or who could be seen lurking in the corridor outside my room.

I remained attached to various monitors, which I'm sure were being closely observed and scrutinised. In addition, my vital signs were monitored what felt like continually throughout the night. It was as if the doctors themselves needed constant verification that their long-term comatose patient had suddenly, inexplicably, decided it was time to wake up. Eventually, Ellen had pulled down the venetian blinds on the internal window of my private room, to prevent some of the medical 'rubber-neckers' from gathering in the corridor. It didn't help; I still felt like a freak at the circus.

The sun had risen several hours before, but it was still early when I heard two familiar voices talking right outside my door. The slats on the venetian blinds allowed me only a shadowy outline of the pair, whose conversation was being conducted in infuriatingly low tones. But even if they had been totally silent, I would still have recognised them. For a single indulgent moment, I allowed myself to drift back six years. *The wedding was only days away and when it came, the man on the left was going to take my arm and together we would walk down a petal-strewn aisle; then he'd remove my hand from the crook in his arm and gently place it in the waiting one of the much taller man on the right, who was preparing to share his life with me.*

I rubbed furiously at the self-pitying tears with the back of my hand, dragging the cannula embedded within it across my face. My cheeks were too red, but at least they were dry when my father knocked lightly on the door, before opening it just wide enough to pop his head through the gap.

'Good morning, Maddie. You're up.' There was such joy in his voice it was practically infectious, and suddenly I found that I was smiling. My emotions were all over the place since waking from the coma. The natural divide between extreme high and plunging low was as thin as gossamer and kept ripping open.

'Awake, not up,' I corrected, looking beyond my father at the shape I could still see loitering on the other side of the blinds. 'Why is Ryan here?'

My father came all the way into the room and carefully closed the door behind him. 'He was worried about you. He said he hadn't been able to sleep last night and that he wanted to see how you were doing today.'

I shook my head slowly. 'He can't do that. He can't be half in my life. That's not fair to anyone: not to me; or him; or even to whatshername – his wife.' I knew perfectly well the name of the woman my fiancé had married. It was engraved forever on the tombstone of my marriage, but I hid behind a feigned nonchalance for self-preservation.

'Chloe, that's her name,' said my father, looking troubled as he leant down and kissed my cheek in greeting.

I pulled back from him as far as the pillows would allow. 'You know her name?' He nodded, and there was a guilty embarrassment in the way his eyes would no longer meet mine. 'Do you *know* her, Dad? Have you ever met her?'

My father had always been a terrible liar, and he certainly hadn't improved during my six-year hibernation. 'Not that well. We've met a few times.' Even without the tell-tale flush bleeding around the collar of his shirt, I realised he was being sparing with the truth. It was disquieting that he appeared to know the woman who had replaced me far better than he was letting on.

He walked to the window and looked out at whatever was beyond it. It would be many weeks before I was able to do that, a fact it was probably just as well I didn't realise right then.

'Why, Dad?'

'Why what?' he asked. *Now who was feigning nonchalance?*

I could feel a tension stretching between us, like a length of elastic. 'Why did you meet Ryan's new wife?'

My dad turned back to me with a sad smile. 'It would have

been rude not to, especially after he'd asked my permission to marry her.'

'You shouldn't be here. You should be at home with your family.'

'*You're* my family too.' And with those words Ryan ran me down, even more effectively than the van had done.

'No, I'm not. Don't say that, because we both know it's not true any more.'

'I didn't stop caring about what happened to you, just because I married someone else.'

'Well you should have done,' I said, my words deliberately sharp and pointed. 'That's how it goes when a relationship ends; you're supposed to put away all those feelings before you move on to the next one.'

'Except we never broke up. We never ended.'

I looked up at him and felt the wall of stone I was trying to hide behind begin to crack. 'Yes, we did. We ended when you married another woman. And what the hell were you doing involving my dad in your proposal?' Ryan looked uncomfortable and glanced towards the door through which my father had recently disappeared, as though hoping for rescue. 'You had no right putting him in that kind of impossible situation. What were you thinking of?'

Ryan looked at me wordlessly for what felt like minutes. Several times he seemed about to say something, only for some internal censor to shut him down at the last second. Finally he replied: 'We all grew very close in the months and years after your accident. We helped each other through an unimaginably difficult time.' He looked down at his feet for a second, shuffling awkwardly, and I was right back on that porch on the day he was about to ask my father's permission for my hand. *This* was why Ryan couldn't be here. Every memory was just too close to the surface. It all hurt too much.

'Your dad feels like my father-in-law,' he confessed. 'He feels like family.'

'Well, he's not. Not yours, anyway. And I'm not sure how pleased your wife would be to hear you talk like this.'

'Actually, she wouldn't—'

'Ryan, no. I can't do this. I don't want to hear any of this. You can't be here. Not yet. *You* might be able to look at me with the fondness of an old love, but seeing you standing there, with half a room between us, is torturing me.'

He went to take a step closer to my bed, but I raised a shaky hand as though stopping traffic. 'No. Don't come any nearer. Because I want you to hold me, and kiss me, and tell me that this has all been some dreadful nightmare, and that I'm going to wake up any minute now, and we'll be right there in your bed, with your arms wound tightly around me.'

If I'd taken a knife and thrown it at him, he couldn't have looked more wounded. 'Maddie—'

'No. Don't say another word, Ryan. I have to focus on getting well and getting out of here. My body is broken and it needs time to heal, and so does my heart.'

He sounded choked as he picked up the jacket he had carelessly thrown over the chair when I'd finally told my father that I would speak to him. 'You *really* don't want to see me any more?'

'I want to see you every day for the rest of my life ... but we both know that I can't,' I said, in a confession that ripped its way free from me.

'I'm not sure I can stay away,' were his final words, spoken at the doorway of my room.

But it turned out that he could, because it was almost three months before I saw him again.

Chapter 4

Three Months Later

'My name is Heidi, and you are going to hate me.' That was how she had introduced herself to me at our first session at the hospital, just days after waking up. 'I'm going to be in charge of your physical therapy, and by the time winter gets here, you are going to be walking out of this hospital without a crutch, a stick, or even the hint of a limp. *Capisce?*'

I remember staring at the short, compact, woman with her military-cropped white-blond hair, nose piercings and the totally incongruous name. A name like that belonged to a rosy-cheeked goatherd, or at least to a Julie Andrews lookalike, running over the Austrian mountainside, singing her heart out. *My* Heidi looked like a marine, and the regime she put me through over the months that followed my awakening gave me no reason to alter that initial impression. I had thought I was fairly fit before the accident. I'd certainly spent many months at the gym ensuring I was wedding-dress-ready, before the unexpected pregnancy had curtailed the spin classes and hardcore workouts.

Apparently that level of fitness had stood me in good stead, although it was hard to appreciate that as I grunted my way through the programme Heidi had devised to reactivate my wasted muscles. 'Your body wants this,' she had a habit of shouting, whenever it looked like all I wanted to do was throw in the towel – which in those early days, had been at practically every session.

But Heidi was nothing if not persistent. 'I tell you what,' she had urged on the day when she'd forced me to take a few faltering steps, leaning heavily upon the guiding handrails. 'When you can make it to the end of this walkway without support, you have my full permission to slap me hard, right across the face.' It had been a tempting carrot which she'd dangled in front of me for months. And yet, when I had finally managed to take those steps unaided, I had fallen into her arms and hugged her tightly, as we both cried. Heidi didn't look like a woman who cried easily, so I knew then what an achievement it was.

They had finally stopped calling my recovery a miracle, but that day it had certainly felt like one all over again.

After a great deal of protest, I had finally persuaded my dad to cut down his visits to one a week. The winning argument which had eventually swung it was that I needed to concentrate on my therapy, and that worrying about him driving back and forth on the motorway every other day was distracting me. But the truth was far simpler than that; my mother's need for him was greater than mine. As heartbreaking as it must have been for him on those days when she failed to remember his name, or the years they had spent together, he said she still looked to the door for him every morning, waiting for the arrival of the man who occasionally she still remembered she loved.

By the start of October, I had progressed to walking with the aid of a frame. 'Practise,' Heidi had urged, parking the new piece of equipment beside my bed. 'The more you practise, the quicker I can stop tormenting you every day.'

'I'm glad you finally agree that's what you're doing,' I had said with a smile.

The rehabilitation team had been amazing. They had painstakingly re-taught me all the things my body had forgotten. Even eating and drinking had to be reintroduced with infinite caution, but finally, when my body was able to tolerate it, I began to regain, if not my curves, then at least some flesh on my bones.

As the weeks slipped from summer to autumn, and then on to winter, I began to reach a level of acceptance that initially I had never imagined I would find. I was finally able to think of Ryan and the life I had so nearly lived, without breaking down in tears. It was still raw, it still felt like a recent break-up, but at least I was moving in the right direction. I didn't need the constant reminders from the medical team to grasp how astounding my recovery had been, and it left me feeling almost morally bound to make something meaningful of this newly returned life of mine, and not to squander the miracle on self-pity and bitterness.

But all that changed on a morning in early November when I received the letter.

I had been sitting in my visitor's chair beside the window, deep in thought, when Ellen had come in carrying the plain white envelope. In my favoured neon-bright, lycra gym clothes, I was probably a garish splash of colour against the muted tones of the hospital decor. I'd felt nothing but relief when I'd finally moved out of the baggy hospital robes and into clothing better suited for physical activity. There's a limit to how many times a person should moon their fellow patients when walking down the corridor, and I had definitely exceeded mine.

I was staring out through the glass, but my thoughts weren't on the small area of parkland I could glimpse out of one quarter of my vista, nor on the large concrete block of the multi-storey car park, which took up the rest of my view. I was too lost in my reflection of what had happened the day before to see anything of the world beyond my window. The incident still made me feel jittery and unsettled, as though a door had opened a crack, and I'd glimpsed something – *a memory?* – which kept niggling at me, like a missing clue in a puzzle.

Over the weeks I'd become confident enough to walk the corridors of the hospital with the aid of just one stick.

There were very few areas of the sprawling complex I hadn't visited as I practised the art of walking, with considerably less skill than the average toddler. After a while most the staff on the wards recognised me, and there was a warm feeling of community that I knew I would definitely miss when I was finally discharged in a couple of weeks. The nurses, doctors and therapists had become much more than mere caregivers, they were now also my friends. Which was fortunate in a way, because very few of the people who'd previously held that title had remained in my life. By the time I'd eventually woken from the coma, my two closest girlfriends had both married and moved away; one to Edinburgh and the other to Australia. Of course there had been a clutch of acquaintances and former work colleagues who had tentatively shown up at hospital visiting time, yet every single one of them had looked distinctly uncomfortable to be there. Their conversation had seemed halting and uncertain, which made me wonder if they felt embarrassed or even guilty that their own lives had all gone on without me, while mine had been frozen in suspended animation. Or perhaps it was simpler than that? Perhaps I was a reminder of their own mortality. Any one of us could have stepped unthinkingly into the path of a speeding vehicle; this time, it just happened to be me.

As usual on my walk, I had forgone the bank of lifts and had laboured patiently up the echoing hospital staircase, pausing to let the occasional octogenarian whistle past me.

I usually went no higher than the fifth floor, but today, in possession of a second wind – *or was it something more meaningful than that?* – I had climbed two more floors, and found myself outside the maternity ward.

I was slightly breathless, and could feel uncomfortable trickles of perspiration crawling lazily down my back, like meandering bugs. Through the glass of the door I could see several patients walking slowly down the length of the corridor, leaning heavily on the arms of their male companions. One of them turned and for just a moment our eyes met, before what I assume must have been a contraction overwhelmed her, and she turned to hang helplessly on her partner's shoulders until it had passed. The gown she wore was stretched tight over her belly, which to my inexperienced eye looked large enough to hold at least half a dozen babies.

Without being aware I was doing so, my hand went to the flat surface of my stomach, and a pain – just as sharp as the woman's contraction – ran through me. That would have been me and Ryan. We would have been that couple, waiting in a frenzy of excitement and fear for the birth of our first child. We could have had that, if only I hadn't been so careless.

Beyond the pregnant women I could see a mother wheeling a Perspex bassinet from a nursery. The baby within it was obscured, but the pale pink blanket told me it was a girl. Suddenly it seemed incredibly wrong that I didn't even know if the baby I still mourned for had been a boy or a girl.

It had been a mistake to come up to this floor. I should turn around right now, and go back to my own room. And yet my feet refused to move, and I remained on the threshold of the ward until – inevitably – someone came up behind me and pressed the button to gain entry. It was a young male nurse, who turned to me as the door swung beckoningly open. 'Are you coming in?'

No, screamed the sensible part of my brain. *Of course I'm not.*

'Yes, I am,' said a voice I hardly recognised as mine.

I walked with a purpose I had no right to feel, past the two labouring couples, stopping only when I reached the doorway from which the young woman pushing the bassinet had emerged. It was the nursery, and my first thought was confusion that it didn't look the way it does in films, with row upon row of babies, all lined up as though they were waiting to be chosen from a shop display. Then I remembered that in UK hospitals, mothers usually keep their babies at their bedside. Probably to protect them from hungry-eyed childless women, who stare longingly through the glass, yearning to be included in a group for which their membership has expired.

However the nursery wasn't entirely empty. There were two mothers seated in a far corner, chatting to each other as they nursed their newborn infants. I glanced down at my own boobs, which were only now regaining some degree of fullness, and wondered how that would have felt. I closed my eyes and saw a yellow-painted nursery, and an old-fashioned rocking chair in which I sat, holding a baby that never was, while Ryan stood by looking—

'Excuse me. Can I help you?'

I turned slowly away from the nursery window, blinking furiously so that the nurse couldn't see my tears.

'You're not a patient on this ward, are you?'

I could have been. Once. A very long time ago. 'No. No, I'm not. I'm on Winchester Ward.'

She opened her mouth, and I was pretty certain it was to ask me what I was doing here, and then her jaw dropped slightly, and an almost visible light bulb of recognition lit up behind her eyes.

'You're Madeline Chambers, aren't you? You're the woman who was in the coma and who—'

'Nurse Martin. A moment of your time, please.'

The young nurse jumped at the summons of the ward sister, and scurried quickly over to the nurses' station. They were too far away for me to hear what was being said, but whatever it was, it certainly looked like a reprimand. The young nurse was shaking her head in clear denial, and at one point they both looked towards me with totally unfathomable expressions on their faces.

It didn't take a genius to work out that – unlike the other wards I had visited – the maternity unit's doors were not open to outsiders. And that was truly how I felt, here among the pregnant and nursing young women. My fingers curled against the glass as I continued to stare blindly into the nursery with unseeing eyes. From somewhere I could hear a baby crying, and something inside me tugged with a mother's instinct to attend to her child. I definitely shouldn't have ventured onto this ward, which was reiterated only moments later when the suitably chastised nurse returned to stand before me.

'I'm sorry, but we have to protect the privacy of the new mums on the ward. Sister has asked me to see you safely back down to Winchester, Miss Chambers.'

The smile I gave her as I politely declined the offer of assistance was brittle and wintry. It was awkward enough that she accompanied me to the door of the ward, as though I couldn't be trusted to follow the instruction to leave. And yet something continued to pull at me, making the effort of walking away from this place of babies so much harder than it should be.

As I began my slow and careful descent back to my own hospital floor, I was filled with conflicting emotions. There was a longing and hunger that I could not entirely ignore or explain. It scared me. And from the worried look on her face as she practically evicted me from the ward, it had also scared the nurse. Was I the type of woman who new mothers would have reason to fear? I thought I had made peace with all the losses in my life, but this one hadn't been overcome at all. Just one glimpse of a maternity ward and all the pain had flooded back, like the twisting gripe of labour which I now had to accept I might never get to experience at all.

*

There's a downside to hospitals being like a small town or community. It doesn't take long before everyone knows everybody else's business. So it came as no real surprise to me when, later that afternoon, Ellen happened to mention with suitably feigned casualness: 'I hear you were up on the maternity ward this morning, Maddie?' I had smiled, because some part of me had been expecting this. I felt like a naughty child, waiting to get her knuckles rapped. 'What took you up there?'

'The stairs,' I quipped.

Ellen laughed, but it didn't quite make it all the way to her eyes. 'I just wondered why you'd gone onto the ward.'

I paused before answering. From an outsider's point of view, perhaps it looked like a weird almost masochistic thing to do. And maybe it was. There was no way I could adequately explain the incredible pull that had drawn me towards the nursery. Perhaps it was the deafening tick of my biological clock, or perhaps for just a moment I felt like I had a right to be there. But how could I possibly explain that? How could anyone possibly understand that, when I didn't understand it myself?

You set in motion chains of events without ever realising exactly what it is that you've done. You attend a boring industry event . . . and meet the man you want to spend the rest of your life with; you inadvertently photograph a stranger . . . and mistakenly convince yourself he's following you; you wander up to a maternity ward . . . and then you get a letter.

Dani Atkins

Ellen extended the business-like white envelope, and even before it had passed from her hand to mine, I knew who it was from. I still recognised his handwriting. The M was tall and sharp, like the peaks of a mountain, and the d's were fashioned like musical notes that had mistakenly wandered off a stave. I'd seen my name written in his hand on numerous birthday, Valentine's Day, and Christmas cards, but this was the first time I had ever seen it on a formal envelope.

There was no surname, no address beneath my name, no stamp and no postmark. So the letter had obviously been delivered by hand. Did that mean Ryan was here now, in the hospital?

'What is this?' I asked ridiculously, setting the envelope carefully down on my legs, as though it was an unexploded bomb. My fingers had trembled slightly, and Ellen was too observant a nurse not to have noticed that.

Her eyes were on my face and there was concern in them, and suddenly that frightened me even more. 'You should open it,' she urged gently.

I looked down at the familiar writing, and felt something flutter in my chest, a tiny warning emotion. 'I will,' I said, trying to sound unbothered, as though receiving letters from the man I'd not heard from in months happened all the time, which we both knew perfectly well was not the case. 'I'll read it later.'

The obvious subtext of my remark was: *I'll read it when I'm alone. That way, if whatever he has to say makes me cry, no one need ever know but me.*

But Ellen was stepping right over the boundaries of her day job now, and speaking only as my friend. 'You need to read this *now*, Maddie.'

There was no brooking the firm note of authority in her voice, so I once again took up the envelope. The adhesive seal parted easily; which meant it had probably been closed only recently. The *possibility* that Ryan was here in the hospital was upgraded to a *probability*.

Ellen turned to the cabinet beside my bed, straightening up the few items upon it, none of which needed straightening. I was grateful for the semblance of privacy she gave me as I pulled out the single sheet of white A4 paper. Even the shape of his handwriting had the power to wound me. It was so familiar that for a moment I didn't bother deciphering the shapes into actual words. Was it because I knew that, once I did, something would change? Or did that reality only occur to me much later?

Maddie,
  Don't tear this letter up, or throw it away without reading it.

As if, I thought, swallowing down a laugh that could well have sounded a little manic if I had released it. I was like a starving person, suddenly presented with a banquet. I was hungry for any contact with him, though I knew I shouldn't be. The good sense that had made me tell him to stay away was a long-forgotten memory. It was galling to realise how willingly I would accept scraps from the table, even if I couldn't have the feast.

I know you told me to stay away. And I've respected that these last few months. But something has happened and I now need to speak to you urgently. I don't want to say anything more in this letter, because what I have to tell you is too important for that. We need to talk face-to-face. I am waiting downstairs in Reception. Please don't send me away, because you need to hear this. You need to hear it today.

I'm sorry, Maddie. I know this is difficult for you to understand, but please can you just trust me? If it's okay for me to come up, ask Ellen to phone down and let me know.

Ryan

I read the letter three times before I spoke. It was as though he was writing in a foreign language and I needed time to try to translate its meaning. There was no point going for a fourth reading, because I remained baffled. The tone of the letter was urgent and slightly ominous. It made me feel as though the news he had to relate might not be welcome. Despite the fact that I attempted to damp it down, a spark of hope kept trying to flicker into life. Was this about his marriage? How terrible was it of me to wish *that* was the reason he was writing to me?

Ellen had finished with her faux tidying and was standing patiently, waiting. 'Will you see him?'

I swallowed noisily. 'Do you know what this is all about?'

The answer flickered in her eyes a millisecond before the lie slipped from her lips. 'No. I don't.'

She knew by the twist of my smile that I didn't believe her.

'What shall I tell him?' she pushed, nudging me inexorably towards the edge of the nest, way too soon. I wasn't ready to fly yet. Or was I?

'Tell him to come up.'

There was no disguising her sigh of relief. Whatever it was Ryan had to share, it was a weight on shoulders other than his, which made the possibility that it was anything to do with his marriage far less likely. Besides, I remembered the way he had sounded when he spoke of her. That depth of feeling only disappeared if one of you went away for a very long time ... about six years, to be precise.

I stopped Ellen just once on her way to the door, ashamed of the question I was about to ask, but asking it anyway. 'Do I look all right? My hair, does it need brushing?'

She smiled sadly and shook her head, her eyes running briefly over the hair falling in a thick dark curtain down my back. 'You look lovely, Maddie.'

He was at my door much quicker than I had been expecting. I'd only just thrown the compact-sized mirror back into my sponge bag, after smearing a thin layer of Vaseline over my suddenly bone-dry lips. The kindest thing I could say about my reflection was that it probably looked a great deal better than it had the last time Ryan had seen me. I'm not even sure why I was so fixated about how I looked. This was the man who'd stood at my shoulder when my head was halfway down the toilet bowl. But that had been another Maddie, and sadly also another Ryan.

Ellen had left the door open, so I knew he'd arrived by the slant of his shadow, which spliced the light from the corridor. We both took a moment. We both needed one. I used mine to try to control my suddenly erratic breathing; his was spent quietly clearing his throat, as though the words he'd come here to say were stuck within it. Ryan knocked lightly on the open door, and I twisted in my chair to face him.

The feelings hit me like a punch. I had spent almost three months convincing myself I would be able to leave him behind in my past, and yet one glimpse of his broad frame; of his slightly dishevelled dark blond hair and tentative smile, and it was like playing Snakes and Ladders. One roll of the dice and I'd slithered all the way back to the start of the board.

'Maddie,' he said softly, walking into the room and carelessly destroying all the barricades I had erected around my heart. 'Thank you for agreeing to see me.'

'You didn't make it sound as though I had much choice.' I nodded towards a second chair on the other side of the room and he pulled it up. He shrugged out of his jacket and took far longer than necessary folding it carefully before lowering himself on to the very edge of the chair. He reminded me of a man standing on the ledge of a high building, still not sure whether or not he had the guts to jump. It was startling to realise that Ryan was possibly even more nervous than me. And I still had no idea why.

'You're looking really good,' he said with a smile. 'Much more like your old self.'

I gave a nod, taking the compliment at face value, because beneath it we both knew that the old version of me had slept through a great many changes and had woken up to a world I scarcely recognised.

'It's been a bit of a process,' I said, which blithely glossed over the numerous occasions I would happily have throttled Heidi, if only I'd been able to get up onto my feet to do so. 'But at least I can now walk again. I should be getting out of here in a few weeks.'

'Yes, I know,' Ryan said unthinkingly. My head shot up and I saw the tightening of his jaw, clamping down too late, for his words had already bolted to freedom.

'How? How do you know?'

He met my eyes and didn't flinch under their scrutiny. 'Because I still speak to your dad on a regular basis. He's been keeping me up-to-date on your progress.'

Twice betrayed, I refused to let him see how disturbed I was by his admission. I suppose part of me should have felt pleased that he still cared enough to ask about me, but a much larger part was suffused with white-hot anger, at both of them. I hated the idea that they were cosily chatting about me, as though I was still lost from them both in an unreachable cocoon.

'Well, there's really no need for you to do that any longer, is there?'

Ryan looked at me for a very long unblinking moment. I tried to read the expression on his face, because I remembered them all so well, but this one was new to me. It had no name.

'Actually, there *is* a reason. A very good one. And that's what I've come here today to talk about.'

My heart began to thud so noisily in my chest, I wondered if he could hear it across the room. When I reached out my hand for a nearby glass of water, the complexity of lifting the drink to my lips without spilling it everywhere was a great deal harder than it should have been.

Ryan leant forward and held his hands out towards me, like a bridge. They were extended palm-side-up, in an obvious invitation, and I knew how easy and how dangerous it would be to lay my own once more within his grip. But they were *her* hands now, not mine. I shook my head, declining the unspoken request, and after a minute he drew them back. They remained resting lightly against his denim-covered knees, and the effort to ignore my own good sense and reach out for them anyway took all of my concentration.

'The hospital telephoned me. They were the ones who asked me to come and see you today.'

Now I was *really* confused and even more annoyed. I could just about come to terms with my dad and Ryan staying in contact, but the doctors in charge of my care had no business getting in touch with my former fiancé. His name had been removed as a contact from my medical records, or so I'd thought.

'I think you'd better explain what this is all about.' My voice sounded cold, but it was fear that was robbing my words of warmth. There was an avalanche coming, a great big wall of ice and snow, and I wasn't going to have time to get out of its way, and from the look in his eyes, neither would Ryan. It was going to bury us both.

His eyes darted towards a small black canvas bag which he'd brought with him. It was propped up against the leg of his chair, but it was impossible to see within it. It wasn't the first time he'd glanced down at it, and I sensed it might be an important prop in the strange play we appeared to be acting out.

'This is very difficult, Maddie. And there's no easy way to break it to you. What I'm going to say will change lives. And I don't just mean yours and mine.'

My heart skipped. It couldn't help it. This *was* about his marriage. It had to be. What else could he be talking about? 'Go on.'

'You went up to the maternity ward yesterday, didn't you?'

Whatever I had been dreading – or even hoping – he was about to say, it certainly had nothing to do with my ill-advised walkabout the previous day. I gave a laugh, which didn't sound real, probably because it wasn't. 'My God, why is everyone going on about that? I didn't do anything wrong. You're all acting as though I was about to snatch a baby or something.'

Ryan's eyes softened, and for a fleeting moment I thought I caught a glimpse of the love he had once felt for me. Then he blinked, and it was gone. 'The doctors thought that maybe there was a reason why you felt drawn to that ward in particular. That it might be some sort of breakthrough.'

I shook my head, still feeling like I was on trial for a crime that no one would reveal to me. 'I went for a walk, that's all. And really, would it be so surprising if I *was* drawn to the nursery? The accident might have been a long time ago for all of you, but for me it's still so recent. I only lost our baby three months ago . . . or at least that's how it seems to me.'

His face twisted in pain, and I wondered how difficult it was for him to hear me speak of 'our baby' when he now had a child with someone else.

'But you didn't,' he said, overriding my earlier refusal, and reaching across the space between us to hold my hands in his. 'You didn't lose our baby three months ago.'

There were tears in my eyes, and there was no point in trying to hide them, because any minute now they were going to flow down my cheeks. 'I know, I know,' I said, my voice hoarse with the truth I had finally learnt to accept. 'It all happened six years ago.'

Ryan was shaking his head, and then unbelievably he

allowed a totally inappropriate smile to form on his lips. 'You didn't lose our baby.'

I heard the words. *Obviously* I heard the words. But they made no sense to me. He might as well have been speaking in Swahili.

'I ... I ...' I had no idea what to say, but Ryan suddenly had more than enough to say for both of us.

'Your injuries were terrible. Both your legs were badly broken, as was one of your arms. There didn't seem to be a single inch of unbruised skin on your entire body. And the injury to your head ... well, no one could tell us what the long-term implications would be. We thought it was a miracle you were alive at all, but actually that *wasn't* the real miracle.'

'You're saying that I ...' The sentence was almost impossible to complete. '... that I *didn't* have a miscarriage?'

Ryan's eyes filled with tears, and he spoke the words the way you would a prayer. 'No, Maddie, you incredible, unbelievable woman. You most definitely *did not*. You kept our baby safe ...' his voice cracked. 'Even with all those terrible injuries, you kept her safe.'

'Her?' My voice was an incredulous whisper.

He was laughing and crying now at the same time, a rainbow through a thunderstorm. 'Yes. Her. A little girl. And somehow you defied everything the doctors predicted and you kept our baby alive. You carried her all the way to the end of the pregnancy.'

The world was spinning, nothing made any sense.

'I was there when she was born. I held her in my arms,

and willed you harder than I had ever done before to open your eyes, so you could see the miracle we had made. We laid her on you, her skin against yours, and for a while I think we all believed that would be the moment. The doctors, the nurses, everyone was in tears as her tiny hands curled against your skin.' He looked down at his feet, as though suddenly the look on my face was too much to take; it was like looking directly into the sun. 'But I guess we'd used up more than our fair share of miracles by then, because you never woke up. You never got to see her.'

I got shakily to my feet. My words sounded jerky and staccato, like discordant notes on an out-of-tune piano. 'I have a daughter? We have a baby? I gave birth whilst still in a coma? Is that even possible?'

Ryan nodded, covering all four of my dazed questions with a single affirmative. 'Except she's not exactly a baby any more. She's five years old now.'

I gripped the back of the chair for support, as though a giant wave — more of tsunami really — had tried to sweep me away. How could I have been so slow to realise what should have been glaringly obvious?

'The daughter you told me about, yours and your wife's; she's not Chloe's child, is she?'

Ryan looked startled to hear his wife's name on my lips. Considering the revelations of the day, that was surely the least shocking of any of them.

'No. She's not. Hope is your daughter. Yours and mine.'

*

I don't remember sinking back down onto my seat, but I clearly must have done. Ryan was leaning forward again, staring anxiously into my face, which I guessed was probably several shades paler than usual.

'Are you all right? Should I call someone?'

I shook my head slowly. 'No, don't. But I'm not all right. Not even a little bit. This is . . . this is . . . a lot.' I seemed to have temporarily lost the ability to string together a coherent sentence.

'I know it must be. I can't even begin to imagine what you're thinking.'

The words were on my lips before I had time to censor them. 'What I'm *thinking* is why didn't you tell me about her straight away? Why wait months to let me know this?'

Ryan shifted awkwardly on his chair, and his eyes seemed suddenly reluctant to meet mine. 'We decided it was better to wait until you were stronger. Everyone was worried that a shock like this could hinder your recovery, or cause a setback.'

'You didn't think that perhaps knowing I *hadn't* lost the child I was carrying might have made some of the hell I was going through an awful a lot more bearable?' There was something on Ryan's face that revealed that was *exactly* what he'd thought. 'I'd lost six years of my life; I'd lost everything I'd planned for . . . I'd lost *you*. Was it fair to let me carry on believing that I'd also lost our baby?'

'It wasn't my decision alone to make,' confessed Ryan reluctantly.

I took a deep breath and forced myself to step away from focusing on who was at fault, because there were other, far more important thoughts screaming to be heard right then. 'Do you have a photograph of her?'

The smile Ryan flashed me opened the door to a hundred forgotten memories, and I slammed it shut just as quickly. Not now. Now wasn't the moment to think about him and me, this moment belonged only to the life we had created together.

'I've got some recent ones on my phone,' he said, reaching into his pocket and pulling out his mobile. 'We went away for a week at half-term.'

I'm pretty sure my expression was blank. I didn't speak 'parent' and had long ago forgotten things like school term dates. But it was a world and a language Ryan was clearly very familiar with. The first spasm of impotent jealousy hit me.

He seemed to take forever switching on the phone and scrolling through the stored images in his library of photographs. 'Ah yes,' he said, his lips curving to form a tender smile as he looked at the device. 'This is the one I was looking for.' I was so impatient I practically snatched the phone from his hand when he held it out towards me.

My own hand was trembling, making the photograph of the girl on the screen a moving target. But my eyes were locked onto her face with missile-like accuracy. I couldn't have looked away from that image if my life had depended upon it.

Perhaps a small, slow, part of my brain had been expect-ing – if not a baby – then certainly a much younger child than the one who grinned up at me from the mobile phone screen. I gasped softly, and pincered my fingers to enlarge the picture, drinking in every detail of her pretty, heart-shaped face. My tears splashed down like silent raindrops and landed on the screen of his phone.

'She looks like me,' I breathed in wonder.

He nodded, and swallowed visibly as though the emotion was rising up like lava within him. 'Heartbreakingly like you. She always has, from the moment she was born.'

My eyes were drinking in every detail of the photograph, afraid to look away. At that moment, if Ryan had wanted his phone back, he would probably have had to wrestle me to the ground to give it up. The skin of my daughter's face was pale, just like mine; she had full pink lips, the same ones I saw whenever I looked in a mirror. Her hair was long and dark and someone – *don't think about who* – had braided it neatly into twin plaits. I'd seen that exact same image in a dozen different school photographs from my past; it was the style I had always worn as a child. That thought shocked me enough to make me raise my head. 'My parents . . . are they a part of her life?'

Ryan looked surprised by the question, as though it was a slightly ridiculous thing to have asked. 'Yes. Of course they are. Your dad absolutely idolises her. It's harder for your mum.' He bit his lip as though unsure how indiscreet he was allowed to be. 'I don't want to speak out of turn here, but because of her condition your mum gets confused. She thinks Hope is you.' I felt a small sick feeling creep into the pit of my stomach. My mother must have deteriorated a great deal more than my dad had chosen to share with me. 'But Hope adores both of them. They're the only grandparents she knows, because my parents still live in the States, and sadly both of Chloe's have passed away.'

I struggled to keep the expression on my face completely neutral, but I could feel my lips and cheeks tightening with irritation. Those people were not her relatives. Those people were not her grandparents. Something small, green and ugly crept up and slithered inside me, like a cancer.

Without bothering to ask for permission, I side-swiped the photograph, eagerly seeking another. And I found one. Ryan's brows drew closer together in concern when he realised what I'd done. The spasm of pain lingered on my face like an angry birthmark as I looked down at this second photograph of our daughter. Except Hope wasn't the only subject in this one. A woman of around my age, wearing a navy swimsuit, was sitting in a large rattan chair beside a glittering-surfaced swimming pool. On her lap, dressed in a cute polka-dot child's bikini was my daughter; my flesh, my blood, my perfect beautiful child. She was mine, you only had to look at her to know that, but the arms wrapped tightly around her belonged to another woman. Both of them were laughing at the camera. They looked happy and carefree, and the knife in my heart twisted viciously.

Ryan had moved to stand behind me. I could feel his

breath gently fanning the back of my neck as he leant forward and also studied the photograph. 'That was the day Chloe taught her to swim. She'd been wanting her to learn for ages. She always panics whenever we're anywhere near water. But she's right; it's an important life skill. Hope had just managed a whole width of "doggy-paddle" when I took that photo.'

I turned my head; it felt slow and heavy as I lifted it to look at him over my shoulder. 'I used to work as a part-time lifeguard at my local pool before I went to university. Did I ever tell you that?'

Ryan's eyes clouded, so I knew the answer before he said it. 'Yes. I believe you did.'

'*I* could have taught her to swim.' It was one more precious moment I'd had to hand over to the woman who was now living my life. I looked back at the photograph, this time concentrating not on the miniature version of me, but on the woman who held her so tightly and securely against her. Chloe's hair was a shade or two lighter than Ryan's. Her eyes were clear and a curious blue-grey colour. They were unadorned by mascara, even the waterproof kind. It was impossible to gauge her height as she was sitting down, but her legs looked shorter than mine, and her frame more gently rounded. The swimsuit was functional rather than sexy, yet still displayed a cleavage way more impressive than my own. How happy Ryan must be; he'd always been a boob man.

Chloe looked like the kind of person who easily made friends wherever she went. She had a smiley openness that came across even through the distortion of pixels. She looked womanly, and motherly. She looked like a perfectly nice, perfectly happy wife to the man I loved.

I hated her with a ferocity that scared me.

They'd warned me about extreme mood swings. Apparently it's not uncommon in patients emerging from a coma. It was my first encounter with how wayward they could be, and I was still in thrall to this new, not-so-nice version of me as I handed Ryan back his phone.

'I've missed so much of her life. There are so many things I'll never know about her and her early years. I don't even know what it felt like to give birth.'

'There are probably a great many women who'd just as soon not remember that,' said Ryan, trying to gently ease me back into good humour. It was a trick he used to be particularly good at, and it was interesting to see that he hadn't lost the knack. He slipped his phone back into the pocket of his jeans and bent to pick up the black canvas bag that was still propped up beside the chair.

'Actually, there might be a way of accessing some of those lost moments,' he said, his hand delving into the bag and extracting a large, leather-bound book.

'What's that?'

'It's something we decided to put together for you shortly after the accident, when we realised you were taking your time waking up.' I smiled slightly at the way he made it sound as if I'd simply decided to have a very long lie-in for the last six years.

'We knew there would be lots of blanks that you would want filled in if—'

Such a small slip, but it changed the smile on his face to an expression of mortification. '*When*,' he corrected hastily. But of course it was too late, the Freudian slip had fallen; there was no pretending it hadn't been said.

'We compiled a photographic memory book for you,' Ryan finished awkwardly, holding out the album to me. I went to flip it open, but his hands reached out to stop me. For a moment they rested on top of mine, and a million nerve endings leapt into life at the memory of his skin.

'Some of them were taken fairly early on after the accident. They might be uncomfortable to look at.' I stared down at the album with slightly less eagerness.

'Okay. I'll bear that in mind,' I said cautiously, taking the unopened book from him and going back to my seat beside the window.

Ryan looked like a man being slowly torn down the middle. He took a step forward, as though intending to go through the album with me, and then abruptly stopped. From somewhere far away I imagined a voice audible only to him was calling him back. 'Actually, you know what, I think I'll go down to the cafeteria and grab a cup of tea and leave you to look at it in peace. Is that okay?'

No. Nothing about any of this was even remotely okay.

'Yes, that's fine,' I replied.

*

I dived into the album before Ryan had pulled the door to a close behind him. For a moment I thought the first few pages held duplicates of the same photograph, until I looked a little closer. The setting was the same hospital room, although not the one I currently inhabited. The bed was close to the window, and I was the only person in the photo. I flipped backwards and forwards through the first half-dozen pages of the album, and it felt remarkably like doing a 'spot-the-difference' puzzle. In the first image the sun was still shining brightly through the window; the boughs of the tree beyond it were heavy with foliage, and both my legs were still in plaster. Ryan had written a caption beneath the photograph, with a date that confirmed it had been taken in the middle of August, eight weeks after the accident.

I flipped over to the next page, which held a photo taken some six weeks later, and saw fewer leaves on the trees and far more clouds in the sky. But the main difference wasn't in the changes of the season, it was in me. In the first photo most of the terrible bruising from the accident had faded to a pale mustard yellow, making me look weirdly like an extra in an episode of *The Simpsons*. In the second photo my skin was back to its normal alabaster white; but I wasn't looking at my skin. The August image showed the outline of a small mound beneath the sheet. Before the accident my baby bump had simply disappeared whenever I lay down, but in the photo before me it now looked like a rolling hillside. I ran my finger wonderingly over its arc and flipped rapidly to the next page, and then the next, and the next. It was strange fast-forwarding through my pregnancy, watching the view from the lower part of the window become increasingly lost behind my ever-growing stomach. What had started as something the size of a small cantaloupe melon had transformed to something more closely resembling a huge Halloween pumpkin.

A soft sigh escaped me. I'd been looking forward to experiencing all the changes my body was going to go through as I grew a tiny human being. I'd wanted to savour and relish every single one of them ... and I had missed them all. For me there had been no sending Ryan out in the middle of the night for chocolate ice cream and pickles to satisfy my weird cravings; no fluttery first movements of the baby stirring inside me; no caressing the child growing steadily within my swollen belly. True, there had also been no heartburn, no backache, or varicose veins, but I'd have traded them all in a heartbeat not to have missed the milestones of my pregnancy.

There was one final photograph before Hope had been born, and in that one I was not alone. Ryan was standing beside the bed, holding one of my limp and unresponsive hands in his. It saddened me to see his hand lovingly rested on my abdomen, and knowing that I'd been unable to feel it. But what upset me even more were the changes the intervening months had wrought on Ryan. He'd lost weight – a lot of weight – and the lines that today radiated from the edges of his eyes had already begun their outward journey. But more than the physical changes, there was an aching melancholy on his face, hiding behind a brave smile. I was the one who'd been struck by the van; I was the one who'd been injured; but that photograph clearly showed that Ryan had been wounded just as badly.

The first photograph of Hope must have been taken when she was only minutes old. The setting was an operating theatre, although I knew from the lack of scars that I hadn't had a Caesarean section. I'd always wanted to experience natural childbirth – and amazingly it would appear that I had, I just couldn't remember doing it. Our baby was held in her father's arms. Ryan was dressed in a green hospital gown, with a funny paper theatre cap on his head, but I scarcely noticed his outfit, for all I could see was the tiny bundle being held so securely in his arms. Not much was visible of her, except for a small wrinkled red face and the hint of an astonishing amount of dark hair. The only thing that eclipsed the sight of our newborn daughter was the expression on Ryan's face. To say it was suffused with love would be an understatement. Lastly my eyes travelled to the third subject in the photograph. Me. My eyes were closed, my lips were slightly parted, and my expression was blank. I had just been part of something truly miraculous, and yet I clearly knew absolutely nothing about it.

The same, apparently, couldn't be said for the readership of several local newspapers and magazines which had run features on Hope's amazing story. It was disconcerting to read the press cuttings that covered the accident, my coma, and then my daughter's arrival into the world. For someone who had been more than willing to share large sections of her life on Facebook and Twitter, I found the personal coverage to be oddly disturbing and intrusive. They say everyone has their fifteen minutes of fame, but I would much rather have earned mine in a far less dramatic way.

If I was doing a book review on the album Ryan had compiled for me, I would have to say that I infinitely preferred the final section. True the photographs of me showed no improvement over the passage of time, but I was almost incidental in those snaps, for the true star of them all was Hope. As a baby being held in the arms of my father or hers, she outshone every other person in the room.

I smiled at one photograph which showed her propped up beside my head, surrounded by pillows. Ryan had been right. Even as a small baby, her resemblance to me was remarkable. It was a small consolation prize given to us by Nature, and I took it gratefully.

Ryan had dutifully tried to capture important moments in our daughter's progress for the memory book. I don't suppose the picture of her crawling on my hospital bed beside my unmoving body was *actually* the first time she had discovered how to move from A to B, but it was still a joy to see. I'm not sure who was holding the camera for the photograph in which Ryan held Hope's two pudgy hands in his, supporting her as she walked beside my bed. I told myself it was probably one of the nurses, because I really didn't want to consider any other possibility. Hope would have been about fourteen months old by that time. Had Ryan already met Chloe by then?

The seasons and occasions I had missed were all catalogued. I saw Hope's first three birthday cakes, I saw the miniature Christmas tree which someone – probably Ryan – had erected in the corner of my hospital room. He'd always known how much I loved Christmas, and decorating my room and hanging fairy lights on a tree for a woman whose eyes remained stubbornly closed, would be just the kind of thing he would do for me. *'There's nothing in the world I wouldn't do for you.'* I could remember him saying those words to me as I lay safe and secure in the circle of his arms in his bed. Did he now say exactly the same thing to her?

There was a lump in my throat as I turned the page after that last photograph, but there was no laughing image of my little girl to dispel it, for the next page was blank. I frowned and flicked through the remaining leaves of the album. They were all empty. For some reason, around two years ago, Ryan had stopped capturing the moments that were passing me by.

I sat with the album closed on my lap for what seemed like a very long time as I waited for its creator to return from the hospital cafeteria. You learn to read people when you're in a relationship. Perhaps his ability to read me had grown rusty after six years of disuse, but my own skills were still pretty sharp. I could tell by the caution in his gait and the smile on his face – which didn't quite meet his eyes – that he was unsure of my reaction.

He glanced at my hands, which were resting on the leather-covered book on my lap, as though I was taking an oath in a court of law. *I promise to tell the truth . . . the whole truth . . .* But *would* he?

'Why are there no recent photographs of our daughter in the album?'

Ryan shifted uncomfortably, and a small part of me felt almost sorry for putting him on the spot like this, but surely he must have known I would ask that question. 'I've got loads of photos at home and quite a few videos too that I can bring in for you.'

It was a valiant effort to send me off down another road altogether, but I wasn't going to be so easily distracted. 'But what about the photographs of her *here* at the hospital, with me? Where are they?'

He ran his tongue over his lower lip. It was a small gesture which I used to find incredibly sexy, in a way I still did, but I also recognised it as a sign that he was nervous. 'There aren't any.'

It was the answer I was expecting, and yet the words still cut me like tiny flying razors, because I knew what they meant. 'You stopped bringing her to the hospital.' It was an accusation, not a question, and we both knew it.

'We had to.'

If I wasn't already cut and bleeding, the pronoun would have finished me off. We.We.We. The word rang out like a shotgun in the room. Him and her. The new Mrs Ryan Turner. Except she wasn't the *new* one, was she, because I

111

had never managed to make it far enough to claim that title. Chloe was the first and *only* Mrs Turner; wife to my fiancé, and mother to my child.

'Why? What possible reason could you have had for separating us?'

He winced at my words, but I wasn't going to retract them, even if they weren't entirely accurate. It was the coma that had separated me from my child, not Ryan. I lifted my head and dared him to contradict me. He said nothing.

'Can't you see how important it was that I remained in her life?'

'It was causing her distress. She started having terrible nightmares. She couldn't understand why you wouldn't wake up for her.'

Now *his* were the words that scythed *me* down. My child had needed me, and I had let her down, not just once but every single day for the last six years.

'We spoke to people, to child experts and to doctors, and the one thing they all said was that we had to do what was best for Hope.'

I suddenly felt very, very, cold, despite the habitually overheated hospital room. 'And what *was* best for Hope? What did you tell her?'

Ryan's eyes were bright with tears. I already knew what he was going to say, but I wasn't going to let him off the hook. 'I'm so sorry, Maddie. We thought what we were doing was for the best. We had no idea—'

'What did you tell her?'

He didn't meet my eyes. Was he really going to make me ask it a third time? He drew in a deep breath and then finally spoke the words that destroyed me: 'We told her that you had passed away.'

Chapter 5

'Have you got everything?'

I pulled up the zip on the large canvas bag, fastening it with a flourish as I ran my eye around the hospital room. My home. But only for the next ten minutes or so.

'I think so, Dad.'

The bag sat on my neatly made hospital bed. There hadn't been much to pack, despite the length of my stay. The contents of the holdall amounted to a couple of toiletry bags, a few paperbacks and a selection of gym outfits. '*These* I am happily going to burn,' I had announced to Heidi after our final session, holding the unpleasantly sweat-drenched top away from my back.

'I wouldn't if I were you, unless exercising naked is your thing.'

I was drinking deeply from the bottle of water that I always drained at the end of Heidi's torturous programmes, so my confused 'Huh?' was a little delayed.

'You're still going to need to attend outpatient sessions twice a week for the next few months, as well as your doctor appointments,' she said, throwing an arm around my shoulders and almost knocking me off my decidedly shaky legs. 'You didn't think you were going to get rid of me *that* easily, did you?' She'd grinned wickedly, and after a moment I realised that, as much as I might dislike her methods, I would have missed the time we spent together. And there was no denying that the credit for getting me back onto my – albeit wobbly – legs, was undoubtedly hers.

My dad's reaction had been less than enthusiastic, when I'd explained I would need to remain close to the hospital when I was finally discharged. 'We could see about getting you transferred to one nearer me? That way I'd be on hand to help and to ...' His words trailed away.

'Keep an eye on me?' I suggested, trying to temper the words with a smile.

He grinned sheepishly, knowing I'd seen through his admittedly flimsy ruse. 'Something like that.'

I shook my head, knowing his offer was well intentioned, but also that it wasn't what I wanted or needed right now. 'If they think I'm well enough to be discharged, then I'm well enough to live on my own. And I don't want to have to get to know a whole new team of doctors and therapists; I like the ones I have.' Somewhere in the hospital I imagined Heidi falling clean off her chair if she heard that one. 'And besides, Dad, we both know that's only part of the reason why I don't want to leave the area. Right now the most important thing is for me to stay here.'

My father bit his lip and looked guilty. The subject of Hope, the granddaughter I hadn't even known I'd given him until recently, was still an extremely tricky one between us. His had been the casting vote in deciding to keep the truth about her birth from me, and as much as I loved him, it was going to take me some time to forgive him for that one.

'You're thinking about what's best for *your* daughter,' he'd said when I'd called him on the night Ryan had dropped his bombshell. 'I totally understand that. But I hope you can see, Maddie, that's exactly what *I* was doing too.'

I hadn't wanted to argue with him then about what I still believed was a very bad decision. I *still* didn't want to. In time I knew I would come to terms with why they'd delayed telling me about Hope's existence. But to tell a three-year-old child that her mother had died, when she hadn't? It didn't matter how much time elapsed, I was never going to be all right with that one.

My father reached for my bag and lifted it easily off the bed. 'Can I just say one last time that I really wish you were coming back to Lingford with me?' He gave a plaintive sigh.

'I know, Dad. But it's time for me to start living the rest of my life. Besides, I'm twenty-eight years old and that's a little too elderly to be moving back home to live with my parents.' There was a lot left unsaid in my reply, but I knew he was perfectly capable of filling in the blanks. For a start, there *was* no family home any more; he lived in a small one-bedroom flat, and his time and energy were already devoted to caring for one woman from the Chambers family, he certainly didn't need to be doubling that quota.

'Thirty-four,' he corrected quietly, almost under his breath.

'Pardon?'

'I was just saying that you're *thirty-four*, not twenty-eight.'

Just when I thought I'd accepted those lost years, a simple mistake like that had the power to stop me in my tracks. I cleared my throat before answering him in an unnaturally chirpy voice. 'Well, all the more reason why I should be standing on my own two legs. Heidi certainly worked hard enough to get me back on them.'

I took one long last look around the room which I'd lived in longer than anywhere else in my adult life, before following my father to the door. I knew I should probably be celebrating this moment. I should be rejoicing that after all this time I was about to rejoin the real world; except all I actually felt was scared. In here I knew the rules, I knew the routine. Out there the goalposts had all shifted and changed. I was like a refugee in my own life and it was going to take some time getting used to that.

The reception committee lying in wait at the door to the ward made the chances of leaving this place dry-eyed totally impossible. They were gathered in a small cluster waiting for me, and as I began walking towards them, Ellen raised her hands and slowly began to clap. It took only a second or two before the rest of them joined in, and by the time my father and I were close enough to fall into the many outstretched arms waiting to hug us, I was in tears. They thrust a huge 'Sorry You're Leaving' card – the kind you usually get when you quit your job – into my hands.

'Er . . . one or two of those comments might be a bit rude,' warned Heidi, when she saw my father looking over my shoulder at the card, which held messages of good wishes in many different styles of handwriting. I smiled at the faint blush on my therapist's cheeks, knowing how much I'd particularly enjoy reading whatever it was she'd written.

Without doubt, the toughest goodbye of all was the one I had to say to Ellen.

'It's not goodbye,' she said fiercely, pulling me against her for a long hard hug. 'We're going to meet for lunch next week, remember?'

I nodded into her bony shoulder, now damp with my tears. 'I don't think I want to go,' I whispered in a terrified confession that only she could hear. 'I'm not sure I'm ready.'

Ellen didn't laugh off my worries, or gloss over them by telling me I'd be fine. That wasn't her style. She leant back and held my upper arms firmly in her strong capable hands. 'You will fall down,' she predicted, nodding her head at her own words for emphasis. 'Physically and emotionally. And not just once, but many times.'

I sniffed and tried to smile, but I think it came out a little crooked. 'Not really making me feel much better here.'

Ellen's smile was full of a confidence I was far from feeling. 'But every time you fall you're going to pick yourself back up and walk on. Do you want to know how I know this?'

'Because Heidi is a great big bully?'

Ellen laughed and glanced over at the short blonde therapist, who was hugging my dad so tightly I feared we might need to stop at A and E on our way out, to get his ribs checked over. 'You'll get back up, Madeline Chambers, because you are the bravest, strongest, woman I have ever had the privilege of nursing back to health.'

It wasn't the moment for a flip or sarcastic rejoinder, so I simply took her hands in mine and spoke from my heart. 'Thank you. For everything.'

'Pwah, you did it yourself. *And* you're going to keep on doing it. There's a whole new life out there, waiting for you to discover it.'

The confidence and buoyancy of Ellen's words stayed with me as my dad tucked my hand in the crook of his arm and led me across the hospital car park. The cold November wind was a refreshing novelty after the heat of the ward, and I allowed myself a moment of pure thankfulness that I was here, alive, when so many people had clearly thought I would never live to see this day. I was finally leaving hospital, and even if it wasn't with the man I had once loved, or the child we had created together, there was still a future ahead for me; there was still a life. It was just going to be different from the one I'd planned to live, that's all.

'It's a decent no-frills kind of a place,' said my father, pulling into the large forecourt of the hotel he'd booked us into. It was one from a well-known budget chain, where he'd frequently stayed when visiting me.

He drove slowly and carefully around the car park, a small frown creasing his forehead as he passed several spaces that all looked plenty big enough to me. Not that I'd be driving myself for a while, at least not until the doctors said I could. It was high on the list of points I wanted to raise at my first check-up.

My dad insisted on carrying my bag once again as we headed for the glass-walled hotel reception. For a man who'd stayed here regularly enough to know many of the staff by name, he appeared to be scoping the area with a curious air of unease. It wasn't until the automatic doors slid open, ushering us into the blue-carpeted foyer, that I realised why.

I turned to my father. 'What's he doing here? Did you know he was coming today?' My voice sounded tight and high, and probably a little too loud in the echoing foyer. The chances of Ryan having missed my less-than-welcoming comment were practically zero.

'No, Maddie, I didn't know he was coming. And I certainly didn't arrange it. I only realised Ryan was here when I saw his car in the car park.'

That explained the worried frown; and there was good reason for his concern, for I'd made it perfectly clear to Ryan that until a solution was found to the problem his unforgivable lie had created, I didn't want to see him. Our last conversation, two weeks earlier, had ended in a frustrating stalemate, and I could see from his eyes that Ryan remembered it as vividly as I did, as my father propelled me across the foyer towards him.

'I want to see my daughter, Ryan.'

He had frowned, and I suspected it was my choice of pronoun that had caused his handsome face to stiffen into a grim and determined expression.

'Obviously you can see her, Maddie. No one's saying you can't,' *he began placatingly, allowing my hopes to rise up like mercury in a barometer, before making them plummet back down again when he added: 'In time.'*

'There's been far too much time spent apart already. I don't want to add to it.'

Ryan had run his hands distractedly through his hair. Dishevelled Ryan had always been far harder to resist than the neatly presented, suited version, and apparently a small thing like a six-year coma hadn't altered that one little bit.

'I understand that,' he had said, making the mistake of reaching out to try to take my hands in his. I'd swatted him away like a wasp; the type you knew was probably going to end up stinging you, whatever you did to avoid it. 'All I'm asking is that you're patient and give us time to figure out how to handle this for the best.'

'I've waited six years, Ryan. It's not fair to ask me to wait any longer.'

His eyes had looked tormented. 'None of this is fair, Maddie. You and I should have been married in 2012. We should have been raising Hope together. And she shouldn't have to be grappling with big life issues like comas, and injuries, and death at five years old.'

His cobalt blue eyes had stared beseechingly into mine. He was asking me to step aside, at least temporarily. But I didn't think that I could do that.

'But no one actually died, did they, Ryan? You just lied, and told our daughter that I had, and now you don't want to undo that lie.'

The last thing I'd been expecting was his brutally honest reply. 'No. I don't want to. Because I'm afraid of what it will do to her, and to her trust in me and her m— and Chloe.'

I'd bitten my lip to prevent it from trembling. Mother. He'd been about to refer to the woman who had everything that once was mine, as Hope's mother.

'At least give us some time to speak to people: to our GP, or a child psychologist? That's not unreasonable, is it?'

'Don't you think it might have been a good idea to have done that before now, so you already had a plan in place?' I'd asked.

Ryan hadn't replied, and it took only a moment for me to realise why. Of course he'd never bothered to consult anyone; there was no contingency plan waiting for this moment. Because this was never meant to happen. I was a sleeping corpse who'd upset everything by waking up.

'Ryan,' greeted my dad warmly, thrusting out his hand into Ryan's waiting one. My father clapped Ryan lightly on the shoulder in a gesture of affection. Instantly I felt wrong-footed. Their relationship had grown in depth while I slept, and the closeness between them made me feel like an inter-loper. This is *my* dad, I wanted to declare childishly. He's *mine*, not yours. Maybe Ryan's caution wasn't misplaced after all. I hardly sounded like someone who was mature enough to be anyone's mother.

'I didn't know you were going to be here today, lad.'

The *lad*, who now had a few threads of silver entwining with the blond at his temples, had kept his eyes fixed firmly on my face throughout their greeting. His expression was guarded and watchful. It was the way you might look if you should suddenly encounter an animal that appeared docile and domesticated, but could turn feral at any moment. We were a very long way from the couple who had once loved each other enough to want to spend the rest of our lives together.

'I thought Maddie might appreciate having some of her old clothes to wear,' Ryan replied, annoyingly talking about me as though I wasn't there, or was that just the way they were used to conversing after my six years of silence?

I glanced down at the floor and felt a lightning bolt of recognition shoot through me. It wasn't just seeing the familiar piece of red luggage that suddenly made me feel like crying. It was the airline tag that was still fastened around its handles. They were from the last holiday Ryan and I had taken together. From our trip to Spain, where Hope had been conceived.

There was a silence which my father was quick to fill. 'Well, that was extremely thoughtful of you. I forgot you'd put her belongings into storage.'

My head sprung up at this revelation.

'Most of your stuff was already at mine before the accident

anyway,' Ryan explained. 'And you'd given notice on your flat, so it made sense to get the rest of your belongings and put them into storage.'

That was the moment when I'm sure I was supposed to say 'thank you', but all I could see were my clothes hanging unworn in his wardrobe. How long had he allowed them to stay there before packing them away into storage with the rest of my possessions? Had they only gone when he'd needed to make space in that same wardrobe for Chloe's clothes instead?

Another awkward moment of silence descended, and once again my father intervened. 'Why don't I go and get us checked in, and take this bag up to your room and leave you two to chat in private?'

I opened my mouth to say that wasn't necessary, but Ryan got his response in first. 'Thank you, Bill.'

I watched my father head towards the reception desk, trundling my case behind him, and tried to feel like a grown woman and less like an abandoned child.

'Could we go and grab a coffee somewhere? We need to talk, Maddie.'

I looked at the dark circles beneath his eyes, which were almost as pronounced as the ones I was currently wearing. Above them his eyes were uncertain, and there was something in his hesitancy that touched me in a way I would rather it did not.

The hotel didn't have its own restaurant, but guests were able to use the establishment next door. As I stepped out into the chilly morning beside Ryan, his hand went automatically to the small of my back, gently guiding me towards the other building. I walked faster than was comfortable, not to get out of the cold, but to escape all the emotions that his remembered touch kept trying to reignite.

Ryan ordered coffees at the bar, while I found a table beside an open fireplace and used the intervening minutes to compose myself. The restaurant was comparatively empty and was as good a place as any for a private discussion. A few minutes later Ryan joined me, carrying a tray with the steaming coffees and an enormous slice of carrot cake. It had always been my particular favourite, and the fact that he had remembered touched me far more than it should. Perhaps there *were* still feelings and memories that affected him almost as much as they did me. However, when he passed me the plate with his left hand, I saw that today he hadn't bothered to remove his wedding ring. It sat like a bright golden reminder of everything I had lost. My appetite for the cake suddenly disappeared.

'It must feel really strange to finally be out of hospital.'

I stabbed at the cake with my fork. 'Yes. It does a bit.'

'How long are you staying at the hotel? Are you going back with your dad?' Ryan's voice sounded hopeful, rather than just politely interested.

The cake was in my mouth; I'm sure it was perfectly delicious, but suddenly it tasted like sawdust. 'No. I have to stay here in town, to be near the hospital. I'll be having monthly check-ups with the doctors and physio. Dad's staying for a couple of nights, then he's going back to be with Mum. Apparently she doesn't do well if she doesn't see him every day.'

'Yes, I know.'

I bit my lip and stared into the fire, hating that he knew so much more about the situation and my mother's condition than I did myself.

'Will you carry on living here?' Ryan asked, gesturing towards the adjacent hotel.

I shook my head, wondering why this whole conversation felt so forced and unnatural. It was like an awkward hybrid between a job interview and a blind date with someone you knew straight away you were never going to click with.

'Only until I find a place to rent,' I said, reaching out and warming my hands in the heat of the flames. After the over-heated hospital, everywhere felt cold to me. 'I understand I have you to thank for sorting out the insurance settlement.'

Ryan waved his hand dismissively, possibly because it was all so long ago he'd most likely forgotten fighting for my very generous settlement, which would allow me the independence of living in a place of my own, and not having to worry about finding a new job for some time. Which was just as well, as I still needed to take at least a couple of naps during the day, and I couldn't see many prospective employers finding that an asset.

'Chloe and I have been trying to figure out how best to manage this situation,' Ryan began, sounding suddenly awkward. *Situation*. Was that what I now was in his life – a *situation*, something that needed to be handled? 'We've spoken to people, and read whatever we can find on the internet, but obviously what we have here is a pretty unique problem.'

I wanted to get to my feet, the way they do in courtroom dramas, and shout *'Objection'*, because he was making it sound as though *I* was the 'problem' here.

'We'd like to tell Hope that you're a distant cousin. That way we can introduce you as a family member, and give you the chance to get to know each other and grow closer, without any additional pressure.'

Or threat to Chloe, I silently added, still determined to cast her as the villain in this story.

'And then, eventually, when you and Hope have spent enough time together and she likes and trusts you, well, then we'll tell her who you really are.'

'So the best solution you can come up with, after having told our daughter the most colossal lie, is to lie to her *again*?' Was it the warmth of the fire that coloured his cheeks, or my cutting observation?

'It's a *white* lie,' he defended, as though the colour sanitised the untruth. 'And it will allow both of you to form a real relationship, without any obstacles getting in your way.'

As much as I didn't want to accept this half-measure of being introduced into my daughter's life, I wasn't stupid. I could see this was a sensible solution. But there *was* one problem Ryan clearly hadn't considered.

'And what happens if she doesn't *ever* get to like me, or trust me? What if she never learns to love me?'

His eyes widened as they looked at me with astonishment. 'Are you serious? She's going to love you. Everyone who meets you always does.'

And just like that I was lost, all over again. Because as much as I tried to tell myself otherwise, I was still every bit as much in love with Chloe's husband as I had ever been.

The red suitcase was the only splash of colour in the neutral-toned decor of the hotel bedroom. My dad had left it for me, at the foot of the double bed. The case *and* the bed looked equally inviting. I was exhausted, and while some of that was no doubt due to my morning of unaccustomed activity, even more of it was a result of my conversation with Ryan. He had left some time ago, and yet his curious proposal was still circling in my head, like a plane looking for a landing spot on rocky terrain. If I accepted his suggestion, I could see Hope as soon as tomorrow, if I felt ready. But if I dug my heels in and insisted that we meet for the first time as mother and daughter, I had no idea how long I'd have to wait.

I looked longingly at the double bed, which appeared as wide as a trampoline after the narrow hospital cots I'd been used to. But the Pandora-pull of the suitcase was too strong to ignore. There was a low-grade excitement gently thrumming through me as I undid the zip and chased it back around the edge of the case. In a world where nothing was the same, where everything and everyone had changed, I was far more excited than a grown woman should probably be at the prospect of seeing something as mundane as a case full of my old familiar clothes. Except the first thing I saw when I flipped back the lid wasn't old or familiar – or even mine, come to that, although I have no doubt it was meant for me. I also had no doubt that *Ryan* wasn't the one who'd put it there.

The name of the high street store was at least familiar, and one of its dark-green carrier bags was sitting on top of my neatly folded clothes. A waft of clean-smelling fragrance had risen like a cloud the moment I'd opened the case. *Someone* had washed and ironed every item of my clothing. The Ryan I remembered had barely known one end of an iron from the other, which made the chances of it having been him highly unlikely.

I reached for the carrier bag and tipped it upside down. The contents fell on to the mattress beside my suitcase. There were two packets of underwear. Nothing fancy, just your regular everyday multi-pack of briefs. There were also two bras in the bag: one white; one beige. Everything appeared to be the right size, which again ruled out Ryan as being responsible. Every clothing gift he'd ever bought me had had to be secretly returned and exchanged for the correct size. The last items to fall out of the carrier bag were a packet of socks and some tights. Everything still had its price tag attached, and the receipt had floated down with the final items, like a leaf from a tree. I looked at the collection of underwear for a long moment. This wasn't the work of a man. Not even a man as thoughtful and loving as Ryan was. *Had been*, I mentally corrected. I had to keep reminding myself that *New Ryan* was still a stranger to me. He was a husband and a father, and the jury was still out as to whether I would like the changes those two new roles had brought about.

Chloe had obviously bought the underwear for me. I tried to give myself a moment not to follow my instinctive knee-jerk reaction and sweep the bought items off the bed in a fit of anger and frustration. She had so much of mine already, was it fair of her to try to take away the tiny shred of autonomy buying my own underwear would have given me? It was a nice thing she had done; a thoughtful gesture, some might say. She certainly didn't have to do it. But she had. She also didn't have to take my fiancé and play mother to my baby, but she'd done that too. Good sense didn't stand much of a chance here. The items flew through the air in a colourful display, each one hitting the adjacent wall before falling in a jumble to the carpet. I too flopped down to the floor, and promptly burst into tears.

A few hours' sleep helped to restore me to a slightly more rational human being. A long hot soak in a bathtub, without a queue of patients waiting to use it after me, did the rest. By the time my father and I went for a very early dinner (my stomach still being on the NHS dining plan) I felt almost normal again.

We managed two entire courses without touching on any topic likely to disturb the peaceful calm of our evening.

'That was absolutely delicious,' I declared, pushing aside

my totally cleared plate. My father's grey and slightly way-ward eyebrows rose questioningly. Food critic was clearly *not* a career I should be considering anytime soon.

'I think a few too many hospital dinners might have affected your judgement,' he said, gently squeezing my hand across the table top.

'You may be right,' I agreed with a rueful smile. 'It's going to take a while to get used to doing ordinary everyday things again: like sleeping in a bed that doesn't have a metal frame; making a cup of tea anytime I fancy one; or having my own front door once more.'

My father's smile faltered on my last comment. 'I'm going to worry about you, living on your own.'

'Dad, I've lived on my own ever since I went away to university,' I reasoned.

'I know, Maddie. But I'm still going to worry. It's what parents do. One day, when you have a—' He stopped abruptly, and his cheeks flushed to the colour of an over-ripe tomato.

'I'm so sorry, Maddie. I didn't mean . . . Obviously I know that . . .'

This time it was my hand that reached for his. 'Don't worry about it, Dad. I know what you meant anyway. Hope might be my flesh and blood, but what do I know about being a mother? Absolutely nothing. As much as it hurts to admit it, I think Ryan might be right. I need to get to know Hope, and she needs to get to know me before we tell her who I really am.'

My father said nothing, but spent a very long time stirring his cup of coffee, which I was pretty sure he'd already done a few minutes earlier.

'What?' I probed, when he failed to lift his head and look at me. 'Don't you agree with that idea? Do you think Ryan's wrong?' There was a clutching-at-straws eagerness to my voice, which I'm sure he easily recognised.

'Not wrong, perhaps. But I think they're seriously under-estimating that little girl. She's uncommonly bright, and I'm not just saying that because she's my granddaughter.' I smiled slowly, wondering if he knew the way his face lit up whenever he spoke about my daughter.

'Do you think she'll work out who I am? Even after everything Ryan has told her?'

My father gave a small shrug of his elderly shoulders. 'For a start, I think she's going to notice she looks an awful lot more like you than she does either of her parents.'

I stared at the woven pattern of my serviette, watching it blur, dance, and then finally crystallise back into fabric. 'When Hope speaks to Chloe, what does she call her, Dad?'

My father looked like he'd rather stab his steak knife straight into his heart than answer me truthfully. What parent would ever want to do or say something that they know will cause their child so much heartbreak or pain?

'She believes what Ryan told her, my love. She believes her natural mother passed away after an accident.'

I shook my head, because he wasn't answering my question. His eyes were washed-out blue pools of anguish when he eventually replied. 'She calls her Mummy. I'm so sorry, sweetheart, but Hope calls her Mummy.'

For someone who had embraced the world of technology and social media so wholeheartedly, I'd been oddly reluctant to re-enter it since I'd woken up in hospital. However, sitting cross-legged on my hotel bed, poring over the infuriatingly small images on my phone's screen, I really missed my laptop and tablet for the first time.

'There's no need to rush into things,' urged my father, who was sitting in the hotel room's only chair. 'You don't want to jump and sign a lease on the very first property you go to see. There'll always be more next week.'

I tried not to smile at his very poorly disguised attempt to discourage me from finding a place of my own to live.

'I know that, Dad. But this flat looks ideal. It's on the ground floor, and it even has a patio area. *And* it's not expensive, either.' The details of the two-bedroom flat had practically leapt off the screen at me, and I had to admit they sounded very encouraging. The rooms looked spacious and as I scrolled through the gallery of images, I got a strange fluttery feeling each time I arrived at the photograph of the small and sunny second bedroom. Would that be the room where one day Hope would come to stay? Was that something that Ryan and Chloe would allow? I shook my head. It was just as Heidi had said the very first time she'd pulled me out of my wheelchair and onto my feet: 'One step at a time.'

I passed the phone to my father and watched him read the property details with so much care you'd have thought he was studying for an imminent exam on them. He swiped through the photographs, not just once but three times, clearly looking for even a modest-sized fly in the ointment, but finding none.

'It does look very promising,' he admitted grudgingly.

'I'm going to phone and see if I can arrange a viewing for today.'

'So soon?' he asked, looking startled. I still didn't think he fully understood my need to take up the reins and regain control, but in order to make sense of this newly returned life, I knew that was what I needed to do. Which made what I had to say next so much harder.

'Dad, would you be terribly offended if I went to see it by myself?'

He coughed unnecessarily for a long moment, which I politely pretended was entirely normal, before answering in a gruff voice. 'No. Of course not. I can drive you there and just wait in the car.' I looked at him from beneath my lowered lashes, until he laughed at his own suggestion. 'Okay, I get it. No interfering parent required.'

I unfurled my legs and crossed the room to put my arms around his neck and kiss the prickly grey bristle on his cheek. 'You're not interfering. But I need to start doing things alone. And this is a good place to begin. If they can arrange a viewing for this afternoon, I'll get the number of a taxi company from the hotel reception.'

'There's no need for that. You might as well *Uber* it. I've got the app on my phone.'

I stopped midway through dialling the number of the estate agent, to look at my father in total confusion. 'I have absolutely no idea what you just said.'

He tapped the side of his nose playfully, and I could see how much he was enjoying this moment of unexpected role reversal. 'I'll explain it to you later,' he said with a wink.

I recognised him straight away. For me it had been just months since we'd last met. It took him a moment or two longer to place me. Some of my father's concern had managed to rub off on me during the twenty-minute journey to the large Victorian property I'd come to see. By the time I'd climbed out of the car, thanked the driver; felt weird about not having to pay him; and stood looking up at the tall imposing building, I was more than just a little jittery.

Had my father been right? Was it foolish for a single woman to have arranged to meet a landlord in an empty property by herself? Was I so doggedly determined to prove I was capable of looking after myself that I'd made a stupid – even dangerous – mistake? Could this man pose a threat to me? My footsteps were slowing as I walked up the black-and-white tiled path. Because suddenly I was back on a June day, when my own paranoia, my own imagination, had turned a perfectly innocent man into a threat. And look how *that* had ended up. There was nothing to fear here.

I pressed the buzzer for the ground-floor flat, and moments later was standing in the tiled hallway outside a black painted front door. I heard the approach of footsteps from within and shifted nervously from one foot to the other. And then the door swung open, and before it had completed its arc, I was smiling broadly. There really *was* nothing at all to fear, because I knew this man, and he knew me.

'Mitch,' I cried, frantically mobilising all of my brain cells to come up with his surname, and failing miserably. I'd only ever known him as 'Mitch', which was a step up from most of my former colleagues, who used to refer to him simply as 'the IT guy . . . you know, the one who looks like Grizzly Adams'.

As though the remembered insult might possibly be written all over my face, I overcompensated slightly, greeting him as enthusiastically as if we were long-lost cousins.

'How amazing to see you again. I had no idea this was your place.'

'Madeline?' he said cautiously, like a diver who wasn't quite ready to jump in at the deep end. 'Madeline Chambers? Maddie? I thought you were . . . I didn't know you had . . .'

It wasn't fair or kind to leave him floundering like that, and I only allowed it to continue for a moment. 'You knew about my accident then?'

His eyebrows rose incredulously. They were thick and dark, like well-fed caterpillars. 'Everyone knew. You were sort of a local celebrity.' He suddenly realised what he'd said and a hint of pink crept onto his face, or as much of it as I could see beneath the beard. 'I guess no one wants to be famous that way though, do they?' he added sympathetically.

We stood for a moment, neither one of us sure how to proceed. What should have been a simple business-like property-viewing had been derailed by our tenuous history, and neither of us knew how to get it back on track.

'Come in, please,' Mitch invited, allowing the door to swing wider. Even so, there wasn't much room to squeeze past him in the narrow hallway. I'd forgotten how huge he was. Not just tall, but broad with it. He'd always reminded me of an American football player who'd idly wandered off the field having forgotten to remove his shoulder pads. It wasn't until I'd followed Mitch down a short passageway, which led to a lovely cosy lounge, that I realised he'd actually lost quite a lot of weight since the last time we'd met. But then again, so had I. Of the two of us, he looked far better for it than I did.

'Sit down,' urged Mitch, gesturing towards a faded chintz-patterned sofa. 'Can I get you something? Tea? Coffee? Something stronger? I think there's a bottle of sherry knocking around here somewhere.' Once again we were way off track, lost in a no-man's-land between business and social niceties.

'No. I'm fine thanks.'

'You look fine. Well, you look a bit pale. But I've got to be truthful, you look a hell of a lot better than you did the last time I saw you.'

I tried not to wince at the brutal honesty. He was clearly a direct, shoot-from-the-hip kind of a person. I pushed away the mountain-man image that my description conjured up, and tried to remember the occasion he was talking about. The company we both worked for had switched its computer operating system, and there'd been an avalanche of glitches and problems that had resulted in Mitch being a very frequent visitor to the Media section where I worked. *Had worked*, I corrected mentally.

'It was pretty tough seeing you like that. I can't imagine how hard it must have been for your fiancé and family.'

I raised my head to look him in the face. It had to travel upwards a considerable distance from my position on the couch to where he stood before me.

'You came to the hospital? I didn't know that.' It wasn't the smartest comment I had ever made, considering there were six whole years which I'd known nothing about, and during one of them I'd even delivered a baby without any recollection of doing so. 'How come . . .? Why did you . . .?' I must have looked as confused as I felt. I'd always got on well with Mitch. We used to chat while he worked at fixing whatever had gone wrong with my computer. And a couple of times I had joined him for coffee, if we both happened to be in the canteen at the same time. But I wouldn't exactly have called us friends. I never saw him out of work. We moved in different circles, and I knew he and his wife had lived in a small village some distance from town.

Once again Mitch's face coloured slightly, and I felt bad that I'd embarrassed him twice in the space of almost as many minutes. I only hoped he wouldn't hold it against me if I wanted to rent his flat, because from the little I'd seen so far, it looked exactly what I was hoping to find.

'I didn't go alone,' he admitted. 'A whole group of us from work went up to see you. I think everyone hoped that the more voices you heard, the more chance there was of something penetrating through to wherever you were lost.' It was an unexpectedly poetic way of describing the nothingness of my coma.

I looked away from the watchful concern in his dark brown eyes. 'Well, that was really nice of you. Thank you. Sorry I didn't wake up for you.'

'I guess you just weren't ready to come back then,' Mitch replied, and there was a sympathy in his voice that told me he probably knew not only about Hope, but also about Ryan's marriage to another fiancée. My five minutes of fame had made my life an open book to everyone who'd known me. The only person who hadn't uncovered all of its secrets yet was me.

'So, the flat,' I said with breezy enthusiasm, that didn't sound entirely natural.

Mitch seized on the safer topic, like a life buoy in the ocean. 'Yes. Absolutely. What do you want to know?'

'Erm, can I see it?'

He flushed for the third time. The poor man was practically allergic to whatever I said. It also told me that he wasn't exactly a practised landlord, something he himself confirmed as he politely held open the door of the lounge for me. 'This place was actually my grandmother's,' he explained. He rested a hand, which felt as large as a dinner plate, on my shoulder to guide me. 'The kitchen's this way.'

It was a reasonable-sized room, and there were certainly enough cabinets and storage for someone who didn't own as much as a single saucepan any more. It was six years too late to regret donating all of my kitchen utensils to a local charity shop, and somehow I doubted the plan to share Ryan's equipment was still an option.

'It's a bit dated, I know,' Mitch apologised. 'I fitted it myself about ten years ago, but these things go out of style so quickly.' He ran his hand thoughtfully along one wooden surface and I could see the affection in his eyes which I'm sure wasn't for the smooth oak worktop, but for the kitchen's former owner.

'You said the flat used to be your grandmother's?' My question dangled in the air, seeking more information.

The sorrow in Mitch's eyes answered it for me, even before he spoke. 'Yes. It was. She passed away six months ago.' He looked around the kitchen, as though he still expected to see its former occupant here. 'She left this place to me. I think she hoped I'd sell it and pay off my mortgage, but ...' His eyes looked a little bright, so I feigned an interest in the wooden grain of the cupboards until he was able to continue. 'I'm not ready to sell it yet and have strangers living here. But I don't want to move in myself. So renting it out – to the right person – seems like the best option.'

'It's a good idea,' I said, surprising myself by reaching out and laying a hand gently on his forearm. My fingers didn't even go halfway around it. Mitch cleared his throat, and I drew back my hand, afraid I'd just overstepped the tenant/landlord boundary.

'There's something I should tell you before you make a decision about whether you're interested in the place.'

I waited, wondering why he suddenly seemed uncomfortable. He looked like someone about to rip off a very big sticking plaster. 'My grandmother died here, in the flat. Not in the bedroom . . .' he added hastily, as though the geography was all important, 'but in the lounge.' I thought of the lovely cosy lounge and waited to see if this breaking news altered my earlier opinion of it. It didn't.

'Some of the people I've shown around have been a bit . . . freaked out when I've told them. They've all said they couldn't possibly live in a place where someone had recently died. One girl told me – quite straight-faced – that the flat was definitely haunted.' Mitch gave a nervous laugh and looked up to see if I was joining in. I smiled weakly, which I hoped would suffice.

'Anyway, in case you're scared of ghosts, or vampires, or zombies, I thought I should tell you this before we go any further.' He had an expression on his face, of a man who couldn't believe he was having this conversation.

I probably spent less than five seconds considering what he'd said, and knew I wasn't in the least bit put off. 'Mitch, I've been about as close to death as it's possible to get for a very long time, and now I've come back. If there *is* a zombie around here, it's probably me.'

The sigh of relief he gave sounded like air escaping from a balloon. But before the subject was lost in a tour of the flat, I was curious about one thing: 'If prospective tenants were put off by what had happened, why did you keep telling them about it?'

Mitch seemed genuinely puzzled by my question. 'Because invariably they asked, and because ...' He gave a shrug of his massive shoulders. '... because I didn't want to deceive anyone. I don't tell lies.'

Mitch's philosophy in life sounded like the polar opposite to Ryan's, and I was never really sure if that was what made me impulsively say: 'I'll take it.'

Mitch looked confused. 'You'll take what?'

'The flat. That's if you're willing to have a quasi-zombie for a tenant.'

'But you haven't even seen the rest of it yet.'

I grinned, unable to explain the exact feeling of 'rightness' that making this decision had suddenly given me. 'I don't need to. I mean, I *will* look, but I don't need to. My mind's made up.'

He laughed, and I'd forgotten how low and deep the sound was. It used to fill the office or the corridors of the building whenever someone cracked a ridiculous joke. The laugh rumbled up from somewhere deep within him, as though it had travelled a long way before it was released. From the height of him – well over six foot four – it probably had.

'Okay,' he said, his eyes still twinkling in merriment. 'But just so no one can accuse me of taking advantage of you, why don't I show you the rest of it anyway?'

We did a whistle-stop tour, and everything I saw I liked. Okay, so the bathroom wasn't particularly modern, and I really would have preferred a separate shower, but there was a charm to the flat that had won me over.

The master bedroom was empty apart from one large wardrobe – which would easily accommodate my very modest suitcase-full of clothes – and a brand-new double bed, its mattress still encased in a plastic wrapper. I gave a small inward sigh of relief. For six years I had slept in beds occupied by goodness-only-knows how many people before me. It would be rather nice to sleep in one that was totally new.

'It's all perfect,' I said, looking around with a smile. 'Where do I sign?'

He looked as though I'd presented him with a very tricky equation. 'I have absolutely no idea. I guess the estate agents will handle all the paperwork. I just wanted to be the one to show the flat, and make sure it went to the right kind of tenant.' He looked down at me, and even though I'm not short, I felt dwarfed by him. 'And I really think that it has.' This time *I* was the one who blushed. I probably owed him that one.

We were walking down the corridor, on our way back to the lounge, when he stopped so suddenly that I walked straight into him. It was like colliding with a brick wall. 'I've just realised, I forgot to show you the second bedroom.'

He pulled open the door immediately to his right, to reveal the small sunny room. True, in real-life the wallpaper was slightly tired and faded, but I was picturing the walls painted bright yellow, with a colourful duvet and cushions thrown across the single bed. I felt the same excited shiver run through me that I'd experienced when I'd seen this room on the internet. This was Hope's bedroom.

The thought led me to a memory that hadn't occurred to me until that very moment. 'I've just remembered, the last time we spoke – it must have been a few weeks before my accident – you and your wife had just had a baby, hadn't you? A little boy, wasn't it?'

Mitch's eyes crinkled when he smiled, and it transformed his whole face into something that wasn't conventionally handsome, but was still quite startlingly attractive. He was lit up from within, in almost the exact same way that Ryan had been whenever he spoke of Hope. Clearly it was a dad thing.

'You've got a good memory.'

'Not really. For me it was only a couple of months ago.'

Mitch shook his head in fascination, as if I were performing some kind of mind-boggling illusion. 'Well, that baby you're talking about isn't a baby any more. Sam is six now.'

'Six?' I said wonderingly, as though it was a number I had never heard before. I had a sudden vivid flashback of Mitch fishing out his mobile phone to show me a photograph of his newborn baby boy, held in the arms of its mother.

Perhaps Mitch shared that memory, for his face suddenly sobered as he added: 'Colleen and I aren't together any more.

We were divorced four years ago, so now I only get to see Sam every other weekend.'

I tried to think of something appropriate to say, but came up blank every time. Instead, I stopped worrying about whether or not it was appropriate, and for the second time that day I laid a hand lightly on his arm. I was out of step with so many people, but here, in this place that was soon to be my new home, beside the man who was soon to be my new landlord, I felt I'd found a kindred spirit. Someone who understood. We had so much more in common than I had realised and while I might not be superstitious, I couldn't help feeling there was a reason why our paths had crossed once again today.

Chapter 6

I moved into Mitch's grandmother's flat the very next day after viewing it. I could probably have moved in that same night if I'd wanted to. As Mitch walked me to the door he was already sliding a front door key from his keyring.

'Don't you think we should wait for the paperwork?' I'd asked, reluctant to take the key he was holding out to me in a hand roughly the size of a bear's paw. 'Won't you need to take up references, or something?'

'I *know* where you've lived for the last six years,' he said with a sympathetic smile. 'And where you last worked. I have all the references I need. Take the key,' he urged, pressing it into the palm of my hand. It was still warm from his touch, and my fingers closed around it, as though I was afraid he might suddenly change his mind.

But he hadn't. And a few days later, the paperwork was all signed and his grandmother's home was officially mine, or at least it was for the next six months.

*

And now, one week later, I was sitting at the table in my new kitchen, wearing an attractive but incredibly itchy bright red jumper, and drinking far more coffee than was good for me, as I prepared to meet my daughter for the very first time.

Ryan had sounded momentarily thrown when I'd phoned him to confirm I was willing to let him introduce me as a cousin. There'd been a long moment of silence which had stretched on and on. 'Are you still there?' I'd eventually had to ask.

'Erm, yes. All right. That's, erm ... that's great.'

Something told me he didn't think it was great at all, and it was only then that it occurred to me that he'd never thought I would accept his suggestion. He'd thought he had more time. 'I'll ... I'll need to talk to Chloe and get back to you about the arrangements.'

Irritation had frizzled through me like an electric shock, because couldn't they have already discussed that?

'I'm not going back on my word, Maddie,' Ryan promised, uncannily picking up my secret thoughts as though they were projected on a screen. 'I *want* you to meet her. I *want* you to see what an incredibly special little girl she is.'

But only as a distant relative. The words were screaming to be let out, but I gritted my teeth and allowed them no exit.

To be fair, Ryan *had* phoned back later that evening with a plan. My heart had jumped annoyingly when I'd seen his name on the screen of my new phone. Would it always do that? Was I always going to feel those emotions whenever we were in a room together? Could he see or sense them? I certainly hoped not. This whole situation was far too uncomfortable for everyone as it was.

'Does Saturday work for you?' he'd asked. 'We thought it was better not to do it on a school day.'

Five days was nothing, I supposed. Not when we'd waited years for this moment. 'Where should we meet?' I asked, panicking that I had no idea how five-year-old girls liked to spend their time.

'Here, of course,' Ryan replied, as though the location had never been in question.

'At your house?' My voice had come out with a revealing squeak. I knew Ryan had moved out of his old flat not long after Hope was born. We'd always said it wasn't a suitable place to raise a baby, but it was unsettling to discover the decisions we'd made together, he'd eventually carried out alone ... or with someone else.

My next question was unavoidable. 'Will ... will Chloe be there as well?' Her name still burnt my tongue every time I had to say it, but it looked as though I was going to have to get over that. Fast.

'Of course she will. Hope would only be suspicious and unsettled if she went out, and what we want to do is to make this all as natural and casual as possible.'

A supposedly deceased mother comes to visit her five-year-old daughter for the very first time, and Ryan was talking about making it natural? Was he serious?

We set a time for the meeting and Ryan gave me his

address, which I wrote down carefully in a small notebook. It wasn't until later that I noticed I'd been gripping the pen so tightly, his address was gouged through almost half the sheets in the pad.

Although my father had wanted to come with me, I'd gently turned him down. I wasn't nearly as adept at pretence as the rest of them so clearly were, and I didn't want to give the game away. Not yet, at least. 'I'll slip up and call you "Dad",' I told him, softening my words with a smile. 'And then if Hope's as bright as you say she is, she'll work out straight away who I am.'

Unable to deny the very real possibility of one of us tripping up over the truth, my dad had reluctantly agreed to stay away. 'I just thought it would be easier for you if there was someone there who was on *your* side.'

I swallowed the uncomfortable lump in my throat, as his words served to confirm what I'd suspected. There would be sides, as in a battle. There would be gains and there would be losses, and possibly casualties. It just wasn't possible to predict yet whose they would be.

Although Ryan had offered to pick me up, I had quietly insisted that I'd prefer to make my own way to his home. That at least spared me the embarrassment of having him look at me the way the taxi driver had done, when I'd made him drive around the block three times before I'd finally said in a shaky voice: 'Okay, this time you can stop. I'll get out now.'

I'd had plenty of opportunity on my circuits past his front door to assess Ryan's new home. It was a large detached property, with a neat front garden featuring an impressive willow tree. I'd told him once, a long time ago, that they were my favourite trees and I wondered if it was sheer coincidence that the house he'd bought had one growing in its front garden. It was a question I knew I would never ask.

The drive was deeply gravelled. I could feel the block heels of my black leather boots sinking into the stones like quicksand, sucking me down. I crunched my way towards the door, my heart hammering so loudly beneath the damn itchy jumper that the sound of the gravel seemed strangely muted and distant. All I could hear was a vague whooshing noise as my blood rushed frantically through a thousand veins and capillaries, doing a passable impression of the sound made by a conch shell. I stepped from the gravel onto a paved porch. The sun had abandoned its position in the sky, which was now thick with heavy grey clouds. It looked cold and unwelcoming. In contrast, the house gave out a warm yellow glow from the many lights shining through its windows. It seemed to be reaching out, beckoning me to come closer, but suddenly I felt like I was about to make a dreadful mistake. I didn't belong here. My chance to be part of this world had come . . . and then gone. I should just leave.

And yet my feet refused to move from their porch. And somehow – without being instructed to do so – my hand was lifting up to the small bell set into the brickwork. I stared unblinkingly at the front door, whose top half was glazed with milky-white glass. It felt like I had been standing out there for minutes, although in reality I'm sure it could only have been seconds. It was too soon to press the bell again, and yet my hand was already on its way to do so, when suddenly the glass revealed a shape in the hallway beyond. A figure approached the door; too short to be Ryan; too tall to be Hope. I heard the rattle of a security chain and the sliding of a bolt.

It was her. She was on the other side of the glass. And when she opened the door, nothing was ever going to be the same . . . for any of us.

PART TWO

Chapter 7

Chloe

My legs were shaking as I walked towards the front door. No, scratch that. My whole body was shaking. I always knew it would feel like this. Whenever it happened, wherever it happened, this was *always* going to be the way my body reacted.

'I'll get it,' I'd said, leaping to my feet before Ryan had a chance to answer the slightly-longer-than-necessary buzz of the doorbell. He'd looked up from his position on the floor, where he and Hope were busy building yet another sprawling Lego structure. It was Hope's favourite pastime, and endless residences had been built, demolished and then reconstructed for her Barbie dolls and cuddly toys. 'That girl's going to be an architect, for sure,' her granddad was fond of saying, his chest swelling up with pride, the way it did whenever he looked at his daughter's daughter.

I like Bill, I always have. And it wasn't just because of the gentle patience and love he freely showered on Hope. Bill was a generous man in all things – not financially, but then Ryan has a good job, so we didn't need that kind of help. No, Bill has a generous heart. It was big enough to love not only his wife, his injured daughter and his grandchild, but Ryan too. I don't think there are many people in this world who would then have held that door open a little bit wider to also invite me into their lives. But Bill had, and he'd never once made me feel like an outsider, or as though I don't belong. But would that all change now? Would the balance of everything be thrown wildly off-kilter after the thing they'd all been praying so very long for had finally come true?

Whenever I watch Bill playing with Hope, and see his gentle patience as he drinks endless cups of invisible tea from miniature plastic beakers, or the love on his face as he sings the theme tune from her favourite animated film – his voice off-key, but knowing all the words – I feel like I'm witnessing an echo from the past. This was the father Maddie had been lucky enough to grow up with, and secretly I've always envied her that. My own dad died when I was so young my memories of him are a curious collage of faded photographs and stories told to me by my mother. I can no longer tell which I genuinely recall, or which I have simply imagined.

'Are you sure?' Ryan had asked when the doorbell had rung, his eyes searching mine, full of warmth, concern, and love. I nodded, and hoped he didn't notice my nervous swallow.

Someone appeared to have stretched the hallway of our comfortable four-bedroom house. Surely it didn't usually take this long to reach the front door? I felt as though I was walking on one of those travelators, the kind they have at airports, except I was walking on it the wrong way. I glanced at the large oak-framed mirror hanging in the hallway, for one last check, and then instantly wished I hadn't. My hair was no longer smooth, and the grey shirt, which I'd thought looked so smart with my new black trousers, made me look as if I was going to a board meeting. I shook my head, watching the poker-straight shoulder-length blond hair fall back into place. There was no time to do anything about the pink flush to my cheeks, or the dryness in my mouth, because suddenly the door was before me. I could see her silhouette beyond the glass, ill-formed and shadowy; a ghost from the past, seeking to slip through the veil into the present.

My fingers trembled, making them clumsy on the bolt. From the lounge behind me I heard the crash of falling bricks and a child's laughter as she exclaimed in exasperation, 'Daddy!' I wanted to run back towards them, because that was my life, *they* were my life. And none of it was ever going to be the same again once I opened this front door. But change was coming, inexorably, like an approaching hurricane. All I could do was hope the foundations my life was built upon were strong enough to withstand the onslaught.

In my head they were unbreakable, but in the quiet secret places in my heart, I saw them tumbling into ruins, like a house made of Lego.

I opened the door.

She was so much taller than I had been expecting. I'd seen her a thousand times before, but always lying down. She would easily be able to look Ryan in the eye when they stood face-to-face, whereas the top of my head scarcely reached his jaw. He had to bend down to kiss me; with her that wouldn't be necessary. It was a bad thought to have in my head as I faced my husband's former lover.

I held out my hand, as though I really *was* at that board meeting. 'Hello. I'm Chloe.' My subconscious urged me to add *Ryan's wife* to the end of that introduction, but I shot it down. She knew that already; it was there in the twin fires burning in her deep blue eyes. They too surprised me. I had never seen her eyes open before, and yet the colour was achingly familiar. It was the colour of my daughter's eyes. *Her daughter's eyes,* I silently corrected.

Was the hand she lifted to join mine a little hesitant and slow to respond? Perhaps it was, just a fraction. I thought I saw a slight tremor in the long thin fingers before they connected with mine. It made me feel slightly better to see that she was as nervous as I was.

'Come in,' I said, hoping my voice sounded more natural to her ears than it did to mine. 'You found us okay?' I asked, suddenly overcome with a need to plug any conversational void with meaningless babble. 'People often get lost. Did you drive yourself?'

Maddie shook her head, and a long silky black curtain of hair moved with her, like a swirling matador's cape. I'd brushed that hair; I'd combed it off her porcelain-white forehead and even plaited it. It was something I was sure she didn't know, and would probably be horrified to discover. It was yet another secret that I'd be keeping to myself.

'I'm not allowed to drive yet. I came by cab.' For years I'd wondered about her voice. And now that I heard it, I could see how well it suited her. There was a soft huskiness in her throaty tones, which made my own sound too high and reedy in comparison.

'Oh, of course,' I said, wondering if she could hear the chipmunk-quality of my reply. 'Can I take your coat?' I held out my hand to take it from her, feeling happier to be back on familiar territory. When visitors came to your home, you greeted them politely; you enquired about their journey; you took their outer garments ... and then you invited them in, to see if they wanted to destroy the happiness you'd thought was yours forever. I was still grappling with the realisation that I might only be a temporary custodian of the life I'd thought was mine.

Maddie was still catwalk-thin from the coma. I could see that despite the chunky bright red jumper, whose colour suited her pale skin and dark hair. It was obvious that she still had a way to go before she reached the end of the road to full recovery, but even so she appeared far healthier than I'd ever seen her look before. For a moment we stood facing each other, unable to stop ourselves from conducting a very natural comparison, in a very unnatural situation. My curves, versus her slender frame; her long dark hair, and my shorter blond locks; her eyes the colour of sapphires, mine the smoky-grey of moonstones. We were nothing alike for two people who had so much in common.

'Ryan and Hope are through here,' I said at last.

Maddie nodded, but didn't move.

'Does she know—' She broke off, as though uncertain how to complete her sentence.

My voice dropped to the same whisper she'd used to ask her question. 'All we've said is that a distant relative might be dropping by today. We kept it deliberately casual.' I saw her wince at the word 'distant', and knew at once it wasn't one Ryan would have chosen.

'Okay.'

I stepped in front of her, expecting her to follow me, but two steps short of the lounge door I realised I was alone. I turned around, and was surprised by the lance of pity I felt at her clearly terrified expression. For a moment I forgot that standing in my home was the woman who could so easily destroy my life.

'I don't think I can do this,' Maddie said, her eyes darting to the front door, the way a cornered animal might do, scoping out its nearest escape route.

I retraced my steps until once again I stood before her. 'Yes you can,' I assured her, wondering how many times I would lie awake at night regretting those words.

A great many, as it turned out.

Ryan got to his feet in one fluid movement as I ushered the first woman he had loved into our lounge. I was watching Maddie carefully, and saw her eyes flash briefly to him before flying towards the dark-haired little girl kneeling on the rug in front of the fire. I felt relief . . . and then terror.

'Maddie, welcome,' said Ryan, walking over to where we both stood. Was that weird for him, I wondered, to see us standing there side by side? The wife he had, and the wife he could have had. It invited comparisons, it had to. And despite the fact that she'd only recently been discharged from hospital, I still thought that if it came to a contest, physically *I'd* be the one to come out wanting.

I saw Ryan hesitate for a moment before placing his hands lightly on her shoulders, and grazing one perfect white cheek with his lips. She flinched as though he'd burnt her. I flinched too, for an entirely different reason.

Hope looked up curiously from her position on the rug, a piece of Lego gripped in one hand. Her eyes went to the newcomer and I swear my heart stopped beating as I saw something that had no name arc across the space between them, like a bolt of electricity. Beside me I heard Maddie's sudden indrawn breath. The air seemed to have left the room, perhaps that's why none of us dared to breathe; why no one moved. And then, as suddenly as it had appeared, that weird invisible connection fizzled out, and Hope reverted to a perfectly ordinary little girl, in the presence of a complete stranger. She got to her feet, a confusion of small bony knees and elbows, and ran to my side, burrowing her face into the curve of my hip. Over the top of her head my eyes went to Ryan's. This wasn't like her. Hope was a bold and sociable child. She hadn't hidden from a stranger like this since her first day at nursery school.

'Hey, what's all this?' cajoled Ryan, his large hand resting gently on his daughter's shoulder. In reaction she burrowed deeper into my side, like a mole caught in a spotlight.

'Give her a minute,' I mouthed silently. *Give us all a minute, or better still, give us all a decade or so to get past this bizarre and unprecedented situation.*

'Maddie, please sit down,' urged Ryan, his eyes concerned as he looked at her. How could someone that pale manage to lose even more colour? You wouldn't have thought it possible, but somehow she had. I watched her sink gratefully onto the deep cushions of the settee, and suddenly a totally inappropriate flashback came to mind. I blinked rapidly, trying to dispel the image of Ryan and me, naked, our limbs glistening from the heat of our lovemaking, on that exact place. Maddie shifted uncomfortably on the settee, as though some residual trace of the passion we had shared lingered like a poltergeist to the spot.

'You're looking really well. Are you all settled in to your new place now?' asked Ryan, still valiantly pretending that this wasn't the weirdest and most uncomfortable experience any of us had ever been a part of.

162

Maddie gave a smile so brief it was gone in a blink. 'Yes. It's a lovely flat.' Her eyes were on the back of Hope's head, and there was a longing on her face that you would have to be made of granite not to see. As scared as I was about how all of this might end, I wasn't made of stone.

My right hand stroked the top of the small head burrowed against me. 'Hope, honey, come and say hello to Maddie. You can show her your Lego house.' In answer the small head shook vigorously from side to side. I wondered if Maddie would think that this uncharacteristic rejection was something I'd deliberately orchestrated. I certainly hoped not.

'Come on, Pumpkin. This is silly.'

'Pumpkin?' said Maddie, her deep red lips curling around the word. 'That's what *my* dad used to call me when I was a little girl.'

My heart sank somewhere into the pit of my stomach. Had I blown this already? From far away I heard Ryan's explanation. 'Pumpkin is Bill's nickname for Hope, and somehow it seems to have stuck.' He looked across at me, and there was concern in his blue eyes. It was too soon to reveal the truth. This wasn't the way it was meant to happen.

Astonishingly it was Maddie who took hold of the dropped reins and steered us back onto solid ground. 'Well, it's a very common nickname. Lots of people get called Pumpkin in my family. And Bill is a relative of mine – not a close one, but still . . .'

I looked with visible gratitude at the woman I had every reason not to trust. She had salvaged the situation, and had lied about her connection to Bill in order to perpetuate the pretence we had insisted upon. I smiled gratefully in acknowledgement, and she nodded briefly in return.

I felt pressure against the palm of my hand as very slowly Hope levered her head away from my hip. She turned to look shyly at her natural mother. 'Did you like being called Pumpkin?'

Maddie's nose wrinkled prettily, and her similarity to Hope intensified so sharply it was all I could do to stifle a gasp. 'Nah. Not really. Who wants to be a big orange vegetable?'

Hope giggled, and I felt the two small arms that had been imprisoning my thighs fall away. And just like that I could tell I was going to lose her.

'We were about to have some tea; would you like a cup, Maddie?'

Maddie tore her eyes away from her daughter with visible reluctance. She was completely entranced, instantly under Hope's unique and magical spell, exactly as I had been from the very first moment Ryan had placed his baby in my arms.

'Thank you, yes. That would be lovely,' she said distractedly. I'd probably have elicited the exact same response if I'd offered her a cup of strychnine, which surely no jury in the land would ever have blamed me for.

I smiled so broadly I could feel my cheeks straining against the impossibly wide beam as I walked from the lounge, leaving the three of them behind me. The smile faltered as I left the room, wobbled a little more as I crossed the hallway, and had completely evaporated by the time I entered the kitchen. *What are you doing, leaving them all alone together?* demanded a furious voice in my head. *Why are you making it so easy for them?*

I turned on the cold tap to full power, splashing the silk of my grey shirt with scores of water droplets. But the thunder of water hitting the bottom of the kettle was nowhere near loud enough to drown out the dark voice that refused to be silent. *Fight for her . . . fight for him. She has rights – of course she does – but so do you. Don't just roll over and hand your life to her.*

My fingers drummed impatiently on the granite worktop as I waited for the kettle to boil. *Did it always take this long?* I threw teabags into the teapot we seldom used, and filled a sugar bowl and milk jug. I ignored the comfortable mismatched assortment of mugs we usually used, and reached instead for the set of best china I'd inherited from my mother. I pulled a sponge cake from its supermarket packaging, and cursed myself for not having made one from scratch. You didn't need a degree in psychology to see what had prompted this sudden drive of domesticity. I was marking my territory, like a wolf in the forest. True, setting a tea tray that would rival one of Mary Berry's finest wasn't quite the same as peeing all around my encampment – but it was probably the suburban equivalent.

I studied my reflection in the brushed aluminium of the kettle's surface. I looked hazy and indistinct, a blurry-edged version of me, as though even this early in the proceedings,

I was already beginning to lose my definition. The image of me shimmered slightly, as tears I hadn't realised were gathering splashed silently down onto the granite worktop.

2012

The first time I saw Ryan he was crying quite openly and unashamedly about another woman. I doubt there are many women who can say that about their first meeting with their future husband. It was at the hospital, of course. It was the place where he'd spent practically every waking (and sleeping) hour since the day of Maddie's accident.

I knew all about her; it would have been impossible not to. Long after the local newspapers and radio stations had stopped reporting on the tragedy of the bride who'd been mown down by a speeding van just days before her wedding, the hospital was still buzzing with talk of her. The nursing staff would idly gossip about her, and once it was revealed that the poor comatose woman was pregnant with her heart-broken fiancé's baby, the story flared into life all over again, like petrol on a dwindling fire. Who couldn't help but feel moved by their tragic tale? I know I certainly was.

'The odds must surely be a million-to-one against her keeping that baby full-term,' I remember overhearing two nurses discuss a little indiscreetly in a lift as I travelled up to the geriatric ward one evening. I shifted the heavy bag of library books I was carrying from one shoulder to the other and listened with open fascination.

'It's a bloody miracle that she didn't lose it straight away,' whispered the second nurse with a degree of stark pragmatism I hoped she never used in front of her patients.

'That's what they're calling her, you know: "The Miracle Girl".'

They got out on the floor before mine, but their words lingered in the small aluminium carriage. There was something incredibly poignant and evocative about both the name and the story. And it stayed with me as the lift pinged to announce my arrival at the ward I visited three evenings a week. It was an intriguing story, and I felt strangely connected to it. It was almost as if in some way I already knew that the life of Madeline Chambers – the Miracle Girl – and mine were destined to be inextricably connected.

Two hours later and my voice had grown hoarse from reading. Gladys Butler's head had begun to nod during the last two chapters of the Agatha Christie book we were currently reading. Or rather, I was the one doing the reading; Gladys was merely listening. I patted her wrinkled, age-spotted hand gently, and got to my feet, trying to unobtrusively straighten out the kinks in my back that were an occupational hazard to my sessions at the hospital. The bright green volunteer badge pinned to my T-shirt glinted in the low lighting beside Gladys's bed.

'Thank you, Carole. That was a real treat. When are you coming back to finish it?'

I smiled gently at the eager expression on the elderly woman's face. I'd stopped correcting her some time ago whenever she got my name wrong. 'I'll be back on Wednesday – that's the day after tomorrow. We can read a few more chapters then, if you like?'

Gladys nodded enthusiastically and gave me a wide tooth-less smile. I was used to her broad gummy grin, although I have to admit the two dentures smiling independently from her in a glass on her bedside cabinet still freaked me out a little whenever I glanced their way.

'I've no idea who's *dunnit*,' said Gladys, nodding at the book I was sliding back into my large tote bag.

'We'll have to wait and see,' I said, hiding the fact that, as it was the second time I'd read her this book, I knew perfectly well who was bumping off the guests at the luxury hotel in the south of France. In a way I almost envied Gladys her forgetfulness. She could hear a book and then happily hear it all over again two weeks later. She could receive the message that once again her family wouldn't be making the two-hour drive to visit her in hospital, and still look forward excitedly to visiting time, waiting for them to arrive. It was patients like Gladys who made volunteering at the hospital so worthwhile.

I walked down the length of the ward, giving the group of nurses sitting at their station a cheery wave as I went past. One of them glanced at the clock with an expression of surprise. 'Leaving so soon, Chloe?' There was still another hour left of visiting time, and I usually stayed until the bell was rung, like the last hardened drinker in a pub when the landlord calls out 'time'.

'Gladys was starting to nod off again, so I thought I'd grab a coffee and then see if anyone else wants me to read them the local paper, or just have a chat.' Each of the three nurses behind the desk smiled at me, and I felt again the familiar warm glow of satisfaction that went hand-in-glove with the way I chose to spend three nights of my week.

When I'd first started volunteering, two years ago, I hadn't been sure how difficult it would be for me. Would thoughts of Mum and those awful last months be in my head every time I walked into the hospital? Surprisingly, they hadn't been. And spending my evenings reading to elderly patients who could no longer read for themselves felt like a very natural and organic extension to my day job.

'Aren't you fed up with books after working here all day?' asked Sally, one of my colleagues at the library, as together we restacked a shelf of biographies. I remember turning and looking at her with genuine bewilderment. Her question was so alien she might as well have asked me if I was fed up with breathing. I *lived* for books. I always had. One of the few memories of my dad that I knew was true and not an illusion was of his deep baritone voice reading me my nightly bedtime story. We'd been halfway through a book when he died. And as much as my mum had tried to fill the space he'd left behind, she'd never been able to bring herself to finish reading me that book.

There was a copy of it in the library where I worked, and each week when I reached for a book to read for the Friday afternoon storytelling session, my hand would hover over its colourfully illustrated spine … and then move on. One day, perhaps, I might actually pick it up and read it to the expectant circle of under-fives waiting for me. But not yet.

I'd inherited my love of literature from my mother, every bit as much as I had the blond of my hair or the grey of my eyes. There had been times over the years when it seemed books were the only thing we had in common. However difficult life became, as gradually she shut out the rest of the world, books were the one place where we could always find each other again. We would discuss the characters from the novels we'd read as though they were newly acquired friends. But in reality her circle of friends was dwindling. In reality there was no immediate family and very few friends left to knock down the walls her agoraphobia had so effectively constructed.

After she died I realised many things – about both of us; some of them uncomfortable to face. We were alike enough for it to frighten me. We were alike enough for me to know that at twenty-seven, with an uninspiring social life and no boyfriend to speak of (Graham from the book club didn't count – even though I suspected he'd like to take our friendship further), I needed to take action. I needed to push the boundaries of my world beyond the four-bedroom house I'd lived in my entire life, and my job at the library. Every time I entered the house and unthinkingly called out 'I'm home' to the empty rooms, I'd feel the aching stab of loneliness pierce me. And so I cauterised those wounds the only way I knew how. With books.

I answered the postcard advertisement on the library noticeboard for volunteer readers at the local hospital. I suppose some people might say I wasn't aiming very high or far away from my comfort zone, but I saw a door opening up, and I slipped through it, never knowing it would one day lead me to become part of a story more incredible than any I had ever read.

Even as I approached the vending machine with my coin-filled purse in hand, I could see that it wasn't working. I came to a stop before the defunct unit and sighed. Some equally exasperated user had scribbled the word *Again!!* beneath the handwritten 'Out of Order' sign. I glanced at my watch and frowned as I realised that the café in the hospital foyer had closed for the evening an hour ago.

'There's a machine down on two and another up on six,' advised a passing orderly helpfully. I glanced over my shoulder and flashed him a grateful smile.

'Thanks, I'll try one of them.'

I didn't even bother waiting to summon the lift. I'd been volunteering at the hospital long enough to know that during visiting hours the stairs were always your best bet. The air felt cooler on my arms and bare legs as I pushed through the heavy swing doors and entered the stairwell. While the wards were usually kept warm enough to grow orchids, here at least the fresh summer evening air could be felt. I paused for a second as I unknowingly arrived at the place where my entire future would be decided. Much, much, later it occurred to me how strange it was to have made such a momentous decision without ever realising it.

Two flights of stairs were before me: one up, one down. I paused for only a moment before running lightly up the stairs, hearing the echo of my summer sandals pick out a tinkling scale on the metal edges of each tread as I dashed up to the sixth floor.

Most of the hospital floors were similar in layout, so I had no need to follow any of the overhead signs directing me to the various areas or wards. I knew where I was. I headed towards the relatives' room, my tread automatically adjusting to the sobering hush this particular floor silently commanded. I hadn't visited the sixth floor since my own mother had been an occupant of one of the intensive care beds, and I was surprised by the goosebumps that had erupted on my forearms as I retraced the steps I had once covered daily.

I kept my head down as I walked swiftly towards the relatives' room and the vending machine which was situated just outside its doors. I was used to places of silence – after all, I worked in a library – but there was something about this particular floor that unsettled me. It felt almost church-like, as though you were walking on hallowed ground, where voices should never be raised above a respectful whisper.

Which made the sound all the more unexpected. It was coming from a man who stood before the vending machine. Even from half the length of the corridor away, I could see the tremor of his broad shoulders as he stood with his arms braced against the sides of the drinks dispenser. It was impossible to say whether he was using it for support, or was about to vandalise it for swallowing his money.

He didn't hear my approach and was unaware that he was no longer alone until my shadow fell across his on the linoleum floor, and he spun around. Immediately his hand came up, and he roughly swiped the back of it against his eyes. It was a largely ineffective manoeuvre, because as soon as he brushed them away, a fresh batch of tears found the tracks of those that had come before, and spilled down his cheeks.

I took an instinctive step backwards, as though I'd carelessly run straight up to the edge of a cliff. The raw naked pain on his face was overwhelming. He was clearly destroyed by grief.

'I . . . I'm sorry,' I said, stumbling over the words as they fell out of my mouth. I'm not even sure what I was apologising for. For witnessing his distress? Or for not knowing how to react to it? I took another faltering step backwards, even as he was shaking his head, dismissing my apology. 'I didn't mean to disturb you,' I mumbled, turning away to escape being witness to something he surely wanted no stranger to see.

I'd only taken two steps when I heard the sound; half groan, half sob. It was the loneliest and most broken cry I'd ever heard in my entire life, and it tugged at my heart and turned my feet around before I knew what I was doing. I'd be surprised if he was aware of my return, for his hands were fisted angrily at his eyes, as though trying to beat the tears back into submission.

'Excuse me,' I said, my voice small and uncertain. 'But are you all right?' I heard the stupidity in my question. *Of course* he wasn't all right. He was a man in his thirties, or thereabouts, sobbing unashamedly in a hospital corridor outside an Intensive Care Unit. It didn't take rocket science to work out what was going on here. I wondered if his grief was for a parent on the ward, as mine had been only a few years before.

His head lifted at my question and the hands fell away from his eyes. They were the brightest blue I'd ever seen, their colour made more brilliant by the bright red lids surrounding them. It was a clashing combination, and yet weirdly didn't detract from the fact that he was an exceptionally good-looking man.

'All right?' he queried, his voice a low rumble. He shook his head, and his dishevelled dark blond hair fell shaggily over his eyes. He swept it back and looked at me properly for the first time. 'No. Not really.'

He said nothing more, and I sensed the next comment was mine to make ... if only I knew what it should be. 'Is there something I can do?'

He shook his head sadly.

'Or someone I can get for you? Are you here with anyone?'

His face contorted in a wince of pain and unconsciously his eyes went to the doors of the Intensive Care Unit. And suddenly I knew *exactly* who he was. I'd seen his photograph in the local newspaper several weeks ago, not long after the accident. But the memory of the picture of him smiling beside a tall beautiful brunette was a million miles removed from the way he looked tonight.

Driven by an unexpected instinct, I reached out my hand and laid it lightly on the man's forearm. His skin was tanned and warm, the hairs soft and unfamiliar against my palm. It had been quite a while, I realised, since I'd last touched a man. 'Well, I was just about to get a coffee,' I said, adopting a tone that I hoped sounded compassionate, but not too pushy. 'Can I get you one?'

He took a long moment, as though my words, so mundane and everyday, had to force their way through a fog of misery to make themselves understood. Then he nodded, just once. I approached the machine and started feeding it coins. I figured asking him how he took his caffeine was going to be too much of a challenge, so I opted for hot, black and sweet.

With the two Styrofoam cups in hand, I turned back to face him again. Thankfully he was no longer crying openly, because if he *had* been there was a good chance that I'd have joined in. This was the real story the newspaper article had failed to cover, this was the truth behind the gossipy snippets overheard in the hospital corridors or lifts. Here was a man who had lost the woman he loved; lost her perhaps for ever – and their unborn child. Who couldn't help but feel his pain?

'Why don't we sit down for a minute?' I suggested, nodding in the direction of the relatives' room. Through the open door I could see it was empty.

He followed me silently, and when I held out one of the blistering hot coffees he took it and immediately began to sip it. It was hot – too hot probably, but he didn't appear to notice. I lowered myself onto a chair and after a moment he took a seat in the row opposite me.

'I'm sorry for that little display out there,' he said, breaking the silence before I had a chance to. He nodded in the direction of the vending machine, as though a trace of his distraught-self still stood there as a reminder. 'I try not to do that in public, if I can help it.'

'There's absolutely no need to apologise. I quite understand. I've been there.' His head came up and I realised how stupid and unthinking my comment had been. Of course I hadn't been *there*. I hadn't lost the person I loved most in the world in a dreadful accident. I hadn't known the pain of realising the future I'd planned had suddenly been ripped out of my grasp.

'My mother . . . she was in this hospital for quite a while before she passed away.'

'I'm sorry for your loss,' he said, strangely reversing the roles and comforting me.

'You're here because of your fiancée, aren't you?' I questioned hesitantly, wondering how many degrees of awkward this was going to be if I had mistakenly placed him. But I knew from the twist of his mouth that my guess had been bullseye-accurate.

'I guess everyone around here has heard about Maddie?' he asked quietly. There was something about the way that he said her name that touched a chord deep within me. For a moment I wondered what it would feel like to have a man love you that much. I'd never even come close.

'Is there . . . has something . . . has there been any change?' I asked clumsily.

He shook his head, looking deep into the bottom of his almost empty cup, as though the words he was looking for were to be found there among the coffee dregs. 'No. No change. None at all,' he answered sadly, and suddenly I thought I understood the reason for his despair. I had no medical training, but I'd spent long enough volunteering at the hospital to know that the longer a patient remains unresponsive, the less optimistic the medical professionals were of a good outcome.

'Are you a doctor here?' he asked.

I gave a small laugh of surprise and then quickly smothered it, because it seemed totally wrong in the presence of such sadness. 'No. Nothing like that. Although I *do* spend an awful lot of my time here.'

He looked up and did a fairly reasonable impersonation of someone who was politely interested. I sat up straighter and pointed at my chest, before realising how totally inappropriate that was. Inviting a man – particularly one grieving for his injured fiancée – to direct his attention to your right boob is always ill-advised.

'Volunteer,' I supplied quickly, before he had need to lean closer and read the word printed on the small green badge. 'I read to the patients – mainly those on the geriatric ward,' I added. I thrust out my hand, like an over-eager candidate at a job interview. 'I'm Chloe. Chloe Barnes.'

A fleeting smile curved on his lips, giving me a glimpse

of how he must look when he wasn't in torment. It was pretty devastating.

'Ryan Turner,' he said, allowing his long firm grip to join with mine across the coffee table that separated us. His mouth twisted wryly. 'But you probably already knew that.'

I nodded sympathetically. 'I can't even begin to imagine how terrible this must be for you and your fiancée's family.'

'The worst of it is there's not a damn thing anyone can do to bring her back quicker,' he said, his voice suddenly bitter. He got to his feet, his pent-up frustration evident in the way he lobbed the empty cup into a nearby bin. 'You'd give everything you own, do anything you could to help someone you love. But having to sit by helplessly and wait, without knowing how long for . . . well, that's what can bring you down, the way it did me tonight.'

'You mustn't give up hope,' I said determinedly, wondering how far I was overstepping the mark, talking like this to someone I didn't even know. 'It sounds like—' for a moment I struggled, before his fiancée's name popped into my head. 'It sounds like *Maddie* has a lot to live for and come back to. I'm sure she'll wake up soon.'

'Thank you.' This time the smile Ryan gave me wasn't twisted in pain. 'I think I needed to hear someone say that tonight.'

'I mean it. I know it might sound weird, particularly as we've only just met, but I've got a really strong feeling that everything's going to work out for you. Everyone here at the hospital is rooting for her – for *all* of you. We're all wishing and hoping that she finds her way back to you. Everyone wants this story to have a happy ending.'

2018

Six years later I stood in my perfect cream-coloured kitchen, my hands trembling so much that I splashed small puddles of boiling water all over the worktop as I attempted to fill my mother's best teapot. It was a little too late in the day to finally remember that old adage about being careful what you wished for ... The words from my past had come back to haunt me, as had the woman who'd inspired them.

I jumped like a red-handed cat burglar as the kitchen door swung open. I must have been a bit too slow wiping the worried expression from my face, because Ryan's eyes darkened in concern.

'Everything okay in here?'

In here was fine. In here it was business as usual. It was only in the warm cosy lounge that everything we took for granted in our lives was being spectacularly rearranged.

'Fine, why?' I asked, trying to remember the exact facial muscles I needed to use to manufacture a smile. I must have found some of them, for Ryan relaxed visibly, his broad shoulders dropping several centimetres as the tension fled from his body. He crossed over to stand behind me and wound his arms around my waist and I leant back against him, allowing the strength of his body to be my buttress. He was like a wall: strong, solid and supporting. At times I leant on him; at others he leant on me. That's what marriage was all about. But what would happen if something (or someone) tore at our foundations, like a tornado. Walls can crumble, and if they do would either of us be left with enough strength to support each other?

'You were taking a long time with the tea.'

'It's the type that you have to let brew,' I replied. As I slipped out of his hold I saw his briefly raised eyebrows as he took in the teapot, the best china, and the neatly set tray.

'Anyone would think we were entertaining royalty,' he said, his voice gently trying to tease me out of the panic he must surely know I was feeling.

'Not really,' I said with a nonchalant shrug that neither of us believed. My eyes went to the closed kitchen door, and took an imaginary journey through its wooden panels to the room on the other side of the hall.

'Shouldn't you be in there with them? Is it safe, leaving her alone with Hope so soon?'

For a second Ryan looked so dumbfounded, I wondered if the words had become garbled on their way out of my mouth. '*Safe?*' he queried, as though he couldn't quite believe what he'd just heard. 'What do you mean "safe"? You're not suggesting that Maddie poses some kind of threat to Hope? That she'd ever harm her in any way?'

He was so defensive, it was all I could do not to gasp. So here it was. So soon. I thought it would have taken much longer before we reached the point where Ryan would consider taking sides. Stupid, stupid, me.

'No. No. Of course not. Well, not physically or anything,' I said, my words tripping over each other as I tried to step out of the quicksand I'd inadvertently walked into. 'I just meant that she might say something that would confuse Hope or worry her. She did seem a little ... *unprepared* ... when she first got here today.'

Ryan's laugh was short and humourless. 'Well you can hardly blame her for that, can you? I think the same could probably be said for all of us. How the fuck are any of us meant to prepare for something like this?'

How indeed?

Ryan stayed with me in the kitchen while I finished making the tea, leaning comfortably against the worktop and swiping the occasional biscuit from the plate I'd carefully arranged. I'd like to think he stayed to keep me company rather than to prevent anything unpleasant finding its way into the bottom of Maddie's teacup, but I could hardly blame him not for trusting me to behave. I *had* been acting a little crazy ever since the night the telephone had rung to say the miracle everyone had stopped waiting for had finally happened.

He held open the kitchen door and I ducked beneath his arm, the items on the tray performing a tuneful percussion of cutlery on china. Ryan's hand rested briefly against my cheek as I passed him, and I turned my face into his palm, inhaling the warm calming smell of him.

'It's all going to work out fine, Chloe. Trust me. I've got a really strong feeling about it.'

I smiled but said nothing, because once, on a night a very long time ago, I'd had one of those too.

My eyes went to Hope the moment I entered the room, it was as instinctive to me as breathing. Down the aisles of a supermarket; by the shoreline at the beach; on the edge of the playground in the park, I kept up a mother's surveillance, 24/7. I always had.

Hope was still on the mat before the fire, crouched low over her colourful brick construction, as she busily created a new wing for Barbie's latest mansion. Only she wasn't alone on the floor. Another head was also bent low, almost touching hers, and I swallowed down a mouthful of something vile-tasting and venomous which threatened to choke me. Long swathes of dark identically coloured hair swung down, like a set of curtains. They entwined and mingled as through their DNA was pulling the strands together like a magnet.

To be fair, as soon as we entered the room Maddie nimbly slid back onto the settee cushions. I set down the tray and apparently must have done all the things a hostess is supposed to do. I even managed a genuine smile when Ryan winked at me from across the room. I could do this; I might not like it, but I could do it.

If Hope had been just a few years older perhaps she'd have been able to detect the underlying current that ran beneath the skin of every topic we covered that afternoon. But a five-year-old isn't interested in the conversation of grown-ups, and frankly I don't think even the adults were paying much attention to what we were talking about. Maddie's eyes were constantly on her daughter, drinking her in like a person dying of thirst, while my own mouth and throat felt dry and scratchy with fear. When Hope suddenly sprang up from the floor and went to sit beside Maddie, a surge of jealousy rushed through my veins, like a virus.

'You've got really pretty hair,' my little girl said, reaching out and picking up a long silky handful.

'Hope,' I cautioned. 'You shouldn't do that without asking.' Hope's small rosebud lips dropped open in surprise. Perhaps my voice had been a bit sharper than was necessary, which made Maddie's automatic response sound like honey on my vinegar.

'That's all right. She's fine.'

Hope wriggled closer to her natural mother, and I died a little inside. This was how it was going to be . . . a multitude of tiny losses as Maddie slowly regained what was hers, and I was left holding just wisps of memories.

'Your hair looks like mine,' Hope declared artlessly.

Maddie's eyes went to Ryan's and I suddenly felt like an intruder in my own home as something private was communicated between them.

'I think *yours* is much prettier,' declared Maddie, and whatever she was about to say next died in her throat as Hope's took a single strand of hair and wound it around her index finger. It was something I knew Ryan used to do whenever he visited Maddie. It was their 'thing'. Had Hope somehow drawn on a memory of seeing her father do that at the hospital when she was only a toddler? I shivered despite the heat from the fire and glanced over to where Ryan stood. I knew his face, every line, every contour, but the expression on it now I'd never seen before.

'Would you read me a story?' Hope asked, shattering the spell that had fallen over the room. I smiled gratefully, like a panicked swimmer who'd just discovered their feet can touch the bottom of the pool. Books were the legacy I had passed on to Hope. Her face, her hair, her eyes, they all came from Maddie, but books were from me.

'Can *Maddie* read me a story, Mummy?' asked my five-year-old, unknowingly finding the sharpest knife in the drawer to slice me with.

'Yes, of course she can. If she'd like to,' I managed to say, past the huge obstruction that suddenly appeared to have lodged in my throat.

'I'd love to.' Maddie didn't even bother pretending she wasn't delighted as her daughter ran from the room to fetch a book. 'You don't mind, do you?' she asked as soon as Hope's feet could be heard thundering up the stairs.

'No. Of course not,' I said, lying as convincingly as I could.

There's a big old-fashioned bookcase in Hope's bedroom. I found it in a junk shop, and painstakingly rubbed it down and painted it bright pink and added silver star-shaped stencils. Each of its five shelves is stacked with books. Some of them are old favourites that we've shared together a hundred times or more. Others are new, with stories and adventures waiting for us to discover.

Hope was back so quickly I felt sure she must have plucked the first random book her small hand fell upon. She entered the room at a run, and leapt up onto the sofa as though it was a trampoline. I glanced over at Ryan, waiting to see if he would chastise her, but his face was a frozen unreadable mask as he watched his daughter inch up to the woman he had once intended to marry. When Maddie raised her arm, Hope wriggled up against her, like a missing piece in a jigsaw finally completing a puzzle. It wasn't until she passed the book into Maddie's hands that I understood the expression on Ryan's face. On the front cover was an instantly recognisable illustration. A beautiful young woman, with porcelain white skin and long black hair, lying in a glass coffin, lost to the world in an unwakeable sleep. Was it coincidence that out of every book in her room, Hope had chosen *Snow White* for Maddie to read to her? No. I really didn't think it was.

Chapter 8

2012

I never made it back down to the geriatric ward on the night I first met Ryan. I didn't even notice the passing of the minutes until I heard a distant clang of a handbell, signalling the end of visiting hours.

I jumped guiltily to my feet. 'I'm so sorry, I've kept you away from your fiancée and now visiting is over.' He smiled kindly down at me as he got to his feet. We'd been sitting down for so long I had forgotten how tall he was.

'Don't worry about it. They're pretty relaxed as far as visiting time goes for Maddie.' He gave a shrug and a small grin, and suddenly I caught a glimpse of the young boy he'd once been, beneath the surface of the man. 'I often spend the night here, sitting by her bed. I just can't bear the thought of her opening her eyes for the first time and not finding me there.'

Inexplicably his admission made me want to cry. To have someone love you with that kind of devotion is the stuff you read about in books, or see in films, it wasn't something I'd ever come across in real life. Despite the tragedy of her accident, Madeline Chambers was still a very lucky woman. I hoped she knew how much this man loved her, how every word, phrase and expression on his face declared it to be true.

'It's been very nice meeting you, Chloe Barnes,' Ryan said, once again holding out his hand to me. This time when our hands locked neither of us moved, which meant for several seconds this tall handsome man, with the world's saddest eyes, simply stood in the hospital relatives' room holding my hand. My heart took a stumble from its normal rhythm, although I'm sure his knew no such malfunction.

'I hope you get good news very soon,' I said, wishing there was something more I could say to let him know how very much I meant that.

Perhaps he did anyway, because his eyes softened and crinkled at the edges as he replied. 'Thank you, Chloe, for saying that *and* for listening to me tonight. It really helped, more than you know.'

The warm glow of his parting words stayed with me, like the lyrics of a song that gets stuck in your head. I heard them again as I walked down the six flights of stairs to the foyer; they followed me as I crossed the hospital grounds in the cool night air, and were still whispering in my ear as I waited alone at the bus stop. I never once stopped to question why a stranger – someone who I would probably never see again – had affected me so much. It was almost as though my body already knew something my head and heart wouldn't discover for a very long time.

For once I hardly noticed the echoing quiet of the empty house as I let myself into the home my mother and I had shared. Even the customary twinge of sadness at the row of empty coat hooks had lost its usual sting. I'd changed nothing since she'd died, keeping the house locked in its own time warp. I'm sure a psychologist would say this reflected an inability to accept that my mother had gone. But they'd be wrong, because she'd been leaving me in small painful increments for years before she died. Her illness had meant that she'd bricked herself up into her own life, and I'd never been able to find the right words or tools to break down the walls she'd built.

'I should get a cat,' I said out loud to the empty house as I crossed to the kitchen, flicking on every light switch I passed. My electricity bills were horrendous, but I hated the dark. 'Or a canary. They'd at least be able to talk back,' I added, knowing very well that I would get neither. What I probably *should* get was a lodger. There were three empty bedrooms in the large Victorian house, which were big enough to bring in some additional income. *And company*, whispered a quiet voice in the back of my mind, which I largely tried to ignore.

I wasn't lonely. I had my job at the library, my friends at my book group, and of course I had the hospital. My life was okay. 'Alone does not mean lonely,' I told the empty kitchen, failing to appreciate the irony of my denial as I spoke to no one at all.

My stomach was grumbling for something more satisfying than the bowl of muesli I usually managed to silence it with, so I pulled a loaf and a slab of cheese from the fridge and piled jagged hunks of cheddar onto slices of bread, and slid them under the grill. As I waited for it to brown, I pulled out the recycling crate from the floor of the larder. The kitchen tiles felt cold against my bare knees as I dropped down and began to rummage through the stack of local newspapers, delving beneath several weeks' worth of editions before finally finding the one I was looking for.

It felt a little odd staring into Ryan's eyes for the second time in one evening. Of course the pixelated black-and-white newspaper image couldn't properly convey the deep blue of his irises, or the warmth that shone through them whenever he spoke of Maddie. With the newspaper propped up against a ketchup bottle, I picked up half a slice of cheesy snack and studied the photograph more closely, this time turning my attention to the other person in the image. I'd remembered that Ryan's fiancée had been attractive, but I realised now that I'd been wrong. She was so much more than that; she was beautiful. Looking closer, I was overwhelmed by the love and happiness that radiated from the couple who smiled back at the camera lens, never knowing that the joy they felt at that moment was destined to be so short-lived. It made me want to crawl into the photo to warn them both to cherish every moment, because tragedy was on its way.

Eventually I tore my attention away from the image and directed it towards the article beneath. I read it twice from start to finish, as though there was a chance I might be quizzed on it later. The three-columned report stuck in my head, like a bur. It would be a while before I could forget the words of the witness who recounted how Maddie had been *thrown through the air like a rag doll*, or the bystander who clearly blamed himself when he told the reporter: '*I should have called out a warning sooner.*' But the line that affected me most was the one where another onlooker spoke of the victim's distraught fiancé, cradling her body on the tarmac as they waited for the ambulance.

I folded up the newspaper, laid it to one side and stared down at my plate. The toast had grown cold, the cheese had congealed unappealingly, and speckled all over the willow-patterned plate were a collection of glittering teardrops that I hadn't even known were falling.

By the following morning I'd gained a little more distance and with it some perspective. It was a sad story, of course it was, but I worked as a volunteer in a hospital; I heard a lot of sad stories. Some of them turned out okay and others didn't . . . but that was life. You couldn't invite every tragedy into your heart. My day job was the place where I could find the 'happy-ever-after' endings, within the pages of a book. In the place where I worked at night, they were considerably rarer.

Not that the library was the calming refuge that it once

had been. For months ominous rumours of closures and cutbacks had circulated like gathering thunderheads. Every head-office memo we received made it impossible to ignore the fact that redundancies might be unavoidable.

I saw Ryan several times over the following weeks, but never to speak to. He was behind the closing lift doors that slid shut as I pressed the call button, or walking out of the cafeteria exit as I was coming through the entrance. After our conversation in the relatives' room it was only natural for me to wonder if there'd been any improvement in his fiancée's condition. What *wouldn't* be natural was for me to actively seek him out. And so I didn't. But that didn't stop me from eavesdropping on conversations, my ears pricking up whenever the word 'miracle' was mentioned. But interest in the accident which had left the young bride-to-be in a coma had begun to fade. In a hospital there's always some new tragedy waiting in the wings to push the last one out of the way.

The lift was taking a very long time, and despite the weight of the book bag cutting painfully into my shoulder, I was considering heading for the stairs when a voice behind me said my name. I'd known who it was before I turned around to face him. How strange to have committed his voice to memory without even realising I'd done so.

'Hello, Ryan,' I said, looking up into his face and hoping I'd been quick enough to mask the shock from showing when I saw the changes the last few weeks had brought about. 'How are you?'

'I'm fine,' he replied, which was clearly far from true. He looked unbelievably tired, and there was a gauntness to his cheeks that I'm sure hadn't been there on the night in the relatives' room. It made me want to ask if he was eating properly, but obviously we were practically strangers, and that was none of my business. I could only hope that question – and others like it – were being asked by his family and friends.

A soft ping sounded behind me, announcing the lift had finally arrived, but I made no move to turn around. 'How's Madeline doing?' I asked, though I already knew the answer to that question. There was always someone on the nursing staff who was willing to answer my frequent enquiries about the comatose patient on the sixth floor. They'd stopped asking why I was so interested, which was just as well because I never had found an adequate answer to that one.

My face remained sympathetic as I allowed Ryan to tell me what I already knew; there'd been no change in Maddie, which was causing her team of doctors continued concern. 'It was her birthday last week,' Ryan confided, his voice so low I had to lean in closer to hear his words. His mouth formed something that resembled a smile. 'I brought in a cake, and a bottle of champagne.' He concentrated his attention for several moments on a nearby noticeboard advertising an upcoming Pilates class, which I was pretty sure he had no intention of joining. 'Pretty stupid, huh?' he said turning back to me with a sound that resembled a laugh gone wrong.

My eyes felt as though someone was pricking them repeatedly with a long fine needle, and I blinked furiously until the sensation faded. 'No,' I said, pleased that there was only a minimal wobble in my voice. 'Not stupid at all. What if she'd opened her eyes right then and you'd not brought her anything? She'd have been furious.'

I wasn't expecting the sound of his laughter, nor the way I felt disproportionately pleased to have broken him free from his sombre mood. I wondered when he'd last laughed like that. It was yet another question that wasn't mine to ask.

Ryan looked at me for a long moment, and there was a similar expression of gratitude on his face to the one I'd seen at our first meeting. 'You're a very good volunteer, Chloe Barnes, and a good listener. The hospital is lucky to have you.' I felt myself fluff up, like a peacock, at the compliment. 'Even if you *have* got a shockingly sweet tooth,' he added with a grin, glancing down at the jumbo-sized packets of jelly babies that I'd totally forgotten were cradled in my arms.

My cheeks flooded with colour as though a switch had been pulled 'Oh these? They're not for me. They're for a friend.'

'Of course they are,' he said, nodding solemnly. It was my first glimpse of his sense of humour.

'They're not mine, honestly,' I assured him, laughing. 'They're for Gladys; she's one of the old ladies I read to here. She has a passion for jelly babies and grisly murder stories. I keep her supplied with both.'

There was an expression on Ryan's face that I knew I

would be trying to decipher long into the evening ahead. 'Like I said, the hospital and the patients are lucky to have you.' He glanced down then at the complex diver-style watch on his wrist, and I felt rather than heard the pull of his fiancée up on the sixth floor. 'I should go,' he said, as though he'd only just realised how many non-Maddie moments he had carelessly squandered in my company.

'Go,' I said, nodding towards the double doors that led to the stairwell. He went through them so rapidly that they continued to swing on their hinges long after his pounding legs had carried him several floors closer to the woman he loved.

'What will you do with the two afternoons you've now got free?' Sally asked me, delving into the carrier bag and passing me one of the cellophane-wrapped sandwiches. We'd headed for a small park just around the corner from the library, for a commiseratory meal-deal picnic lunch following the meeting at the library that morning. Although none of the staff had been laid off, we were all going to have to reduce our hours.

Apart from a few buggy-pushing mothers, and duck-feeding OAPs, we had the park to ourselves. The schools had gone back several weeks earlier, and although we were enjoying an unexpectedly warm September, autumn was quietly knocking on the door. She'd already left her calling card in the scattering of russet-brown leaves that littered the grass.

'Me?' I said, throwing the crust from my chicken sandwich towards a hopeful duck who'd headed our way at the sight of brown paper bags. 'I'm not sure. Maybe I'll do some more hours at the hospital.'

Sally took a long swig of drink from her can, before replying. 'You should join a club or something. Meet some new people.'

I smiled at her as I lobbed the duck yet another chunk of bread. 'Meet a man, you mean?' I teased.

Sally shrugged as though this idea hadn't occurred to her, and then grinned mischievously. 'I don't know how come you haven't snaffled up a hot doctor, or even one of the patients by now,' she declared.

'Most of the patients I meet are in their eighties,' I said, balling up the remains of my sandwich bag and dropping it into the bin beside us. 'And the doctors are either straight out of university and barely shaving, or happily married middle-aged men. In real life it's nothing like *Grey's Anatomy*, you know.'

'I just think you're not looking hard enough,' Sally said, getting to her feet with obvious reluctance. 'I bet the right man is out there – he's probably right under your nose.'

I laughed and linked my arm through hers. 'You weren't tidying up the Mills and Boon shelf by any chance this morning, were you?' I teased, trying to divert her away from a topic that was starting to make the back of my neck feel prickly and uncomfortable.

'Is something wrong? I thought you'd be pleased with the suggestion. After all, you *are* always asking about her.'

That is definitely going to have to stop, I thought, staring at the kindly ward sister, sitting behind a desk fast-disappearing under a mountain of hospital files and paperwork. I shook my head and summoned an innocuous smile to my lips, when what I felt like doing was chewing on them anxiously. It wasn't that I *didn't* want to spend some of my volunteer hours on the sixth floor. What worried me more, was just how much I *did*. Was my interest in the love story of a couple I knew virtually nothing about in danger of tipping over into an obsession? Why was I so fascinated about a woman I had never met? And why should the tragedy of two total strangers continue to keep slowly infiltrating into my thoughts?

'Look, why don't you go up to the sixth floor and have a chat with the patient's fiancé. I hear he's a really nice guy, and he'll be able to give you a better idea of the kind of assistance you could offer them.' It was a reasonable suggestion and there wasn't a single thing about it that should have made my heart suddenly pound like crazy, or the palms of my hands turn sticky with sweat. And yet it did.

'If you don't feel comfortable helping them out after you've spoken to him, we can always work out some polite excuse between us. But to be perfectly honest, Chloe, I think you're going to be of far more value to them in the afternoons than you are down here.' She made a valid point. The patients on the geriatric ward seemed to have more visitors in the afternoons than they did in the evenings, making me largely surplus to requirements.

I got carefully to my feet in the small office, which wasn't much bigger than a broom cupboard. How could I possibly explain to the woman on the other side of the desk the peculiar feeling of serendipity that had overwhelmed me as I listened to her suggestion? It was as if threads of coincidence were once again stitching my life to Ryan and his pregnant fiancé.

'Okay. I'll go and see if I can find him,' I said.

'Good girl,' said Sister with a satisfied sigh. I could practically see her drawing a thick black line through *Sort out Volunteer Request* on her mental 'to do' list.

I didn't run up the steps to the sixth floor. I took each tread slowly and carefully, as though my sedate pace would somehow calm my racing thoughts. I could feel an inner tug of war going on, which made my stomach twist and knot uncomfortably. One side of the rope was trying to pull me further into Maddie's world, and the other end was desperately trying to anchor me as far away from it as I could get.

I didn't need to ask anyone which was the room where the comatose patient Madeline Chambers lay, and yet I still hesitated in the corridor. I stood hovering for a minute, until I felt a hand lightly touch my shoulder. I turned around, and knew an unexpected moment of disappointment when I saw that the person standing in front of me was one of the nurses who used to work on the geriatric ward.

'Hey, Chloe. How are you?'

I mumbled something about being fine, which was such a lie you would have thought a member of the medical profession would have been able to instantly tell that I was most definitely *not fine*. The nurse however continued to smile at me warmly, guessing nothing at all of my inner turmoil.

'Are you here about spending some of your voluntary hours with Maddie Chambers?'

It threw me for a moment that everybody in the hospital seemed to know everyone else's business. It was a reminder that a secret here would be almost impossible to keep.

'Yes, I am.' I glanced towards Maddie's closed door. 'But I don't want to disturb her fiancé when he's here visiting her.'

The nurse, whose name I suddenly remembered was Abby, shook her head and laughed quietly. 'I wouldn't worry about that. He practically *lives* here. He's always with her.'

Then why do they need me? That was the question that sprang to mind, but never actually made it to my lips. It was probably one that Ryan could best answer himself.

'I think I'll wait in the relatives' room for a bit,' I suggested. 'But if you get a free moment, Abby, would you mind letting him know that I'm here?'

Abby looked a little surprised by my request, but after a moment gave a friendly toothy smile and a small shrug. 'Okay, sure. No problem.'

I sat on the same chair in the relatives' room that I'd occupied on the night I'd first met Ryan, but after a few seconds I jumped up and moved to another. I wanted our meeting today to feel totally different to that first one; to feel professional. I certainly had no intention of letting him see how conflicted I was about getting further drawn in to their story.

I would give him ten minutes, I resolved, checking my watch against the clock on the wall. If he hadn't shown up by then, I'd go back down to my regular ward and catch him at another time. *Or not at all,* a quiet voice whispered in the back of my head.

He arrived in less than four minutes.

'Chloe. How are you? You're looking well,' Ryan said with a welcoming smile, as he walked through the door.

I thought he might possibly be confusing my warm flustered flush with good health, but I wasn't going to contradict him. The polite thing to say in response was *Thank you*, or *So do you*, except I couldn't say that in all conscience, because he didn't look very well at all. I did a quick mental calculation to work out how long he'd been living on this particular knife-edge, and realised it must now be over ten weeks. No wonder the poor man looked haggard.

'I was really hoping the volunteer would be you. I thought about asking specifically, but wasn't sure if that'd be a bit weird.'

I looked into the warm, but tired, eyes of the man who crossed my mind on practically a daily basis, and I still had no idea why. I was definitely not the right person to talk to about *weird*.

'I'm happy to help, if I can. How is Madeline doing?'

'Her friends call her Maddie,' Ryan said, by way of an answer, as though lifting up a corner of a blanket and inviting me under it. 'Physically, she's made a remarkable recovery from the terrible injuries she received in the accident.'

For a horrible moment I pictured it. The ugly phrase from the newspaper about 'flying through the air like a rag doll' was a hard one to shake off. I swallowed uncomfortably. 'And . . . and the baby?' I asked hesitantly.

Ryan's smile softened and became something so beautiful I could have stared at it for hours and never got bored. 'Our little miracle?' he said, and even the words he used were warm and glowing, as though they'd been glazed in honey. 'She's doing very, very, well.'

'You know it's a girl then?'

He nodded, and there was a father's pride in his eyes for the child he had yet to meet. 'She's a survivor. Just like her mum. The doctors can't quite believe it, but Maddie's having a textbook pregnancy.'

I had a burning curiosity – or nosiness, to give it its true name – to ask what would happen when the time came for the baby to be born, but that felt like a step too far into their personal life. So instead I sat up a little straighter in my seat, and tried to sound brisk and professional.

'So how exactly can I help out during my volunteer hours? What do you need from me?'

Ryan, who had until then been leaning casually against the wall, crossed the small room to drop down onto the chair beside me. I could feel the heat of his arm as it brushed against mine on the shared armrest.

'Up until now I've been able to spend pretty much all of

my time here with Maddie.' I kept my face politely blank, because this wasn't something I was supposed to know. 'But there's only so much leave or goodwill my company are able to give me.' Ryan sighed, and I heard concern in the sound. 'Basically, if I want to keep my job – and I *need* to keep my job – I'm going to have to go back to work, at least part-time.'

I thought I could see where the role he was asking me to play was going to come in, but I just nodded encouragingly and waited for him to continue.

'Maddie's parents live quite a distance away, and her mum is—' He broke off suddenly as though he'd thought better of whatever it was he'd been about to say. 'She's not able to do the journey that often, so her dad is only able to come and visit Maddie for a couple of days a week.'

Ryan leant back in his chair, lifted both arms and began to rub distractedly at the stiff knotted muscles of his neck. Too many nights spent sleeping upright in an uncomfortable hospital chair will do that, I thought sympathetically.

'I'm not sure how much you know about patients who're in a coma,' he said.

More than I probably should, and more than I'm willing to admit to. 'A little,' I replied.

'Well, one of the few things they've told us we can do to help is to keep giving Maddie as much sensory stimulation as possible. The more we talk to her, touch her hand, play her music and just generally interact with her, well . . . the better the chances are of her coming out of it sooner.' There was a sadness around his eyes as he sighed and added: 'Or so they say.'

'And you'd like me to sit with Maddie when you're not able to be here?'

He nodded, and drew his lower lip in between his teeth. I addressed my reply to a particularly interesting fire notice fixed to the wall. 'I'd be happy to do that. It's very similar to what I do down on the other ward anyway.'

Relief exuded from him, like heat from a fire. 'Oh, that's really great news. I was hoping you'd say yes.'

I gave something that I hoped looked like a casual shrug. 'It's what I do. I'm happy to help.'

'I know, and I also know that it shouldn't matter *who* it is, but I wanted Maddie to spend time with someone I felt sure she'd like.' He gave a slightly embarrassed laugh. 'I must be getting a bit punchy from lack of sleep. I don't want to come across like some kind of idiot, but I just feel like you and Maddie would get on together.' He looked me straight in the eyes. 'We tend to have similar tastes in people.'

There was a compliment in there, and I didn't have to excavate too deep to uncover it, but with admirable restraint I kept it safely buried.

'So when would you like me to start?'

He got to his feet, and I followed suit. It felt like that moment at the end of a job interview, when he was meant to say *We'll be in touch*, and I'd hold out my hand and say something like *It was a pleasure meeting you*.

'How about right now?'

'Now?' My voice sounded like a parrot who'd taken a sneaky draught of helium.

'If you're free? I'd like to introduce the two of you – if that doesn't sound too strange?'

I shook my head, and felt the ends of my long bob graze the skin between my shoulder blades. 'Her room's this way,' Ryan said, heading towards the door, which he held open for me.

I smiled, and successfully managed not to say: *Yes, I know.* This is just another patient, I kept telling myself as I walked behind Ryan down the glaringly bright fluorescent-lit corridor. I'd helped scores and scores of them during my time as a volunteer. This was no different. Maddie was just another patient.

Except of course, she wasn't. I think I already knew that, even before Ryan's hand paused momentarily on the door handle. 'Okay?' he asked, looking down at me with an encouraging smile.

'Okay,' I confirmed. His fingers tightened around the handle and the door began to open. And with my first step over the threshold, my future took on a whole new direction.

'Maddie, hello sweetheart. It's Ryan. I've brought someone to meet you.'

Chapter 9

2018

'I think today went really well. Don't you?'

I carried on tipping strawberry-scented bubble bath under the running water from the taps, with the precision of a scientist in a laboratory. In the room next door I could hear Hope singing happily. The first meeting with her birth mother had left no scar, no damage. At least not on her, and that was what was important here, I reminded myself.

'I'm sorry about next Saturday. I should probably have checked with you first.'

Yes, you should, I said silently to the mini-torrent cascading into the bathtub. I turned and looked over my shoulder at Ryan. 'No. That was fine. It's perfectly natural to have asked her. I would probably have suggested it myself if it had occurred to me.' *Really?* questioned a voice that only I could hear. I tucked a loose strand of hair behind my ear and got up from my kneeling position on the cool tiles of the bathroom floor.

'I'll need to have a quiet word with the other mums first. Just to make sure they know not to say anything.'

I could see a reflection of Ryan's puzzled expression in the steam-covered bathroom mirror. He looked like a man lost in a mist. 'The resemblance between them is even more noticeable now that Maddie is awake.' I explained. 'We don't want one of them saying anything.'

Ryan pulled me gently into his arms. 'My hands are all soapy,' I said in a token protest as they pressed up against the material of his shirt. Beneath my palms I could feel the slow and steady beat of his heart. Its familiar rhythm calmed me, the way it did late at night when he pulled me against him in our big double bed, and I fell asleep with my cheek resting against his chest.

'You won't lose her,' he whispered into the wisps of blond hair tickling beneath his chin. 'I won't let you lose her,' he promised. My soapy hands slid around him, leaving a small damp trail to show their passage.

'I know that,' I said calmly. Except I saw the reflection of my face in that same bathroom mirror, and it wasn't calm at all. It looked terrified.

We had successfully navigated almost two hours of what had to be one of the most unusual mother-and-child reunions to have ever taken place. The only awkward moment had come after Maddie had finished reading yet another chapter to Hope, and had closed the book with a sad look in her eyes. She glanced down at her watch, and I tried not to heave a sigh of relief that the ordeal was almost over.

'This has been a lovely afternoon. Thank you for inviting me Ryan – and Chloe, of course,' Maddie added hurriedly. My polite smile didn't wobble, which I was very pleased about.

'We're so glad you were able to come,' said Ryan, getting easily to his feet and putting his arm casually around my shoulders. *Don't do that*, I silently tried to telegraph, by tensing up beneath his touch. He must have realised, because he allowed his hand to slide off my shoulder and down my arm. But it was too late, Maddie had seen it, and there was a brief stricken look on her face.

It disappeared the only way that it possibly could, when her daughter leapt off the seat they had shared and placed her hand in Maddie's. Maddie looked down, and the genuine delight on her face at Hope's generous heart broke mine a little bit more.

'Will you come back again? We haven't finished the story and I've lots more books in my room that I want to hear again.'

I couldn't blame Hope for her enthusiasm. She had a new and exciting relation who clearly wanted to spend time with her. She was new and shiny . . . and I was just—

'Mummy.' My head shot up, and so did Maddie's. Ryan looked uncomfortable.

'Yes, Pumpkin?' I replied.

'Can Maddie come back again soon?'

'Yes, of course she can.' I looked into the grown-up version of my daughter's beautiful blue eyes, and saw gratitude in their sapphire depths. This was the plan we'd agreed on, I was just sticking to it, that's all. But perhaps she had doubted that we would keep to our word.

'Why don't you join us next Saturday?' suggested Ryan innocently. My eyes darted to his, and it was only then that he realised his invitation was something we should probably have discussed in advance.

'What's happening next Saturday?' asked Maddie, her glance going from Ryan to me. An unexpected stab of pity slipped between my ribs and pierced the shell around my heart. It was so wrong that she didn't know. All of it was so very wrong.

It was probably Ryan's place to answer, not mine, but neither of us got the chance, because a much younger voice piped up with the answer.

'It's my birthday,' Hope declared with an infectious giggle and a dance of pure excitement. 'It's the day I was born.'

The look in Maddie's eyes still haunted me as I held my little girl's hand to steady her as she stepped into the deep sea of white bubbles of her evening bath. Maddie's pale face had looked shocked, and then her eyes had started to glisten like polished gemstones. She hadn't known. And why should she? Perhaps the maths simply hadn't occurred to her. After all, she'd had a lot to cope with recently. But I could see the guilt beneath the pain. Maddie's emotions were all new, and it was obvious she hadn't yet mastered the art of hiding them very well. She was a mother who hadn't even known the date of her own child's birthday.

'I . . . I didn't know,' her eyes went to Ryan, and some of the sympathy I felt for her withered as they exchanged a look that felt as though it held a thousand memories.

'That's okay. You've still got time to buy me a present,' said Hope, effectively defusing the bomb in the room with a very childlike response.

'Hope!' I cried, sounding shocked, but actually feeling relieved that the moment had been neutralised so effectively. 'You can't say something like that to someone you don't—'

Maddie turned to me, and finished the sentence I should never have started '—know very well?'

Hope looked up at the three adults who were all exchanging looks. For the first time, perhaps she sensed something of the undercurrent of emotions bubbling quietly beneath the seemingly tranquil surface of the afternoon.

'But Maddie's *not* a stranger, Mummy, is she? I would never say that to a *proper* stranger. But Maddie is kind of like my new relative, so doesn't that make her part of our family? Wasn't that what you said this morning?'

She had me there, that clever little girl of mine who saw so much without realising what she was seeing.

'Yes I did, Pumpkin. I did.'

Hours later, when the house was dark and quiet, when Hope was fast asleep in the room beside ours, Ryan's hands slid around my body and drew me against him. I wriggled back into the curve of him, my body and his automatically responding to our closeness. 'You did good today, Mrs Turner. I was so proud of the way you were with Maddie.'

'How did you expect me to be?' I whispered into my pillow, feeling a single tear escape from the corner of my eye and disappear into the soft cotton cover.

'Exactly the way you were,' he said, and I felt the sadness ebb away a little at his faith in me.

'She was my friend,' I whispered softly into the darkness of our room. 'She may not remember it; she certainly won't want to hear about it – especially now. But for a long time that was the way I thought of her. She was my sleeping friend.'

'I guess that was always going to end whenever she woke up,' Ryan said sadly, and for a moment I wondered why – even now – he still didn't get it.

I turned in his arms, my lips soft as they kissed his shoulder. 'No, it ended a long time before that.'

Ryan kissed me then, and neither of us needed to finish that sentence, because some things don't have to be spoken out loud to be true.

My friendship with Maddie Chambers faltered and then failed when I fell in love with the man she had planned to marry.

2012

'Why don't I go and get us some coffee and leave you two to chat for a bit?'

I looked across the room at Ryan, certain the surprise on my face was as prominent as a blush. My glance dropped to the figure lying motionless and silent on the bed and then back to him. Any 'chatting' going on here was definitely going to be of the one-sided variety.

And yet from the moment I'd followed him into her room, I'd been impressed and incredibly moved by the very natural and loving way Ryan was with Maddie. He'd crossed to her bedside and very gently pressed his mouth to her lips. 'Hello, baby,' he said so softly, that I knew his words had been meant for her unhearing ears only. When he introduced me, and explained that I'd be coming in to visit her from time to time, Ryan held Maddie's immobile hand in his, his thumb running slowly in a caress across her palm as he spoke. My own hand tingled as though it could feel his touch upon it, but Maddie's never moved.

He chatted so comfortably to the woman in the bed, he made it very easy to believe that at any moment those ivory-white eyelids were about to spring open, or the slightly parted lips would curve into a smile at something he'd said. If I hadn't been around hospitals for as long as I had, I would almost have believed it myself.

But after spending several minutes recounting an amusing story about something that had happened to one of their friends, only *two* voices joined together in laughter at the end of the anecdote: his and mine. For a moment I glimpsed the raw pain on Ryan's face at her lack of reaction, but he masked it so quickly, that afterwards I wondered if I'd simply imagined it.

I'd taken up an unobtrusive position in one corner of the room, feeling strangely as if I was watching the two of them act out a scene in a terribly sad film; the kind that you know is going to have you reaching for the tissues by the time the credits are rolling. Here was a man whose heart was clearly breaking, over and over again; who was fighting to bring back the woman he loved the only way he knew how. The enormity of his feelings filled the room, making it hard to breathe.

With uncanny intuition, Ryan must have picked up on my vague discomfort, which I'm sure was why he'd left Maddie and me alone for a while. I stood silently at the edge of the room for several moments after he'd left, closing the door quietly behind him. I felt nervous and awkward in a way I don't ever remember being before with a hospital patient. I cast my eyes around the room, taking in the line of get-well cards on the window ledge, and the collection of shiny foil helium balloons tied to the handles of a locker. Maddie was clearly popular and had many friends. It was only when I looked a little closer that I noticed the corners of several of the cards had begun to curl at the edges, and their print was starting to fade. The balloons too showed signs of age, their words of greeting now blurred in the wrinkles of the foil. I sighed sadly. It happened this way, when patients had been in hospital for as long as Maddie had. People didn't stop *caring*, but eventually they went back to their own lives. Life went on. *This is why they need you here*, an inner voice quietly reminded me. It was the impetus I needed to push myself away from the wall and approach the bed.

For a moment I said nothing, just stared down at the woman whose tragedy had reached out and touched a chord deep within me, and had inexplicably refused to let go. I cleared my throat, as though I was about to say something really important, when in fact nothing could have been further from the truth.

'Erm ... do you mind if I sit down?' I asked the beautiful young woman in the high hospital bed. I pulled out a chair, paused for a ridiculous moment, as though expecting a reply, and then lowered myself onto the seat with a small embarrassed cough.

'You're much younger than the people I normally spend time with here,' I told Maddie, my eyes going to the unmistakable bump on her stomach, which rose like a dome beneath the blanket. 'I'm more used to asking people about their grandchildren and families, or listening to them talk about what they did when they were my age.' I gave a small laugh. 'I don't suppose you and I can do that, can we? I'm twenty-seven, by the way, in case you were wondering. I guess we must be about the same age.' I sighed and closed my eyes. I was babbling, and if Maddie *could* hear me, I imagined she'd be rolling her comatose eyes in despair. This *is the most interesting person you could find to sit with me?* she'd silently be asking Ryan. And truthfully, based on what she had to go on so far, I could hardly blame her.

Working on an instinct so strong it wouldn't allow me to ignore it, I suddenly bent down to the girl lying in the bed. Up close her skin was the perfect white of a carved statue; her dark hair gleamed with a shine that could have featured in any commercial. The life growing within her was enhancing a beauty that I suspected had been there long before her pregnancy. She had so much, and yet strangely she had nothing at all.

On the bedside cabinet was an enormous vase of deep red roses, with a small white card nestling among the stems, a single word written upon it: *Ryan*. Did Maddie know that her fiancé filled her room with flowers, even though she couldn't see them? On impulse I reached for the heavy vase, lifting it down so that the fragrant blooms were just beneath her nose. 'These are from him,' I whispered. Our faces were so close that my own hair had swung down and had fallen onto her pillow, mingling with hers. My wrists began to ache and my arms started to tremble, but I held the flowers to her face for as long as I could, hoping to find a way – any way – to reach her that might not have been tried before.

Eventually I replaced the vase, and looked down sadly at the woman whose life had already entwined itself inextricably around mine, like a fast-growing ivy.

'When I come next time I'll bring some books from the library. What do you like to read, Maddie?' I smiled and reached out and gently touched her shoulder. Beneath the skin I could feel the sharpness of her collarbone. 'Don't worry, I'll find something you like,' I assured her. I was still smiling down at her when Ryan returned carrying two cups of steaming coffee. It was almost a surprise that there weren't *three* drinks on the cardboard tray.

There are all sorts of things you're not meant to do if you undertake any type of voluntary work at a hospital. Most of them you probably don't need to be told, because they're basic common sense. But the one they make a point of telling you anyway, spelling it out in big bold letters on your very first day, is *don't* get emotionally attached to the patients. If you do, it's going to end up breaking your heart. For two years I'd successfully managed to keep that instruction at the forefront of my mind. But that autumn I broke that rule spectacularly, not once, but twice.

Surprisingly for someone who was spending so much of her free time with his fiancée, I saw very little of Ryan over the next month. I knew from the nurses on the ward that he'd gone back to work; apparently he was there early every morning for about an hour, dressed in a suit and tie, and then back again in the evening, similarly attired, presumably having come straight from his office. Normal visiting hours had long been waived for the devoted partner of the long-term coma patient on the sixth floor. The ward staff said that some evenings he was there well beyond midnight, before reluctantly saying goodnight to the woman he never wanted to leave. I had no idea how he was able to carry on like that, and neither did the nursing staff.

'He's going to burn out or collapse for sure,' commented a sparky, freckle-faced nurse called Ellen who'd recently joined the hospital. 'Then we'll end up with *both* of them in hospital!' It was a worrying thought.

The rain hit me like an assault as I ran head-down through the hospital sliding doors. It had only been spitting when I'd got off the bus just twenty minutes ago, but a lot had changed in that brief period of time. The paved walkway was now scattered with deep puddles which reflected the orange glow from the street lamps. The hospital car park was now filled to capacity with the cohort of evening visitors. And the life of a patient who I'd grown far closer to than I should was now over.

A sound escaped me, part sob, part cry of injustice. She shouldn't have died, not like that, not all alone. A pain – so real it felt almost physical – tore through me. My tote bag slipped from my shoulder, and the book we'd been in the middle of reading fell face-down onto the wet tarmac. It felt heartbreakingly symbolic. I stood staring down at the book, making no move to retrieve it as the rain mingled with the tears falling relentlessly down my cheeks. A hand came into view, a man's hand. It picked up the book, shaking the ruined pages as they dripped water. The grisly cover image of a bloodstained dagger, protected beneath its plastic jacket, was still intact.

'Chloe.' I didn't look up, though I knew who it was. 'Chloe, what's wrong?'

I gave an involuntary shudder, although it wasn't really cold, despite the rain. 'You ran right past me in the doorway. I called your name, but I don't think you even heard me.'

I hadn't, but I probably wouldn't have stopped even if I had. All I'd wanted to do was to get as far away from the hospital as possible, because tonight it didn't feel like a place of healing, it felt like a place of death. The memory of arriving on the ward and seeing the stripped hospital bed, and the locker bare of her personal effects was still raw. I'd worked there long enough to know what it meant. The jumbo-size bag of jelly babies I'd been holding slipped from my fingers, and I left it where it fell at my feet, like a marker. From the corner of my eye I could see one of the nurses walking towards me, her rubber-soled shoes soundless as she crossed to where I stood. My hand reached out and curled tightly around the cool metal of the bed frame. I looked for the glass holding the grinning dentures of the ward's longest-serving resident, but it too was gone.

'Gladys?' I asked, making the elderly woman's name a question that didn't need to be asked.

'I'm sorry, Chloe,' said the nurse kindly, her hand briefly squeezing my shoulder. 'It happened this afternoon,' she added, pre-empting my next question.

'Was anyone . . .' my voice cracked, as tears which I rarely shed for patients began to pool in my eyes. 'Was anyone with her?'

The hand squeezed one last time before dropping away. 'No. She went quietly,' the nurse replied, her voice sombre, but not sad. She was used to this in a way I realised I never would be. The nurse bent to pick up the dropped bag of sweets, Gladys's favourites. 'Shall I get rid of these for you?'

I nodded, unable to take my eyes away from the bed. 'Why don't you go home?' the nurse suggested kindly, and I couldn't help feeling that her concern was as much for the other patients as it was for me. No one needed to be reminded about the fragility of life on this ward; its occupants knew that only too well.

I'd been okay as I walked slowly down the first flight of stairs. This had happened before, many times. It would happen again. My pace increased, and my descent grew quicker, as though I was trying to outrun my emotions. But they caught up with me anyway, even though I was practically running by the time I reached the ground floor. I charged out into the wet October night, knowing I would be of no use to anyone that evening.

'You're getting drenched,' Ryan said, his hand resting lightly on the sodden sleeve of my jacket. 'Why don't we go inside, to the cafeteria, and you can tell me what's wrong.' I shook my head so violently droplets of water sprayed in twin arcs around my face. I still didn't trust my voice.

'Okay,' said Ryan, showing incredible patience for a man who was getting practically drowned. 'But you really need to get out of this rain. If you don't want to go inside, why don't we sit in my car for a moment?'

I looked into Ryan's concerned face. Raindrops had gathered like jewels on his eyelashes. I wasn't the only one who needed to get out of the deluge. He nodded his head towards the row of parked vehicles. 'I'm just over there.'

I gave a single sharp nod, and he reached for my elbow, guiding me towards the bay where a sleek black car was parked. He blipped to open the door and gently helped me into the passenger seat before I realised I was dripping all over the cream fabric upholstery.

'Don't worry about that,' assured Ryan, slipping into the driver's seat. The darkened car offered a cavern-like refuge, which could have been peaceful if it weren't for the embarrassingly loud clattering noise that appeared to be coming from me, as my teeth chattered in a way I'd never heard before.

'You're freezing,' declared Ryan, switching on the engine and allowing the air from the blowers to fill the car.

'I'm f-f-fine,' I protested.

His eyebrows rose, and that was all it took to knock the fight out of me. I sank back against the cushioned seat like a deflating crash dummy. Ryan reached behind him, and a moment later a luxuriously soft jumper was placed in my hands. 'Here, use this to dry your face and hair.'

'No, I'm fine,' I repeated, trying to pass the garment back to him. I knew cashmere when I felt it, even if none of my own clothes were made from it.

'It's okay, it's clean,' he reassured, gently forcing the soft woollen sweater back to me. Our hands were touching as we played pass-the-parcel with the expensive jumper. I could see the name of a designer in the label, and an uncanny instinct told me Maddie had bought this for him.

I abandoned my protests and used the soft folds of fabric to dry my face and the dripping ends of my hair. Ryan sat back in his own seat, as though watching me ruin his top was exactly how he'd planned to spend his evening.

'What happened?' he asked quietly.

For a second I considered not telling him the truth. Does a man whose own fiancée was lying in limbo in a hospital bed really need to hear about someone dying? 'One of the old ladies on the ward passed away this afternoon,' I said quietly, my eyes not on him, but on the windscreen. The wipers weren't turned on, and the rain was falling so heavily that the hospital and the rest of the car park were completely obscured. 'I know it sounds stupid. It's a geriatric ward; people pass away all the time. But this lady . . .' My voice trailed away, unable to articulate or explain – even to myself – why this one death had affected me in this way.

'Was it the jelly-baby lady? The one with the taste for grisly thrillers?'

I gave a small broken laugh, though his words had brought a lump to my throat. 'It was. I can't believe you remembered that.'

Ryan gave a small shrug, but I remained impressed. 'Her family weren't with her. They don't visit often. *Didn't* visit often,' I corrected sadly.

There was a wealth of sympathy on Ryan's face for an old

lady he'd never met, but then he was a man whose whole life revolved around not neglecting a loved-one in hospital.

'The stupid thing is,' I said, and then shook my head as I started to cry again. I looked down at my lap, where his expensive cashmere jumper was twisted like a wrung-out rag in my agitated hands. Absently I wondered how much it was going to cost me to replace it. 'The stupid thing is, she was so excited because I'd found a book we'd not read before. And she was really enjoying it. And now . . . now she's never going to know who committed the murder.' We both looked at the sodden book which Ryan had placed on the dashboard. 'It's ridiculous to get so upset about something like that, isn't it?'

Ryan shook his head, and there was an expression in his eyes as he looked at me that warmed me far more than all the hot air blowing through the jets of his car had done. 'No. It's not ridiculous at all. In fact it just proves that asking you to spend time with Maddie was the best decision I've made in a long time.'

He reached for his seat belt and looped it over his shoulder. 'Buckle up,' he instructed.

'What? Why? Where are we going?'

'I'm driving you home,' Ryan replied as though it was obvious.

'No. No, you don't have to do that. I can get the bus.'

'Absolutely not. I can come back to the hospital after I've dropped you home. I'm sure Maddie will understand and forgive me for being late,' he added with a smile. And the weird thing was that after four weeks of talking, reading, and idly chatting to the woman he loved, I found myself agreeing with him. Maddie *would* understand.

'This is all yours?' there was no mistaking the surprise in his voice. I looked through the windscreen at the large four-bedroom house which appeared and then disappeared behind the sweep of the wipers. I suppose it *was* a very large property for just one person. 'It's where I've lived all my life,' I said by way of explanation, my hand reaching for the car door.

'You don't share it with anyone?'

'I've thought about getting a lodger—' I began, and then felt my cheeks begin to grow warm, as I realised that probably wasn't what he was asking me. 'I don't have a boyfriend. I mean, I don't live with anyone,' I finished clumsily, giving him all sorts of information he'd never asked for.

'I know that.' This time it was *his* turn to look embarrassed. 'I wasn't prying,' he assured me quickly. 'One of the nurses mentioned it in passing.' I was trying to imagine how that topic could possibly have come up, when Ryan explained: 'I think I said something about how spending so much time at the hospital must be really hard on your personal life.' Ryan looked uncomfortable, like someone who wished he'd never taken this conversational side-street. That made two of us.

'No boyfriend. Well, no one significant. Not for a while,' I said lightly, my hand pressing down on the door handle.

He'd wanted to walk me to the door, but I wouldn't let him. There was no need for both of us to get wet again. 'Thanks again for the lift home,' I said through the rolled-down passenger window. 'And also for listening, about Gladys, I mean.'

'It's the least I can do after everything you're doing for us,' Ryan said gratefully.

Us. Even though he'd not heard her voice or felt the touch of her hand in almost four months, Ryan still felt the enduring bond of being part of a couple; part of an 'us'. I had no idea how that felt, I thought sadly, as I let myself into my house and watched his tail lights disappear into the falling rain. I'd been economical with the truth in my reply. What I should have said was that there'd *never* been a boyfriend of any significance. Not one.

It wasn't the first time I'd attended the funeral of a patient. Some deaths go by without touching you; while others will always leave their mark. Gladys had been such a colourful character on the ward it hadn't surprised me that several of us had wanted to pay our respects and say goodbye.

I recognised some members of Gladys's family at the church from the pages of the well-thumbed photograph album she'd often shown me. *Have you seen these pictures of my grandchildren?* she'd ask, her wrinkled fingers grazing over the faces of people I'd never seen visit her bedside. Perhaps I was being unfair; perhaps they visited her when I wasn't there.

They were here today though, dressed in black and

looking sombre. I tried not to judge them as I listened to the vicar speak about a completely different Gladys to the one I knew; one without her wicked sense of humour or penchant for bloodthirsty crimes. It was still a moving ceremony, and the nurses who'd accompanied me were dabbing at their watery eyes almost as much as I was by the end of it.

'We're going to have to go straight back to the hospital,' Diana apologised as the strains of the final hymn faded away. 'Are you staying?' I nodded, and after hugging them both goodbye I went to join the shuffling line of mourners waiting to pay their respects to the family.

'Thank you so much for coming,' said the middle-aged woman, who I recognised as Gladys's daughter. Behind her glasses her eyes were red-rimmed and her nose was shiny. 'How did you know Mum exactly?'

'I'm one of the volunteers at the hospital,' I explained.

'Oh, you must be Chloe,' she exclaimed. 'Mum spoke about you all the time. I know she really appreciated your visits with her.'

'It was my pleasure. She was a lovely old lady.'

Her daughter looked slightly baffled by my words, and I felt sad that perhaps *she* was the one who'd missed out by not visiting more often.

'Well, thank you for all that you did, and for coming today. It means a lot.' I was about to walk away when she stopped me in my tracks with her parting words. 'Oh, and please thank your friend too for the lovely flowers. That was very thoughtful.'

'My friend?' I asked, certain she was muddling me up with someone else.

'Brian? Is that his name? Or something like that? Anyway, it was very kind of him. You can see the flowers. All the floral tributes have been laid out in the courtyard.'

Brian. I knew no one of that name. It was surely just a coincidence that it sounded like the name of someone I *did* know, I told myself as I walked down the path lined with floral bouquets and wreaths.

I found it at the very end of the row of tributes; a bright yellow arrangement, its colour defiantly cheerful among the blood-red roses and waxy white lilies. I crouched down, wobbling a little in my black dress and high-heeled shoes. There was a black-edged card, nestled among the yellow blooms, and I pulled it out to read with fingers that were trembling from a peculiar emotion I scarcely recognised. *To Gladys,* it said, in bold black penmanship. *Wishing you the safest of journeys for your next adventure. With warmest best wishes, Ryan (Chloe's friend).*

My hand went to my throat, as though to silence the small sob that I knew was going to escape anyway, whatever I did. But even as I began to cry, I was smiling widely at the final line of Ryan's message: *Just thought you would like to know . . . it was the brother-in-law who did it.*

Chapter 10

2012

I held the book in my hands and flicked through its pages, flipping past the glossy illustrations and concentrating mainly on the text. I gave a little nod of approval and added it to the growing pile on the table beside me. There was quite a gap on the shelf by the time I'd finished, and when Sally's face suddenly appeared within it my heart jumped so violently, several years were probably shaved off my life expectancy.

'I hate to be the one to tell you this,' she hissed, in a huge faux whisper, leaning even further into the space the books had left, 'but you don't actually work here today.'

I smiled into the empty space as Sally scooted around the library bookshelf. 'I just popped in to pick up a couple of books on my way to the hospital,' I explained, gathering up the pile from the table. Sally glanced down at the topmost book, which showed a pair of hands lovingly cradling a hugely swollen abdomen. Her eyebrows rose expressively.

'Something you want to share with me?' She cast a quick glance at the other titles, which all covered the same topic.

'These aren't for me,' I replied. 'They're for Maddie.'

For a second Sally looked almost as concerned by my reply as if I *had* been the one in need of the pregnancy manuals. 'Weren't you at the hospital only yesterday?'

I shifted from one foot to the other, feeling like a naughty school child called into the headteacher's office. 'So?' I said, playing a hand of cards I was never going to win.

'So, I'm concerned that you might be getting a tad over-involved with this one particular patient, that's all.' She softened her words with a gentle squeeze of my shoulder. 'You do seem to spend most of your free time there these days.' I shrugged, but the innocent dart had found its target. 'Just ignore me. It's none of my business,' Sally said with a smile that didn't quite find its way to her eyes. 'I'm probably just jealous that you've gone and got yourself a new best friend.'

I reached out for humour, and threw it over our conversation like a fire blanket. 'Well she's certainly not as nosy as you are,' I said, heading towards the desk to scan my own books. 'And pretty good at keeping secrets,' I added, giving my sometimes less-than-discreet friend a cheeky grin.

It was just after lunchtime and the library was practically deserted; the morning browsers and newspaper-readers had long gone, and the after-school children and parents were yet to arrive. I could have done with a few customers around for distraction, I thought as I loaded the books into a sturdy jute bag, aware of Sally's watchful gaze upon me.

'What does her husband think about you reading her books about babies and childbirth?' she asked, with all the finesse of someone poking a rattlesnake with a long stick.

'Fiancé,' I corrected automatically, and then inwardly cursed, because I was sure Sally knew perfectly well that Maddie and Ryan weren't married. 'Actually, I've no idea what he thinks. I haven't run it by him. Our paths rarely cross at the hospital. That's the whole reason why I'm there; to sit with her when no one else can.'

Sally nodded, but said nothing, at least not with her voice. Her eyes however, they had plenty to say. 'Just be careful, hon, that's all. I know how upset you were when your OAP friend passed away. I'm worried that you're getting too attached to someone who may not—'

'I'm fine,' I interrupted, not wanting to hear the end of that sentence, not even wanting to *think* about it. The possibility of Maddie *or* her baby not surviving filled me with the kind of dread they'd specifically warned volunteers about. But it was too late. I was involved; way over-my-head involved. And yet still I tried to hide it.

'If *I* was the one who was pregnant, I'd want to read every book ever written on the subject. I'd have a thousand questions. Wouldn't you?' I countered.

'If *I* was pregnant,' Sally said, deciding the conversation was in dire need of some levity, 'the only question I'd be asking is: *What happened to that damn condom?'*

It started with Maddie's Kindle, and grew from there.

'What kind of books does she like to read?' I'd asked Ryan before my first visit.

He'd looked from me to his motionless fiancée, as if expecting her to open her eyes – just for a moment – to help him out. 'Do you know, I have absolutely no idea. That's pretty awful to admit, isn't it?'

If that was his only area of negligence, it was an easy one to forgive. 'Don't worry,' I told him. 'I'm sure I'll find something she likes. *And it's not like she's going to tell you if she doesn't,* a silent voice whispered in my head. 'But if she happens to have a Kindle or something similar, it might give me a clue.'

When I knocked lightly on the door of Maddie's room a few days later, pausing for an invitation to enter that would never come, the Kindle was sitting on her bedside cabinet, waiting for me. I'd introduced myself clumsily as I crossed the room, still feeling self-conscious as I conducted our one-way conversation. 'I'll get better at this, I promise,' I assured her. *Do it fast* I imagined her replying. My lips curled. Imaginary Maddie had quite the sense of humour.

When I picked up her Kindle and switched it on, it felt like a passport allowing me entry into a foreign country. I reached for a chair and pulled it up close to the bed, asking its silent occupant if it was okay for me to sit down. She seemed to have no objection, so I sat and began to scan through the library on her device. Maddie's choice of books was as distinctive and as personal as a fingerprint. My smile grew broader as I went down the list of titles, surprised by how many were also to be found on my own bookshelf. We might lead completely different lives, but *this* we had in common. It cemented a foundation between us that I could build on.

'I couldn't finish that one either,' I confessed, lightly touching her hand as though to gain her straying attention. I searched her exquisite face for the smallest sign of acknowledgement. How did her family and Ryan continue to remain so positive about her recovery, when there was so little evidence that there was anything left beyond a beautiful shell that was once Madeline Chambers.

Well, if they could do it, then so could I, I told myself firmly. I'd seen enough to decide what books to bring next time, and was about to switch off the reader when I noticed a book that was probably one of Maddie's last purchases; a compendium of baby names. The row of grey dots beneath its title told me she'd never started reading it. I stared at the Kindle sadly, knowing why.

The decision was easily made, and felt fully formed and satisfying, almost as though the idea hadn't even been mine. Perhaps Maddie *couldn't* hear me; perhaps she *was* so deeply lost that no voice could penetrate the silence. But perhaps not.

I clicked to open the book, and settled back more comfortably in my chair. 'Okay, Maddie, we'll start with the As today and then work our way through the alphabet.' She said nothing, which I took as her unspoken agreement. I often held the hands of the patients I visited, but it felt different when the skin brushing mine wasn't paper-dry or wrinkled. I slid my hand around hers. Her nails were neater than mine, her skin softer and about three shades paler. 'If I get to one you really like, try to give my hand a squeeze,' I said as I began to slowly read out names for her unborn daughter.

It was the second week of October and we had now reached the Ls in the alphabet. Maddie was making medical history, a fact she remained blissfully unaware of. She'd been in a coma for fifteen weeks, and was now thirty-one weeks pregnant. She was probably the only person on the sixth floor of the hospital who didn't find those two facts both miraculous and astounding.

'Laura, Laurel, Laverne—' I screwed up my nose, 'Don't call her Laverne.' I looked down at the hand held in mine. It remained motionless, as it had done for the first half of the alphabet, which we'd systematically covered over the last five weeks.

'Leanne, Lesley, Letitia—'

'That has to be the most boring book ever written!'

The Kindle slipped from my fingers and landed on the floor with a dull thud. I hadn't heard the opening of the door, much less anyone entering the room. I automatically glanced at my watch. It was almost four in the afternoon.

'What are you doing here?' I questioned the man who had every right to visit his comatose fiancée at any time of the day or night. Ryan's unexpected arrival had startled me. Fortunately he didn't appear to take offence at my slightly confrontational greeting. He smiled warmly at Maddie, and perhaps at me too, it was hard to tell. He crossed over to the bed and ran his finger lightly over one ivory cheek. 'Hello, sweetheart.'

I swooped down to retrieve Maddie's Kindle, which meant I heard rather than saw the kiss he pressed upon her unmoving lips. I got to my feet, and immediately began looking around the room for my bag and coat.

'There's no need for you to rush away,' Ryan said easily, shrugging off his suit jacket and reaching up to loosen and then pull off his tie. 'I had a meeting over on this side of town and it wound up earlier than I was expecting. So I thought I'd surprise my girls by getting here earlier.'

I swallowed so loudly it sounded deafening to my ears. I'd been surprised when he'd walked in, but to hear myself referred to as one of Ryan's 'girls' was nothing short of a shock. I was still trying to work out how I felt about it, when I saw his hand go to the waffle blanket covering Maddie and then come to rest on the mound beneath it, which seemed to be growing almost daily.

'Hello, little girl. How are you today?'

The baby. *Of course* the baby, I thought, feeling stupid and very, very, embarrassed. God, what if I'd said something? I could feel my cheeks growing warm at the thought.

The hand resting on Maddie's stomach gently caressed the child inside her. My eyes were fixed on its slow backward and forward motion, so I saw the sharp kick that jolted the blanket upward and brought an expression of pure joy onto Ryan's face. He looked over at me with delight plastered all over his features.

'Did you see that?'

I nodded, unable to say anything beyond the huge lump that had mysteriously settled in my throat.

The baby kicked again, so hard that Ryan's hand was momentarily displaced. He shook his head in wonder, smiling as he looked down at Maddie's unmoving face. 'Can you feel that?' he asked her. 'You *must* be able to feel that.' The disappointment that momentarily doused the joy in his eyes was so intense I could feel it like the blast from an explosion. I got to my feet, without knowing why. I can only think his need to share this moment with someone – anyone – was the reason why Ryan did what he did next.

'Feel this,' he urged, holding out his free hand for mine. I shook my head so vigorously that my dangling earrings slapped against my cheeks.

'No. That's okay, I'm fine,' I replied stupidly, as though implying that I'd already felt my share of kicking infants that day, and couldn't possibly manage another.

More disappointment in his eyes, and this time I was the one who'd put it there. I saw the very human need he felt to share this moment with someone. With someone who was able to respond.

I took a shaky step towards the bed. I saw my arm lifting and my hand stretching out towards his, almost as though it was doing so of its own volition. He reached for my hand, and his skin felt warm and something weird happened to my breathing. Very gently he placed my hand on Maddie's belly. The room seemed to go unnaturally quiet. I could no longer hear the muted sounds from the hospital corridor. The chatter of nurses and doctors had all faded away. The only sound to be heard was the breathing of three people. Nothing happened, and after about twenty seconds I went to remove my hand, but Ryan placed his own directly on top of it, preventing me from doing so.

'Wait a moment,' he urged. 'I think sometimes she just needs to hear a voice.' He moved his hand gently backwards and forwards, taking mine with it. His action was a caress, but it wasn't my hand he was caressing, even though my stupid heart clearly thought it was by the way it was racing. 'Hey, baby girl. Daddy's here,' Ryan spoke gently. He was standing so close I could feel his breath ruffling my hair. And then suddenly it came, not just once, but twice. Fierce and unmistakable, two sharp little kicks fell squarely into the palm of my hand.

My mouth dropped open in a small O of surprise and wonder. Was that the moment when I fell in love with Maddie's baby? It might have been. I'd certainly never felt an emotion like it before in my entire life. I felt like I was standing on the edge of something so bright and beautiful that looking too closely would damage my eyes. Damage all of me. Inexplicably and embarrassingly, I burst into tears.

*

It took about three weeks for me to stop jumping every time the door opened to Maddie's room whenever I was with her. Each time it did, and a member of the medical team came in, I heaved a small sigh of relief which strangely left a lingering taste of disappointment on my tongue. I'd been hugely embarrassed by the fool I'd made of myself when the baby had kicked. And yet whenever I thought back to what had happened – which I did with excruciating regularity, it was the aftermath I remembered more vividly than the incident itself.

Ryan had been so sweet and kind. Without a thought, his arm had come around my shoulders, and he'd pulled me to his side. I shouldn't have gone there. Being held and comforted by him wasn't a place where I belonged. That was Maddie's position, even if she was currently unable to claim it. Yet Ryan clearly saw nothing wrong in offering comfort to someone in distress. Even if it was someone he didn't know very well. Perhaps some men are like that, but none that I'd ever met before.

That still didn't excuse my actions, because instead of pulling away and apologising for being all kinds of stupid, I did something totally unforgivable and buried my face against his chest as I continued to cry. For a moment I felt him pause, stiffen awkwardly, and then his body relaxed and I felt his hand come up to pat my shoulder comfortingly. Perhaps that was when I realised how many lines I was stepping over. Too many to count.

'It's hormones,' I heard him say from somewhere far above

my head, which was now beginning to realise it had no business being rested so closely against him that I could hear the thud of his heartbeat beneath my ear. 'Pregnancy does things to people's hormones,' he declared.

He'd found the right note to hit, so when I finally pulled back and grabbed a handful of tissues from the box he was offering, I was able to produce a sound that almost resembled a laugh. 'I think it's only the pregnant person's hormones that are meant to go haywire,' I said. I depleted Maddie's box of tissues by blowing my nose repeatedly and then swabbing at my eyes. The black stains smeared on the tissues that I lobbed into the bin told me there was very little left of the mascara I'd applied that morning. I didn't need to look in the small mirror positioned above the hand basin to know my cheeks would be red and blotchy, and my eyes puffy and swollen. Crying never looked good on me.

'Ryan, I am so sorry. I have no idea why I reacted like that. It was totally unprofessional of me.'

I looked down at my feet, so I didn't see the compassion in his eyes, but I still heard it in his voice. 'That's what makes you exactly the right person to be with Maddie right now.' I slowly lifted my head. 'It's because you're *not* professional.'

It was a damning thing to hear for someone who'd been a hospital volunteer for over two years. 'You may have picked the wrong way to make me feel better,' I said. Ryan responded with a throaty chuckle.

'Maddie has a legion of doctors, nurses, physios, and God-only-knows-who-else to meet all of her medical needs. They're doing a fantastic job, and yet they're still failing her.'

I stood up a little straighter, feeling I should come to the defence of my colleagues, but not wanting to contradict him.

'What she needs,' he continued, 'is someone who'll brush her hair when the nurses haven't got time to do it; who'll file her nails; who has a very questionable taste in music, but plays it to her anyway; who reads to her from books about pregnancy – when no one else had thought about doing that.' I felt my already-hot cheeks go very, very, pink. I had no idea he knew about all of that. The nurses had clearly been talking.

'But more than any of that, what Maddie really needs is someone with a big enough heart to cry the first time she feels our baby kick.' I bit my lower lip, certain he was just being kind. 'What Maddie needs most of all, Chloe Barnes, is you. And thank God she has you.'

I spent so long imagining my next encounter with Ryan at the hospital, that when our paths crossed again at my *other* place of work, I was totally unprepared.

It was Friday afternoon, which was my favourite time of the week at the library. The staff happily swapped and changed roles and duties all the time, but the storytelling session was all mine. I was the one who decorated the walls of the cosy nook in the children's section with collages and pictures of characters from favourite books. I set out the semi-circle of low bright-red plastic seats, even though I knew my fidgety audience would probably not stay on them for long. I picked the stories: sometimes new titles; and sometimes old favourites that I had loved as a child.

I glanced out through the large plate-glass library windows. Rain was lashing viciously against them. The parks and playgrounds would hold no appeal this afternoon. I went back to the storytelling corner and added an extra row of seats. At just after three o'clock my excited audience started to arrive. There was always an element of herding cats as we tried to persuade the group of enthusiastic under-fives to stay in their seats until the session officially began. Today was no different, but I wasn't worried. Once I sat down on the chair facing them and opened up today's book, their brief attention span would be all mine – at least for half an hour.

Although it wasn't a requirement, most of the parents elected to stay, forming a solid barrier behind their listening offspring, which explains why I didn't see Ryan straightaway. I was halfway through a story about a lost toy – a gripping suspenseful thriller, if you happen to be under five – when I looked over the top of the illustration I was holding up to show the children, and saw him. He was leaning against one of the bookcases, standing a little apart from the waiting parents, like a lone wolf watching the rest of the pack.

His eye caught mine and he smiled, as though it was perfectly natural for him to be there, when nothing could be further from the truth. I turned the book back around, my connection with the story momentarily broken.

'Who's taken the bear?'

'How will he find his way back home?'

'Why have you stopped reading?'

Hurriedly I scanned the page looking for my place. Nursery-age children are notorious hecklers, and today's audience was no exception. Somehow or other I managed to get to the end of the book, but I stumbled over words an eight-year-old would have managed with ease, and was informed by at least two disgruntled listeners that I was *doing the voice wrong* for the toy giraffe.

'Tough crowd,' Ryan sympathised, weaving his way through the small bodies and grateful parents at the end of the session. 'Are they always like that?'

I gave a smile, feeling slightly more in control now that several dozen pairs of eyes were no longer on me. 'No, sometimes they can be quite critical.'

He shook his head and looked down in perplexed admiration as parents manoeuvred small resisting limbs into raincoats and feet into wellie boots. 'I can't believe we're soon going to have one of these.'

I looked down at the children, some of whom were running around the library like possessed monkeys, expending the energy they'd been forced to suppress for the last thirty minutes. 'Yours won't be like this for a good few years. You'll be an expert by the time she's ready to come along to something like this.'

I'd made the comment lightly, but there was nothing light about the look on Ryan's face. 'I haven't got a clue about any of this. What I do I know about babies, or toddlers, or little girls? Absolutely nothing.'

It was easy to see his worries weren't being voiced carelessly, they ran deep like veins of silver in bedrock. 'I'm sure every new parent thinks exactly the same thing,' I said, perfectly aware that his unique circumstances made him nothing at all like most new parents.

'Except most of them are doing it as part of a duo, they're a team. But unless Maddie miraculously wakes up just in the nick of time, there's a very good chance I'm going to be doing this all by myself. At least for now.'

I bit my lip, and said nothing.

'The baby's due in six weeks,' he said, the fear of that countdown showing in his eyes. He wasn't telling me anything I didn't already know. The buzz around Maddie had increased dramatically the closer she got to her due date. Plans were being made for the delivery, which must surely be exciting and terrifying for Ryan. Particularly if he'd heard the same whispers that I had.

I was very careful to make sure no trace of them showed on my face, as I looked up and gave him my most reassuring *everything-will-be-fine* smile. But there were shadows everywhere: in his eyes, beneath them, and hanging over him like a spectre. There was a real and tangible concern that Maddie might not survive the birth of her child, and I could tell that Ryan was well aware of that.

I grappled to erase that look from his face any way that I could. 'Not that I blame you for wanting to know how the lost bear managed to make it back home, but what *exactly* are you doing here, Ryan?'

He shook his head as though he couldn't believe he hadn't already made that clear, and dug deep into the pocket of his jacket to pull out a small red leather purse. *My* purse.

I stared at it for a second, as though he'd just performed a magic trick that I couldn't quite figure out. 'Where——? How——?'

'I found it late last night; it had slipped down the side of Maddie's bed.'

I smiled gratefully and reached for the purse that I hadn't even realised was missing from my bag. 'Thank you so much. But you didn't have to come all this way to return it. Although you *have* probably saved me hours of tearing my house apart looking for it.'

'It was no problem,' Ryan said easily.

He looked around the library curiously, like a man who hasn't been inside one for a very long time. He didn't appear uncomfortable exactly, but there was a weird feeling of displacement, having him here in my world. It was as though we were two actors who'd accidentally walked on to the stage of the wrong play. When he glanced down at his watch, I wondered if he was anxious to leave.

'Are you off to the hospital now?'

'Actually, I'm not. Not for a couple of hours, anyway,' he replied, sounding regretful. It made me think of a comment I'd overheard one of the nurses say recently: 'If that man could live at the hospital he'd move in in a heartbeat.'

'Maddie's parents have come up to stay for a couple days, so I'm giving them some time alone with her.'

'I've seen her dad a few times,' I said, recalling the quietly spoken man who held himself so rigidly upright when he walked that you had to look twice to realise how badly he was broken. 'But I don't think I've met her mum.'

'It's ... it's difficult for Faye,' Ryan said diplomatically. There was genuine affection in his voice when he spoke about his future in-laws. 'But with the baby coming so soon, Bill wanted to bring her up to see Maddie again.' Ryan swallowed visibly and looked away for a long moment.

'So, it left me with some free time to return your lost property,' Ryan said, trying to shake off the fear that had dug its claws so deeply into him, the scars would be with him forever.

He glanced across the library to the desk, where Sally and another of my colleagues were sitting, doing a very poor job of pretending they weren't watching us. 'I should probably let you get back to work,' Ryan said, with a slightly guilty expression.

'Thanks again, for this,' I said holding up my purse as though it was a trophy. I was still holding it aloft as my eyes followed Ryan when he walked out of the library into the driving rain, striding into the torrent almost as though he couldn't feel it pounding against him.

That was the last time I saw Ryan Turner until the night before he became a father.

I'd stayed later than usual on the geriatric ward and when I was finally about to leave, a couple of the nurses had waylaid me. 'Come and join us in the office for a bit. We're celebrating Viv's last shift before she gets hitched.' There had been cake, non-alcoholic fizz, and a selection of gifts of underwear that all looked far too uncomfortable to wear, and had *certainly* not come from any high street store. Viv gamely modelled the skimpy scraps of lace and leather, holding them up against her uniform to the delight of her colleagues. Among the bawdy jokes and raucous laughter it was easy to forget that two floors above us was a woman who'd probably had a similar hen-night celebration . . . for a wedding that never was.

I'd seen Maddie only the day before. It had felt weird sitting beside her knowing that the next time I visited, the huge mound that now seemed to dominate her slender frame would be gone, and a tiny new human being would be in its place. If all went well.

'Still thinking about the Miracle Girl upstairs?' guessed Diana astutely, coming up beside me with an open box of chocolates in her hand.

I shook my head, turning down the offer of the sweets, but unable to deny her assumption. 'It's hard not to. I can't believe this time tomorrow it will all be over.' My throat swallowed convulsively, not liking the choice of words that had come out of it.

Diana looked at me for a long considering moment. 'If I told you not to get too involved with this one, would I be too late?'

I looked around the room at the small group of women

who all knew far better than I did how to separate their emotions from their work. 'Way too late,' I admitted sadly.

'That's what I was afraid of,' Diana said, popping a chocolate into her mouth.

'It just sounds so risky, trying to deliver the baby normally.'

'Less risky than surgery would be,' Diana replied, repeating a party line I'd heard in many overheard conversations over the last few weeks. The truth of it was, *no one* really knew what was best to do, because Maddie's condition was so unique. I wondered if Ryan had even been given a say in this decision. What if only one of them could be saved? Who would make that choice? Ryan? Maddie's parents? Or the doctors themselves? I shook my head, trying to dislodge that thought, but it had burrowed in deep, like a tick.

Despite having said my goodbyes to Maddie the day before, when I eventually shrugged into my coat and left the nurses' impromptu hen party, I felt an overwhelming urge to whisper one final 'good luck' into her unhearing ear.

My feet knew their way to Maddie's room, but I diverted them first to the nurses' station. Ellen looked up from a chart she was filling in under a small pool of light from the desk lamp. The ward was quiet and we both spoke in whispers, as if we were sharing secrets in church.

'Goodness, Chloe, what are you still doing here at this hour?'

'I thought I'd pop in to see Maddie before—' *Before what?* questioned a persistent voice in my head that simply wouldn't shut-up. 'Before tomorrow,' I completed firmly.

Ellen nodded with gentle acceptance. Of all the nurses on the ward, I knew she'd be the one who'd best understand why I was still there so late that night. There was something about the way she was with Maddie that I'd not witnessed with any of the other nurses.

'Has Ryan gone home already? Because I don't want to disturb his time with her.'

'I don't think he's gone home, but he did go outside for a walk about fifteen minutes ago. He looked pretty choked-up and I think he needed some air to clear his head.' I glanced out through the windows at the cold night. That air was probably just above freezing, for the topmost branches of the trees and the roofs of the parked cars were glazed with a shimmer of ice. Somewhere out there in the cold and darkness I imagined a man so full of fear and uncertainty he was probably striking all kinds of bargains with anyone who would listen, to save the woman he loved.

'That's great. I'll just nip in for a moment, if that's okay?'

'You know the way.'

I did indeed. And because the ward was so silent and I didn't want to disturb anyone, for once I didn't bother knocking or announcing myself as I opened the door to Maddie's room and slipped into its darkened interior.

My shocked gasp sounded raw, but nowhere near as raw as the sounds coming from the man who wasn't wandering the pathways of the hospital grounds at all, but was sitting by Maddie's bedside, his face deeply burrowed against her chest. The blankets had muffed the sound of his sobs from the corridor, but in here they could be heard with heartbreaking clarity. They came from somewhere deep within him, and their force rocked me on my feet.

For a moment I wondered if I could slip back out of the room without him noticing me, but the slice of light I'd let into the room when I'd opened the door had made that easy exit impossible. Ryan raised his head slowly and looked towards the door, so lost in his pain that he didn't seem to think it was odd that I was here at the hospital many hours after I should have gone home.

'What if this is it, Chloe?' he asked, his voice a hoarse whisper. 'What if this is the last time I'll ever be able to do this? The last kiss; the last touch; the last chance to tell her I love her?'

I crossed over to the bed without even realising I was moving. 'You can't think like that. You have to keep believing that it's all going to be all right.' My hand didn't stop to think whether it had any right to be there, for it was already on his back, squeezing his shoulder in reassurance. It was hard to know if the rock-hard muscle beneath my palm was the result of tension or hours spent at the gym.

I stayed longer than I probably should have done, murmuring all kinds of assurances I had no business giving. It was like trying to plug a gaping hole in a dam with tissue-paper hopes and positivity. Maybe I helped. I'd like to think I did, a little.

When eventually I glanced down at my watch I was amazed to discover it was long past midnight. 'What time are you leaving here?' I asked.

'I'm not. Not tonight,' Ryan said with quiet resolution. I certainly wouldn't have wanted to be the hospital employee who tried to challenge that decision. 'I'm not leaving her side until the baby is born.'

And probably not even then, I added silently, getting to my feet and putting out a hand to steady myself on the bed frame. I was so exhausted I was practically sleep-walking.

'I'm sorry, Chloe, I've kept you here for far too long,' Ryan apologised.

My head felt twice as heavy as usual as I shook it in denial. 'No. Not at all. I wanted to be here. I hope I've helped.'

Ryan took his eyes from Maddie for a moment to meet mine. 'You have no idea how much, Chloe. You're a very calming person to be around.'

It was a measure of how tired I must have been that I felt my eyes smart with tears at his words. I was in danger of confusing heartfelt gratitude with something else altogether. It was definitely time for me to leave.

'Good luck for tomorrow,' I said.

Ryan lifted one of Maddie's lifeless hands and threaded his fingers through hers. 'Thank you. I think we'll need it.' On his face was the saddest smile I had ever seen. It stayed with me throughout the taxi ride home, and was still burning inside my closed lids when I eventually shut them and fell into a disturbed and restless sleep.

By mid-afternoon the following day I'd still had no news from the hospital. I held out for as long as I could, but when

I went to the staffroom to make tea, I headed straight for my phone and not the kettle. I'd always thought fathers anxiously pacing maternity wards was just a cliché, but as I waited for my phone to pick up signal, I found myself walking in circuits around the perimeter of the room. Four new messages had landed in my inbox while I was busy pretending to be cataloguing books – and getting it spectacularly wrong. I'd been aware of Sally working silently beside me, correcting every error I'd made throughout the day.

She slipped into the staffroom now, glanced towards the kitchenette where the mugs had neither teabags nor water in them, and took over the task, while I stood on the opposite side of the room, my phone cradled in my palm. From what seemed like a very long way away, I heard her asking if everything was okay. I still didn't know. My trembling finger hovered over the unopened messages, coming to a stop at the one from Ryan. It took two attempts before I managed to open it: *Maddie and I have a daughter.* I devoured the words hungrily, never realising then how they would end up changing my life.

There was a photograph attached to the message, and I scrolled down to study it with a sound that could have been either a laugh or a sob. It drew Sally across the room, and she hung over my shoulder to look at the screen. From the angle of the photo, I suspected Ryan must have taken it with his newborn daughter cradled in his arms. The infant's face was unbelievably small and screwed up, a new arrival to the world who was already missing the warmth and quiet of her mother's womb. The soft folds of pink blanket cocooning her couldn't hide the incredible shock of short spiky hair, which looked long enough to need combing. But it wasn't the hair that made my heart beat faster, it was her face; so tiny, so perfect, and so very beautiful. Maddie's stunning features looked even more amazing on her newborn daughter than they did on her own face.

Hope. They called her Hope. But of course they did. Afterwards I wondered how I could possibly have skipped through the H section of that book of names, without ever realising it was the only one in the world they could possibly have chosen for her.

I didn't see her for several days, and by that time I was probably the only person who worked at the hospital who hadn't done so. Apparently there'd been a never-ending stream of staff from almost every other ward, who'd suddenly discovered a need to visit the sixth floor on some pretext or another. It was telling that Maddie's circumstances were so unusual that no one had suggested that Baby Chambers might be better off staying in the hospital's nursery on the maternity ward. Maddie and Hope just kept breaking all the rules ... and no one seemed to care.

My knock on Maddie's door was more tentative than usual. I could hear voices talking on the other side, and in the seconds that passed before I recognised Ryan's voice, calling out for me to 'come in', I wondered if I should be there at all.

Surprisingly there was no one else in the room, apart from Ryan who was talking into his mobile phone; Maddie; and a small Perspex crib beside the bed, which held the room's third occupant. Ryan beckoned me in, indicating with hand signals that he was almost finished on his call.

'Yes, Mum, I know. It took my breath away when I saw her too.' The mobile was pressed firmly against his ear, but I could still make out the sound of a woman's voice speaking very loudly into her phone. Ryan's eye caught mine and he flashed me a quick grin before returning to his conversation.

I tiptoed further into the room, and headed straight for Maddie. Keeping my voice to a whisper so I didn't disturb Ryan, I bent down low towards her pillow.

'Hello, Maddie, it's Chloe.'

I always paused when I did that, as though allowing her time to silently greet me. But then I did something that wasn't usual, normal, or probably even allowed if I'd stopped to think about it, which I didn't. I leant in a little closer and placed a single kiss on her perfect white alabaster cheek. 'Congratulations, Maddie. You're a mummy. Everyone is so proud of you.'

My hair had fallen across my face, but not enough to hide the single tear of happiness that trickled down my cheek and dropped onto hers. I erased it gently with my fingertip, but when I straightened up I saw Ryan, whose call had now finished, looking at me with a surprising expression on his face.

I took a step backwards, feeling flustered, and skirted quickly around to the other side of the bed, to meet the youngest person in the room. 'Hello there, baby girl.'

Two bright blue eyes looked up straight into mine. Her tiny rosebud mouth wobbled for a second and then seemed to widen into a smile. I'd read the baby books to her mother; I *knew* that I wasn't standing close enough for Hope to be able to focus on my face; I *knew* what I believed to be a smile was most probably just wind, but for once I refused to accept that the books knew best. I swore that those sparkling blue eyes were looking directly at me, as though she recognised my voice, and that the gummy smile was her saying hello, the only way that she could.

'How are they both?' I asked, my voice sounding both hushed and awed.

Ryan smiled and bent to lift his daughter from her plastic crib. He didn't look entirely natural with her yet, spending a great deal of time settling his large hands beneath her head and bottom before daring to lift her up from the mattress. I wasn't even aware I was holding my breath, until I heard him exhale slowly in relief at exactly the same time.

'The midwives keep telling me I won't drop her ... but I'm not so sure.'

'I'm certain you're doing just fine,' I said watching as he slowly and carefully settled his newborn baby more securely in the crook of his arm, cradling her against the warmth of his body. She looked perfectly content to be there. 'The good thing about babies is that they haven't read the books we have,' I joked. 'They don't know when you're doing it wrong.'

Ryan smiled, but his eyes were on the infant in his arms and not on me. If a man could be mesmerised by his own child, then that's what I was witnessing right there in that quiet hospital room. Ryan was falling even more deeply in love with his daughter, right before my eyes. I wished with all my heart that Maddie could see this. This was *their* moment, not mine. I glanced over towards her, but she looked exactly the same as ever. Minus the enormous bump, of course.

'I'm so glad everything went well with the delivery.'

Ryan nodded, and this time he did look away from his daughter's face, towards Maddie. 'Everything went as they'd hoped. Except . . .' his voice trailed off, and I knew the end of that sentence, because it hadn't been just *his* deepest wish. It had been what everyone in the hospital had been hoping for: one more miracle.

'Except Maddie didn't wake up,' I completed sadly.

He nodded, and neither of us spoke for several minutes. Ryan filled his staring deeply into his daughter's face. I spent mine looking around the room, wondering why I'd failed to notice its recent transformation to a miniature florist's. The window ledge, the bedside cabinet – practically every surface – was covered with bouquets, huge teddy bears, or bright pink helium balloons.

'You must have had loads of visitors,' I observed.

Ryan's expression was rueful. 'Just family and a few close friends.' He nodded to indicate the flowers, gifts and cards. 'Most of these are from total strangers. People have been very generous. There were so many I had to ask the nurses to distribute them to some of the other wards.'

'I guess everyone is interested in Hope,' I said, looking down at the tiny scrap in her white towelling babygro, who was falling asleep as I watched.

Ryan lifted his gaze from his daughter and there was a sudden softness blurring the new lines around his eyes when he looked at me. 'Except you.' For a moment I thought he was criticising me, and I could feel my pulse racing as I wondered what it was I'd done wrong. 'When you came in here today, you didn't go straight to the baby, the way every other visitor has done. You went to Maddie; you congratulated her; you even kissed her.' I could feel the flush burning my cheeks, despite the over-warm room. I *knew* that kiss had been a step too far.

But instead of censure, there was only admiration in Ryan's eyes. 'You treated Maddie the same way you would treat any other new mum. That meant more than you can possibly know, Chloe. She deserves that.'

I was still wondering how to respond to his unexpected praise, when thankfully I didn't have to, for the door opened behind me and the soft fall of footsteps sounded in the room. I turned around and recognised Maddie's parents. Her father paused when he saw me, and I could see him trying to place me. Her mother walked past me as though

I was invisible, her eyes only on her daughter and the child in Ryan's arms.

'Hello,' greeted Bill politely, his bushy brows joining together for a moment to form one long grey caterpillar. 'It's ... Chloe, isn't it?'

I smiled back at him, suddenly feeling very much like the one person in the room who didn't belong there. 'Yes, it is,' I said, extending my hand, which he shook formally. 'I just popped in to see your lovely new granddaughter,' I explained, my words tumbling out in a guilty rush, and I had no idea why.

Bill's eyes became misty as they looked over at his own child, his own baby, lying in her hospital bed. This scene should be so very different, I thought sadly.

On the other side of the room I was aware of Ryan settling Hope into her grandmother's waiting arms. It wasn't my place to worry about whether that was a good idea, and it was definitely time for me to go before I voiced my concern, which would be the second inappropriate thing I'd done that day.

'I have to be going now, but it was very nice meeting you again Mr and Mrs Chambers.'

'That's Bill and Faye,' Maddie's father corrected kindly. 'You're a friend of the family.'

Am I? I quietly asked myself as I ran lightly back down to the fourth floor to spend my afternoon with patients approaching the end of their days, rather than one at the beginning of hers. Somehow I seemed to have slipped out of

the role I usually played, and into one I didn't entirely rec-
ognise. Friend? Companion? Or something else altogether?
Something that the board of administrators at the hospital
would definitely never approve of. Maddie, Ryan, and now
Hope had somehow become an important part of my life.
And when they left the hospital, which inevitably they would
soon do, a piece of me was going to go with them, whether
I wanted it to or not.

Chapter 11

2012

I heard the crash first. Then came the voices – at least two of them – raised in anger, in a place where everyone walked softly and spoke in whispers. There was a long, loud scraping noise, as if the metal legs of a chair had travelled at speed over the linoleum floor of the corridor. Then came a loud thud and the sound of something breaking, I wasn't sure what.

My steps faltered for a second and then quickened, hurrying *towards* the commotion, even though common sense was telling me I should be going in the opposite direction. I rounded the corner and came to a stop, so abruptly that I almost stumbled forward from my own momentum. It took several moments for me to process what I was seeing, because it all looked so improbable and out of place. It was like a scene from a movie. A violent movie.

Two plastic chairs that were usually positioned in the corridor outside Maddie's room were now on their sides, skewed at weird angles down the wide passageway. One appeared to have collided with a small trolley, which was also on its side. But it wasn't the displaced hospital furniture that caused my eyes to widen like saucers and my mouth to drop open. Two men were facing off in the corridor. Both were breathing heavily, and the fury and rage emanating from them pulsated through the air like a sound wave.

'What the fuck were you doing?' thundered Ryan, in a voice I'd never heard from him before. It was also the first time I'd ever heard him swear.

'Get out of my way,' yelled a greasy-haired man, trying to push past Ryan. *Yeah, good luck with that, my friend*, I thought, seeing the immovable wall of muscle, cemented with the type of fury that was scary to see. *I* was scared, and I still didn't even know what had happened.

In the distance, beyond the two men, I could hear a voice which I thought might possibly be Ellen's, shouting urgently into the telephone. 'Security. I need Security up on Six straight away. We have an intruder.'

'Oh no you don't,' Ryan said, through gritted teeth, pushing the man back against the wall with the flat of his hand when it looked like he was about to escape.

'That's assault. You all saw that, didn't you?' the man yelled, his eyes going to me and then to the three nurses gathered around the desk, one of whom I could now see was definitely Ellen. He couldn't have called upon a collection of more *unreliable* witnesses, if he was hoping to make that one stick.

'Assault?' roared Ryan. 'I'll give you assault. What were you doing in there, with your hands on my baby?'

Suddenly my feet had wings. I was running down the corridor towards the open door of Maddie's room, my heart almost bursting out of my chest in terror. What had this man done?

I stepped over something that was broken in a great many pieces next to the doorway. Something that was clearly never going to function again. I dived into the room, ignoring the two men who were only a metre or so away from me. There was a large brown pool of something on the floor just inside Maddie's room. I stepped in it, almost slipped, and then righted myself. I glanced down and saw the familiar logo of a well-known coffee chain on the dropped takeout cup. I was still moving at speed, yet a separate part of my brain was already piecing together the picture. Ryan had come into the room, carrying his drink, and had disturbed this man and whatever it was he was doing here.

My frantic glance went first to Hope in her crib, and then to Maddie. For a terrifying moment I thought the absolute worst, and then forced myself to look at each of them in turn, carefully. Two chests, both rising and falling in a regular and seemingly normal fashion. The only thing wrong about the room that I could see, apart from the pool of coffee on the floor, was that the blanket that should have been swaddled around Hope was now bunched down around her tiny feet.

'I didn't touch the kid, I just moved the blanket,' the man answered aggressively from the corridor behind me.

There followed a heavy thudding noise, and suddenly I was terrified that something truly dreadful was about to happen. Uncaring of whether I was putting myself in any danger, I ran back out into the corridor.

'They're fine Ryan, they're both fine. I checked.' The fist he had raised stopped in mid-air, never completing its arc. It hung there at shoulder height, its line of trajectory putting it squarely in the middle of the other man's face.

'Mr Turner!' shouted a new voice, coming from the direction of the bank of lifts. 'Mr Turner, no!' For a second I thought Ryan was so incensed he was going to take the swing anyway. 'He's not worth it, Mr Turner. Don't do it,' the security guard implored, still running towards the men. I recognised him. His name was Jerry, and he'd started at the hospital not long after I had. I seemed to remember him telling me once that he was a retired policeman. I just hoped whatever skills he'd learnt while he was on the force weren't so far in the past that he couldn't call on them when he needed to.

The intruder, clearly still feeling *he* was the victim here, turned towards the uniformed guard who had now reached the two men, and had laid his hand firmly upon Ryan's upraised arm. 'Leave him.'

The man, who was sweating profusely, nodded his head vehemently. 'You should do as he says, mate,' he said, his voice as oily as his hair.

'Because *I'm* allowed to use reasonable restraint if he puts up a struggle . . . and I most certainly will,' Jerry promised, his eyes glittering dangerously.

The man against the wall seemed to suddenly realise how little help he was going to get from the new arrival, and decided to take a different tack. He looked down at the collection of broken pieces scattered on the floor by his feet. 'Do you know how much that camera cost? How am I meant to earn a living now? I'm going to bloody sue you for damages, you know,' he threatened.

'And I'm filing a charge against you for molesting a newborn baby,' promised Ryan.

Finally the man seemed to comprehend exactly how much trouble he was in.

'Mr Turner, I want you to walk away now. Leave him to me,' urged Jerry. 'Mr Turner . . . Ryan . . . please.'

Very slowly I saw Ryan lower his arm. It was still trembling. From beyond him I heard Ellen's voice speaking in a tone that sounded a great deal calmer than it had done just a few minutes earlier. 'Chloe, why don't you take Ryan outside to cool off while we get this all sorted out?'

Ryan shook his head, but I could see that removing him from the scene was not only sensible, it was vital. Clearly, Ellen thought so too. 'I'm going to go and sit with Maddie and Hope, and I won't leave their room until you get back. You have my word on it.'

Her eyes went to mine, and I nodded determinedly and reached for Ryan's elbow. For a moment I thought he was going to resist me, but then much to my surprise he allowed me to drag him away, towards the staircase.

Neither of us spoke on the six-flight descent to the ground floor. I don't think Ryan was capable of speech, and I certainly had no idea what to say. By the time we had emerged into the cold December afternoon, I had pieced it all together. As terrifying as it must have been for Ryan to find someone leaning over his newborn daughter, with his hands in her crib, I was sure the intruder was nothing more than the gutter element of the press, whose basic humanity seemed easily forgotten when an exclusive 'photo-op' presented itself.

Reporters had been crowding around the hospital entrance for several days since Maddie's story had been resurrected, following the birth of Hope. Ryan had imposed a strict no-interviews, no-photographs ruling, and I could only imagine that the man today had thought those rules didn't apply to him. It had been a dangerous and costly mistake.

Ryan walked quickly along the hospital pathway, forcing me to trot just to keep up with him. His jaw looked tight and clenched, and when I glanced down at his hands I saw that they were both still fisted, as though the fight was still ongoing. From the expression on his face, I rather suspected that for him, it still was. When we came to a bench, and I reached out and grasped his sleeve to bring him to a stop. 'Why don't we sit down here for a minute?'

Ryan looked like he might be about to disagree, but I

knew that if we carried on at that pace I was either going to get the world's worst stitch, or we'd end up halfway back to town. I sat down hurriedly, forcing him to join me. The icy-cold slats of the bench cut straight through the lightweight wool of my skirt. I thought longingly of my coat, scarf and gloves which I'd left up on the fourth floor.

Ryan sat down beside me, leaning forward with his elbows on his knees, and put his head in his hands. I tried to think of something to say; considered about half a dozen possibilities, and ended up dismissing them all. Perhaps silence was the most calming thing I could offer here.

Eventually Ryan was the one who broke it. 'I still can't seem to stop shaking.' It was true. I could see the tremors running through his frame as though he was in the throes of a raging fever. He allowed one hand to fall away from his face and turned to me with a twisted expression, which might have been an attempt at a smile. 'It's not very Bruce Willis, is it? Shaking like a leaf after a confrontation?'

'I think it's perfectly understandable. And I totally disagree. I think what you did up there was very heroic and protective.'

This time his smile looked slightly less weird. 'As you can probably guess, I don't really "do" violent. I don't think I've been in a fight since I was sixteen years old, and that one was on a football pitch.'

'Well, I'm not aggressive either, but if Jerry hadn't come along when he did, I think I'd have decked that guy myself.'

Ryan's hand reached across and briefly squeezed mine in

a gesture of friendship. 'The one he *really* would have had to worry about is Maddie. If she'd been awake . . . she would probably have torn his head off.'

I tried to imagine the ever-silent, ever-motionless, Maddie in a tearing temper or a fiery rage, and just couldn't picture it.

'I suppose I should have been expecting something like this,' Ryan said sadly, running his fingers through his dark blond hair. 'Somehow the reporters got hold of my mobile number, and every time I set foot outside the hospital they're waiting to pounce, like a pack of hyenas.'

'I knew the press were being a nuisance, but I've no idea how that guy managed to get into Maddie's room without anyone stopping him.'

'It won't happen again,' Ryan said darkly. I shivered, and this time it had nothing to do with the falling temperature or the biting wind. 'The hospital tried to warn me about keeping Hope with Maddie,' Ryan continued, and I could see that there was going to be an awful lot of self-blame that he'd chosen not to listen to that advice. 'They kept saying that the Maternity Unit was far more secure. You can't just waltz up and gain access to anyone up there.'

'You're not meant to be able to do that *anywhere* in the hospital,' I defended.

'Well, that scumbag today proved all too easily that you can.' Ryan sat up straighter and I could tell from the set of his spine that he'd finally stopped trembling, and something else was running through him, washing out the adrenalin that had pumped through his veins and replacing it with liquid steel.

'Well, they're not going to get a second chance. I'm getting her out of there.'

His words jolted me upright, like an electric shock. 'Maddie? You're taking Maddie out of the hospital?'

Ryan's eyes looked unbelievably sad, and I cursed myself for not thinking before I opened my mouth. Of course he couldn't take Maddie anywhere. 'Oh, you mean Hope.'

He nodded, and I could see the bitterness on his face that he was being forced into separating mother and daughter. 'I mean, I know I was going to have to do that eventually. It's not like all three of us can permanently live at the hospital.' He left his words dangling in the air, as though waiting for me to reach up and grab them and say something like, 'Yes, you could.' But I couldn't say that, because I honestly didn't believe it *was* what was best for Hope. Admittedly all my knowledge about babies was purely theoretical and had come from the books I'd read to Maddie, but they all seemed to agree that babies needed to have a stable routine. And keeping a perfectly healthy infant in hospital long after the time she should have gone home wasn't something I imagined you'd find any book recommending. But in this, as in everything else he did, Ryan was trying to do what was best for Maddie. He still hoped their baby could do the one thing that so far he'd failed to achieve: that she'd be able to bring Maddie back.

263

'How will you manage? Will you get a nanny?'

Ryan's eyebrows rose slightly, and I clumsily tried to remove the foot I had effectively rammed into my own mouth. Would I even have thought of making that suggestion if *Maddie* was the single parent left to care for their baby? No, of course I wouldn't have.

'I don't mean that you're not perfectly capable of—'

Once again Ryan's hand reached out and squeezed mine. 'It's okay, Chloe. And for the record, I don't think you're going to be the only one who questions whether I'll be able to manage.'

'I didn't—'

His smile silenced me. 'I read all the books you left in Maddie's room. And the midwives here have been pretty fantastic. They've been on a mission to train me. I think it's safe to say that if they put a nappy-changing event in the next Olympics, I'll be coming home with a medal.'

I gave a small laugh which the wind tried to whip away.

'I can bathe, bottle feed, and burp. All the Bs in fact . . . except breastfeeding, of course. That one is still beyond me.' I wasn't sure if I was meant to laugh at that or not, so I just smiled weakly.

'What will you do about work?' I asked, wondering if that was too personal a question, although Ryan didn't appear offended by it.

'My company has a pretty good paternity scheme, and because of my unique circumstances I should be okay for the next three months or so. After that . . .' he shrugged. 'I guess I'll just have to see how things go and look into day care – or see about getting my own Mrs Doubtfire.' I knew he was teasing me now, but I was okay with that.

'I'm obviously still going to bring Hope to the hospital every day, because she needs to be near her mum.' My eyes felt a little watery as I filled in the part of that sentence that Ryan didn't complete: *As do I.*

'But I'm definitely going to need some help making this work,' he admitted, looking straight at me. My heart started to beat faster, while something that felt like a snake writhed in the pit of my stomach. 'Ryan, I'm not sure I'm the right person to ask. I really don't know much about babies.'

His blue eyes clouded in confusion for a moment, and before they cleared I'd realised my mistake. 'Oh, no. What I meant was that I'm not going to be able to spend as much time with Maddie as I've done up until now. So I wanted to ask if you'd be willing to carry on visiting her.'

If a sudden convenient earthquake had decided to strike the hospital grounds at that precise moment and swallow me down into a yawning chasm, I wouldn't have minded one bit. As it didn't, I just had to put up with feeling like the world's biggest idiot.

I forced my lips to form a smile, which must have done a passable job of hiding not only my feelings of embarrassment, but also the lingering disappointment I was still struggling to understand. 'I'd be happy to.'

*

I trained for the next major career change in my life without ever knowing I was doing so. I was on an interview for over four months, and still didn't have a clue. Sometimes it's the things you *can't* control that shape your future, like a van driving too fast on a busy road; or a local authority making cutbacks.

Over the weeks and months that followed I saw and shared a great many moments that weren't mine to treasure, but they were there, happening all around me. I never set out to take something that wasn't mine. I never expected to feel love like that. Never. But Hope stole my heart, and I gave it to her with a willingness that scared me.

I saw those early smiles – the ones you knew had nothing to do with wind. I felt the surprisingly strong grip as her tiny hand, with its miniature shell-pink nails, held on to my finger. Ryan was partly to blame. His reluctance to leave Maddie's side meant there was frequently a crossover period between the end of his visits and the beginning of mine. He would linger and chat, asking me about my day as he packed away the extraordinary amount of equipment one small person appeared to require for travel. He sounded surprisingly interested when I rambled on about my job at the library and the continued threat of further cutbacks, and even *I* was bored with that topic.

'Actually, Chloe, there is a favour I'd like to ask,' Ryan said one day, expertly collapsing down Hope's travel cot single-handedly while balancing his daughter on one hip. He'd come a very long way from the man who took several minutes carefully positioning his hands before daring to pick her up.

'You don't work at the library on Thursdays, do you?'

I shook my head, thinking, *And possibly not for the other four days of the week, the way things are going.*

'There's a conference I need to attend before going back to work next month, and I'm not sure how comfortable I feel about leaving Hope at the day-care place when she hasn't been for her trial session yet.'

I nodded and looked over at Hope, who Ryan had now tucked up securely against Maddie's side. There was a wall of blankets and the bed's guard rail keeping her safe, and yet I still worried about her falling. I wasn't normally a paranoid kind of person, but when it came to Hope's well-being I turned into the worst kind of psychic, seeing a world of disasters just waiting to happen. What on earth was I going to be like when I had kids of my own?

'Would you be willing to look after her for the day?' asked Ryan, with an engaging smile.

My reply was one hundred per cent enthusiastic. 'Of course I would. I'd *love* to.'

It was early. Shortly after seven o'clock in the morning, and yet several of Ryan's neighbours had already passed me in the hallway. They were all dressed smartly, in formal office-style clothing. My old but comfortable jeans and thick jumper made me look even more of an outsider than I already felt. This was the kind of building where the residents had careers rather than jobs. And it didn't look particularly child-friendly, I decided, doing an unconscious risk-assessment of the hallway as I pressed the button to summon the lift to the fifth floor. In fact, I was willing to put money on Hope being the only baby in the entire building.

Ryan was waiting for me by the open door of his apartment. He was dressed in the same uniform as his neighbours: smart grey suit, crisp white shirt and pale blue silk tie. His companion was more casually attired, in teddy bear pyjamas.

'I'm sorry,' Ryan apologised, transferring his sleepy daughter into my arms as soon as I crossed the threshold. 'For the first time in ... well ever, actually ... she didn't wake me up at the crack of dawn. So I've not given her a bottle, or sorted out her things, or done anything.' He took a worried glance at his watch. 'And my train is due to leave in twenty-seven minutes.'

'Go,' I said, urging him towards the door, with a gentle shove.

He looked hesitant and uncertain. 'But I haven't even shown you where everything is kept, or—'

'It's not a big place. I'm sure I'll figure it out,' I said with surprising confidence.

It appeared to fool him as much as it did me. He paused, nodded, and then reached into the pocket of his suit and drew out a small bundle of keys. 'Door key; car key; and fob thing to get out of the underground car park. You're sure you're okay about driving to the hospital later?'

'Yes. No problem. The ban was lifted a couple of months ago.'

It was too cruel really, watching his expression change. Then he realised I was joking.

'You're hilarious,' he deadpanned, bending his head down towards me. For one crazy moment I thought he was about to kiss me goodbye. But the cheek which received the touch of his lips was Hope's, who was nestled in my arms. We were so close I could feel the warmth of Ryan's breath on my face. I saw the fleeting flare in his cobalt eyes, and knew he'd been as wrong-footed by the move as I'd been.

He straightened quickly. 'I should be back by no later than seven this evening. You have my mobile number if there's any problem.'

'Twenty-four minutes now until that train,' I advised, watching him pick up a leather briefcase and heavy top coat that were waiting by the front door.

'See you tonight,' he said, disappearing out of the door in a blur of expensive suit and subtle aftershave.

I leant back against the closed door, cradling the sleepy infant in my arms. To be fair, she seemed totally unconcerned that the only parent she'd ever known had walked out and abandoned her.

'Just you and me then, kiddo,' I said, dropping a kiss on the same cheek her father's mouth had grazed. That felt all kinds of wrong, and I wiped my fingers furiously over my lips as though erasing any lingering trace of the man who today had entrusted me with his most precious possession.

269

Buoyed up by the false confidence I had effectively sold to Ryan, I set off in search of a bottle for Hope. I passed through what once must have been a fairly spacious living room before it was overtaken by all manner of baby paraphernalia. I bounced a slightly grizzly Hope on my hip as I surveyed the room, which bore a striking resemblance to the shop floor of a Mothercare store. I counted a stroller, a Moses basket, a baby swing, a rocker chair, a multi-activity play mat, and a travel cot.

'You need all this, do you?' I asked the increasingly grouchy infant. Hope's small gummy mouth opened like a baby bird's.

'Okay, let's go find you some breakfast.'

Ryan's kitchen told an equally interesting story. I particularly liked the wine rack in the fridge where a neat line of prepared bottles of formula sat, where once I imagined the Chardonnay might have lived. A very fancy-looking coffee maker that wouldn't have been out of place in a Starbucks was currently unplugged and decommissioned in order to make space on the worktop for an enormous electric sterilising unit.

'You really have turned your daddy's life upside down, haven't you?' I asked the happily guzzling baby in my arms, as I sat on Ryan's black leather settee and fed his hungry daughter. While Hope made short work of the bottle, my eyes travelled the room, looking beyond the masculine decor and catching glimpses of the small touches I imagined Maddie had left behind. The vibrant multicoloured scatter cushions relieving the sombre funereal furniture were surely hers. And I couldn't see Ryan putting those brightly patterned throws on the back of the sofa, or the tall scented candles in the holders. You didn't need a degree in forensics to be able to find Maddie in this place. She was everywhere.

After eliciting a burp from Hope that a burly lorry driver would be proud of, I set off in search of the place where her belongings were kept. The flat had two bedrooms, but when I opened the door to the smallest of them, I found only a room that was part home-office and part storage facility. There was a desk, piled high with files and folders, and a wall full of carefully stacked and labelled cardboard boxes: *Maddie's Winter Scarves*; *Maddie's DVDs*; *Maddie's Books*. Much of Maddie's life and a great many of her personal belongings were catalogued and stored in this room, just waiting for her to open her eyes and reclaim them. I touched the top of one box and my finger left a visible trail in ten months' worth of accumulated dust. For some reason that made me incredibly sad.

I found where Hope slept easily enough. I should have known it was the only place Ryan would consider suitable. The cot was pushed up close against the left-hand side of the large double bed. The pillows on that side were undisturbed, and bore no indent of a head, unlike their mangled counterparts on the other side of the mattress. Ryan was clearly an extremely restless sleeper. Knowing that made me feel strangely uncomfortable, like I'd been caught prying.

I changed Hope and found her clothes in one of the

deep drawers of the dresser. Pushed far into the back of the drawer were a few items of women's underwear. Maddie's obviously, unless I'd accidentally uncovered a secret that Ryan really didn't want to share. The thought made me smile, and Hope happily mimicked it as she watched me from the changing mat. 'Oh, so you think that's funny, do you?' I asked, scooping her up into my arms. I'm glad I had a good firm hold of my tiny wriggling charge, because when I turned around to leave the room I suddenly found myself face-to-face with Madeline Chambers. Or as close as I imagined I was ever likely to be, with her eyes wide open.

The photograph had been enlarged, placed inside a light oak frame, and hung proudly on the wall. I could see why. Maddie looked absolutely gorgeous in it. She must have been on holiday somewhere, for a palm tree and a glimmer of ocean were visible beyond her shoulder. She was certainly dressed for the beach in the photograph, which cut off just below two impossibly tiny triangles of her bikini top. It was the kind of swimwear Nature had decided I would never be able to wear – at least not without getting arrested. But I couldn't deny that on Maddie it looked amazing. Her long dark hair was blowing in a gentle breeze, and was held back from her face by an oversized pair of sunglasses perched on top of her head. But what elevated the photo above that of any attractive young woman on holiday was the happiness radiating out of her sparkling blue eyes. That was what turned beautiful into something ethereal. I didn't doubt for a moment who had been on the other side of the camera taking that shot. The love Maddie shone back at him was breathtaking to see. And Ryan had captured it perfectly.

Of course, once I'd noticed that photograph, I realised that images of Maddie were everywhere in Ryan's flat. There was one in a silver frame on the bedside table by Hope's cot, making it the very first thing she would see whenever her head was turned that way. There was another on Ryan's bedside table, presumably for exactly the same reason.

I carried Hope back into the lounge, passing a few other smiling Maddies on the way. Of all the dangers I ever feared for Hope, not knowing who her mother was could safely be scratched off the list. I laid Hope down on the activity mat, and sat cross-legged on the floor beside her as she amused herself swiping at the colourful mobiles hanging above her. The day stretched out before me, and I felt like a learner driver who'd accidentally strayed onto the motorway and now had no idea what to do next.

Sunlight slanted in through the glass of the floor-to-ceiling balcony doors. April was giving an impressive audition and pretending to be summer, and the idea of taking Hope out for some fresh air seemed like a perfect solution for how to spend our morning.

Fifteen minutes later I was beginning to question that decision as I struggled to turn the intricate collapsed framework propped up against the wall into a working pushchair. Convinced it must have been designed by a rocket scientist, I would probably have given up if it hadn't been for Maddie's watchful eyes staring down at me in judgement from a dozen photo frames. Finally my fingers found a small silver lever and then, as if by magic, the jumbled conundrum of gleaming chrome turned into a stroller.

Ryan lived in an area of town I wasn't particularly familiar with, but following the directions from a particularly chirpy traffic warden, I headed to the nearest shops. I'd never pushed a pram before, so I had no idea if everyone always smiled at young women who did so. I must have received at least four *good mornings* from random strangers, and countless warm glances from many of the women I passed. It was as if I had gained entry to some exclusive sisterhood that I didn't even realise existed.

I spent an enjoyable few hours window-shopping, before returning to the flat with a very sleepy Hope and a carrier bag full of ingredients that I'd purchased from a small delicatessen. Besides the bottles of formula, Ryan's fridge held nothing more than a stack of microwaveable dinners, making me wonder how often he bothered with a home-cooked meal. That at least was something I could do with my time today. It would be a nice surprise for him when he got back from the conference.

Hope obligingly fell into a deep sleep as soon as we were back at the flat, which lasted just long enough for me to look up a recipe on my phone for a foolproof Beef Bourguignon and then prepare it. From the pristine state of Ryan's oven I guessed he was either seriously OCD about kitchen hygiene, or his oven saw even less action than mine did.

I set the timer so that it would be ready for seven thirty that evening, and then after eating the sandwich I'd bought in town and feeding Hope, it was time to head for the hospital.

I drove along the familiar roads as nervously as an eighty-year-old woman on her driving test, and hadn't realised how tightly I'd been gripping the steering wheel until I felt the cramp in my fingers when I eventually unfurled them in the hospital car park.

'Hello, Chloe. Is that little Hope you have there?' asked Jerry with a warm beam as we passed him at the hospital entrance. Ever since the incident with the intruder, I had more time and respect for the friendly security guard. I never did get to find out what he'd said to the reporter after we'd left, but I *did* know that he'd never pressed charges about his smashed camera. In turn, Ryan had chosen not to pursue an official complaint; a decision which I found more than a little dissatisfying.

'It would be pouring even more petrol onto a fire that I'd just as soon burnt out,' he had reasoned. It was the one and only time I had raised the subject, and all I could do was simply shrug and let it go. It was his decision to make, not mine.

'Have you got yourself a new job there?' Jerry asked, gently chucking Hope under the soft folds of her chin.

I'm sure I must have looked a bit bewildered for a moment before I corrected him, but his innocent enquiry had lit a spark, and it flickered and grew throughout my afternoon at the hospital with Maddie and her daughter.

*

The sound of Ryan's key in the door alerted me. I swivelled around, holding Hope securely against my shoulder. It was almost dusk, and although I hadn't drawn any of the curtains, I had turned on all the table lamps, giving the room a warm and welcoming glow. The door opened and Ryan stood for a moment in its frame. He looked tired. He'd loosened his tie, revealing the open top button of his shirt. The coat, which probably cost more than I made in a month at the library, was carelessly held in one hand, its sleeves dragging along the floor.

For a very long moment Ryan didn't move, and I saw his gaze taking everything in. I'd tidied up a little, but nothing to warrant the startled look on his face. I wondered if I'd done something wrong, because whatever he was seeing was clearly causing him pain. And then I saw it all through his eyes. The flat was warm and welcoming; the fragrant smell of bourguignon was wafting from the kitchen; and his fed, bathed and sleepy daughter was smiling at him . . . from the arms of the *wrong woman*. What a fool I had been. What I was showing him was a painful glimpse of all the things that *could* have been, that *should* have been . . . and might never actually happen.

I'm sure he read the distraught look on my face, because he quickly composed himself and reached for humour to disguise his reaction. 'I feel like I ought to be saying, "Honey, I'm home."'

I smiled nervously, still not sure if I should be apologising. But for what? For not being Maddie?

'How has your day been?' Ryan asked, carelessly dropping

his briefcase and coat onto the settee and walking towards us. Hope pushed against my restraining hands, craning her entire body towards her daddy. Her little arms were out-stretched; a miniature superman preparing to launch through the air to reach him. He plucked her from me and folded his arms around her in an enveloping cuddle. He burrowed his face against the top of her head, breathing her in as though they'd been separated for years instead of hours.

'You've no idea how much I missed her today,' he said, his eyes looking suspiciously bright when he finally raised his head. My heart melted as I saw and felt the love between them. 'But I bet she didn't miss me one bit,' he said with a rueful smile.

'No, she definitely did. She kept looking for you,' I lied, just to make him smile again. And he did.

'And what is that smell?' asked Ryan, sniffing in an exag-gerated fashion.

'Oh no, I only just changed her,' I lamented.

Ryan laughed and began to literally follow his nose towards the kitchen, inhaling deeply as he went, like a blood-hound on a mission. '*That* smell,' he declared, stopping in front of the cooker.

'Oh. Oh, that's something I made for your dinner tonight.'

Ryan crouched down, still holding Hope, and together they peered through the glass door at the bubbling French dish, which would be ready in about fifteen minutes' time.

He rose up in one fluid movement. 'Who knew my oven could do that?' he joked.

Ryan walked back into the lounge and flopped down on

the settee, shrugging off his suit jacket before settling Hope into the crook of his arm. Her long dark eyelashes fluttered slowly down, resting on her cheeks and then flying open, as she fought an unwinnable battle with sleep.

'Has everything been all right today? Did you find everything you needed?'

'Everything has been great. We went for a walk this morning, did some shopping, and then spent the afternoon with Maddie at the hospital.' Ryan nodded, and there was a very thoughtful expression on his face.

'Was it a good conference?'

'It was okay. It felt a bit like I was testing the water again after so long out of the office. Still, it was nice to engage in some intelligent conversation for a change.' He realised his gaffe as soon as it had fallen from his lips. I laughed, not taking offence in the slightest.

'Thanks for that,' I teased, thinking of the countless conversations we'd had in Maddie's hospital room over the last four months.

Ryan's blue eyes twinkled in amusement. 'Male conversation,' he amended.

For a second his face sobered, and I could see an earnest look upon it. 'I think I needed this trial run, almost as much as Hope is going to need hers at the day-care place. As much as I enjoyed being back in a business environment today, I don't think I could have done it without you.'

'Me?' I questioned, my voice a surprised squawk. 'What did I do?'

'You gave me peace of mind. I knew Hope was in safe hands. As much as I wanted to be with her, knowing she was here with you was the next best thing – well, second only to Maddie being here and being able to look after her.'

'Of course,' I said slowly.

'Actually,' said Ryan, drawing the word out. Are you in a hurry to dash off anywhere, Chloe?' his eyes went towards the kitchen, and I was pretty sure he was about to invite me to join him for dinner. I certainly hoped that was what he was thinking, because the smell of cooking red wine had been making my mouth water for the last hour.

'No. I've no plans for this evening.'

He smiled and looked pleased. 'Well, if your delicious dinner could possibly be reheated, would you mind staying on a while longer so I can spend a couple of hours with Maddie at the hospital? I rarely get the chance to see her in the evenings any more and it would be great to say goodnight to her, the way I used to do.'

My features were all to be commended. They betrayed none of my disappointment; but that didn't mean I didn't feel it.

'Of course. I'd be happy to stay with Hope until you get back.'

Ryan looked as though he'd been given a perfect gift, and I felt guilty that all I was thinking about was the stupid beef dish in the oven. He carried Hope into his bedroom and settled her in her cot, winding up the musical mobile fixed to its bars.

By the time he emerged from the bedroom, he'd tugged

off his tie, and undone a second button on his shirt, but hadn't bothered changing. 'Please don't wait for me,' he urged, nodding towards the kitchen. 'Eat yours now; it really does smell wonderful.'

'It does, doesn't it?' I said brightly, hoping my false cheery voice masked the fact that I'd suddenly lost my appetite.

A librarian is always prepared: train delays; long queues at the post office; busy doctors' waiting rooms; meals for one in a restaurant. A librarian always has at least one ongoing book with them to while away the time. I didn't bother turning on Ryan's truly enormous television after he left. As soon as I'd checked that Hope was still fast asleep and that the state-of-the-art baby monitor was switched on (it even had a camera, for goodness' sake), I pulled the latest bestseller I was reading from my handbag. I plucked off my boots and settled at one end of the black leather settee, where the pool of light from the table lamp would fall perfectly on my open page.

I read the same paragraph at least three times, and yet still would have failed miserably if you'd asked me a single thing about it. The words were dancing tipsily on the line and nothing was going in. My eyes felt heavy, as though weighted down with lead. *Just for a few minutes*, I promised myself foolishly as they gave up the battle to stay open. *Just a few minutes*.

The smell of toast woke me. I could smell it everywhere. My eyes opened, but I saw nothing except a vibrant collage of orange and purple. I blinked at the garish kaleidoscope of colours, my brain taking several moments to recognise and place them. They were the pattern on the throw on the back of Ryan's settee.

I pulled the cover from my face. The room was bathed in light, and it wasn't coming from the overhead fitment. Because it was no longer night-time.

'Ah, you're awake. Just in time for toast and coffee. Only instant, I'm afraid,' Ryan apologised, placing a plate and a mug on the small table beside me.

'Why didn't you wake me?' I protested, struggling to get into an upright position. Someone had slipped one of the soft satin pillows beneath my head and covered me with the throw, and I very much doubted it was Hope.

'I got back later than I'd said, and you were fast asleep,' Ryan replied with an easy-going shrug. He reached for the mug and put it in my hands, and I caught a fleeting whiff of shampoo and shower gel. His hair was a couple of shades darker than normal, still damp from the shower. I glanced down at my watch and saw it was after eight o'clock.

'I never sleep in this late. *Never.*'

Ryan's laugh was sympathetic. 'You don't normally look after a very demanding infant for an entire day either. They take it out of you. Believe me, I know.'

I took a long reviving gulp of the coffee and looked up at him through lowered lids. 'Well you still should have woken me, however late it was. I would have happily got a cab.'

'Ah, but I couldn't risk having you wake up to discover my guilty secret.'

I smiled, liking the friendly banter between us. 'What secret?'

'I ate the bourguignon. All of it,' he confessed.

I gave a tiny splutter into my coffee. 'No! The recipe said it should feed four.'

He gave an easy shrug. 'After cardboard British Rail sandwiches, it was too tempting to leave.'

'I'm glad you liked it.'

'And I'm glad you're awake, because I have something important I'd like to discuss with you.'

Afterwards we never could agree whose idea it had been. I always claimed that Jerry had given me the first nudge towards suggesting it. But Ryan said it was when his employer had mentioned at the conference that he might be able to work from home for two days a week that the idea had begun to germinate.

The solution to so many problems is often right there under your nose, you just need to let it form and crystallise in its own time. Ryan needed someone to look after Hope for three days a week; the library was asking for staff to cut their hours or take voluntary redundancy. The salary he was offering me for the job was twice what I was earning at the library. But it was never about the money.

'So, you'll do it?' asked Ryan, and for just a second he looked like a much younger, almost schoolboy version of himself. 'You'll be my Mrs Doubtfire?'

'I will,' I said happily.

And for the first two years of my employment that was exactly what I did.

And then we fell in love ... and I took on another, far more important role.

PART THREE

Chapter 12

Maddie

It was too big. It looked too try-hard. And it was wrapped in the wrong sort of paper. The expensive silver-foil gift wrap had been a mistake. All the other presents were wrapped in colourful paper with Disney princesses or cartoon characters on them. The large square box, with the bright red ribbon around it just showed more than anything else that I knew nothing at all about six-year-old little girls. Somehow I suspected it wouldn't be the only mistake I made that day.

This was nothing like the childhood birthday parties I remembered. There was no clumsily drawn donkey waiting for his missing tail to be pinned into place; no newspaper-wrapped bundle for pass-the-parcel. This was slick and efficiently organised. Almost as though they'd hired a professional party planner. Perhaps they had. Maybe that was a 'thing' these days. From my unobtrusive position on a small padded bench, I looked across the large converted barn (the kind of place people might book for a wedding reception) and watched Chloe efficiently masterminding the event. No. She looked as if she'd need no help in organising something like this, she was clearly a natural.

From the moment I'd woken that morning I'd felt a peculiar sensation building within me. More nerves than excitement; more fear than anticipation. When I'd stood before the full-length mirror in my bedroom, still trying to decide what to wear, I'd run my hands over the smooth white skin of my stomach, that was still just a little bit concave, and tried to imagine it stretched and swollen with the child I'd given birth to six years earlier. I'd shaken my head, as though dismissing the idea as some kind of improbable myth. If it hadn't been for the photographic evidence in the memory book, I would truly have doubted it had ever happened. My fingers slid over the unblemished skin, longing for a single whispery silver thread of a stretch mark, but there wasn't one. I was probably the only woman in the world to feel sad about dodging that particular bullet.

But of course there *was* evidence, real irrefutable evidence, that I'd been a mother. *Was* a mother. For there was Hope. And today was about celebrating that she was here, that she'd been born against the thousands of odds stacked against her. It wasn't about me, I told the sad-faced reflection in the mirror with a decisive nod. She nodded back at me, so I guessed she got it.

Ryan had phoned during the week to give me details about the party. 'There's going to be about thirty kids there,' he said, his voice making that sound like a problem.

'Okay.'

'I just thought you should know; these parties tend to be a bit full-on.'

'In a rock and roll, and too much alcohol kind of way?' I joked.

There was a pause, and then suddenly the familiar sound of his laughter travelled down the phone and filled my head with a million memories I would do far better to forget.

'More in a too much sugar, and someone throwing up on the floor kind of a way,' he said, still sounding amused.

'Well, I've been to that kind too . . . although obviously not for a while,' I said, my thoughts running away on a tangent as I tried to remember the last party he and I had been to together. My grip on my mobile tightened as I realised when that would have been. Our engagement party.

'I just wanted to make sure you knew what to expect.'

I paused for a moment, waiting for him to say something more, but there was only a long moment of silence on the other end of the line. Sometimes it's easier to work out what someone is thinking by the things they *don't* say, rather than the things they do.

'Have you and Chloe changed your mind about me coming to Hope's party?'

Ryan's answer was too quick, too vehement and a little too hearty to be entirely believable. 'No. Not at all. Absolutely not. We're all looking forward to having you there. So . . . I guess we'll see you on Saturday then.'

The taxi driver smiled cheekily. 'This'll be the place,' he said with a wink, his head nodding towards the rows of virtually identical four-by-four vehicles. 'No self-respecting mum would drive anything else for the school run.'

I gave a slightly uncertain smile, not sure exactly which side of the fence he thought I might be on. To be honest, I wasn't sure myself. I tried to imagine waiting at a school gate for Hope; buckling her safely into the car, and hearing her chatter excitedly about her day. The image kept fading out of view, like a station you couldn't quite manage to tune in to.

I shivered when I climbed out of the cab, as the December wind found the places where my soft wool tunic and leggings didn't provide sufficient coverage. 'Do you need a hand with that?' the driver asked, watching me reach towards the back seat to retrieve the enormous red-ribboned gift.

'No thank you. I've got it,' I said, adjusting my hold on the cumbersome box. I was half expecting him to ask me what on earth I'd bought, which was a question I would prefer not to answer, because I was already worried enough about my chosen birthday present for Hope.

'Well, enjoy the party,' the driver said cheerily, before

heading back down the long gravelled drive. I wobbled a little on my way towards the barn's entrance, feeling the stone chips sucking hungrily on the heels of my boots with every step I took. I might have been a bit steadier if I'd been able to see my own feet, but they were lost beneath the enormous gift, the one that was probably a colossal mistake. I should have asked Ryan what to buy her . . . although Chloe would probably have been the one who best knew the answer to that. Perhaps that was why the question had remained unasked.

I passed beneath a canopy of bobbing pink balloons that had been carefully tied to the oak-beamed porch, but the very first thing I saw in the foyer stopped me in my tracks. It was a photograph, a recent one I guessed, that had been enlarged and pinned to a felt-covered board in the barn's reception. My fingers itched to reach out and trace every feature of the dark-haired little girl who wore my face and a happy grin. There was a cartoon-style caption beneath the image: *'Today is my birthday,' says Hope.*

'I know it is, baby,' I said softly to the empty foyer.

Before I could break the hold the photograph held on me, I felt a sudden rush of cold air at my back. I half turned around, expecting to see a late-arriving party guest.

'Maddie,' cried a voice that my senses hadn't yet learnt how to ignore. My breath still quickened, my heart still began to race, and palms that moments earlier had been perfectly dry, suddenly felt damp enough to drop the present I was carrying. Perhaps Ryan thought that too, because he reached out and took the heavy box from me without bothering to ask.

I was rather glad we had an obstacle between us, because it prevented any of that awkward indecision as to whether it was appropriate to hug, air kiss, or just pretend to ignore the fact that once – a very long time ago – we had scarcely been able to keep our hands off each other.

'You made it!' Ryan cried, with a little too much false enthusiasm to sound natural.

'Of course. I've been looking forward to it.' My voice sounded peculiar, as though someone was doing a fairly good impersonation of me, but hadn't quite got it right.

'Hope's really been looking forward to seeing you again.'

'Has she?' The simple delight in my question seemed to touch him, and for a moment neither of us knew where we were, except that the ground beneath our feet felt nowhere near as steady as it should.

'Well, come on in and meet everyone,' Ryan said, taking one hand off the box he was carrying and placing it lightly at my back.

There was a time – which felt so very recent to me – when a room full of people wouldn't have fazed me in the slightest. But things had changed for me in ways I was still discovering, and something else I appeared to have lost along the way was the ability to walk confidently into a room full of strangers. Even when the majority of them were only six years old.

I'm sure the eyes of all the other parents, who were

chatting sociably in one corner of the room, didn't *actually* swivel in unison in our direction. It just felt like they did.

The junior party guests were nowhere near as interested. They were far too busy engaging in something that might have been either hardcore aerobics or dancing – it was difficult to tell which. Standing to one side of the wooden dance floor, apparently judging their efforts, was Chloe. She was laughing happily as she surveyed Maddie's little school friends, handing out consolation prizes to every single loser, rather than the winner. It was a novel idea, and seemed to be going down well with the children.

Ryan smiled across at his wife and I saw her responding grin, saw the way it wavered for a moment as she realised who was standing beside him, and the brief wave she then sent in our direction. As soon as the music stopped, Chloe began marshalling the group to their next activity. I watched, fascinated by her multi-tasking skills, as she crouched to deal with a tearful child, directed another one speedily to the toilets, and listened to at least three others who were shouting out questions.

'Was Chloe ever a teacher?' I asked, marvelling at the way she appeared to be able to deal with ten queries at once.

'No. A librarian,' Ryan replied, which was funny enough to make me laugh if I hadn't been distracted by the look of love and admiration in his eyes as he watched her. *Did he ever look at you that way?* A voice in my head silently asked. *As though you'd just done something truly amazing?* A memory suddenly unfolded, like an inflating lifeboat, and filled my head with the answer. Just once. Ryan had looked at me in a very similar way when I'd told him that I was pregnant. That was a good day. The *best* day, I remembered sadly.

A small shape dressed in pink suddenly detached itself from the group of children, and came hurtling across the width of the room towards us, like a tiny guided Exocet missile. Hope's face was split with a wide grin, and I was pretty certain mine held an exact mirror image of it.

'Maddie. You came to my birthday party!' my child cried with such obvious delight that I felt something – that might have been either joy or pain – catch in my throat. I dropped down to my knees and was almost knocked over when her small body collided with mine, like a magnet, finding its way home. I burrowed my face into her shoulder, until I was sure my eyes were bright, but dry. I was still down at Hope's height when a pair of slim legs in dark denim jeans came into view. I got to my feet, rising up through a cloud of Chloe's perfume, wondering why it seemed so distinctively familiar.

'Mummy,' cried Hope with delight, pulling away from me and reaching for Chloe's hand. 'Look, Maddie's here, she *did* come.'

Ryan shot a slightly concerned look at the woman he'd replaced me with, but he was worrying unnecessarily. Whatever Chloe really felt about me being there was buried deep beneath her perfectly pleasant manner.

'It's good to see you again, Maddie. Thank you so much for coming.' Those words would have stuck in my throat like a fish hook, but Chloe certainly sounded sincere enough.

Strangely she looked more comfortable here on neutral territory than she had the week before in her own home. Her cheeks were flushed to a soft, becoming pink, which looked undeniably attractive against the pale blue of her jumper. It also made her look about sixteen years old, and made me feel ancient. She bent her head to drop a kiss on Hope's forehead, and her blond hair swung like a fluffy cloud upon her shoulders. If she was a storybook character, she'd be the Good Fairy, and me . . . I glanced down at what I was wearing, and regretted my choice of black . . . I guess that made me the Wicked Witch.

It was certainly something I felt I could read on the faces of several of the mothers when Chloe led me towards them.

'There's tea and coffee, or wine, if you'd prefer,' she said. She gave a small high laugh, and it was only then that I realised she was nowhere near as comfortable around me as I had first thought. 'Keeping the children happy is easy; it's the mothers you have to worry about.'

I glanced up and saw many of those mothers staring at us as we approached the lounge area where they were sitting out the party. I swear I caught glimpses of disappointment on the faces of a few of them. Were they hoping that Hope's natural mother and her stepmother would make a scene at their daughter's birthday party?

The thought jabbed at me suddenly like an electric shock. *Our* daughter. Not just Ryan's and mine – that was obvious, but also Chloe's and mine. From now and going forward, we were both going to have to learn how to share something that I already knew was the most precious thing in the world . . . to both of us.

There were a few too many Charlottes and Emmas among the group of fashionably dressed mothers for me to remember who was whose mummy. So I just smiled and nodded and tried not to feel like the outsider they clearly all knew that I was. There was only one truly awkward moment when a husband of one of the Charlottes came up and thrust a neatly manicured, slightly pudgy hand towards me like a weapon.

'Don't think we've been introduced. I'm Lawrence. Francesca's dad.'

I smiled politely, having no idea which particular six-year-old he was referring to, and realising it didn't matter. My hand lifted to shake his, but before I could introduce myself he gave a loud and hearty guffaw. 'And we don't need to ask who you are. You're obviously little Hope's—'

'—*cousin*,' cut in an Emma or a Kate sharply. 'This is Maddie, Lawrence. She's a relative of Hope's. Second, or third cousin, isn't it?'

She had bright green eyes, more brilliant than a cat's, and I was pierced under their emerald glare like a bug on a stick. I glanced down at her expensive-looking top, fully expecting to see it emblazoned with the words *Team Chloe*. 'That's right, isn't it?' she pressed. Her eyes dropped down meaningfully and I suddenly saw that several party guests had made their way back to their parents' side. There was a saying my own mother used when I was a child; something about little pitchers having big ears. It had always struck me as a slightly ridiculous expression, which had suddenly become exceedingly wise. I was surrounded by far too many people who could blow my daughter's safe little world apart. It was for *her* I lied, not for Ryan or Chloe.

'Yes. I'm a cousin,' I said, lying more convincingly than a professional poker player.

I cried when they brought out the birthday cake. It was made in the shape of a castle, and I knew without even bothering to ask any of the surrounding mothers that Chloe had made it herself. The lights had been dimmed and when Chloe walked in proudly holding the creation with its six blazing candles, my eyes went to where Ryan was standing with his arm securely around Hope's waist as she stood on a chair, little cheeks puffed out far too early in readiness.

There had to be ten metres and about twenty people between us, but they all seemed to suddenly evaporate away as Ryan looked across the distance at me. He was smiling with his lips, while his eyes were saying sorry, two thousand sorries, one for almost every day that I'd missed.

It's hard to sing 'Happy Birthday' when you're crying. But I did the best I could.

*

'Can I open Maddie's one next?' Hope asked, running over to the box she had no chance of lifting down unaided. Ryan smiled and crossed the lounge to the enormous pile of birthday presents, lifting mine down for her. He ruffled her hair affectionately before stepping back. 'You can open whichever one you want, Pumpkin. They're all yours.'

Hope's small hands ran excitedly over the ribbons, and like an efficient scrub nurse in an operating theatre, Chloe was suddenly beside her with a pair of sharp scissors, ready and waiting. She sliced through ribbons and foil paper, and then stepped back to allow her little girl to do the rest.

I hadn't anticipated coming back to Ryan and Chloe's home following the party. To be honest, I'd been more than ready for the peace and solitude of my new home. I was used to hospital, I was used to quiet, I was used to six years of silence. At some point during the party I finally understood why Ryan had tried to warn me in advance. When you're a parent, you get a slow indoctrination into the world of children, but when you're suddenly dropped into it, it feels as if you've unexpectedly crash-landed on Mars.

'Maddie *is* coming back to our house, isn't she?' Hope had asked, putting Chloe in an impossibly awkward position. Good manners meant she had to say: 'Of course, if she wants to,' though I suspected the response she'd much rather have given was: 'Over my dead body.'

The party had been an education, and not just in the habits of six-year-olds, which I watched with all the fascination of a David Attenborough documentary. *And here we have the lesser-hyperactive six-year-old* . . . As interesting as it was to watch Hope and her posse of friends, watching Chloe and Ryan had been even more illuminating. Ryan had become exactly the kind of father I'd always known he would be. He was caring and loving, firm at times – when he needed to be – but also fun. 'I want to be a good dad,' I remembered him whispering in the dark of the night, as we snuggled together in his bed. His hands had glided over the almost imperceptible bump, low on my stomach. 'I want to give this baby everything I have; all of my heart, all of my love, all of my time.' My hands had slid down and linked with his over the tiny human we had made together. 'Lucky baby, look who you've got as a daddy,' I'd said softly, happily content in the safe haven of a life I never got to live in the end.

Watching Chloe at the party had been even more poignant. She had an aura about her, as though she was exactly where she belonged. She was loving, patient, and kind. She was the mother I had planned to be: always there with a smile, a kiss, or a tender cuddle. The kind who would be on hand to share every last special moment in her child's life. She was the better version of what I had planned and hoped to be. She was a better *me* than I think I could have been.

'What is it?' squealed Hope, ripping open the tape holding the flaps of the cardboard box and finally revealing the gift that had cost me far more than you're probably meant to spend on a child's birthday, unless you happen to have recently won the lottery, that is.

'Oh wow, oh wow, oh wow!' I smiled and breathed a huge sigh of relief. Three wows had to mean I'd got it right, didn't it? Hope had circled the huge carved wooden pumpkin, as though expecting it to magically change into a coach at any moment. It was a good present, but not quite *that* good. I got out of my chair and went over to her.

'There's a little catch here,' I said, guiding her fingers to a small brass fixing. 'You have to slide it over like this.' Together we opened the pumpkin, allowing the two halves to swing apart on their carefully crafted hinges.

'It's a doll's house,' she breathed in wonder, dropping to her knees to study the labyrinth of tiny rooms, each fitted out with miniature intricately carved woodland creatures, living in fully furnished splendour.

'I got the idea when I saw your Lego house last week,' I said, my words lost as Hope launched herself into my arms. 'I love it, Maddie. It's the best present ... *ever*.' That alone was worth spending the next month eating beans on toast for, I thought, turning to Ryan and Chloe as Hope once again began to examine every single occupant of the unique doll's house.

'It's a lovely present. Very original. Hope's going to have a lot of fun playing with it.' It was exactly the right thing to say, and I wondered how much it had cost Chloe to say it.

Hope suddenly sprang to her feet and raced for the door. 'I'm going to get some of the toys from my room. I want to put them in the Pumpkin House too.' There was a slightly awkward silence after she left.

'It really *is* a very special present,' said Ryan kindly. His hand, I noticed, had come to rest on Chloe's shoulder, as though soothing away a tension that perhaps I'd put there. 'Where on earth did you find it?'

'That's the funny thing. I remembered there was a specialist shop down that road with the Italian restaurant we used to go to. We went in there a couple of times last year, just to look at the wonderful doll's houses the guy made. Do you remember?'

The room was quiet for a moment, the only sound was the crackling of the log fire and the beat of my heart, that for some reason sounded so much louder than usual.

'Not last year,' corrected Ryan quietly, and I don't know what was worse, the sadness in his voice or the sudden flash of sympathy on Chloe's face. 'I know the place you mean, Maddie, but it was seven years ago that we went there.'

Chloe

'Why didn't you tell me about that place?'

Ryan's sleepy mumble told me he'd already fallen asleep. He was way ahead of me.

'Blurgh?'

'That place. The place that sells the fancy doll's houses. Why had you never mentioned it to me?'

Ryan yawned, not yet all-the-way awake. 'I suppose I forgot about it. It's been years and years since I was there.

301

If I'd remembered it existed, I would have told you about it, hon.'

I was silent for a few moments. Let it drop, or keep worrying away at it, like a wound you won't allow to heal? Good sense didn't stand a chance.

'Well, *Maddie* remembered it.'

Ryan sighed and I knew he was now with me one hundred per cent.

'For Maddie, it *was* only recent,' Ryan reasoned.

His words opened a door on a corridor I knew better than to walk down, and yet I took that first dangerous step anyway. 'That's how it is for her though, isn't it? All of her memories, all of her emotions … all of her feelings … they're not in the past at all, are they? They're still real to her. Everything she felt back then, she still feels now.'

I didn't need to elaborate. Even half asleep and late at night, he knew what I meant.

'Is that what this is all about?' Ryan's arms reached out for me and pulled me against him. But for once there was no comfort to be found being held against the slow and steady beat of his heart. 'I can't help what Maddie might or might not be feeling,' he whispered into my hair. 'All I can tell you is that those feelings don't exist any more for me. They haven't for a very long time. You know that.'

I was crying now, and I really hoped he couldn't tell, because I knew I was being foolish, I didn't need to provide corroborating evidence.

'*I* would have liked to have bought her that doll's house, that's all,' I said peevishly.

'You bought her a kitten,' Ryan countered, trying to gently tease me out of the spiral that was sucking me down. 'You nuked the doll's house with the kitten,' he said solemnly.

I smiled, even as the tears were tumbling into my pillow, remembering Hope's face when I'd told her that we had one last present for her. How I'd run to our neighbour's house to retrieve the carrier they'd been safely storing for me, the one with the tiny eight-week-old smoke-coloured kitten, that Ryan and I had bought for Hope.

'Yes, I suppose we did,' I said. This time even I could hear the smile in my voice.

'And this way Hope has *two* amazing presents, from two amazing mothers. One of whom, incidentally, I am about to make love to.'

I should have gone to him then. But my husband's words had conjured up an image of him making love to Maddie, even if was over six years in the past. It hung in the air between us like a spectre; there would be no getting rid of it tonight.

I turned my face and tenderly kissed his naked shoulder. 'I'm sorry. Would you mind if I have a rain check on that? I have a horrible headache right now.'

And it wasn't just an excuse I realised, because suddenly I really and truly did.

Maddie

'My birthday present got gazumped.'

A rumbling laugh came from somewhere beneath my kitchen sink. 'I think that expression only applies to houses,' said Mitch, and despite the fact all I could see of him was a pair of incredibly long legs protruding from the cabinet, I knew he was grinning widely.

'Yes, well, my present was a doll's house, so I believe it's still applicable.'

'Fair enough. Can you pass me the mole grip,' Mitch requested, holding out his hand in readiness for the tool.

'That sounds like something you'd find in Farthing Wood,' I said, staring helplessly at the array of tools scattered across the kitchen floor.

'They're the ones next to the Stillson wrench,' he added uselessly.

'You're speaking in a foreign language. Do you mean the thing with the red handle, or the thing with the blue one?'

Once again Mitch laughed. 'The blue one,' he confirmed.

I passed him the tool and looked over at his young apprentice, who was making small explosive sounds as he played an enthusiastic game involving a toy truck and a robot on my kitchen table.

'Would you like some more milk or biscuits, Sam?' I asked, feeling more than a little guilty that his weekend with his dad had been hijacked in order to fix my leaking pipe.

'No thank you,' the seven-year-old replied politely, before returning to his game of mass destruction.

I'd been greeted with the sight of a steadily growing puddle of water, trickling slowly across my kitchen floor, when I'd returned from Hope's birthday party the evening before. After mopping up the best I could, I offered a silent apology to Mitch's late grandmother before placing her large fancy soup tureen beneath the dripping pipe. Her grandson must have been out, because he didn't answer his mobile, so I left him a message explaining that I had a problem. I'd just climbed sleepily into bed when he messaged back, to advise me that someone would come round the next day to fix it. He certainly hadn't hinted in that message that the 'someone' would be him.

It only occurred to me as I packed the final items into my overnight bag the next morning that I should probably have told Mitch I was going away for a few days, particularly if he was arranging for the repair to be done. I looked around for my mobile to call him, but before I managed to locate it, there were two resounding raps on my front door. If that was the plumber, it sounded as if he must have used a wrench to knock on it. I hurried to let him in, before he moved on to a heftier tool.

But when I pulled open the door no one was there; at least that's what I initially thought, until I lowered my gaze and saw a small, dark-haired child standing beside a huge metal toolbox, which probably weighed almost as much as he did. They say you know you're getting old when policemen start to look impossibly young, but I wasn't sure *what* it meant when tradesmen looked like they still attended primary school.

'Hello,' I said, craning my head out into the hall to see who it was who'd left the miniature workman at my door. A few seconds later, heavy-booted footsteps crossed the chequered tiled hallway.

'Sam. You were meant to wait in the car,' said Mitch reprovingly, shaking his head, and looking more than ever like a large shaggy bear. My less-than-conventional-landlord placed an arm around the shoulders of the young boy, pulling him close.

I smiled down at the child, before looking up and sharing it with Mitch. 'I'm not sure the plumber you've hired is actually *old* enough to drive.'

Mitch's laughter boomed around the hallway like a runaway echo. I half expected one of my new neighbours (none of whom I'd met yet) to open their front door to investigate the thunderous sound.

'Sorry, Maddie. I hope we're not too early.' As I hadn't even realised they were coming, there really wasn't an answer to that one, and it didn't look as if Mitch expected one as he bent to retrieve the tool box, lifting it easily, as though it contained nothing heavier than feathers.

He strode towards the kitchen, his young son at his heels. 'I couldn't get hold of an emergency plumber for today, so Sam and I decided it would be fun to fix your leak ourselves.'

I glanced down at the solemn-faced little boy, who looked like he might need convincing on the 'fun' element of that particular activity, and reminded myself not to bother asking Mitch for tips on how to amuse young children.

'You'll be like Bob the Builder,' I said, smiling engagingly at Sam. He gave me a look as if he was almost sorry for me. I guessed Bob's appeal must be with a younger demographic. If I'd needed further proof that I knew absolutely nothing at all about children, it was right there on Sam's face.

'You didn't have to give up your Sunday morning to do this,' I said, turning to Mitch as he began to lay out an impressive array of tools onto a large cloth. I wondered if the number of wrenches required was an indicator of how long it would take to fix the leak. As surreptitiously as I could, I glanced at my watch and chewed worriedly on my lip. Was it too rude to ask how long this would all take?

'It's no problem at all,' Mitch said breezily. 'It shouldn't take us too long and then we're off to the park to kick a football around.' His smile wavered when he caught the expression on my face. Suddenly he looked awkward, and the top half of his cheeks – the only bit visible above his beard – coloured. I'd made him blush. *Again*. 'Unless now isn't a good time ...' he said, glancing around him as if it had only just occurred to him that he might have been interrupting something. I flushed myself when I realised he thought I might not be alone in the flat. The unlikeliness of that almost made me laugh out loud.

'Now is fine,' I assured him, crossing to the coffee maker and switching it on. 'It's only that I have a train to catch later. I'm going to spend a couple of days with my dad,' I added, supplying an explanation he hadn't asked for.

'Ah, that'll be nice,' Mitch declared, dropping to the floor and disappearing beneath my sink. 'I'll work fast then, and get out of your way.'

'So did your daughter enjoy her birthday party?' asked Mitch, treading carelessly with his huge size thirteen feet, all over the secret I was having to keep.

I glanced around the room and almost laughed at my own jumpiness. Here, at least, it was safe to admit to being Hope's mother.

'I think so. Of course, I don't know how these things usually go. It was my first children's party for several decades.'

'You'll get the hang of them,' Mitch said assuredly.

It had been surprisingly easy chatting to him about the events of the previous day, including the doll's house versus kitten climax. It reminded me of all the times we used to chat in the past; the only difference now was that he was fixing my sink and not my computer.

'How do you do it, Mitch?' I asked, dropping my voice down low so that his son couldn't hear us above the crashing noises as robot and truck repeatedly collided. 'How do you get used to not being there in their life, all the time?'

Mitch scooted out from beneath the cupboard, and for once the easy, ready, twinkle had disappeared from his eyes. 'It's about the *quality* of the time you spend with your child, not the *quantity*. It's about giving up your ego and realising it's not a territory battle. It's about making them realise a boy with two dads gets *twice* as much love. There are fathers who live under the same roof as their kids who have no idea about the things that matter to them.' Mitch looked over at his son, who was happily munching on what had to be his tenth chocolate biscuit. I might not know much about children, but I was pretty sure *that* wasn't a good idea.

'Sam is the most important person in my world. I know it, and more importantly, *he* knows it.' Mitch's voice dropped, and I crouched down low beside him to hear whatever secret he was about to share. 'Sam gets nightmares, real scary-monsters-under-the-bed ones. So a few months ago I gave him an old mobile phone of mine, with my number programmed in it. Now, when a scary dream wakes him in the night, he can call out for his mum or his step-dad, or he can phone me, and I'll do my monster-chasing spell over the phone.' He looked sheepish, as if waiting for me to laugh at this giant of a man who chanted incantations to dispel scary goblins in the middle of the night. But laughing was the last thing I felt like doing. I was much more likely to cry.

'You're a very good dad, Mitch.' His face split with a grin; a delighted grizzly bear, sitting on my kitchen floor with a wrench in his hand.

'Okay, try that tap,' he commanded, his voice gruff with

embarrassment. Water gushed into the sink, and not a single drop leaked out from the joint he'd fixed.

'And you're not a bad plumber either,' I added with a smile.

It must have been a difficult and painful decision for my dad *not* to bring my mum to the hospital when I'd finally woken up from the coma. He'd had to balance my need to see her with the impact it would have on her peace of mind. And as painful as it was to accept, I hadn't been in a position to argue when he'd said he thought it would be better to wait until I was well enough to go to the home and visit her.

'She has a routine, Maddie, and any departure from it throws her.'

'Don't you think she'd want to see me though?' I'd asked, my eyes filling with tears, like a small abandoned child in need of her mum, instead of a grown woman who should know better.

'If your mum was who she once was, a squadron of marines couldn't keep her from your bedside, my love,' my dad had replied, picking up my hand and holding it gently. 'But she's not that person any more. She just looks like her.'

It had been a very long wait from the time I'd first opened my eyes until today. And it was strange to realise that my separation from my mother was about as long as my own daughter's had been from me. Our lives had become a tangled ball of string, and the weird serendipity made my head hurt whenever I tried to unravel it.

It wasn't the unfamiliarity of my father's new home that I found so heartbreaking. It was actually seeing once again the few familiar cherished possessions he'd taken from his old life, to transplant into his new one. I ran my hand over a small side table, a lamp with a tasselled shade, and a remembered painting, as though reacquainting myself with old friends. I tried not to think about all the things that should have been here in his new home with him, the most notable of which being my mother.

'You need to keep your expectations low,' my father had advised, as we'd walked together up the drive of the single-storey white building where my mother now lived. I'd nodded, but despite his words of caution, there was no stopping my expectations from bobbing persistently up to the surface, like tiny unsinkable buoys.

'Be prepared for her not to recognise you, my love,' he warned, signing us both in at the reception desk. 'There are days when she doesn't even know me. And she gets confused sometimes when Ryan and Chloe bring Hope for a visit.'

The cut of jealousy had gone deep as I thought of Chloe spending time with my mother, while I had slept on, oblivious to a world slipping away through my fingers. That's why the timing of my visit was important, because Ryan,

Chloe and Hope had plans to visit the following week, for a belated celebration of Hope's birthday with her grand-parents. I wasn't invited to that one, which I knew was sensible because it would only confuse both my mother and my daughter. But it stung nonetheless. I'd spent so much time on the outside because of my coma, and now that I was awake it didn't seem fair that I was still there, with my face pressed up against the window of the life that should have been mine.

My nose twitched involuntarily as we walked side by side down a maze of twisting corridors to my mother's room. My father spotted it, and offered an apology. 'You get used to it after a while. I hardly notice the smell at all these days.'

The smile I gave him in reply was a little sad. 'Actually, I was thinking that it smelled like home ... like the hospital,' I amended. I'd have given anything to wipe that particular expression from his eyes, but there was no time, because he'd already come to a halt beside a white panelled door. A small card bearing my mother's name was set into a slot beside the frame.

The room was bigger than I'd been expecting, separated into two distinct areas by an archway. My mother was in the section that was furnished as a lounge. My eyes flew past coffee tables, a bookcase and a television, to settle hungrily on the grey-haired woman staring out through a set of French windows at the bleak barren gardens. She was smiling wistfully, as if what she saw *wasn't* bare winter branches and grey skies, but lush green grass and trees full of foliage and flowers. She always had loved her garden. She took a long time turning around, the vista beyond the panes clearly more of a draw than the sound of the opening door.

I didn't realise I was holding my breath until I began to feel slightly light-headed from doing so. Her face strangely looked no older, although the grey in her hair had quad-rupled. Her back was still ramrod straight, and I heard the echo of a thousand reminders flying back through the years of her constantly telling me to stand tall and not to slouch. Unconsciously I found myself drawing up straighter and pulling my shoulders back to greet the mother whose eyes showed no flicker of recognition as they fluttered over me. They went straight to my father, and on seeing his smile, she mimicked it.

'Hello, Faye. How are you today, my darling?' Her brow furrowed, and I realised she was giving his question her most serious consideration.

'I'm well, thank you . . .' My heart broke a little as I saw her grappling to remember my father's name.

'Bill,' provided my father, crossing the room to take the hand of the woman he loved in his. How did he do this, day after day? Where did he find the strength?

'I've brought someone very special with me today,' said my dad carefully. 'Do you know who this is?'

My mother's eyes travelled over me, strangely starting at my booted feet and working their way upwards. I could tell when they reached my face, for the furrows on her brow deepened. The lump in my throat made it hard to swallow

as I stood, mannequin still, waiting for my mother to recognise her only daughter. Slowly, with polite regret, she
shook her head.

'Are you one of my doctors?' she guessed, her hand
coming up and toying with the neckline of her silky blouse.

'No, my love. Look closer,' urged my father. 'You *know*
who this is.' With his free hand he beckoned me to come
further into the room. My legs felt shaky as I took three
steps towards the window.

Her eyes examined me, feature by feature, as though a
clue was cunningly concealed among them. The arch of my
eyebrows was the same as hers, the bright blue of my eyes
was different from the milky opal of her irises, but their
shape was practically identical. Her fingers fluttered at her
throat, and I saw the tremor of a pulse beating behind the
restless digits. 'You don't work here, do you,' she said, more
statement than question.

I shook my head, bracing myself for the impact of her
denouncement, which I could see was coming. Her seeking
hand slid around her neck. And suddenly my heart started
to beat a little faster.

'I'm sorry. I feel I *should* know who you are, but I can't
quite place you.'

I saw my father's lips part, to reveal my identity, but I
shook my head slightly. There were tears in my eyes, but a
small smile on my lips. My mother had finally found what
she'd been searching for, and gently tugged on a thin silver
chain, pulling free the necklace that I'd given her when I

was sixteen years old. She ran the chain through her fingers, until she reached the silver pendant with the word 'Mum' on it. Her fingertips grazed backwards and forwards over it, as though reading it in Braille.

'No, dear. I'm sorry. I don't remember you.'

Except somewhere, somehow, I felt that just maybe, she did.

My dad caved after an hour, and to be honest I'm surprised he lasted that long. As we'd sat drinking the cups of tea he'd fetched from the residents' lounge, I could practically feel the pulse of his thought waves, trying to telepathically identify me to my mother. I would have been just as happy to allow her to remember me in her own time. The important thing for me was that I was *here* spending time with her, even if she didn't know who I was. But perhaps I was deluding myself into thinking this was only a temporary obstacle.

'What did you say your name was again, dear?' asked my mother, her face wearing a politely interested expression.

My eyes went to hers and didn't fall away as I repeated the name she had chosen for me thirty-four years earlier. 'Madeline. My name is Madeline.'

Her eyes fluttered, like a frightened bird's, and then automatically went to my father, her source of calm and stability. His face was beseeching her to remember, but all she appeared to be was confused.

'Well. How very strange. That's my daughter's name.'

I tried to turn my small sob into a cough, but I don't think I did a very good job of it. I knew I should have been expecting this, but it was still a shock.

My father got out of his seat to crouch down beside her armchair. Very tenderly he took one of her wrinkled hands in his. 'This *is* Maddie, Faye. This is our daughter. She came back to us.'

For a moment I thought he'd broken through the walls her dementia had built, but then she shook her head in denial. 'No. Of course this isn't Maddie. Don't be ridiculous. Maddie's at school,' she declared, looking across the room at the gold carriage clock on top of the bookcase, and from there to two silver-framed photographs showing a pretty little girl with bright blue eyes and long dark hair. One of them was Hope, the other one was me.

'So, now you see how it is.'

I walked over to the French windows and stood shoulder to shoulder with the only parent who knew I had returned. It was starting to snow, and the floodlights in the care home grounds were picking up the falling flakes, making it look like a fiercely shaken snow globe.

'I thought that when she saw me ... when she realised I'd come out of the coma ...'

His arm came up around me, and my head fell onto his shoulder, as if it was suddenly too heavy for my neck. 'She doesn't remember any of that, Maddie. She *did* for a while, she certainly understood what was going on when Hope was born, but then . . .' His voice trailed away and I could tell by the gruffness of his tone that he was determined not to cry in front of me. But the thought of him crying alone was even harder to bear. 'I think this was the only way she could cope with what happened to you, to let her illness take it all away.'

'But what about you? How do *you* cope? How do you manage to keep coming here, day after day, knowing that some days she can't even remember your name?'

My father was of a generation that always kept a neatly laundered handkerchief in a pocket, and he extracted it now and pressed it into my hand. 'Where else would I be except at the side of the woman I love? Somewhere inside there is still the girl I fell in love with. She's still the bride I couldn't wait to marry; she's the one I promised to grow old with. The goalposts might have moved, but there's nowhere else I could be in the world, except at her side.'

Something deep inside me began to tear very slowly apart, like the ripping of a seam. Because those were the words I once believed Ryan would have said . . . about me. Until the day came when he stopped waiting and made the decision to move on without me.

My mother's return from her evening meal made us both turn towards the door. The carer who'd escorted her to her room settled her in a chair. 'I'll be back to get you ready for bed when your family have gone, my lovely,' she promised before slipping out of the room to allow us to say our goodbyes.

My mother stared curiously after the woman, and I could see something glimmer briefly in her eyes like the sputtering of a match in the dark. I don't think my father saw, for he bent to kiss her cheek and reached for his thick woollen coat. 'I'm going to go and bring the car to the front entrance. I don't want you trudging around in the cold and ending up back in hospital.' He was being over-protective, but I knew better than to argue with him on this one. I nodded and watched him go.

I wasn't aware that my mother had heard his comment until I turned back to face her. That light was back in her eyes, burning more brightly now, trying to shine a spotlight through the fog of confusion.

'You've been in hospital?' her question was tentative.

I nodded. 'For quite a long time.'

'You were sick?' she asked, but there was doubt in her voice, as if she knew that wasn't quite right. The room went very still. It felt as if something almost supernatural was happening and I wished my father was here to see it, because it felt ephemeral and fleeting, as if I was trying to grasp hold of wisps of smoke with my bare hands.

'You were in an accident?' she queried hesitantly.

I nodded, because this time I was too choked to speak. She was remembering. I had no idea how long this precious moment would last before the veils of forgetfulness fell over her memory, and I was too scared to do or say anything that might break the spell.

Her face softened and then suddenly there was

recognition. It was the moment I had come here for and I flew into her arms with a broken sob.

'Maddie, Maddie, Maddie,' she crooned into my hair. I was eight years old, crying in my mother's arms; I was a child who knew with absolute certainty this woman would never leave me.

She leant back to look at me, her age-worn hands cradling my cheeks, her eyes drinking me in. 'You grew up. When did you do that?'

There was no answer I could give that would make sense to her.

'Have I been asleep? Is that what happened?' she asked. Heartbreakingly I could see the clouds coming back, covering the fleeting breakthrough with forgetfulness again.

I kissed her cheek tenderly, trying to imprint the soft velvet of her skin into my memory. 'No, Mum. You weren't the one who was asleep. I was.'

Chapter 13

Chloe

'Are we nearly there yet?'

'Isn't that supposed to be your daughter's line?'

Ryan laughed and looked up at the rear-view mirror to glance at Hope, who was sitting on the back seat of the car, happily singing away to herself as she filled in a colouring book.

'I was just wondering if we should message Bill and tell him that we've been delayed.'

'Already done it,' I said. I peered out through the windscreen at the unfamiliar countryside, or as much of it as I could see through the falling sleet. We had made the journey to visit Bill and Faye innumerable times, but today there'd been a serious pile-up on the motorway, and we'd been diverted onto roads we didn't know, and were now running late.

I thought of the cakes carefully stored in the boot of the car, in a collection of tins and plastic containers. I'd spent the last two days busily baking for this visit, but if we didn't get there soon, the residents of Faye's home would be having them for breakfast instead of afternoon tea. Some people might have thought it strange, but I really *enjoyed* my visits to the care home to see the woman who felt like my mother-in-law – even though she wasn't.

I'd had to cut back on my volunteering at the hospital when I'd first agreed to work for Ryan. I'd obviously continued to visit Maddie – taking her baby with me every time – but the hours I spent on the geriatric ward had sadly had to be reduced. And I'd really missed it. I'd missed the company; I'd missed reading to them; but most of all I'd missed the amazing stories they loved to share, of lives so very different to mine.

So, after Bill had made the agonising decision that he could no longer care for Faye alone, visits to the care home to allow Faye to spend time with her granddaughter had become a regular event, but they'd never been a strain or a hardship for me. Quite the opposite, in fact. And it has to be said, I was a huge hit there. I still remembered the first time we had visited, how I'd packed the car full of treats – much as it was packed today – and how Ryan had stood looking at the trays of chocolate brownies and cupcakes and had scratched his chin thoughtfully. 'I really don't think Faye is going to be able to get through this lot.' I'd smiled knowingly. 'Ah, but all her friends at the care home will love them – and the staff too.' He'd still looked doubtful. 'Trust me,' I'd said confidently. 'These are my people.' And I'd been proved right.

At first Faye had been understandably mistrustful of the woman Ryan had hired to look after her grandchild. She was nowhere near as welcoming as Bill had been, but I didn't blame her for that. And then over the years, as the dementia had slowly shredded away the person she had been, she had softened and now greeted Ryan and me with equal enthusiasm. Not because she was pleased to see us, I knew that, but because of what we would be bringing with us: a delightful grandchild who was the image of her own daughter ... and cakes. They were two very valuable currencies.

'Does your phone say what time we should get there?' Ryan asked, his concentration totally on the road. Despite the alarming way the tyres were skating upon the sleet-covered tarmac, Ryan's grip on the wheel seemed remarkably relaxed and nowhere near as white-knuckled as mine would have been. He even found time to flash me a reassuring smile.

'The worst that's going to happen today is that we'll be a bit late,' he said confidently. I nodded, not doubting for a moment his ability to deliver all three of us safely to our destination, but unable to shake the nerve-tingling presentiment that something bad was going to happen.

I bent my head lower, peering at the phone in the poor light, cowardly hiding the concern on my face behind the swinging curtain of my hair.

'So how much longer until we get there, babe?'

I blinked rapidly several times, hoping that might help to clear my suddenly blurry vision. It didn't. My voice sounded unnaturally chipper when I replied: 'I can't tell you, just now.'

'Sure you can,' Ryan joked. 'I'm your husband. You can tell me anything.'

I ground the pad of my thumb against my right eyelid, which instantly improved the blur of my vision but probably did very little to improve my eye make-up. 'Another twenty minutes, I think,' I said, squinting at the screen.

Ryan's eyes left the road for a moment, just long enough for me to see the concern in them. 'Did you ever make that optician's appointment you were talking about?'

For a moment I was annoyed. There'd been so much going on recently, it was hardly surprising that I'd let some non-urgent matters slide. And I had a feeling – a pretty strong one – that the problems I was having with my eyes were largely stress-related. But with Hope sitting right behind us in the back seat of the car, it was definitely not the time to be discussing why I might be feeling like that. 'Things have been a bit ... *busy* ... one way and another recently,' I euphemised. 'It's not been high up on my list of priorities.'

'It will be when we have to trade in Hope's new kitten for a guide dog.'

'Are we getting a dog?' Hope piped up from the back seat. Despite the serious undertones of our conversation, I couldn't help but smile. That little girl of ours missed nothing at all.

'I don't think Elsa would like us getting a dog, not when

we've only just got her,' I reasoned to Hope, before swivel-ling back to look out through the windscreen.

'I think you'd look very cute in glasses,' said Ryan softly, with a slight sexy tease in his voice. 'Like a proper librarian.'

'I *was* a proper librarian,' I defended, feeling a warm glow at the twinkle in his eyes.

'That's probably why your eyes are bad. Too many hours spent poring over books.'

'Books don't ruin your eyes, they improve your mind.'

He laughed, and was still doing so when the signpost directing us to the care home came into view. The subject of the opticians and whether or not I would look good in glasses was once again forgotten. For now.

'She knows.'

I glanced back over my shoulder from my position halfway up the stairs, with Hope fast asleep in my arms. My eyes flared at Ryan, who saw me, gave a quick apologetic nod and strode into the kitchen to continue his phone call with Maddie in private.

Hope murmured something in her sleep, and a stab of unease cut through me. I'd been so anxious today that either Faye or Bill would accidentally reveal the truth to Hope about Maddie's identity, that it hadn't even occurred to me that someone else had already told her.

For the entire journey home I kept reliving the moment when Hope had stood in her grandmother's room, looking at the two practically identical photographs in their silver frames and innocently asked: 'Which one is me, and which one is Maddie my dead mummy?'

We handled it badly, I could see that now. There are lies you can get over. There are lies that you can sneakily sweep under the carpet, and then there are other lies that are so enormous they're like giant boulders that come crashing down off a mountain to crush you. Someone gasped – that might have been me; someone groaned softly – I think that was Ryan; and someone else struggled valiantly to clear the army of frogs that appeared to be lodged in their throat. I imagine that was Bill.

'Hope,' I said softly, dropping down to my knees in front of her so that our faces were level. 'Did someone tell you that about Maddie?' I'd read countless books about child psychology, but nothing could ever have prepared me for this. 'Did *Maddie* tell you that?'

Hope's bright blue eyes, her mother's eyes, filled instantly with fearful tears. There was a genuinely distraught expression on her face, which no child should ever have to wear. I glanced up at Ryan; he looked mortified. This guilt was ours, we were the ones who'd done this to our little girl.

'I'm sorry, Mummy. I forgot it was a secret. I forgot I wasn't supposed to tell you that I knew.'

I pulled her small body into my arms, shocked to realise she was trembling as if she had a fever. 'It's all right. Nobody's cross with you.'

'Who told you Maddie was your mummy, Pumpkin?' Ryan questioned, his voice more gravelly than usual, the way it always goes when he gets emotional.

'Francesca did,' Hope's voice was a terrified whisper. 'At school. She said she heard her mum and dad talking about it after my birthday party. She said Maddie must be a ghost. She's not, is she, Mummy?'

I should have known something was wrong. The nightmares she'd woken from twice this week, and the feeling that something wasn't quite right now all made sense. I'd thought she was coming down with something. I'd even bought two extra bottles of Calpol in readiness. How could I have missed the signs? I was a bad mother ... except I wasn't at all, not really. And now everyone knew the truth. I wasn't Hope's mother, I never had been. Maddie was.

Maddie

'She knows,' said Ryan, his voice dark and solemn at the other end of the phone.

'Oh my God. How did that happen?'

'Some kid at school overheard her parents talking. And she told Hope.'

'Oh my God,' I repeated. There was a good chance that I might keep saying that for hours, and still be no further forward. 'Is Hope all right?'

Ryan's sigh sounded as though it was being ripped from him. 'To be perfectly honest, Maddie, I don't know. She seemed more upset that she'd forgotten she was supposed to be keeping it a secret, than anything else.' There was a long moment of silence and then he gave a small sharp laugh that held very little humour. 'Oh yes, and apparently she thought that you were a ghost.'

'I'm a *what*? Why would she think that?'

The question didn't need to be asked though, not when I thought about it. Of course Hope would think I was a ghost. Why wouldn't she, when everyone she loved and trusted in the world had told her that I'd died?

'We'll work this out,' I said, with a confidence I didn't feel.

'We have to,' said Ryan, and for the first time since he'd revealed the lie he'd told our daughter, I felt sorry for the torment he was going through. 'Because I don't know how we're going to live with ourselves if we've done something to screw her up. She could end up with trust issues ... she could end up hating us—'

'That won't happen. We're three intelligent and caring adults, who only want what's best for her. We'll work this out.'

Ryan's voice sounded suddenly younger, more the man I'd met and fallen in love with than the man who was now Chloe's husband. 'I hope you're right, Maddie. I guess we'll find out tomorrow.'

I was dressed hours before Ryan was due to collect me. I'd accepted his offer of a lift, knowing we'd need that time to discuss how to handle the conversation with Hope. I imagined he and Chloe would have spent much of the previous night strategising.

When the buzzer went on my door, I glanced at my watch,

pleased to see that for once he was actually early. That was a new departure from the Ryan I remembered.

'I guess you couldn't sleep either?' I said, as I pulled open the door, only to find the wrong man waiting on my doorstep.

'As a matter of fact, I sleep like a baby – I always have,' admitted Mitch with a sheepish expression. 'But I imagine you were expecting it to be someone else?'

I looked at the empty hallway behind him. Ryan wasn't late – at least not yet, so it was irrational to feel irritated that he wasn't the one who had knocked on my door.

'Sorry. I thought you were Ryan. I'm going round to his house this morning.' *Ryan and Chloe's house*, reminded a voice in my head. She wasn't a walk-on character in this play, she had a leading role, and I should be trying much harder to remember that.

'Oh, okay. Well, I won't stay then,' said Mitch, and then flushed as we both realised that I hadn't actually invited him to do so. I blushed almost as deeply as him. It was becoming contagious.

'Mitch. I'm so sorry, that was terribly rude of me. Please, come in,' I said, stepping back into the flat and holding the door wide open in invitation. He shook his head, and seemed suddenly uncomfortable standing on the threshold of a property that was actually his, rather than mine.

'No. Another time, maybe. I was only calling round to see if you'd had any more trouble with the pipes after last week.'

'Pipes?' I said, distractedly, and then shook my head in amazement that his visit the previous week had completely slipped from my memory. 'Sorry. I'm not with it this morning.'

Mitch's warm brown eyes – bear's eyes, I told myself stupidly – crinkled at the edges in concern. 'Are you feeling all right, Maddie? You're not sick or anything?' There was genuine anxiety in his voice, which I found quite touching, because I remembered him telling me once that he wasn't very comfortable around sick people. And sick was definitely something I was feeling right then ... it was how I'd felt every single minute since the night before, when Ryan's telephone call had shattered the illusion he'd been forcing me to live.

'Not in the way you mean,' I said, reaching out and touching his arm lightly. His forearm felt as solid as a small log. 'Hope has discovered the truth. She's found out that I'm her mum.'

Mitch's lips pursed and a long soundless whistle blew from them. I felt the tail end of it touch my face, as soft as a spring breeze. 'Phew. That's big,' he said, succinctly summing up the dilemma we found ourselves in, in three words.

'It is, rather.'

He was silent for a moment, considering. 'But it's a good thing. I never could understand why you were all keeping it a secret.' Somewhere deep within his thick beard I saw him draw in his lower lip, and there was a definite increase in the pink of his cheeks as he added brusquely: 'Although obviously it's none of my business.' It wasn't, but perhaps talking to someone who wasn't involved was something I should have done right from the very beginning. 'All I will say,' said Mitch, battling on despite his heightened colour, 'is that from my experience with Sam, the one thing I've come to realise is that kids are far stronger than you think they are. They can deal with all kinds of things, in ways far more mature than adults do. They can handle separation, divorce . . . even death. As long as you tell it to them straight. As long as you're honest with them.'

His eyes met mine, and there was apology in them, but for once his skin colour remained normal. He didn't need to say anything more, it wasn't necessary. Because being honest with Hope was the one thing that *hadn't* happened; not from Ryan, not from Chloe, or her grandfather, and ultimately not from me either.

'Sorry I'm late,' said an achingly familiar voice from somewhere unseen. Mitch stepped hastily to one side to reveal Ryan, who'd been totally hidden behind him. It was odd seeing them together like that at my door. Ryan was tall, muscular and extremely fit, and yet he seemed oddly diminished in the hallway beside Mitch.

Ryan didn't say anything further until we were walking down the pavement towards his car. 'Who was the guy? The one who looks like Hagrid?'

The sudden urge to rush to the defence of a man who was probably strong enough to uproot small trees with one hand took me by surprise. 'That was my landlord. His name is Mitch, and was that *Harry Potter* jibe really necessary?'

Ryan was instantly apologetic. 'Sorry. Chloe and I have just started reading the books to Hope, so I guess the characters are on my mind. I apologise. I wasn't trying to be rude.'

'I'm not sure that comparing someone to a hairy giant could ever be anything *except* derogatory.'

To be fair, Ryan did appear genuinely contrite. 'I guess I was just surprised to find him there, that's all.'

'He's a good friend,' I said, promoting Mitch to a status he didn't know he'd achieved. But as we drove the short distance to Ryan and Chloe's home, I realised that I hadn't been exaggerating; well, not that much. Mitch *did* feel like a friend, and right then I certainly felt in need of one.

'Will I have to go and live somewhere else?'

'No. Absolutely not.' Ryan's reply was faster than a bullet, shooting down Hope's concerns and my secret fantasies with marksman accuracy. 'This is your home. This is where you live, where you'll always live ... with Mummy and Daddy.'

Hope took a moment to think about this, and then looked up with the question we should have been expecting.

'Which mummy?'

It was a very good question, but not one that any of the adults in the room were capable of answering. This whole situation was all so new, so unchartered, that no one had thought of discussing it on a formal, or even legal basis. Words like custody, visitation and shared care were a language none of us spoke. At least not yet.

My eyes went from Ryan to Chloe, and the sight of the

woman I thought of as my enemy fighting back tears shook me far more than I cared to admit. Perhaps that was what made me jump in headfirst with my own reassurances. I reached across their kitchen table to take Hope's small hand in mine, while a separate part of me quietly marvelled that even our fingernails were the same shape. 'Well, I've only just moved into my new home, so right now there isn't a bedroom pretty enough for you to stay in. But maybe, in time, you could help me pick out some things you like, so that when you feel ready you could come for a sleepover sometimes, or maybe for the whole weekend. But only if you want to. No one is going to make you do anything you don't want to do.'

There was a hint of a challenge in my eyes when I lifted them to gauge Ryan's reaction, but his were warm in response, and his slight nod confirmed his unspoken agreement. I exhaled in relief, and braced myself for a totally different reaction from the woman he'd married. But surprisingly, Chloe too was nodding in agreement.

'And could I bring Elsa with me when I come?' Hope questioned.

I smiled, feeling the relief rush through me like adrenalin. Could it really be this simple? 'Of course you can, honey. You can bring anything that you want.'

Hope seemed to consider this for a moment, and then nodded, a tiny six-year-old judge, who found the prosecution had put forward a reasonable suggestion. 'Okay.' She fidgeted on the pine chair, and I sensed this was probably as much 'serious' as she was capable of coping with right then. The fine details were something that her father and I needed to work out. And of course, Chloe. Always Chloe.

'Can I go and play with Elsa now?' she asked Chloe, already slithering off her seat.

Chloe nodded and smiled, and the two of them shared a special look which made me feel as if I was right back on the outside of their special circle again, despite Hope's willingness to accept this new and dramatic change in her life. But we weren't getting off quite that easily, for she paused at the door and looked back at all three of us for a long moment, before turning to Ryan.

'Why did you say my mummy had died?'

It was the unseen right hook, the flying jab you hadn't noticed your opponent was launching your way. To his credit, Ryan didn't dress up his answer to paint himself in a better light. I had to admire him for that. 'That was a *big* mistake, and I was the one who made it, not your mummy, or Maddie. The doctors said Maddie was in a sleep so deep that she couldn't wake up from it, however much she wanted to; however much she wanted to come back to you.'

'Like Snow White or Sleeping Beauty?' Hope asked innocently.

'Kind of,' I said, smiling at the child I would happily surrender this new reclaimed life of mine for in a heartbeat. The depth of love I felt for her was like nothing I had ever experienced before. If Chloe felt just one hundredth of these emotions, no wonder she looked as if the foundations of her entire world were crumbling. Who could have something as precious as this in their life and bear to lose it?

'So did a handsome prince come and kiss you and make you wake up?' This time the smile I gave her was broad enough to make it all the way to my eyes. 'Actually, Pumpkin, I didn't need any dumb old prince. I woke up all by myself.'

Ryan's eyes widened a fraction, but it was Chloe's reaction that I found the most surprising, for her eyes met mine, and she nodded firmly in approval. And somehow that felt like a very small step on a long journey we would all be taking together.

Chapter 14

Chloe

I replaced the phone handset on its base, and gave a small disappointed sigh. I glanced at my watch, though I knew there was little point in trying to find a substitute babysitter at such short notice. And Megan was the only one I felt comfortable leaving Hope with anyway. Even if we miraculously managed to find a last-minute replacement, I probably wouldn't be able to relax enough to enjoy the evening. Which was a shame, because I'd really been looking forward to it.

I thought of the expensive floor-length dress hanging up on the back of our bedroom door, and felt a small selfish pang of longing. Of course Megan couldn't help coming down with a sickness bug, and I quite understood why she'd had to cancel, but with only half an hour until we were due to leave, there wasn't any other option except for us to stay at home.

I climbed the staircase, catching a glimpse of my reflection in the hall mirror as I passed. I was looking far more glamorous than I usually did when clad in my towelling robe. Tonight long dangling earrings sparkled from my ears, and my hair was pinned into a complex and sophisticated up-do, courtesy of several hours spent at the hair salon that afternoon. The style was going to accentuate the low scooped-out back of my evening dress, but the effect didn't work quite so well with dressing gown and slippers.

I crossed the upstairs hallway, automatically glancing through Hope's open bedroom door, where I could see her sitting cross-legged on the floor beside the pumpkin house. It looked as if she might be trying to persuade her new kitten to climb inside. It was a plan that I suspected wouldn't end well.

I opened our bedroom door and slipped into the room. Ryan must have only just got out of the shower, for he was wearing nothing more than a small towel, knotted low on his hips. Even after two years of marriage, I still found myself deeply affected by the sight of him semi-naked. Droplets of water that he hadn't bothered to dry off glinted like tiny jewels over his chest and shoulders, but it was the taut muscles of his stomach which drew my gaze, and the vague shadowy trail of hair that speared downwards. The trail which I knew grew darker and denser beneath the towel.

Ryan smiled as I entered the room and crossed to our queen-size bed, where his white evening shirt was lying in readiness.

'There's no need for you to wear that,' I said matter-of-factly. 'Or your dinner suit, come to that.'

He paused with his arm outstretched to grab the shirt and raised one eyebrow in humour. 'I don't think my company are hosting *that* kind of party tonight, hon. They normally ask us to at least *arrive* fully clothed for the Christmas bash.'

Despite my feelings of disappointment, I laughed. Ryan's employers hosted *amazing* parties, and this year's venue for their Christmas ball was the British Library, which I'd been excited about for months. My librarian's heart had been understandably giddy at the prospect of vintage champagne and every book ever published in the UK, all in one place. And they would both be there tonight. But sadly it looked as if Ryan and I wouldn't be.

'That was Megan on the phone. She's sick and can't babysit for us tonight.'

Ryan's forehead creased, and he sat down heavily on the edge of the bed. The towel gaped slightly, which was a distraction I refused to succumb to, not with our daughter just down the hall.

'Bugger. That's a shame. I don't suppose she has any friends who'd be willing to step in at short notice?' He saw the way my eyebrows rose, and shot down his own suggestion before I had a chance to. 'But you wouldn't want anyone we hadn't used before, would you?'

I shook my head and felt the dangling earrings swing and brush my cheek like diamanté chandeliers. Ryan reached for my hand and pulled me down to sit beside him. 'I'm sorry, my love. I know how much you were looking forward to this.' I gave a *c'est la vie* shrug, but he wasn't fooled. 'What about one of the mums from school?'

I shook my head once again. Although I knew them well enough for conversations at the school gates, I'd never got into the coffee morning or ladies-who-lunch crowd, and I wasn't comfortable phoning up and asking a cheeky favour just because we were in a fix.

Ryan traced his finger down the curve of my cheek, his gaze taking in the hair, the carefully applied make-up and also the disappointment in my eyes. 'Got it!' he said, getting to his feet and looking around the room for his phone. 'You *will* go to the ball,' he said with a cheerful grin as he began scrolling through his directory. He looked so pleased with his idea, I tried very hard not to reveal my true feelings as he pressed the green button on his phone, so obviously delighted that he'd found a solution. A solution I'd already considered and rejected.

'Maddie, it's Ryan. Do you happen to have any plans for this evening? No? That's great, because I have a big favour to ask ...'

With hindsight, I'd much rather have asked one of the school-gate mums.

Maddie

'Tonight? Oh, right now? Oh, okay, er ... yes. That's fine. I'll call a cab.' I hung up the phone with his offer not to bother, and that he was on his way to collect me, ringing in my ears.

Ryan had been so delighted that I'd said yes, it had taken me right back to the first time he'd ever asked me out. For reasons I'd never fully understood, I hadn't given him my number on the night we'd first met, forcing him to track it down through various industry colleagues. Perhaps I was testing him; trying to see just how motivated he was to see me again. The answer had been: extremely motivated. He'd utilised some pretty impressive detective skills to get hold of my number, and when he'd called to ask me out, I already knew I was going to say yes, and keep on saying yes to this man whatever he suggested, before he'd even asked me the question. I'd been *that* sure of him.

I shook off the memory, like an annoying buzzing insect, and dashed into my bedroom to pull on boots and grab my bag. I was standing there wondering if I should have changed out of my old but comfortable pre-coma jeans and jumper, when the buzzer on my front door made the decision for me. So, he *could* be on time, when he wanted to be.

I flicked off the light switches behind me as I went through the flat to the front door, so that when I opened it and saw Ryan silhouetted in the soft light of the hallway table lamp, he was backlit by an amber glow, which made him look devastatingly attractive. Like someone in a TV advert for expensive male cologne, I thought. The dinner suit and bow tie look was unfamiliar, but it suited him enough for me to feel all kinds of things that should have been dead and buried a very long time ago.

'Not just a night out at the cinema then?' I said lightly, my eyes on the perfectly fitting suit.

'Company Christmas ball,' he said succinctly, waiting as I double-locked my front door.

'Do you still work at the same place?' I asked, wondering how we'd never covered this kind of small talk up until now. Probably because we'd been occupied with far more pressing *big talk*, I imagined.

'Yes. They've been pretty good to me over the years since—' He looked as if he was about to say something else then, and some sixth sense told me it was probably about my accident or the early years of my hospital stay. 'They throw pretty impressive parties for their staff each year,' he added instead.

'I remember,' I said quietly. And suddenly, in a way I don't believe either of us intended, we were both back at the last black-tie event we'd attended together, the Christmas party organised by his company seven years earlier. The party itself was a blur of expensive caviar and the kind of champagne they haul out of dusty crates, and not down off the supermarket shelves. While the first part of the evening might have faded away in both of our minds, I could see that we were both suddenly remembering the cab drive home from the fancy venue. I could almost feel the warm touch of his hand sliding up my leg, his fingers dipping dangerously beneath the thigh-length split on my tight sequinned sheath dress. And the kiss that started as we pulled away from the party and only broke off when a slightly embarrassed cab driver had cleared his throat meaningfully and announced that we had got to our destination. 'And not a minute too soon,' he'd added. Did Ryan remember how we'd still been laughing about that as he'd pushed the front door shut and we stumbled back against it, taking up where we'd left off in the cab?

There was a look in his eyes now, and his pupils looked larger, almost swallowing up the colour of his irises. Oh yes. He was remembering it every bit as clearly as I was, and I don't think either of us knew what to do about that.

Chloe looked pretty, and I silently congratulated myself for managing to tell her so without sounding the smallest bit insincere. It was probably because I was still feeling the shock waves of guilt from the memory I had no business recalling. I had absolutely no idea what was going on in Ryan's head, because he'd spent the entire drive talking about a recent news story that I think we both knew was only a smokescreen.

'It's a lovely dress,' I said, and I wasn't lying, because it was. The deep aquamarine colour suited her blond hair, and she was wearing more make-up than I'd ever seen her use before.

'Mummy looks so beautiful,' said Hope, coming down the stairs one careful step at a time, cradling the kitten in her arms.

'She certainly does, Pumpkin,' replied Ryan from his position on the other side of the hall. He was looking at Chloe, not me, I had to keep reminding myself as I stood right beside her.

Perhaps Chloe sensed the sudden awkwardness of the moment. 'I need to sort out a couple of things in the kitchen, then we ought to be on our way,' she declared. She disappeared down the hallway, her recently applied perfume leaving an intriguing aroma jet trail in the air behind her. It was so elusively familiar. Perhaps someone I'd once known had worn that same fragrance?

I was just asking Hope what she'd like to do for the rest of the evening, when a sudden crash and a loud cry came from the room Chloe had disappeared into. Ryan was gone in a blur of expensive dinner suit as he ran into the kitchen. Hope and I weren't far behind him.

Chloe was crouched on the floor, on the edge of a pool of spreading water, which was strewn with large jagged shards of crystal and floating long-stemmed red roses.

What happened? seemed a stupid question, but Ryan asked it anyway.

'I was moving the flowers you bought me, and then … I don't know, perhaps my hand was slippery or something, because for no reason at all I lost my grip on it and the vase slipped out of my hand.'

She had gathered up a handful of broken pieces of glass which glittered like a tiny dangerous mountain on her open palm.

'Hope, stay back,' Chloe said firmly, as her daughter inched further into the room to see what had happened. 'There's glass everywhere.'

'There is,' said Ryan firmly, lifting the pieces from Chloe's hand with no regard for his own safety. 'So step back before you cut yourself, or ruin that pretty dress. *I'll* do this.'

Chloe straightened, but her eyes were on the broken vase, which somehow seemed to have virtually exploded across her tiled kitchen floor. 'That vase was my mother's. She got it as a wedding gift. I can't believe I've broken it.' She looked so close to tears that I found my own eyes welling up. I suppose when you've lost both parents, the mementos you have from them became that much more precious. I was lucky, I thought, I still had both of mine, even if one of them was permanently confused about my identity. Perhaps that was why I found myself unexpectedly stepping up to the plate.

'Tell you what, why don't you *both* just get out of here, and leave me to clear up this mess?'

'Maddie, we couldn't do that,' said Ryan, bending down to resume picking up the shards of glass.

I crouched down beside him and reached for one of the broken pieces. 'I don't mind. Honestly. And I'm more suitably dressed for domestic stuff than either of you. So why don't you both get out of here, or you're going to be late for your party.'

'The cab *is* waiting outside,' Ryan conceded, still looking troubled. Another cab, seven years after the one he and I had shared. For a moment the memory was back; I saw it in his eyes, and he saw it in mine.

'Okay then. Let's go,' he said, taking Chloe's hand and leading her away from her mother's shattered vase.

'You have both of our numbers if you need them,' Chloe

couldn't help adding as Ryan ushered her hastily away. As I carefully cleaned up their kitchen, swabbing every last inch of the floor for any stray shards, I couldn't help but wonder if he'd been hurrying her away for her protection, or his own.

So this is what it feels like to be a mother, I thought exhaustedly. I collapsed onto the lounge sofa that in a different life, with a different turn of the dice, could have been mine.

Hope and I had played an extensive game with the pumpkin house, which I'd like to think wasn't *just* because I happened to be the one who'd given it to her. Every last penny I'd spent on the gift was entirely justified, I thought, as I watched her happily position the tiny carved woodland creatures in the miniature furnished rooms.

Hope had eaten before I arrived, but persuaded me that her mummy often let her have a bedtime snack of milk and biscuits. I knew I was being played, but the novelty of sitting at the table across from her, enjoying her big milky smiles and chocolate-smeared lips was so rewarding I was happy to be hoodwinked.

I'm sure I allowed her to stay up later than her usual bedtime, which she solemnly told me was 'fourteen o'clock'. I grinned at that, admiring this small replica of me for her cheek and ingenuity. We compromised in the end when I persuaded her we could read twice as many bedtime stories if she went upstairs without argument.

Standing in the bathroom, watching Hope's look of deep concentration as she brushed her teeth, I was struck by a feeling of aching poignancy. I looked around the family bathroom, and everywhere there were small sharp darts waiting to wound me. There was the brand of shampoo and deodorant I remembered Ryan favoured, only now they stood on a shelf next to products I neither recognised nor used. On the unit beside the basin was a glass tumbler that held two adult-size toothbrushes, and for some reason they had the power to cut me deepest of all. I tried to focus on my daughter diligently brushing away, but my eyes kept going back to the pink and blue toothbrushes, their bristles touching intimately in the glass. It was strange: I could see the gold ring on her finger; I could watch them disappear out of the house, his arm around her waist, and tell myself that I was fine, I'd moved on. But those two damn toothbrushes had the power to undo me.

Hope raced ahead to her room and I followed, keeping my gaze firmly fixed on the pile of the carpet and away from the adjacent room, whose door was slightly ajar. Stepping over the threshold into the room which the man I was going to marry now shared with his wife crossed a very dangerous line from curious to creepy.

Hope's bedroom was far safer territory. Decorated in pastel shades, it was a proper little girl's paradise, and I spent several moments taking it all in. Painted cartoon characters and cheerful woodland animals covered the walls; not quite good enough to be the work of a professional artist, but far too good to have been done by Ryan, whose drawing skills peaked at stick men with oversized heads. Chloe had created a true fairy-tale room for Hope to play, sleep and dream in, and though I tried my best to swallow it down, I could taste the bitter tang of jealousy, like bile, at the back of my throat. This was the room *I* would have created for her, if only her other mummy hadn't done it before me.

Hope raced over to the bookcase in the corner of her room and plucked a book for me to read. I was rather glad she hadn't asked for the next excerpt from her *Harry Potter* book, because I didn't think I'd be able to say Hagrid's name without visualising Mitch for some time to come. Damn Ryan and his stupid little jibe.

I read until my throat was dry and Hope's eyes were struggling to stay open. I would happily have read to her until dawn, or at least until I heard her parents' key in the front door. Having her snuggled against my side, smelling the clean fragrance of her freshly washed hair, feeling the alien yet weirdly familiar sensation of having her body once again nestled against mine, was the best feeling I'd experienced in a very long time.

Even when I knew she was asleep, I continued to sit on the edge of her bed, mesmerised by the simple pleasure of watching her chest rise and fall. Eventually I forced myself to my feet, carefully levering off the mattress, not wanting to wake her, and yet half hoping that she would. I tiptoed across the oasis of pink carpet and back out into the hallway.

I took one last wistful glance back at Hope's door before heading for the stairs, and almost managed to wake her up after all as my hip collided with a small table positioned against the wall. I reached out to right a silver-framed photograph that had fallen when I'd bumped into the table. Thankfully it wasn't damaged, because frankly there was no way they'd ever have believed I hadn't done that deliberately. I carried it to the top of the stairs, where the light was brighter, and sank slowly down onto the top step, holding the frame away from my body, as if I was carrying dynamite.

Chloe's wedding dress was very different from the one I had chosen. Hers was a simple ivory sheath, full-length but with no embellishments or decoration. Her hair was worn loose, held back from her face by a single slide entwined with gypsophila, or Baby's Breath as it was more commonly known. My mouth twisted in irony.

Ryan looked handsome in a grey suit and tie, although more aged than perhaps he should have done. I traced the outline of his face beneath the glass with my fingertip, looking for . . . I'm not sure what . . . a sign that he wasn't entirely happy? That the bride beside him wasn't the one he'd wanted to spend the rest of his life with? A single tear trickled down my cheek and landed, somewhat poetically, upon his smiling face, which showed no sign of any such emotion. He looked as ecstatically happy as any groom should on his wedding day. His face was tilted towards the smiling bride beside him, and the look of love that shone from his eyes tore the skin from my heart in long jagged rips. Ryan had one arm around Chloe, and in the other he held our daughter. Was it unreasonable to feel hurt that she'd been a flower girl at their wedding? Or that this was how I had discovered that fact, sitting alone at the top of their staircase, crying over a stupid photograph.

I was about to put the frame back where it belonged, when I noticed a face at the back of the crowd of people standing behind the newlyweds on the registry office steps. Half obscured by a tall, broad-shouldered stranger and a woman in a big floppy hat, was a face I knew well and seeing it there felt much more than a shock, it felt like a betrayal. How many more pieces of my life had Chloe silently pilfered from me? The list seemed never-ending: my fiancé, my baby, my own parents and now, unbelievably, standing at the back of the crowd of wedding guests was Ellen, the friend it would appear we also shared.

'I thought you knew.'

'How could I possibly have known?'

Ellen spent longer than necessary meticulously tearing open a small sachet of sugar and stirring it into her coffee. 'I thought that someone might have mentioned it.'

'Perhaps *you* should have mentioned it,' I said, hurt making my voice small and tight.

To be fair, when she raised her head, Ellen didn't deny it, but merely nodded sadly. 'You're right, Maddie. I *should* have told you. But I didn't want to hurt you, any more than you'd already been hurt.'

She looked awkward, her freckles standing out like blemishes against her suddenly pale cheeks. 'During those first three years Ryan was at the hospital every single day.' Ellen smiled fleetingly. 'I think I probably saw more of *your* fiancé than I did of my own at that time. And he began to feel more like a work colleague than a visiting relative – not just to me, but to everyone on the ward,' she explained.

I nodded. Hearing how devoted Ryan had once been had become a double-edged sword, because now I also knew that it hadn't lasted.

'He became a friend,' Ellen said simply.

'A good enough friend to invite you to his wedding?'

There was a fleeting look of guilt on Ellen's face, and suddenly I knew I wasn't going to like whatever it was she was about to say. 'Maddie, Ryan wasn't the one who invited me to the wedding. It was Chloe.'

'Chloe?' My voice was an incredulous whisper. I was the one they'd thought was as good as dead, but she was a living ghost, haunting me at every turn. 'You knew her before she married Ryan?' It felt as if everything was spinning. Up was now down, friend was now foe and truth . . . well, truth didn't seem to exist any more.

'I've known Chloe for years,' Ellen admitted. 'She'd worked at the hospital even longer than I had.'

'Chloe was a nurse?' I asked, genuinely confused. 'I thought she worked in a library?'

Ellen shook her head and took a bite out of her toasted sandwich. My own was growing unappealingly cold on the plate before me. Not surprisingly, I seemed to have lost my appetite.

'Chloe *did* work in a library, but she was also a part-time hospital volunteer.'

Something cold crept into my stomach and squirmed there. 'A volunteer? Doing what?'

'Reading to the patients. She worked mainly on the geriatric ward, but also ...' Her voice trailed away, as if only now did she realise that she was about to say something that might change everything.

'Go on,' I urged, my voice low and thick. 'Where else did Chloe work?'

'On our ward. She was asked by the family to work with one specific patient. She sat with them several times a week, reading, chatting, playing music ... that kind of thing.'

A waitress came to clear away our plates and it seemed like an agonisingly long wait before I could ask the question I already knew the answer to.

'This patient ...' I began. Ellen looked at me and slowly nodded. But somehow it still wouldn't be real until I'd heard the words spoken out loud.

'The patient was me, wasn't it?'

'Yes, Maddie, it was.'

Chapter 15

Chloe

I flopped back onto the airplane seat and waited for my heart to stop feeling as if it was about to explode out of my chest. My breathing was ragged as I turned to look over the top of Hope's head, and met Ryan's eyes. We were lucky to have caught the flight, and if we'd missed it there would have been no one to blame but me. I still couldn't believe that I'd managed to misread the gate number on the boarding pass, and directed us off in completely the wrong direction, with only minutes left until the gate closed.

'Still think you don't need glasses?' Ryan had teased, collapsing onto his own seat with visible relief. I'd smiled, because he thought it was a simple mistake, and I didn't want to ruin the start of our holiday by telling him that the instances of blurred vision in my right eye seemed to be increasing.

Equally worrying was the thought that I might have sub-consciously tried to *make* us miss the plane, to answer the guilt I felt for taking Hope so far away from Maddie, on what would have been their first Christmas together.

'Even if we *hadn't* booked this holiday months before Maddie woke up from her coma, would we really have asked her to join us for Christmas day? Don't you think that would have been weird?' Ryan had reasoned.

'Everything about this is weird,' I'd countered. 'But Christmas is about family, and I don't like the idea of *anyone* spending it alone.'

'I'm sure she'll end up changing her mind and spending it with Bill and Faye,' Ryan had assured me, sliding his arms around my waist and whispering into the curve of my neck. 'I love you for caring, but Maddie's not *your* responsibility,' he'd reminded me gently.

I nodded, and zipped up the case I was packing for our much-anticipated Christmas trip to Lapland. But my ears were ringing with the unspoken end to that sentence, as clearly as if he'd said the words out loud: *She's mine.*

During our six-night stay, we experienced everything the tour brochure had promised us, and more. Bundled up warmly against the sub-zero temperature, each day felt as if we were stepping straight into a quintessential Christmas card. Not surprisingly, Hope fell in love with the reindeers pulling our sleigh, even if disappointingly they *couldn't* actu-ally fly, and then lost her heart to the team of huskies who drove us through a snowy landscape, which was lit by flaming lanterns flickering like beacons in the snow. While the highlight of her stay was the visit to Santa's cabin, my own took place on the final night of our holiday, when Hope was fast asleep in bed.

Ryan and I were snuggled together on the deep comfortable settee before a crackling open fire. Two empty brandy glasses were on the table beside us, the warmth from the alcohol warming us almost as much as the blazing logs. It would have been easy to have drifted off to sleep, limbs entwined around each other, but thankfully we didn't.

Just before midnight, Ryan leapt to his feet, so unexpectedly that I collapsed into the space he'd left behind. 'The lights!' he exclaimed, reaching for my hand and pulling me up beside him. Once upright, he spun me around to face the huge window, where a vague greenish streak was staining the black of the sky. We struggled into our outer clothes so fast that jumpers went on backwards, or inside out, and somehow I managed to put my snow boots on the wrong feet, wasting several precious minutes having to sort them out.

'Hurry,' urged Ryan as he waited by the door, his face wearing an identical expression of excitement to the one I'd seen hours earlier on Hope's, when she'd met Santa Claus.

I was worried we'd taken too long, that the lights in the sky would have grown impatient and cut short their spectacular show, but they were still there, as if they'd been waiting for us. Hand in hand we ran towards the lake and then turned back to stare at the sky above our darkened cabin, to see something so incredible, I knew the memory of it would stay with me for the rest of my life.

Neither of us spoke as we stood awestruck watching the dancing green curtain of the aurora borealis undulate and ripple above us. The night was silent, and there was something special in the air, and it wasn't just the northern lights. Without either of us saying a word, I knew we were both remembering another night sky two and a half years earlier.

It was the night of the meteor shower, and it was also the night when everything had first begun to change. Ryan and I were in his garden on that warm summer evening, a blanket spread upon the lawn, so we'd get the best view of the night sky. I never could decide if the glowing streaks painting the velvet blackness above us made it happen, or whether it was destined to have happened anyway; as unstoppable as a comet.

We watched for hours, speaking in hushed whispers, as though terrified of breaking the spell. And when Ryan's hand had hesitantly crossed the expanse of blanket between us to reach for mine, my fingers were unfurled, waiting for him. It would be weeks before we kissed, even longer before he finally took me to his bed, but for both of us, that was the night when we realised that something we'd never engineered or planned had happened. We had fallen in love.

Maddie

I hadn't expected to spend Christmas with my landlord; in fact there was probably something written in my tenancy agreement specifically advising against it. But then a lot of things happening in my life lately weren't exactly what I'd planned or expected either. I was learning to go with the flow.

I'd had other options for Christmas. I could have spent it with my parents at the care home, or with Ellen at the hospital, but I'd turned them both down as tactfully as I could. 'I'm looking forward to spending the day in my pyjamas, watching *White Christmas* on the telly and chilling out,' I'd told my father.

With Ellen, I'd been more honest. 'Don't take this the wrong way,' I'd said, hugging her tightly as we said goodbye on the pavement outside the café where we'd met for lunch. 'But I've spent more than enough Christmases at the hospital, so I might just pass on joining you, if you don't mind.'

'Okay,' she'd replied, scrutinising me carefully; more nurse than friend, I suspected, by the concerned look in her eyes. 'But if you change your mind, promise you'll let me know.' She hugged me fiercely one last time and whispered the words she used to say every single time she left my hospital room. 'You stay awake now, Miracle Girl.'

The words were poignant, and my smile couldn't entirely dispel the memory of those early terrifying weeks, when the doctors weren't able to assure me that I wouldn't slip back

355

into a coma. How could they, when there'd never been a case like mine before?

'Always,' I assured her, the reply falling from my lips like the chorus of a familiar song. It was what I always said.

There were things I'd obviously forgotten during the six years I'd been in a coma, and the fact that supermarket shopping on Christmas Eve is *always* a bad idea was clearly one of them. The lack of trolleys should have warned me it was going to be busy, but I continued into the store anyway, carried on a tide of fellow shoppers.

Noddy Holder was screeching out from the overhead speakers, informing me (in case I hadn't figured it out for myself) '*It's Christmaaaaas*'. I paused inside the doorway and smiled. It was my first Christmas for seven years, and it was good to know that some things hadn't changed.

Like a salmon making its way upstream, I negotiated my way to the frozen goods aisle, past shoppers with trolleys loaded so high they could scarcely see over the top of them. I was leaning into a deep freezer cabinet, trying to haul out the only remaining frozen turkey that wasn't the size of a small emu, when someone's trolley collided into my legs and I felt my feet lift off the floor. In the brief seconds before Mitch pulled me back, I was already visualising the headlines: *Coma girl breaks neck after freak freezer accident.* Fortunately the timely arrival of my landlord saved me from featuring once again in the local newspaper.

The five bruises I felt sure I would find where his fingers

had bitten into my shoulder and saved me from falling, were a small price to pay for retaining my dignity. Being unexpectedly inverted into a freezer had brought twin spots of colour to my cheeks, which stayed there as I repeatedly thanked Mitch.

'No problem,' he said easily, glaring at the offender who'd barged into me and who was already at the other end of the aisle, presumably looking for new shoppers to mow down.

'I wasn't expecting it to be so busy,' I said, flustered. 'I guess this is what happens when you leave your shopping to the last minute.'

'I'm a man, I know no other way,' said Mitch with a smile.

I laughed, noticing for the first time his loaded trolley which held not only food but also a remote-control car and several hi-tech toys.

'Looks like Sam's going to have a great Christmas,' I said with a smile.

Mitch gave a disarming shrug, and for a second he looked more like a kid than a father himself. Admittedly, a very big kid. 'I hope so. But I'm not actually seeing him tomorrow. It's not my turn this year.'

Was that what made the offer jump straight to my lips, totally bypassing my brain for a quick censor before being voiced? There were surely thousands of parents in similar situations all over the world, but the common ground Mitch and I stood on seemed to suddenly have constructed a bridge between us.

'I'm sure you probably have something arranged, but if

you don't, do you feel like spending Christmas day with me?'

I hadn't planned on inviting him, and I certainly hadn't expected him to say yes, but somehow both of those things happened, and by the time I left the supermarket and headed back home, my plans for a solitary Christmas day had been totally rewritten.

For two people who didn't know each other particularly well, we spent a remarkably comfortable day together. He'd arrived on time, bringing wine, more food than we could possibly manage to eat, and an enormous bunch of out-of-season sunflowers. 'A friend of mine owns a nursery; he grows them in greenhouses all year round for hotels and weddings, that kind of thing. I thought if we're having a non-traditional Christmas, I should bring non-traditional flowers.'

I smiled at the blooms, whose cheerfulness always seemed like an instant antidote to gloom or despondency. I couldn't think of a better flower for him to have brought. He found a vase in his grandmother's kitchen when I couldn't locate one, and while I arranged the sunflowers in the tall crystal container my curiosity got the better of me.

'Is it weird for you, seeing me here in this flat, instead of your grandmother?'

Mitch was putting the cheeses he'd brought into the fridge, and perhaps his reply was a bit slow in coming, and when it did his voice was slightly gruff. Oh God, I was like cyanide to this man; if I wasn't making him blush furiously, I was choking him with emotion.

'No. It's not weird at all. It's comforting in a way, especially as you've kept the place pretty much as she had it. It's given the flat continuity, but also breathed new life into it. And I think she'd be happy about that.' He paused for a moment. 'She'd have liked you, you know,' he added with quiet certainty.

Without bothering to consider whether or not I should, I leant across the worktop and laid my hand lightly on the thick breadth of his forearm. 'I'm sure it would have been mutual.'

We steered a careful path that day around all possible minefield topics. Mitch never spoke of his ex-wife, or their divorce; and I stayed away from all mention of Ryan or my accident, as though it was conversational Kryptonite. And yet we never ran out of things to talk about. It helped having worked for the same company for several years, but as I listened to Mitch's deep rumbling voice talking about the day-to-day trivia of the office which had once been such an important part of my life, a realisation that had been crystallising for some time now finally became an undeniable truth. I was done with that kind of job. Whatever I did next would have to be something completely different, something more meaningful. That's the thing about coming back from the dead, which was how I still felt about my awakening. It made you realise that there had to be a reason you were here. A reason you'd come back. I might not know what that was yet, but I was sure that sooner or later it would reveal itself.

*

'Don't cross anywhere except at the zebra crossing,' said Chloe worriedly, as she tucked a warm scarf securely around Hope's neck.

'Maddie knows how to cross a road,' said Ryan reasonably, leaning back against the wall with an easy smile.

Chloe straightened from double-checking that Hope's coat was buttoned up, and her eyebrows rose meaningfully.

Okay, fair enough. She had me there. My experience with road-crossing skills wasn't exactly a shining advertisement for the Green Cross Code.

'We'll *only* cross at zebras,' I assured Chloe, 'and we won't walk by the edge of the pavement, and we won't—'

'Okay. I'm sorry,' cut in Chloe, sounding apologetic, yet still worried. Clearly she wasn't used to handing over the care of her daughter to someone else, outside the house.

'I'll be careful,' I reiterated. 'I'll look after her as if she was ...' my voice trailed off as all three adults exchanged an identical and uncomfortable look. 'I'll look after her,' I finished instead.

There was a strangely liberating feeling in closing the front door and walking down the path to the pavement with Hope's hand held firmly in mine. I felt like a prisoner on the day when the jail gates are finally flung open and freedom stretches before you like an unfurled carpet. We could go anywhere, my daughter and me. We could jump in a car, drive to the coast, drive to an airport, we could— I snapped off that train of thought before it got truly dangerous. And it was all totally ridiculous anyway. I wasn't going to kidnap my own child and take her away from the only home she had ever known. Plus, on a purely practical level, I didn't actually have a car, and although my doctors had now cleared me to drive, I didn't yet have my licence back. Far better to stick to the original plan, and spend the afternoon at the park, I decided.

Nevertheless, sooner rather than later, we were all going to have to sit down together and figure out something a bit more structured with regard to the amount of time I could spend with Hope. I hadn't liked the way it had felt as if I was begging for crumbs at their table when I'd phoned Ryan to ask if I could see Hope today.

'I'd like to give her my Christmas present, before it seems like an afterthought,' I'd said. I realised how anxious I was by the way I kept shifting my weight from one foot to the other as I stood staring unseeingly out of my kitchen window, waiting for Ryan's reply. *And you did just have her exclusively for the last six days*, I wanted to add, when the silence at the end of the line grew uncomfortably long. *Actually, you've had her exclusively for the last six years*, an advocating devil corrected in my head. I was bracing myself for his refusal, so he took the wind completely out of my sails when he eventually replied: 'Yes. That should be absolutely fine. How about this afternoon?'

The park had seemed like an excellent choice, and Hope skipped happily along beside me as we walked the twenty minutes or so to reach our destination. I smiled as she chattered enthusiastically about her recent holiday, the favourite bits of which seemed to involve either reindeers or huskies. Animals were clearly a passion with her, and I wondered how Mitch felt about his tenants keeping a pet. *I could ask*, I thought, already knowing it was a bad idea. I shouldn't be trying to buy Hope's affections, or attempting to lure her into visiting me. When the time was right, she should *want* to come and stay with me, regardless of how many furry creatures shared my home.

I let Hope decide where we should head first, and she didn't hesitate. 'Swings!' she cried gleefully, pulling me by the hand and tugging me across the grass, which was frosted with a thin crust of snow. I committed my first faux-pas when I tried to steer Hope towards the enclosed toddler-seat swings.

'I haven't been in those for *years*,' she said, with a disparaging sigh, and for a moment I caught a brief glimpse of the petulant teenager she might one day become. My grin was difficult to stifle, because she'd looked and sounded exactly like me. My mother had once said it would serve me right if I had a stroppy teenager of my own one day, and I wondered if she was going to get her wish, and how sad it was that I wouldn't be able to share that joke with her.

'I'm sorry, Pumpkin. Of course you're too grown-up for those.' Hope raced across the artificial safety surface and leapt like a tiny stuntwoman onto the wooden seat of a far more substantial two-swing set. I watched her settle herself onto the plank and curl her hands around the thick metal chains. Before I had a chance to ask whether she'd like me to push her, she was kicking out her legs and swinging forward to gain momentum.

I watched her for a moment, but she seemed utterly competent, so I gave a shrug, dropped my handbag on the ground and climbed onto the vacant swing beside her.

'Maddieeeee!' Hope exclaimed delightedly, as she watched me launch myself into the air, my long legs swallowing up, and then overtaking her head start. 'You're swinging. Are grown-ups allowed to do that?'

To be honest, that thought hadn't even occurred to me. There was probably a stuffy council notice nailed to the play area railings, prohibiting adults from climbing all over the apparatus. I shrugged my shoulders mischievously, which made me wobble slightly on my trajectory through the air.

'I don't know, kiddo. But I can't see anyone around who's going to tell me off, so let's not worry about it,' I replied, aware I was probably straying as far away from Chloe's sensible parenting guidelines as it was possible to get.

'When Mummy brings me here she just stands on the side and watches, or sometimes she pushes me,' declared Hope as we passed each other through the air. 'But this is *much* more fun.'

I was smiling, and trying very hard not to mentally lick my finger and mark down a point for me. It wasn't a contest, Mitch had said, and he was right. 'You're much more fun than a regular mummy,' Hope declared, with all the honesty and innocence of youth. To hell with it, I thought, metaphorically licking that finger and noting down my score anyway.

My legs were trembling from the unaccustomed activity by the time Hope eventually grew tired of the swings. Heidi should introduce *this* into her rehab exercises, I thought as I followed Hope on shaky legs towards a tall climbing frame with a slide on the side. This time I decided not to join her, worried that the slide's narrow trough was designed for bottoms far younger – and slimmer – than mine. I liked firemen as much as the next girl, but I had no desire to meet a bunch of them while they were cutting me free from a piece of playground equipment.

A little boy, around Hope's age, joined her on the frame, and for a while I was happy to watch them tirelessly clamber and race over the structure, small hands and feet scrabbling like mountain goats over the rungs. But as much as I wanted to be the cool and nonchalant grown-up, some of Chloe's over-protectiveness must have rubbed off on me. *Was that frame too high for her? Was she too young to be on it?* And shouldn't I have asked those questions *before* I allowed her to climb on it?

'They're fearless at that age, aren't they?' said a woman a year or so younger than me, who I assumed was the little boy's mum. 'But I'd really rather not spend *another* afternoon at Accident and Emergency,' she said, sounding almost resigned.

My eyes widened in alarm. Hope had now reached the topmost rungs and was attempting to swing monkey-style, using only one hand to support her weight.

'Hope,' I called out anxiously, and perhaps it was the

sharpness of my tone, or perhaps she was always going to find it impossible to support her body with one tiny hand. She twisted to face me and in that second her equilibrium shifted and the next moment she wasn't on the frame at all, but was tumbling down onto the ground some two metres below.

Her howl of pain split the air, and I felt it ricocheting around the play area like an echo of blame as I raced across the distance to reach her. She was screaming so loudly I was convinced that at the very least bones had to be broken. 'Don't move,' I cried out as I threw myself onto the ground beside her. Because that's what you're meant to say to casualties when they're injured, isn't it?

I doubt Hope heard me over the impressive decibel level she was currently achieving with her cries, for she drew both her legs up protectively towards her body. The fact that everything appeared to move the way it was supposed to was only a small consolation when I saw the ripped tights and the blood pouring freely from two nastily grazed knees. Despite the safety surface, Hope had somehow managed to fall onto an earthy patch of frozen ground, and particles of dirt peppered the twin wounds like buckshot. The guilt smacked me like punch. This was my watch. This was my chance to show I knew how to look after her, and I'd failed miserably.

'It's okay,' I said, sounding more distraught than she did as I scrabbled in the depths of my handbag. 'Let's find something to get you cleaned up.' I rummaged frantically among the detritus of my bag, as though it was a high-stakes lucky-dip, but all I could find were a couple of used tissues and some panty liners. Even my *handbag* didn't know how to be a proper mother.

The other mum knew no such deficiency, and she quickly passed me antiseptic wipes and a couple of oversized plasters from her own bag. My fingers trembled as I ripped open the packets, thanking her without looking up.

'No worries. It's every mother's survival kit,' she said with a smile.

Except mine, I added silently, head bent low as I concentrated on cleaning up Hope's injuries. Scared of hurting her further, I just covered the grazes with the wipes and tucked them into the gaping holes in her tights, watching with alarm as the squares turned from white to pink, and then red with worrying speed.

'I want to go home. I don't want to be with you. I want my real mummy,' Hope wailed miserably, and I felt rather than saw the woman beside me stiffen and grip her own little boy's hand more securely. Her expression of concern was replaced with one of immediate suspicion.

'I'm her cousin,' I said, answering the unspoken question in the stranger's eyes, as I rose to my feet with Hope cradled in my arms. I hated the way Ryan's lie suddenly felt more comfortable than the truth.

'Come on, Pumpkin, let's get you back home,' I said to my daughter, who was now snivelling quietly against my shoulder. 'Let's get you back to your mummy.'

*

I'd seen Ryan angry before. Well, I thought I had. There was the time when I reversed his brand-new car straight into a concrete bollard, marring the perfect paintwork. Then there was the time when I'd somehow muddled up our travel plans, and we'd gone to the wrong London airport, and missed our flight. Or the time I'd put my new red top in a wash load of his white shirts. But, despite whatever I might have thought at the time, *that* hadn't been angry. *This* was angry.

I didn't say a word. I just let his words lash me like a whip. I flinched at some of them, how could I not. I caught *irresponsible* at least three times; *inept* made an appearance twice, but *negligent* was the one that cut the deepest.

It didn't seem to matter that Hope was now desperately trying to convince her father that it was all her fault, because he wasn't listening. He wasn't ever going to forgive me for this, and that was fine, because neither was I. And I couldn't deny the truth. I shouldn't have allowed Hope to climb like that. For God's sake, she could have fallen and broken her neck. The thought made me feel physically sick.

'Please don't tell Maddie off,' said Hope, from the safety of her position, fixed – as if by glue – to Chloe's hip. It was where she'd been from the moment her parents had opened the front door and found two figures with long dark hair and tear-stained ashen faces standing on the step.

'I shouldn't have gone on the big children's frame.'

'No, you shouldn't,' agreed Chloe, the hand stroking her daughter's head, soothing the sting from her words.

'You know we don't let you go on it. But Maddie didn't know that.'

Ryan was shaking his head, as though it was all too much to take in. 'Well, one thing's for certain. It won't happen again. You're clearly not ready to take Hope out on your own.'

'Daddy,' pleaded Hope, looking very much as if she was about to start crying again.

'Ryan, please,' I began, not knowing how on earth I could get him to trust me, when *I* didn't even trust me now.

But the words which finally pierced the red mist of his anger were surprisingly Chloe's, not mine. 'Come on now. Let's keep this all in proportion.'

'What? Are you serious?' Ryan said, turning to his wife, who seemed to suddenly grow in stature as I watched her shoulders pull back when she answered him.

'Kids do this kind of stuff all the time. They run off, they go where they're not meant to go. It doesn't make you a negligent parent.'

'Well it doesn't make you a terrific one either,' countered Ryan.

Chloe was quiet for a long moment, as though considering. 'Nor does dropping her, when she's only a baby,' she said softly.

I felt as if I'd walked into a play that had started several scenes ago, and I had no idea what was going on.

'She fell onto the bed.' Ryan's voice was so quiet, I could hardly hear him.

'Or the time you shut her finger in the cupboard door?'

'What?' Ryan sounded startled to hear his parenting misdemeanours being presented as evidence. 'What has that got to do with anything?'

'Or taking off the training wheels on her bike, when she wasn't ready?'

'All kids graze their knees when they're learning to ride.'

'Exactly,' said Chloe, as though she was an attorney in a court of law, who'd just made a very valid closing argument. 'We *all* make mistakes when we're learning to be a parent.' Her eyes went from Ryan to me. 'We've all done it.'

There was something in Chloe's eyes that I'd never expected to see there. If I had to name it, it would be called kindness. 'Maddie's coming to all this very late in the day. The mistakes you and I made are years in the past. Maddie's playing catch-up, and she's going to make a few of her own. The important thing here,' she paused and her eyes went to her husband's, and for a moment I felt totally excluded by the bond they shared. 'The important thing is no one was seriously hurt. Apart from a few grazes, everything is fine.'

She turned away from the man we'd both fallen in love with, to face me. 'Hope rolled off the settee when I was changing her nappy once. I'd only looked away for a second to grab the wipes, but when I looked back she was staring up at me from the carpet. Then, when she was three, I lost her in a busy shopping centre. I was running up and down the stairs like a lunatic. They'd even put a message out on the tannoy when a security guard came up to me, carrying

369

her in his arms.' She looked at me for a very long moment. 'We *all* do it. And we all beat ourselves up about it. But the important thing is that we all *learn* from it.'

I nodded fiercely as though taking an oath.

'Then let's put today behind us, and move on,' Chloe said firmly.

Chloe

He waited much longer than I'd been expecting, almost five hours in fact, to raise the subject once more. I was in the kitchen, loading the final items into the dishwasher. I heard the click of the kitchen door and slowly straightened. The overhead lights were switched off, leaving the room bathed in a soft glow from the cabinet lights.

'Is she asleep?' I asked.

Ryan nodded and came to stand opposite me, leaning back against the worktop. There was an unreadable expression on his face.

'Hope never fell off the settee when you were changing her.'

It might have sounded like an odd way to begin a conversation, but I'd been expecting it. I stared into the blue eyes I loved so much, and said nothing.

'You never lost her at the shopping centre. I *know* you didn't.'

The room seemed very silent, with only the quiet hum of the dishwasher as a backdrop to our conversation. I didn't bother denying his accusations. We knew each other too well.

'And your point is?'

Ryan pushed away from the worktop and crossed to where I stood. His arms slid around me slowly, as if it was the very first time he'd ever held me.

'The point is . . .' he said, his voice and his head lowering almost simultaneously, '. . . the point is, is that I love you for lying. I love you for trying to make her feel better. I love you for *not* taking my side. I love you for making me see I was wrong.' His mouth was so close to mine, I could feel the warmth of his words as his breath brushed my lips. 'I just love you,' he said finally, before his mouth found mine and words at last became redundant.

Chapter 16

Chloe

She came running up the road towards us, her long dark hair flying out behind her like a streamer. I saw several men turn their heads – and a couple of women too. Maddie didn't appear to notice. I guessed it had always been that way for her.

'I'm so sorry I'm late, I must have misread the bus timetable.'

'We've been waiting *ages*,' grumbled Hope. It was one of those parenting moments when you really regret telling them they should always be truthful.

Maddie dropped lithely down to Hope's level and kissed her cheek. 'I'm sorry, Pumpkin,' she said, lightly touching Hope's face with her fingertips. 'Oh, you *are* cold.'

Hope shook her head, making her own hair fly in an

action replay of her mother's. 'No. Not really. It's not as cold as Lapland,' she declared, smiling back into Maddie's face. The grizzly child who'd moaned that she was turning into an icicle appeared to have suddenly melted away. Maddie rose smoothly up to my height, apparently unaware that she'd once again worked her own particular brand of magic.

'I'm sorry. I should have offered to pick you up.'

A fleeting look of relief flashed over her features that I'd done nothing of the sort. I had to admit, I felt the same way.

'I'll be driving again soon, anyway,' Maddie said. 'The doctors gave me the go-ahead at my last check-up.'

My smile was neutral, hiding the fact I was a long way from comfortable about the idea of Hope being in a car with her. This letting-go-and-sharing business was turning out to be a lot harder than I had expected.

'So, new school shoes?' Maddie declared excitedly, directing her attention back to Hope. 'That's fun. I love shoe shopping.'

I couldn't help thinking that Maddie's enthusiasm was probably borne from the type of expedition where you ended up with a pair of Jimmy Choos or Louboutins rather than Clarks' finest, but her excitement must have been infectious, because Hope jumped up and down gleefully. Maddie turned to me as we walked three abreast towards the shoe shop. 'It was so nice of you to ask me to come with you today, Chloe.'

I shrugged as though it was nothing, which I don't think

either of us believed. Ryan had certainly been surprised, and had stared at me incredulously when I'd suggested it.

'You're volunteering to spend time alone with Maddie? When I'm not with you?'

I carried on folding up the pile of laundry that was still warm from the dryer. 'I've spent *hundreds* of hours with Maddie when you weren't there,' I reminded him.

'Not when she was conscious,' he replied. It was a checkmate comment and I had no rebuttal.

'It's an hour or two out of my day. I think I can be the bigger person here and ask her to join us. She might not even want to come,' I'd replied. But of course Maddie had said yes, so enthusiastically it made me feel guilty how I'd almost changed my mind right up to the moment when I'd dialled her number.

The shoe shop was warm and smelled of leather, with an undertone of sweaty feet. Hope raced ahead as we climbed the stairs to the children's department and by the time we joined her, she was already staring lovingly at a shelf of sequinned party shoes.

'These are so pretty, like Cinderella shoes,' she cried, touching the glittering footwear reverently as if they were treasure.

'They're lovely,' Maddie agreed, before catching the subtle shake of my head. 'But I bet there are some even *nicer* ones if we keep looking.'

I gave an imperceptible nod of thanks and was rewarded with a smile that took me by surprise, and not just because it looked so much like Hope's. There was something in it that for a moment made me forget that this woman could so easily steal everything precious in the world away from me. Ryan had once told me, long before he and I got together, that Maddie could charm just about anyone with her smile. People were drawn to her, they always had been, he'd said. I'd dismissed his words as the exaggeration of a man mourning the woman he loved, but today, on the receiving end of that smile, I could see he'd spoken the truth.

I turned away from her, momentarily unsettled. 'How about these, Hope?' I asked, pulling a pair of Mary Janes from the shelf.

'Yuck,' declared Hope.

Maddie's eyebrows rose. Perhaps she'd not seen this side of her daughter before. Maybe inviting her along wasn't so foolish or crazy after all.

'These, then?' I suggested. Hope pulled the kind of face she usually reserved for bad-tasting medicine. But before she had a chance to kick them to the kerb, Maddie piped up.

'Oh they're lovely. I had a pair just like them when I was your age.'

Ten minutes later I was passing the assistant my credit card, still dumbfounded at how easy it had been. It was yet another aspect of 'the Maddie effect'.

'I may have to rope you in on all of our shopping trips,' I said, taking the carrier bag from the young assistant.

'I really hope you do,' said Maddie, with such open longing that I instantly felt bad, because I'd only been joking.

As we made our way towards the exit, a woman in a

smart black dress, who I took to be the store manager, smiled warmly at us.

'Did you find a pair of shoes you and your mummy liked?' she asked Hope.

'Which mummy do you mean?' said Hope, looking first up at me and then at Maddie. 'I have two,' she said proudly.

The coffee shop was warm and welcoming, and although I was going to say no when Maddie suggested it, I somehow found myself agreeing to go.

'They have muffins there as big as your head,' she told Hope, which was an exciting enough prospect to delight any six-year-old, and mine was no exception. *Ours* was no exception, I mentally corrected.

'I think that store manager might have thought we were a couple,' I said, taking a small sip from the caramel latte in front of me.

'No? *Really*?' said Maddie, blinking in surprise. I saw her mentally replaying the conversation and then the amusement which danced in her eyes and curled her lips. 'Ryan would find that hilarious,' she said, and the smile I gave was suddenly much harder to maintain. Because she was absolutely right. Ryan *would* find it funny, and it was disconcerting when you found yourself face-to-face with a woman who knew your husband as well as you did. Possibly better.

I glanced over at Hope, who was busily devouring an enormous chocolate muffin. She wasn't listening to our conversation. 'He felt bad about the things he said the other day, after Hope fell off the climbing frame.'

The humour slid off Maddie's face as though it had never been there. 'Did he? I'm not so sure.'

'He's always been very protective of her,' I said, my face softening as I glanced over at Hope, who was now creating chocolate cake crumb mountains on her plate. 'He practically beat up a photographer who'd got into your room soon after Hope was born.'

Why did I tell you that? I thought, as I watched my words find a home within her. Was I *trying* to make her love him all over again?

'That doesn't sound like him.'

'He overcompensates, even now. Back then he was worried about all the things Hope would miss out on by having only one parent.'

Maddie looked away across the busy coffee shop for a long moment. When she turned back to face me, her eyes were bright with tears I knew she wouldn't allow to spill.

'But Hope didn't miss out in the end, did she? You've been in her life since she was a baby. So in fact she's always had *two* parents.'

I swallowed both my coffee and my pride. 'And now she has three,' I said quietly.

We turned and looked at the child we both so obviously loved.

'Yes, she does,' agreed Maddie softly.

*

Maddie picked up the bill while I was taking Hope to the toilet, and refused to take anything for our share. Not that I'd have known what our portion of the bill was, because although it was sitting on a saucer right in front of me, the numbers were indistinguishable blurs on the paper. Perhaps that was why, when we walked along the high street and found ourselves outside the opticians, I made a sudden snap decision.

'Would you mind waiting out here with Hope for a moment while I go in and make an appointment? I've been meaning to get my eyes checked for a while now.'

'Sure, no problem,' said Maddie easily, taking Hope's hand the very second I released it. The incident in the park had clearly left its mark on her.

'Can I help you?' asked a cheery-faced redhead behind the optician's counter.

'I'd like to make an appointment for a sight test, please,' I said, glancing back over my shoulder where I could see Maddie and Hope on the pavement outside, chatting animatedly. 'I've been having a bit of a problem with my eyes.'

The girl behind the counter rattled something into the computer in front of her, and then smiled at whatever she was reading on the screen. 'Hey. You're in luck. We had a last-minute cancellation this morning. So the optician could fit you in right now, if you like.'

'Are you sure you don't mind? I don't know how long I'll

be. Forty-five minutes, maybe? Possibly longer, if I end up needing to choose some frames.'

'Take as long as you need,' said Maddie, obviously delighted to be gaining some unexpected time alone with Hope. 'I think there's a pet shop down the road, so maybe Hope and I can go there and buy that kitten of hers some new toys.'

I watched them head off down the road, Hope's hand practically super-glued to Maddie's. Sharing my daughter was hard, but I would learn how to do it, for Ryan, for Hope and even for Maddie. It wasn't the worst thing to happen in my life, I thought, never for a moment thinking that the very first worst thing was a great deal closer than I knew.

'Okay, Mrs Turner, if you could just lean forward and look at the green cross for me.'

I dutifully peered into the aperture on the machine, while Mr Ingram the optician stared at a monitor. The eye exam was taking far longer than I'd thought, and we hadn't yet got to the bit where I'd read letters off a chart, which was all I'd been expecting. I should have realised when I saw the consultation room crammed with state-of-the-art diagnostic equipment that eye tests had moved on a lot since I'd last had one.

The room was quiet except for the sound of the optician's slightly stertorous breathing. 'And now the left eye.'

Nobody could accuse this man of not being thorough, I

thought, as I saw him draw his chair closer to the screen, as though *he* was the one having trouble with his vision instead of me. I almost giggled at that, but suddenly there was something in his voice that sucked the humour from me like a vacuum.

'And once more with the right.' He stared unblinkingly at the screen and I knew, even before he rolled back his seat to look at me, that something was wrong.

'Is anything the matter?' I asked in a voice that didn't sound like mine at all.

'How long is it that you've been having problems with your vision in this eye?'

It was a reasonable question and shouldn't have alarmed me, but the small muscle twitching revealingly at the corner of his eye did. His foot was also jiggling up and down, performing a stationary tap dance against the metal frame of his chair.

'A few months, I suppose,' I answered, trying to quell an instinctive wave of panic that was rising up like nausea within me. 'Is anything the matter?' I asked again.

'I'm sure it's nothing,' Mr Ingram began. *That's* when I knew that whatever it was he'd seen on the screen, it was definitely *not* nothing. This man should never cheat on his wife, play poker, or try to evade his taxes, I thought, because he was an absolutely appalling liar.

'What's causing my blurred vision?'

Instead of answering me, Mr Ingram swivelled the monitor around to reveal a screenshot of the image he'd been looking at on the machine, which according to the plate on its side scanned optical coherence tomography. I had no idea what that was.

'This area here,' he said, pointing one long thin finger to a section of the frozen image, 'is a great deal . . . lighter . . . than we would expect to see on an OCT. I'd like to ask one of my colleagues to have a look at it later on today.'

'Can't they look now?' my voice was full of the fear I could taste at the back of my throat.

'I'm afraid he's out for a few hours, but as soon as he returns I'll share this with him and give you a call.' He looked down at his notes to check my phone number was on them.

'Can't you at least tell me what you think might be wrong?'

'I'd rather not, until I'm sure. I wouldn't want to worry you unnecessarily.'

He was already way too late on that score.

'Was everything all right?' asked Maddie, as I joined her and Hope on the pavement.

'Fine,' I lied, far more convincingly than the optician had been able to do.

'Do you need glasses, Mummy?' asked Hope. I bent down and kissed the top of her head, closing my eyes tightly like a child hiding from something scary. When I opened them I saw Maddie studying me curiously.

'No, no glasses for me,' I said with forced cheerfulness.

'My eyes are fine.' The lies were piling up so high, I soon wouldn't be able to see over the top of them.

Good manners made me offer to drive Maddie home; good sense made her decline. 'Be sure to tell me what Elsa thinks of those new toys,' she said, enfolding Hope in a long hug.

'When will I see you again?' Hope asked, taking the bulging pet shop bag from Maddie's hands.

'Soon,' her mother promised.

Sooner than either of us expected, as it turned out.

The phone rang when I was chopping onions, which meant there were already tears running down my cheeks long before the optician got to deliver his message.

'I don't want you to worry,' he said, as Ryan walked into the kitchen. He looked instantly concerned at the tears coursing down my face.

'What's wrong?' he mouthed. In answer I pointed at the chopping board and the pile of diced onions waiting to go into our bolognaise sauce.

He smiled, immediately relieved, grabbed a beer from the fridge and headed back towards the lounge. I waited until I was sure he couldn't hear me before continuing with the call. 'I'm sorry. What were you saying?'

'I've spoken to your GP and also to a friend of mine who's a consultant at Queen Mary's. He's moved some appointments around, and you're lucky, Mrs Turner, they can see you tomorrow.'

I felt a great many emotions as I shakily noted down the name of the doctor and where I should go on arrival at the neurology department the following day, but *lucky* certainly wasn't one of them.

'Who was that on the phone?'

I twirled the long strands of spaghetti round and round on my spoon. So far I'd done a pretty good job of simply repositioning it from one side of my plate to the other.

'When?' I asked, buying for time.

'Earlier on. When you were cooking.'

I delayed my answer by lifting the spoon of pasta to my lips. Tonight I had no stomach for what was usually one of my favourite dishes. I slid the spoon into my mouth and somehow managed not to gag as I swallowed what felt like a mouthful of slithering worms.

'Just one of the school mums. Why do you ask?'

I didn't feel so guilty about this lie, because I could justify why I was telling it. I was protecting him. Surprisingly, Ryan was the one who suddenly looked uncomfortable.

'I wondered if it might have been Maddie, that's all.' Strangely I welcomed the shard of jealousy that stabbed my heart. It stopped me thinking about the hospital appointment and what I already feared the tests would find. That's the problem with the internet. It's all too easy to rattle in your symptoms and self-diagnose. And you never consider going for the innocuous or innocent illnesses. Armed with not a single jot of medical knowledge, you always go straight for the very worst, scariest diagnosis possible. It was what I'd done as soon as we'd returned home.

'Why would you think it was Maddie calling?'

Ryan looked even more uncomfortable. 'I don't know. You had a kind of look on your face that you only seem to get . . .' The hole he was digging himself into was going to be impossible to climb out of, so he stopped trying.

'No. Like I said, it was one of the mums from school. More spaghetti, anyone?'

Hospitals are familiar to me. I feel at home there. I like the smell, the noise, the constant buzz of everyone moving with a purpose. This used to be a large part of my world. So walking through the automatic doors and feeling my heart pound – not just in my chest, but all the way up to my throat; and feeling my stomach churn, even though I hadn't touched a single mouthful of breakfast that morning, was both unexpected and unsettling.

My steps were slow and hesitant as I scanned the overhead signs. I felt small and lost, and suddenly very much alone. Why hadn't I told Ryan I was coming here today? There had been time and opportunity. The day had begun like a thousand others before it: he showered, I showered; I woke Hope; together Ryan and I made breakfast while I packed Hope's lunch and fed her kitten. I was busy, but no more so than on any other day.

When Ryan came quietly up behind me and stealthily swiped the slice of toast I was probably never going to eat from my plate, I could have turned my head and whispered into his ear. When he poured me my morning coffee and passed me the cup with a tender smile, *that* could have been the time to speak. And even if I'd missed every one of those opportunities, when he'd casually asked: 'And what are you doing today, Mrs Turner?' that was when I should have shared the truth with him. But instead I'd feigned a casual shrug, not easy with the crushing weight of the lie sitting across my shoulders like a yoke. 'Nothing much,' I'd said. 'A few errands, that's all.'

And now here I was, on the one and only errand I had to complete today. Too confused by the signs to work out where to go, I asked at the information desk for directions. My heels clicked noisily as I walked along the hospital corridors, passing numerous clinics, many of which I'd much rather be visiting than the one I was heading for. Dermatology – that would be all right, I could cope with a rash or two. Allergy Clinic – I would just buy more tissues. Obesity clinic – I could probably do with losing a pound or two. Instead, my feet took me past all of those, until I arrived at a set of double doors that led to a department with not just one name, but many: Neurosciences; Neuro Critical Care Unit; Neuro Surgery.

I swallowed, but my mouth was so dry, even that didn't feel normal.

'Good morning. Can I help you?' The receptionist was young and smiley; her voice was the sing-song chant airline check-in staff have in films, but rarely in real life.

'Hello. My name is Chloe Turner and I've—'

'Ah, Mrs Turner, good. We've been expecting you.' She reached for a clipboard, on which I saw a patient information sheet bearing my name. I should have felt heartened by the efficiency. I should be feeling grateful for the wheels that had turned, and stops that had been pulled out, to get me this early appointment. Bizarrely, I realised I would far rather have been left waiting for hours to be seen, or sent back home because a patient with a case more urgent than mine required treatment. As I followed a nurse down the hallway to an examination room, I realised sadly that today that patient was probably me.

The room was empty. In one corner there was an examination table covered by a roll of paper, on the other side of the room was a desk with two chairs lined up beside it. I went for the chairs.

'Is anyone here with you today?' the nurse asked, her eyes going to the vacant seat beside me.

'No. I came alone. Should I have brought someone?' I tried to read her face to judge if coming alone was a bad thing.

'No. Some people like to have someone with them; others prefer to do this kind of thing by themselves.' I almost asked her then what *this kind of thing* was, but I was suddenly afraid I knew the answer to that one. 'Someone will be in to see you shortly.'

There wasn't much in the room to occupy or distract me. The wall behind the desk was dominated by a huge poster depicting the anatomy of the human brain. I tried to dispel my mounting fear by telling myself it looked no more sinister than the pieces of coral we'd seen on holiday while snorkelling in the warm waters of the ocean. I closed my eyes and let my memories carry me back to days bathed in sunshine, the smell of the sea and suncream lingering like perfume on the air. Where the only worry you had was what cocktail you wanted to try next.

The door opened and I came back to reality with an unpleasant jolt. A tall man with a slight stoop, iron-grey hair and a neatly groomed moustache entered the room. I committed his features to memory, as though I might later be called on to pick him out of a line-up. He was the first neurologist I had ever seen. I strongly suspected that he wouldn't be the last.

Dr Higgins was softly spoken, everything he said sounded almost like an apology. I found myself craning forward at every question he asked, anxious not to miss anything. I craned a lot, because he had a great many questions. And when they were finally done, the physical examination began. He looked into my eyes with a machine similar to one the optician had used. He asked me to touch my nose with my index finger – and then with every other finger in turn. I felt like a particularly unexciting circus performer as Dr Higgins and his team of doctors studied me silently as I did as he asked. Sometimes he nodded, occasionally he muttered an encouraging noise, but at no time did he suddenly interrupt the examination by interjecting *Oh, this is absolutely nothing at all for you to worry about*. He was clearly a doctor who didn't believe in lying to his patients.

'I think at this point, we need to arrange for you to have a CT scan, to give us a better idea of what exactly is going on.'

I should have been expecting this, I *was* expecting this, and yet I still felt my heart sink. 'Today?'

Dr Higgins looked almost startled by my question. 'Yes indeed, today.'

'It's just . . .' I started, knowing how ridiculous my next words were going to sound. 'I didn't know how long I was going to be here. I only paid for three hours' car parking.'

Several of the team of junior doctors smiled kindly at me at that, which only made me feel more foolish.

'Perhaps one of the nurses could arrange for someone to get you a different ticket,' Dr Higgins suggested, already heading for the door. 'I'll see you later, after your scan.'

It was just as well they found a work experience student to top up my car park ticket. I'm not sure I could have entirely trusted myself to go back to my car, keys in hand, and not drive away, in a last-ditch attempt to pretend that none of this was happening.

Instead, while the helpful schoolgirl was extending my ticket, I was changing into a hospital gown in the radiology department. *Now* was when I needed Ryan to be there. Now I needed him beside me, cracking some stupid joke about how sexy I looked in my pale blue coverall, still wearing my knee-high leather boots. I needed that humour, I needed that humanisation, I needed . . . I needed *him*.

My first thought on entering the room beside the ginger-haired radiographer was that the CT machine looked like a giant polo mint. It was a better comparison than thinking of it as a huge gaping white mouth, waiting to swallow me up. I climbed onto the motorised bed, trying to concentrate on the instructions the radiographer – 'Call me Mike' – was giving, and knowing that nothing was really going in. Mike had clearly seen that kind of rabbit-in-the-headlights fear before. 'Pretty much all you have to do is lie down and not move,' he said, giving my forearm a gentle squeeze. 'It'll be over before you know it.'

Lunchtime came and went. Someone brought me a sandwich, but I never even bothered breaking the cellophane seal. As soon as I returned to the neurology ward, I tried to phone Ryan. Having fought – and lost – a battle with my conscience about worrying him, the disappointment at not being able to reach him crushed me like a boulder. I held several conversations with his voicemail, each one sounding a little less nonchalant than the one before. I didn't want to alarm him, so I never said where I was calling from, just asked him to phone me as soon as he got the message. Two hours later, I'd still heard nothing, despite employing every means of contact my phone was capable of performing.

The hands of the clock were creeping menacingly around

the dial, and at quarter past two, when I was still waiting to see Dr Higgins, I finally asked a passing nurse if she knew when I'd be able to leave. 'You see, I didn't realise I'd need to be here this long, and I have to pick up my little girl from school very soon.'

I wasn't sure whether her look of pity was because of the length of my wait, or for what the doctors would tell me when they did eventually return. 'I'm sorry, there's no way of saying how much longer it will be. Could someone else collect her? Your husband, perhaps?'

My smile was tight. It wasn't the poor woman's fault that I had no idea where Ryan was, or why he wasn't picking up his messages. Why hadn't I listened properly when he'd mentioned being out of the office today? Probably because I'd been too preoccupied thinking about what my own day would entail. It was only now I wished I'd paid better attention to the details of his.

At two thirty, I knew I was going to have to call in a favour and ask someone else to collect Hope for me. My phone directory held the numbers of the mothers I chatted to most frequently at the school gates. There were several who I was sure would be more than happy to take Hope back home that afternoon. But as my finger scrolled down the list of names, I already knew that I wouldn't be asking any of them.

She answered on the second ring, almost as if she'd been sitting by her phone, waiting for my call. 'Hello, Maddie, it's Chloe. I have a huge favour to ask you.'

Maddie

'I have a huge favour to ask you.'

She was the last person I'd been expecting to hear from. After inviting me to join them on the shoe-shopping trip, I suspected Chloe's to-do list had a big fat tick beside 'Include Maddie in something'. I wasn't expecting a repeat performance, and certainly not one so soon.

'Go on,' I urged.

'I'm at . . . an appointment, and it's overrun, and I was wondering—' I didn't catch the rest of that sentence for it was lost under a peculiar loud trundling noise. Wherever Chloe was calling from, it was certainly noisy.

'Sorry. Could you say that again?'

'It doesn't look as if I'm going to get away from here in time to pick up Hope from school, and I was wondering if there was any chance you could collect her and take her back to yours?'

There was something in her voice that should probably have alerted me, even that early, but I was honestly too taken aback by her suggestion to figure out what it was.

'Of course I can.'

'You know where the school is?'

'Yes. Ryan pointed it out when he picked me up to babysit that time.'

There was clear guilt in Chloe's voice. 'I'm really sorry to be calling on you at the last minute once again.'

'Don't be silly. I'm really happy that you asked me.'

'I thought about asking one of the other mums,' Chloe began, artlessly making it clear I hadn't been her first choice, 'but I don't know how long—'

'Mrs Turner?' interrupted a voice from somewhere nearby. Chloe must have placed her hand over her phone, but not effectively enough to muffle the words, for I managed to hear her say: 'Just one moment.' In the background a bell began to ring, well, more of a beeping alarm than a bell. Wherever she was, it certainly sounded chaotic.

'Sorry, Maddie. I'm going to have to go. I'll get word to Ryan and he'll pick Hope up from you later, but I don't know when that will be exactly.'

'It's no problem. Tell him whenever it suits him will be fine.' Chloe made a small sound, which might have been a cough. Then again, it might not. 'Chloe?' I said, aware that I was stepping forward onto ice so thin it was sure to crack beneath my feet. 'Is everything all right?'

'Yes. Everything's perfect,' she said, and this time I heard the thread of a sob in her voice. 'I have to go now. I need to phone the school and let them know you'll be collecting her.'

'Oh, right. Do I need to take ID?'

This time she did laugh, though it was heavily laced with irony. 'I think your face is identification enough.'

'Okay. Right, well, I guess I'll see Ryan later then.'

They were words I'm sure his wife never wanted to hear me say, but she allowed them to slide straight over her, as though they simply didn't matter any more. 'Take good care of Hope. Tell her everything is fine and I'll see her soon.'

That's when I knew that, whatever was going on, it wasn't fine at all. I stood in the quiet of my lounge staring at my phone long after Chloe had gone. I didn't blame her for not wanting to share her secrets with me. It's not as if we were exactly friends; our connection was far closer, and far more distant than that. It was so unique, it didn't even have a name. Chloe might have thought she'd been speaking in carefully guarded riddles, but the background noise, the soundtrack of the last six years of my life, had revealed her location to me. Chloe was in a hospital, and for reasons she chose not to share with me, I realised something was very, very wrong.

'You're okay waiting here for me?' I asked, as I climbed out of the car. The Uber driver reached for a folded newspaper on the passenger seat. 'Sure. No worries.'

I pushed open the heavy metal gate that led to the school playground and walked towards the clusters of mothers congregated around the school's exit. I saw several heads turn my way. There were a couple of faces I recognised from Hope's birthday party, but if I'd ever known any of their names, I'd certainly forgotten them by now. A few people smiled vaguely in my direction, but no one invited me to join them, so I stood a little apart in the cold January afternoon and enjoyed my very first experience of collecting my daughter from school.

From somewhere within the building I heard the distant trill of a bell, and then several moments later a middle-aged woman came to the glass doors, threw them open and an excitable horde of primary school children dashed past her into the playground to find their parents.

The first wave of escapees didn't include Hope, so I silently skirted behind the throng and approached the door from the side. 'Excuse me,' I said to the slightly harassed-looking teacher who was on door sentry duty. 'I'm here to collect—'

'Hope Turner,' she finished for me. 'Her mother called a short while ago. Hope's just getting her coat on.' She glanced back into the building, checking that Hope wasn't already there. 'I do hope everything is all right. Mrs Turner sounded a bit ... stressed.'

'Everything is fine,' I said, as I caught sight of my pretty little girl hurtling down the corridor towards the doorway, coat undone and pigtails flying. She cannoned into me, and flung her arms around my waist as though it had been far longer than twenty-four hours since we'd last seen each other. I held her close, savouring this special moment, which Chloe got to experience every single day. 'Everything is absolutely fine,' I reiterated to Hope's teacher, proving there was yet one more thing that Hope's two very different mothers had in common: we were both pretty good at lying.

'Is this one your bedroom?' asked Hope, barrelling into that room, like a sniffer dog following a scent. She jumped onto my double bed, trampolining on it in her thick grey school socks, in a way I was pretty sure wasn't allowed in her own home.

She executed a fairly impressive seat-drop onto my duvet and then stopped suddenly. The mattress rippled from the impact, but her attention was on the twin bedside cabinets and the collection of framed photographs upon them. Too late, I realised my mistake.

'It's me!' she cried joyfully, her eyes going to the collection of snaps I'd extracted from the album Ryan had created for me.

'It *is* you,' I agreed, holding out my hand, hoping to entice her away from the bed, but I should have known I wasn't going to be that lucky.

'And that's Daddy!' she cried. I nodded, feeling the tiniest bit sick, for Hope's eyes were riveted on the photograph I should have had the good sense to have hidden away. 'And it's you,' she exclaimed, her voice a curious blend of surprise and confusion. It was one of the last photographs taken of us together, on our final holiday. The holiday when Hope had been conceived – a fact she was definitely never going to hear from me.

Ryan's arms were around me in the photo, and we were half turned towards each other. I remember that he'd kissed me only seconds before that photograph had been taken, and my lips were still parted and pink, as though waiting for more. Every other photograph of us had been securely locked away in an old suitcase, but this one, when we were both so obviously in love, so obviously together, refused to stay hidden. It screamed out to me from the bottom of my jumper drawer. It called from the depths of the back of the wardrobe. The only way to silence it was to allow it to sit beside my bed as a reminder of things that once were, and would never be again. But how do you explain that to a six-year-old?

It turned out you didn't have to. 'Daddy's hair looks funny. But you look pretty,' she declared innocently, turning away from the frame and leaping off my bed like a small Russian gymnast. 'Can I have a snack?'

'You can have anything you want,' I said, which I'm sure no parenting manual will tell you to say. But what the hell.

Chloe

There's a phrase I've often read in books which talks about a phone ringing urgently. It's always struck me as an odd description. A ring is surely just a ring; it has no ability to convey emotion. And yet when Ryan finally called me back, the ring wasn't just urgent, it was imperative.

'Chloe?' My name had become a question, a whole jumble of questions, but I knew which one he needed answering first.

'Hope is absolutely fine,' I reassured him.

I heard the exhalation and his relief. 'Where are you? Is something wrong?'

I'd practised how to tell him in the hours while I waited for his call, and yet when I finally had my cue, I fluffed my lines, getting them all wrong.

'I don't want you to panic—' That was a terrible way to start. *Of course* he was going to panic, when a sentence began like that.

'What's happened?'

'I'm at the hospital.'

'Has there been an accident?' Ryan's voice was heavy with dread. Naturally that's what he would think. How could a man see the woman he loved thrown through the air after colliding with a van, and not automatically assume that was the worst thing that could ever happen?

'No. It's not an accident. I . . . I had an appointment here today.'

'You did? What for? Why didn't you tell me?' And then, before I could stop him, he jumped to completely the wrong conclusion. 'Are you . . . Are we going to have . . . ?'

Stupid, stupid, me. We'd been talking about trying for a baby, and although we'd put those plans on hold after Maddie woke up, it was still an understandable mistake for him to have made.

'No. It's not that. I wish it was. I'm in the Neurology Unit.'

'Are you hurt?' The concern was back in his voice.

'No. They're doing some tests. It would be . . .' And that's when I started to cry. 'It would be really good if you could get here as soon as possible.'

*

I don't want to think how fast he drove to achieve it, but he was there quick enough to have left a trail of speed camera fines behind him. I heard his voice asking for me, and moments later he was standing in the doorway, his eyes the only colour in a face bleached of all pigment.

The nurse who'd led him to the bay where I was waiting, faded away like a ghost. I swung my legs off the bed I was lying on, but he was quicker, covering the distance between us in a blur and gathering me into his arms. We didn't speak for what felt like minutes, we just stood, clinging to each other like shipwreck survivors *before* the collision.

'Tell me,' he said at last, taking my hand and pulling us towards the bed. We sat on the edge, my feet not quite managing to reach the floor. 'Tell me everything.'

I rewound the last twenty-four hours – had it really only been that long? This time filling him in on all the details I'd kept hidden the night before. His hands were holding mine as I spoke, so tightly I could see the white outline of every knuckle bone.

'And then they gave me a CT scan.' Ryan nodded. There was no asking what that was, or what was its purpose. He knew, because this wasn't the first time he'd been through this kind of nightmare.

'When will they have the results?' His voice was a memory from the past. It was his anxious hospital voice, and I'd thought I'd never hear it again.

'I've already had them,' I said.

*

'Are you here alone?' Dr Higgins had asked when he'd returned to see me that afternoon. The question told me all that I needed to know. There was no need for him to flip open the buff-coloured folder cradled in his arm to reveal the test results.

'I haven't been able to reach my husband yet.'

'Would you rather we wait until he's here with you?'

It had to be bad for him to suggest that. 'No. Tell me now.'

Dr Higgins had sat on the edge of the bed, in exactly the same place Ryan would occupy several hours later. His deliberate casualness alarmed me, because it filled in any lingering gaps of hope I was holding on to. Dr Higgins wasn't a sitting-on-the-bed kind of doctor, unless the news was really bad.

'Your scans show us something is definitely causing worrying levels of pressure inside your head. As you may know, CT results aren't detailed enough to give us a full picture, so we've scheduled you in for an MRI in the morning. We'll talk again after that, when I hope to have a far better idea of what we're dealing with here.'

I stared at him for several seconds, bizarrely focusing my attention on a small grease spot on his pale blue silk tie that definitely hadn't been there that morning. Whatever he'd eaten for lunch, some of it had spilled on his clothing. Should I be placing my survival in the hands of a man who couldn't successfully negotiate a pathway to his own mouth?

'We're arranging for a bed for you up on Neuro,' advised Dr Higgins, his voice soft and sympathetic.

'Couldn't I just go home and come back tomorrow for the MRI? I have a little girl,' I added, as though that might earn me some special dispensation.

The stoop temporarily disappeared as his spine straightened. 'No. I'm afraid that won't be possible. The level of pressure is concerning us, and we need to keep you monitored. I'm sorry, but leaving at this time could be extremely dangerous.'

'Dangerous?' echoed Ryan, his voice almost as disbelieving as my own had been. How was it possible to go from not knowing anything was wrong, to critical care in the blink of an eye . . . or the blurring of an eye, to be more precise?

Once again Ryan pulled me into his arms. 'Whatever it is, we'll deal with it. You're young and strong and healthy. Whatever it is they find, we'll fight it together, and beat it together.'

I wanted to believe him. I wanted to believe that Maddie hadn't used up all the available miracles in his life . . . but I was very much afraid that she just might have done.

Maddie

There was a bittersweet quality to the hours I spent with Hope waiting for Ryan to arrive. As much as I treasured the time alone with her, doing normal everyday things like watching children's TV programmes, making her dinner, and then giving her a bath in a tub so full of bubbles it was hard to find her among the frothy white peaks, I was only marking time. And dodging questions – not terribly effectively, as it turned out.

'But where are Mummy and Daddy right now?' Hope asked, and for the first time I heard the wobble of uncertainty in her voice. Up until then it had all been an exciting adventure, but she was tired, and ready to go home to her own cosy bedroom. And the longer the evening went on without word from either Chloe or Ryan, the more afraid I was that normal wasn't going to be a part of her life in the foreseeable future.

I wrapped her in a big fluffy towel and combed through her hair, breathing in the clean smell of it as I dried and carefully plaited it. She yawned sleepily, and surprisingly when I suggested she lie down on my bed until her daddy arrived to collect her, she didn't put up an argument.

'I think Elsa is scared,' she whispered into my neck as I tucked her up in my bed, dressed in one of my old T-shirts for a nightdress. 'She'll be frightened without Mummy in the house.' Her bright blue eyes were sparkling with tears. 'Mummy's the only one who knows how to look after her properly,' Hope declared, her small voice cracking.

'Your mummy will be home very soon to look after both *you* and Elsa,' I replied, kicking off my shoes and climbing up onto the bed beside her. 'Why don't you close your eyes for a minute, and I bet when you open them again, your daddy will be here to take you home.'

I switched on one of the bedside lamps, bathing the room in a warm soft golden glow.

'Will you stay here with me, until he gets here? Will you stay with me, Maddie?'

I kissed the smooth velvet of her forehead. 'Forever and always,' I promised, knowing those words would have meant so much more to her if they'd come from her other mother's lips.

It was almost nine o'clock when I finally heard the knock on my door. I carefully removed my arm from where it had been cradling Hope, and inched slowly off the bed, so I wouldn't disturb her.

Ryan's hand was raised to knock again when I pulled open the front door. I'd seen him look ill on the night we discovered that neither of us could handle tequila; I'd seen him exhausted after working through the night on an important presentation; and I'd seen him worried, the way he'd always looked whenever morning sickness had me racing for the bathroom. But I don't think I'd ever seen all those emotions on his face at the same time. Until now.

I held the door open wide and he half-walked, half-stumbled into the narrow hallway.

Are you all right? hovered on my lips, but I was sensible enough not to ask it. He obviously was not. I walked to the kitchen and he followed me, collapsing heavily onto one of the pine chairs.

I made tea in silence, memory serving me well as to how he took it. I placed the cup on the table in front of him. 'Drink,' I commanded.

He raised his head, and I saw a tell-tale ring of red circling his eyes. Extreme tiredness could do that, as could many hours spent behind the wheel of a car. I didn't believe either of those reasons had put that redness there.

'Where's Hope?' he asked, scanning the room, as though she might possibly be concealed in one of the kitchen cabinets. I put that one down to his preoccupied state of mind, rather than a judgement on my parenting skills.

'She's fast asleep in my bed.'

He nodded, satisfied. 'What did you tell her?'

'Nothing, really. Except what Chloe said to me: that she'd been delayed and that you would be coming to pick her up later.'

He took a sip of the tea, not seeming to notice it was probably far too hot to drink.

'Which hospital is she in, Ryan?'

He spilled the tea as he put the cup back down with a jerky hand.

'Who said Chloe was in a hospital?'

My eyes spoke for me. He gave a small sound, which was the closest I think he was going to get to a laugh for a considerable period of time.

'Queen Mary's.'

'What's wrong with her?'

He looked towards the door, checking our daughter

403

hadn't put in an unfortunate, ill-timed appearance. The frame was empty.

'They think it might be a brain tumour. She's having an MRI tomorrow, and after that an angiogram. We'll know more after that.'

I crossed over to the place where he sat. His head was bent, the hair I'd run my hands through a thousand times was dishevelled and awry. His shoulders were shaking, not much, but enough for me to know he was crying. My hand reached out tentatively and touched his back. He turned to me with a low animal-like moan, which was largely muffled as he buried his face against my stomach.

The man I had loved and lost was in my arms, crying in fear of losing the woman he now loved, and I couldn't think of a weirder or more bizarre situation for any of us to be in. There were no rules or guidelines of how we should behave. So I did the only thing that I could. I let my arms find their way around the familiar shape of him, and I held him close as he wept.

Chapter 17

Chloe

I thought having a CT scan was the most frightening thing I'd ever done; that was until the next day when they wheeled me down for an MRI. The operators dutifully ask all patients if they're claustrophobic before they begin, but unless you've ever been stuck inside a narrow tunnel, with a noise like a jet engine taking off beside you, you probably don't know that you are, until it's too late.

'The headphones we give you will muffle the noise,' the operator said kindly, leading me towards the machine which looked like something out of one of those science-fiction films Ryan was so fond of watching. 'Did you bring a CD to listen to?'

I shook my head. I hadn't even brought a toothbrush, a nightdress, or a change of underwear with me. I was woefully unprepared for absolutely everything that was happening to me. But as I walked on shaky legs towards the enormous scanner, I suddenly remembered that there *was* a CD in my handbag, though it wasn't mine.

The operator was far too professional to look surprised when she took the flat plastic case from me, but I still felt the need to justify my slightly peculiar taste in music. 'It's my daughter's, she likes to listen to it on the journey to school.' I glanced over at the MRI with apprehension. 'Maybe it'll make me feel like she's close by, if I hear it playing.'

So, while the machine took detailed images of my brain, revealing the sizeable tumour that had been stealthily growing in the meninges inside my skull, I hummed brokenly along to the soundtrack, until I could no longer hear the deafening cacophony of machinery, but instead heard Hope's voice singing lustily through the headphones that she was Moana. Nothing in my own CD collection could possibly have given me greater comfort.

Ryan was waiting for me by the time they wheeled me back up to the ward. I was the one who was sick, but *he* looked absolutely terrible.

'You don't look well,' I said, my hand grazing down his unshaved cheek, as he pulled back from our kiss.

'Isn't that what I'm meant to say?'

My smile was sad. 'Did you get any sleep?'

For a moment I could see him consider lying, before he shook his head. 'No. Turns out I can't do it unless you're there beside me.'

I found his hand on the mattress and threaded my fingers through his. 'Me neither,' I said softly. 'How was Hope when you took her to school this morning?'

'Better, after she'd spoken to you,' Ryan answered honestly.

It had been hard to find a way of explaining why I had suddenly disappeared, without even saying goodbye to her. You're just not meant to do that to a six-year-old. I looked over at Ryan, who was doing a very poor job of hiding his own fears from me. You also shouldn't do it to a thirty-six-year-old, as it turns out.

'But *why* are you in hospital, Mummy? You're not sick. You're not throwing up or sneezing.' Hope's yardstick for good health was a little different to the one the neurology department used. 'Can't you have some Calpol and come home?'

I'd smiled into my phone at her treatment plan. 'I don't think that works very well on grown-ups, Pumpkin. I think the doctors want me to stay here and get some stronger medicine to make me well.'

'Will it taste bad?'

I laughed, even though I felt like crying. Hearing her voice and not being able to reach out and hug her was a new kind of torture I was afraid I might have to get used to. For a moment I felt like I was walking in Maddie's shoes, and they weren't comfortable at all. 'It'll probably taste very bad indeed,' I confirmed.

'Maddie's going to pick her up again after school,' Ryan said, as though just thinking about her had summoned up her presence into my hospital room. He saw the beginnings of a protest on my face, and shot it down before I had formed the words. 'I'm *not* leaving your side today. Whatever tests they have to do, whatever conversations the doctors want to have, I'm going to be right there beside you.'

I was glad of that later on when they performed the lumbar puncture. Curled up like a foetus on the bed, waiting for the needle to be inserted between the bones at the base of my spine, I could feel my fear level rising, like lava in a volcano.

'Look at me. Don't look anywhere else. Just at me.' The pressure in my back faded away as his hands gripped mine and I lost myself in the brilliant deep blue depths of his eyes. The room was full of doctors, nurses, and technicians, but none of them heard the words of love that Ryan's eyes silently declared. Only me.

Maddie

'I didn't take you for a chicken-nugget kind of a girl.'

I spun around, still holding the frozen packet, as though I'd been caught red-handed by the nutrition police.

Mitch was grinning, so widely I could actually see his mouth beneath the dense foliage of his beard. He had nice teeth, I noticed; even, and very white.

I suppose I shouldn't have been surprised to run into him here once again. It was, after all, the closest supermarket to both of our homes. 'We have to stop meeting like this,' he said cheesily.

'Do people still use that line?' I asked, and then instantly regretted my sassy response when his face began to turn tomato red, as though he had – just maybe – been flirting with me. No, surely not? Not Mitch. I felt awkward and clumsy, like a mean girl who'd been cruel to the nerdy kid in the class. 'Do you know if these are any good?' I asked, thrusting the bag of nuggets towards him.

He seemed more than happy with the conversational diversion. 'Nutritionally . . . not so much. Taste-wise, Sam loves 'em.' The grin came back, and I was relieved to see I'd not chased it out of town completely. 'I do too, come to that.'

It was enough of a recommendation for me. I dropped the nuggets into my basket, where they fell on top of the smiley-face potato thingies, the packets of sweets, and the two cartoon DVDs I'd picked up from the entertainment aisle.

'I'm going to be taking care of Hope after school today,' I explained unnecessarily.

Mitch smiled, and his eyes crinkled into the folds that were always present beside them. He must either squint or smile a lot for them to be that deep, I thought distractedly, entirely missing what he was saying.

'Sorry?' I said, tearing my eyes away from his face and hoping I hadn't been staring rudely.

'I said you must be happy about that.'

I gave a slightly uncomfortable shrug. 'Yes and no. Her mum – I mean, Chloe – isn't well. She's in hospital, which is why they've asked me to step in. It seems wrong to be happy that because of that I get to spend some more time with Hope,' I added guiltily.

'You're a nice person, Maddie. Don't feel guilty when something good happens to you. You're owed it.' For once, his skin didn't colour, though it was possibly one of the most personal things he'd ever said to me.

I swallowed, surprisingly pleased by his words. 'Actually, I was going to give you a call later. I was wondering if you had any objection to me decorating the second bedroom. I'd like to make it a bit more appealing for Hope, if she ever stays over.' Mitch's eyebrows were thick and bushy, and they almost disappeared into his hairline at my words. 'Not that there's anything *wrong* with your grandmother's choice of decor,' I added hurriedly.

Mitch shook his head and his hair settled messily back into place; it was getting rather long and shaggy, and I wondered if he knew he was overdue for a haircut. Was there anyone in his life to tell him that, I wondered. We'd spoken of many things, but I had no idea if he currently had a girlfriend.

'Do you know how to do it?'

'How to do what?' I asked artlessly.

'Decorate.'

I must have looked taken aback. 'You put paint on a brush, and then put the brush on the walls. How hard can it be?'

He laughed, and several people half an aisle away turned their heads at the deep rumbling explosion of sound. 'Yeah,

I thought as much. I tell you what: you pick out the colour scheme, or wallpaper or whatever, and *I'll* do the decorating. I've got some leave coming up that I have to either take or lose.'

'Oh no,' I said, hoping he hadn't thought I'd been angling for him to volunteer all along. 'I wouldn't want to put you to the trouble.'

'It's no trouble,' Mitch assured me, reaching into the freezer cabinet and plucking up his own packet of nuggets with a boyish grin. 'I'm only protecting my investment. I'm going to need to let the flat out after you've gone.'

'I'm not planning on going anywhere for a while.'

He smiled, looking suddenly far more at ease. 'That's good to know.' And then, as though hearing his own words through another's ears, he added hurriedly: 'From a landlord's point of view.'

Not quite so many heads turned when I walked into the school playground for the second day running. Hope was one of the first out the door, one arm raised in the air, as though she was about to ask a question. Tightly gripped in her hand was a colourful piece of artwork, fluttering above her head like a flag. An extremely colourful flag, I observed, noting that many of her small friends were carrying similar paintings aloft. In my totally unbiased opinion, Hope's was definitely the best.

Even as she threw her arms around me in an enthusiastic hug, I could see Hope's eyes scanning the crowd of parents, and I knew without asking what, or rather who, she was looking for.

'I thought Mummy would be here with you today,' she confessed quietly, her lower lip trembling on the admission. 'I wanted to show her my painting.'

Two mums who were chatting close by both turned their heads at Hope's words. I recognised them as friends of Chloe, and got the distinct impression that whatever I did or said next would eventually find its way back to her.

'I tell you what, when we get back to my flat, I'll take a photo of it on my phone and then we can send it to her with a message from you. How would that be?'

Hope nodded, satisfied with my solution, and when I glanced at Chloe's friends I was pleased to see that they were doing likewise. It might have been a small test, but I felt immensely grateful to have passed it.

We stopped at the swings on our way home, taking advantage of the fading afternoon light and the fact that today I'd come on foot to collect her. We stayed in the park until our normally pale cheeks were flushed red with the cold. And she didn't fall off of anything. Another test passed with flying colours.

Back at my flat, we warmed ourselves with mugs of hot chocolate, lost under a bobbing froth of mini marshmallows. When Hope had drained her mug, her normally pink lips had disappeared beneath a cocoa moustache, so I pulled out my phone and took a photo, which we sent to Chloe, along with one of the painting.

'Do you think she'll message us back?' Hope asked, her eyes never straying far from my phone, which I'd left out on the kitchen table.

'If she can, I'm sure she will,' I said. I don't know which of us was more disappointed as the hours of the afternoon slipped by, and my phone remained silent.

I was arranging a regimental line of nuggets onto the grill tray when Ryan arrived, far earlier than he'd been the day before. Hope had run to the door with me, which meant my questions about Chloe had to be asked by a series of non-verbal eye and facial expressions as he lifted Hope up into his arms and hugged her tightly. She wrapped her skinny legs and arms around him like a baby monkey, and when he tried to lower her back to the ground, she shook her head fiercely and clung on tighter. If proof was needed how much she was missing her mother, it was there in her death-grip on her remaining parent. Except of course he wasn't her only remaining parent, I thought sadly, as I followed them down the corridor to the kitchen.

There was an ominous smell of burning coming from my oven, and when I pushed past Ryan and yanked out the grill tray, the golden-brown colour the instructions had told me to aim for had been . . . and gone.

'I was making Hope's supper,' I said, stupidly feeling like crying as I looked down at the line of charred bread-crumbed shapes.

'Looks delicious,' said Ryan in a deadpan way that once, a thousand years ago, would have had me laughing. Today it had the exact opposite effect. I was no good at any of this. I was no good at pretending I was anything other than a very poor substitute for the woman both Ryan and Hope would rather be with.

'What kind of idiot can't even grill some bloody nuggets?' I said despondently.

Hope gasped, and leant closer to Ryan's ear. 'Maddie said a rude word,' she whispered, in case it had passed him by. My daughter, the supergrass. I laughed, and thankfully the downward spiral of doubt I could easily have got sucked into was avoided.

'Tell you what,' Ryan suggested, 'why don't we order a takeaway pizza for all of us, and then you and I can go home so you can call Mummy and say goodnight to her before you go to bed.' It was quite a feat, finding a solution that could satisfy all three women in his life, but somehow Ryan pulled it off.

It was, I realised, the first meal he and I had shared in six years, but the tiny chaperone, who was half him, half me, prevented either of us from commenting on it. We ate the fragrant cheese and tomato pizza straight from the box, sitting in the lounge, which was warmer and cosier than the kitchen. It also allowed Hope to watch the last half-hour of the film I'd bought her, sitting cross-legged on the floor in front of the TV.

'How were things today?' I asked softly, glancing over to see if the talking mouse on the screen was holding our daughter's attention. It was.

'Grim. Scary, and confusing. You have no idea how many tests they put you through in there.'

'Actually, I do,' I said quietly.

Ryan reached over to briefly touch the back of my hand, and then almost immediately drew his arm back, as though he couldn't quite believe his limb had been so irresponsible.

'I'm sorry, Maddie, I forget. Of course, you know about all this better than *anyone*.'

I shrugged, but couldn't deny that many of the tests and investigations Chloe was undergoing were ones I'd been through myself – not just once, but many times, after waking from the coma and in my regular check-ups.

I looked closely at Ryan, who'd taken no more than a couple of bites from his slice of the wagon-wheel-sized pizza. He might be putting on a show for Hope's sake, but I knew him better than that. He wasn't coping well, and that was hardly surprising, given that this was the *second* time he'd had to live through this kind of nightmare. How could that possibly be fair?

'She has a cerebral angiogram scheduled for the morning,' Ryan said, his eyes on the back of Hope's head, which was still avidly fixed on the screen. I tried to hide my instinctive grimace, knowing how little fun *that* was going to be. 'Then in the afternoon we're meeting with the doctor to go through all the results.'

'Try not to worry,' I said, which might possibly have been the most ridiculous thing I had ever said to Ryan, or to anyone.

Chloe

The worst thing about the angiogram wasn't the room full of scary equipment; it wasn't the bank of monitors that looked like they belonged in a television studio control room; it wasn't even the lopsided shaving, which made me look like I'd chickened out halfway through a Brazilian wax. No, the worst thing was seeing Ryan's face when the nurse very firmly steered him towards the door of the room and back into the corridor. Because it mirrored every one of my worst fears. I needed someone to tell me everything was going to be all right, that this wasn't going to change our lives in ways I didn't yet know or understand. But on Ryan's face I could see only tortured concern and pain, the same expressions he'd once worn for Maddie. Like a suit I'd never really liked, it was disconcerting to see how easily he'd slipped it back on.

'Don't you worry, we'll take good care of her,' the nurse said, her hand squarely placed in the middle of Ryan's broad back. She ejected him from the room with the slick efficiency of a nightclub bouncer, but as she walked towards the narrow treatment bed on which I lay, she glanced over her shoulder at the doors several times, as though she didn't entirely trust him not to come barging through them at any moment.

As the doctor began preparing the catheter for its meandering journey through my body from groin to brain, the nurse did her best to calm me. Gripped tightly in one hand I held the photograph I'd asked Ryan to bring from home.

Freed from the frame in which it usually sat, I stared at the snap of the three of us, taken on our last beach holiday. Our faces were tanned and carefree. I remember that we'd hijacked a passing stranger to take the picture, who'd perfectly captured three people whose biggest worry was whether to spend the afternoon at the beach or the pool. The photograph had been taken only weeks before the person they'd once called the Miracle Girl had lived up to her name one last time, and had come back.

'Is that your little girl?' asked the nurse, trying to distract me from the very weird sensation of the contrast dye coursing through the catheter. It was hard holding a conversation when you felt as though you'd just peed yourself for the first time in over thirty years.

I nodded, and tried to focus on her words and not the weird scratching sound I swore I could hear as the thin plastic tube journeying inside me travelled past my ear. 'Yes, it is. Her name is Hope; she's just turned six.'

The nurse squeezed my wrist warmly and even while I knew her conversation was more to distract me from looking at the bank of screens showing images of the inside of my head, I still welcomed the human contact in this impersonal, clean and sterile room.

She bent down closer and studied the photograph with care. 'She looks like you,' she said, because isn't that what mothers always want to hear? I smiled sadly, and for once I pretended that Hope actually did.

*

'Imagine it like a motorway – the M25, if you will,' said Dr Higgins, clearly pleased with his analogy. He reached for a large sketch pad and a thick black marker pen and began drawing in quick bold strokes. 'This long vein in your head is like the M25, and the mass you have – the meningioma – is blocking it.' He broke off to grapple in the desk drawer for a different coloured pen. The one he found was green, and was almost the exact same shade as bile. 'And all of these slip roads here are now trying to take the traffic from the blocked motorway . . . but they can't cope with the pressure.' He sat back in his chair, his eyes looking approvingly at his own artwork.

Ryan and I stared back at him from the other side of the desk, both wearing the expression of bomb-blast survivors.

'The good news is: your tumour isn't malignant; it hasn't caused you to have seizures; and we now know exactly where it is and how we can relieve the pressure.'

The hours after the angiogram had been an excruciating wait. My body might have been forced to lie totally immobile on a bed while it recovered from the procedure, but my brain had been all too active. Despite the nurse's admirable diversionary tactics, I'd seen the screens and upon them the ugly white . . . thing . . . that had insidiously taken up residence inside my head.

'Our first priority is to unblock these roads, and get the traffic moving again,' continued Dr Higgins, determined to run with his highway theme.

Ryan's hand squeezed mine tightly, but *I* was the one who

asked the question. 'But you're going to take it out, right?' Of the three people in the room, you could hear only one of them exhale, for the other two were suddenly holding their breath.

'No, we're not. At this moment in time, I'm afraid that isn't our best course of action.'

I leant forward in my chair, feeling the scratchiness of the hospital gown against my skin beneath the fleecy dressing gown Ryan had brought from home. It's hard to sound decisive and commanding when you're not fully dressed, but I gave it my best shot. 'Dr Higgins, I want it taken *out*. I don't want to "wait and see", or monitor and observe it. I just want it gone.'

Dr Higgins sighed sadly, and his features reordered themselves into an expression of sympathy, which I uncharacteristically wanted to slap off him. 'I understand why you feel surgery would be your best option, Chloe, but you have to believe us when we say that for now inserting stents to relieve the pressure is our best plan of action. The position and size of the mass makes anything else far too risky. Surgery will have to be our very last resort. And it won't be a decision we make hurriedly, if we make it at all. But we're not there yet.'

Ryan and I looked at each other sadly, because the rest of the doctor's words were hanging in the air, like a speech bubble in a silent movie. For it seemed clear that one day, perhaps not too much further down the line, we *would* be there.

Maddie

I had a new routine; a new normal. Except nothing about it felt at all normal. When I looked back, my days before Chloe's illness seemed squandered and self-indulgent, while those since seemed curiously stolen or at least borrowed without permission. More than anything – since the very first moment I'd learned of her existence – I'd yearned for Hope to be a permanent part of my world . . . but not this way. Not by default.

I think everyone had imagined that after the stents had been successfully implanted, Chloe would be allowed out of hospital. Yet six days after the procedure, she was still a patient, imprisoned on the ward until they'd successfully stabilised her medication.

As hard as I tried, I'd always known it would be impossible to fill Chloe's shoes, but what worried me more than failing in that task was seeing the light in Hope's eyes gradually being dialled down. It happened each day when I turned up alone at the school gates; it happened every night when it was only Ryan standing on my doorstep to take her home.

'I really think you need to take her to the hospital to see Chloe,' I said one evening, my voice a whisper as we stood closer than I felt comfortable with, in my narrow hallway.

'Hope *does* see Chloe, every night and every morning.'

'Skype or FaceTime, or whatever other technology you're using, isn't the same. It's not good enough. Being online isn't real human contact.'

420

For a moment he almost smiled, and I knew we were both remembering a time when I'd happily shared much of my life online. These days I didn't even have a Twitter or Facebook account. It was yet another example of how my old life and my new one were worlds apart. Ryan shook his head, and his bright blue eyes looked troubled, but then they'd scarcely looked anything else since the day Chloe had gone into hospital.

'We've both agreed that seeing her mum in a hospital ward – particularly *that* type of ward – would be too much for her to cope with. It would do more harm than good.'

I let the small wounds he'd casually inflicted go untended. *They'd both agreed ... seeing her mum ...* There'd be time enough later during the long wakeful hours of the night for me to examine exactly how alone they'd made me feel.

'We won't risk having her distressed by being in that type of environment. Not again,' Ryan said resolutely.

I felt the weight of his unspoken blame settling on me like a cloak. This was the reason why Hope hadn't been taken to see Chloe at the hospital. *I* was the reason.

'Hope was only a toddler when she reacted like that. Don't you think you owe it to her to give her another chance now she's older and can better understand what's going on?'

Ryan's mouth had drawn into a tight and uncompromising line. Words at this point were virtually redundant, because I knew he wasn't going to change his mind.

'You weren't there. You didn't see how bad it was.'

Two stabs with the sword this time, instead of one. My

absence and my ignorance of the pain I'd caused my own child were the weapons he now used to stop me fighting for her. My artillery was empty and I knew his mind was made up.

I padded barefoot down the hallway, a cup of tea in one hand and a slice of toast in the other. Even after several months, I still relished the indulgence of starting each day slowly. It was my small quiet rebellion against the early-rising regimen that the hospital had insisted on. It was after half-past eight, I hadn't showered, and was wearing the oversized gym T-shirt that I'd stolen from Ryan years before. The fabric was soft from a hundred cycles in the washing machine, the seams were starting to fray, and it was indecently short – but as no one ever saw me in it, what did that matter?

I was contemplating whether going back to bed with a second slice of toast was decadent or just plain lazy, when the sound of the letterbox opening and then slapping shut caught my attention. It was too early for the post, which normally arrived mid-morning, yet the coconut door mat was scattered with brightly coloured cards someone had posted through my door. Holding the toast between my teeth, I bent down to retrieve the collection of glossy cards from the mat. They were paint colour charts, and I smiled slightly around the crust in my mouth when I realised who must have delivered them. I was still smiling when one last card was popped through the flap and landed on my bare feet.

Without thinking, I opened the door and greeted Mitch, forgetting about my inappropriate state of undress, or the fact that my teeth were clamped around my toast.

'Oh, Maddie,' he said, taking one startled step backwards into the communal hallway. 'I didn't expect to see you.'

His eyes ran fleetingly up my body, from the painted red of my toenails, past the long still-too-skinny legs, before hurriedly skimming over the soft material of the old T-shirt, through which my breasts were clearly outlined. I rather imagined what Mitch might *actually* have meant was: *I didn't expect to see quite* so much *of you.*

He'd left the main front door standing open, and a cold draught of morning air whistled past him, speckling my arms with goosebumps, and making the view of my breasts through the grey marl suddenly more interesting.

I pulled the toast from my teeth, leaving behind a small mouthful that I hastily chewed and swallowed before speaking. 'I wasn't expecting anyone,' I said, which from the way I was dressed was probably perfectly clear. I wondered if pulling down on the hem of the T-shirt would cover up my semi-nudity, or merely draw further attention to it. To be fair, Mitch was making a deliberate point of not allowing his gaze to drop below my chin, so I left the T-shirt alone.

'It's very early to be calling,' I said, before realising that sounded both critical and rude. 'Not that it isn't great to see you,' I added hastily. 'Can I offer you a cup of tea?'

'I can't stop, I'm afraid. I'm on my way to work.' It was only then that I noticed his normal casual wear was replaced by a more formal shirt and tie. The shirt was stretched so tightly across the breadth of his shoulders, I doubted he ever needed to iron it.

'I picked up some colour charts from the DIY shop the other day,' he explained, glancing down at the bundle of cards, which I was holding at the same level as my hemline. Mitch looked uncomfortable as his eyes quickly returned to my face. It might be a race to see which one of us blushed first today, I found myself thinking randomly.

'If there's anything there you like, I could probably pick up the paint this weekend and make a start on the second bedroom for you.'

I bit my lip, feeling suddenly awkward. 'Actually, Mitch, I don't think it's a great idea to go ahead with that right now.'

A look skittered across his eyes. It was a look of resignation and inevitability. He thought I was brushing him off. And suddenly I saw him not as the grown man who now stood before me, but as a big gangly teenager, who'd walked nervously across the dance floor only to be turned down by the cool girl, who'd laughed with her friends as he skulked back into the shadows.

'I *do* still want you to help me,' I said, my guilt making me sound over-enthusiastic. 'It's just that right now Hope's so upset about Chloe being in hospital, I'd worry that if she saw me getting a room ready for her here, she'll think her mother is *never* coming back.'

Mitch's smile was slow and understanding. '*You're* her

mother,' he corrected loyally, pinning his colours firmly to the *Team Maddie* mast.

'We *both* are,' I answered, knowing the only team who could win this particular contest would be the one that pulled *with* the other side, instead of against it.

I wasn't sure if it was lingering pangs of guilt or the desire for companionship which made me suddenly call out as he was walking away. 'Look, if you're not busy tonight, why don't you come over for a drink and we could discuss ... match pots, or ... whatever.' If he'd needed proof of my ignorance of all things DIY, I'd clearly given it to him. 'Ryan usually picks up Chloe by seven o'clock, so if you got here around eight?'

'That sounds good,' Mitch said, looking surprised by my unexpected invitation. That made two of us. At the last moment I suddenly worried I might be sending out the wrong signals. 'Nothing fancy. Just a casual friendly drink. Don't worry about getting dressed up or anything.'

Mitch's golden brown eyes twinkled, and all at once he looked much more teddy than grizzly bear. 'You nei-ther.' There was definitely a hint of mischief in his eyes and voice.

After he'd gone, I leant back on the front door for several minutes, rewinding our parting words through my head, as though deciphering code. Was that flirting, or was that just being funny? I'd been out of the game for so long, I could no longer tell the difference.

*

'Why don't I treat us all to burgers tonight? There's a new place that's just opened on the High Street.' Ryan had arrived half an hour earlier than usual to collect Hope, before I'd begun cooking or cremating a meal for her.

'Yes, burgers!' exclaimed Hope delightedly.

Ryan pulled his daughter against him, and I saw the deep lines of strain etched beside his mouth ease slightly. He'd come straight from the hospital and looked in need of some decompression time. I was itching to ask what had happened during his visit, but with Hope standing right beside him, my tongue was silenced.

'What do you say, Maddie? Do you still like burgers?' There was no faulting his memory of my love of junk food.

'Does a bear—' I broke off suddenly, and not just because the rest of that sentence contained language I should *definitely* not be using in front of Hope. I broke off because the image of a bear suddenly reminded me that I had plans for the evening.

'I'm sorry Ryan, but I can't. I've made other arrangements for tonight.' There was a curiosity in his gaze that rankled a little. I was entitled to a life of my own; friendships of my own; ones that had nothing to do with him. His right to know the details about my social life had long since passed its expiration date.

'You can't cancel them?' he asked.

Hope looked up at me pleadingly, and I almost wavered, because I knew she wanted me to join them – and I *did* want to. But then a snapshot memory flashed in my head of Mitch's face, anticipating rejection.

'No, I'm sorry, I can't. Not tonight.'

He brought sunflowers again. And I smiled, because who can't *help* but smile at a giant of a man who awkwardly hands you a large bunch of oversized yellow-faced blooms.

Some decisions, the type that seem like such a good idea in the small hours of the night, don't sound quite so wonderful when the sun rises the following day. Similarly, the kind you reach after drinking more wine than your body has consumed in years are equally untrustworthy.

I didn't rush things. I drank hot strong black coffee, nibbled on toast and stayed longer than usual under the flat's surprisingly efficient shower, waiting for the idea to be washed out of my head and swirl away down the drain. But instead it stuck. I couldn't even remember if the suggestion had been mine or Mitch's, I realised as I briskly rubbed myself dry.

We'd talked for hours. I'd always known Mitch was a good listener, but last night I discovered that he was also insightful and perceptive. Perhaps it's easier to see past all the obstacles and objections when you're not emotionally involved. Admittedly, after three glasses of wine my thinking was a bit fuzzy around the edges, while Mitch, who appeared to have the constitution of a small rhinoceros, didn't seem affected at all.

'You need to go to the hospital,' I remember him saying.

'Why? I'm perfectly okay,' I told him, and then felt extremely foolish when I saw his face split into a wide grin. I noticed he didn't replenish my glass quite so much after that.

'You and Chloe need to talk ... without Ryan being there,' he advised. 'After all, you both only want what's best for Hope.'

I nodded vigorously, waited a moment for the room to stop bobbing up and down, before saying: 'We do. But it's not possible because I have to look after Hope each day, and Ryan's there in the evenings. Plus, the hospital is miles away,' I added, aware that I was now throwing pretty pathetic spanners into the works, to get me out of doing something I didn't want to do.

'I could always drive you there,' Mitch offered.

In the end I decided not to rush my decision. I would sit on it, like a hen on an egg, and let events unfold as they would. But before I'd finished dressing, my phone had pinged with an incoming message. I perched on the side of my bed to read the first text Ryan had ever sent me that didn't have a kiss at the end of it. It was brisk and to the point, curt even, in a way that was so unfamiliar, it jarred. The essence of the message was that Hope was attending a classmate's birthday party after school that day, which he would collect her from. My services were therefore not required, which left my afternoon unexpectedly free. I tried not to see it as a sign. It was merely a coincidence.

I tidied the lounge, clearing away the wine glasses and empty bottles, and spent quite some time pummelling the Mitch-sized dent out of the worn sofa cushions. As I repeatedly struck the upholstery, my thoughts kept circling and then returning to visiting Chloe at the hospital. I knew from Ryan she hadn't wanted visitors, and that her closest friend, an old work colleague, had moved abroad several years ago. So why would she want to see me? The answer was obvious: she wouldn't.

The decision was finally made when the postman dropped the mail through my front door. There were a couple of bills, which I put to the bottom of the pile, and turned instead to an A5 brown envelope with DVLA stamped on the postmark. I knew what it was before I pulled out the contents. My driving licence had finally been returned, with all of the restrictions my condition had imposed removed. I now had the means to go wherever I wanted, whenever I wanted.

I looked upwards, addressing my comment to the ceiling. 'Okay, Universe, I get it. That's enough signs. I'll go to the damn hospital.' I'm not sure if the universe heard me, or if my words were only picked up by the people who lived in the flat above, but it didn't much matter. Today I would visit Chloe.

Hiring a car for the week was surprisingly easy. The guy in the rental office was a bit sleazy and kept smiling and winking at me as we went through the paperwork, in a way I doubt he'd have done if Mitch had been beside me. It was only as I slid into the driver's seat, and breathed in that freshly valeted new car smell, that I realised how odd it was that Mitch was the person who'd come to mind, rather than Ryan.

I stopped only once on my journey, pulling into the car park of a large shopping centre. There was a huge branch of Boots which had everything I wanted, and twenty minutes and two laden carrier bags later, I was back on the road to visit the sick bed of the woman who I now knew had visited *me* a great many times when our roles were reversed. Serendipity felt like an improbably strong elastic band, continually pulling our lives together.

She was sitting on the edge of her bed, staring out the window at the fine drizzle that threatened to turn into a downpour at any moment. Her shoulders were slumped and her hair looked in need of brushing – maybe washing too, if I was being brutally honest. A nurse had directed me to her bed, but to reach it I'd had to pass several other bays. There was a man in one, shouting out belligerently, and in another an elderly gentleman who either didn't know, or care, that his bottom was on display to anyone who happened to be walking past. A strident alarm began to sound from the far end of the ward and a nurse ran past me, her flat sensible shoes slapping on the linoleum. Ryan was right; this wasn't a place that Hope should visit.

I cleared my throat awkwardly, but I was pretty sure she must have heard the sound of my footsteps as I entered her bay. 'Hello, Maddie,' she said quietly, startling me, for she hadn't yet turned around. I stepped closer to her bed and saw my silhouette reflected in the glass of the window. She turned her head, very slowly, as though afraid to jar anything within it.

I should have known better than to gasp. I'd seen photographs of how *I'd* looked after the accident: bruised and battered, my skin a rainbow of blues, greys and purples; colours nature had never intended it to be. It was probably extremely uncool of me to inhale sharply in shock when I saw the thick band of bruises which circled Chloe's throat like a scarf.

Her fingers went to her neck, and the pretty diamond ring on her left hand twinkled incongruously against the discoloured skin. 'They went in through the jugular,' she said, her voice flat and tired. My eyes went to the small white wound dressing, which showed up even more vividly against the grey bruises. 'I look like someone tried to strangle me,' Chloe said.

I pulled up a chair and sat down without waiting for an invitation, because I was fairly certain one wasn't going to be forthcoming. 'More like you've been attacked by a very inept vampire,' I countered.

Her lips twisted into a fleeting smile, as though they'd almost forgotten how to do it. 'What are you doing here, Maddie?'

'Hope has a party after school today, so I don't need—' Chloe shook her head and I realised she was probably perfectly aware of Hope's social diary, which was far busier than my own had ever been. 'I brought some things you might need,' I said, not wanting to launch straight into the purpose of my visit. Chloe glanced down briefly at the carrier bags I'd placed on the bed beside her, but she didn't delve into them.

'Thank you. But whatever I need, Ryan has brought in.'

I counted to ten and bit my lip to make sure my instinctive retort didn't accidentally come bursting out of my mouth. 'Not *everything* you need,' I contradicted. Chloe looked briefly at the bags once more, but I shook my head. 'Ryan hasn't brought you Hope.'

Chloe sighed, and a look of irritation passed over her face. She really didn't want me there, and if truth be told I didn't want to be there either. But what either of us wanted faded into insignificance weighed up against what Hope needed, and that was to see Chloe, the only mother she'd ever known.

'Hope isn't doing very well. She needs to see you.' Chloe opened her mouth to reply, but I jumped in before she could speak. 'And don't tell me she can do that via a phone or a laptop, because I've already heard that shit from Ryan.'

Chloe looked at me for a long moment, blinking slowly. 'Do you swear like that in front of Hope?'

'All the fucking time,' I replied, adopting a taunting tone to match the challenging gleam in my eye. 'In fact, if you don't step in pretty soon, she'll be cursing like a marine by the time you see her next.'

I hadn't expected to make her laugh, and I didn't know what to do with that small victory, except to forge ahead with my mission. 'I know that you're both worried about how she'll react. I know what happened when she was younger, but she's suffering right now. She needs to feel your arms around her.' I gave a small sound, like a defeated laugh. 'And mine just won't do.'

Chloe's eyes went to the other beds in her bay. The one directly opposite her held a middle-aged woman who appeared to be in a comatose state; to her left was a teenager whose head was swathed in bandages. The third bed, the one next to Chloe's, was stripped bare.

'The woman in that bed died this morning.'

I stared at the stripped mattress, and for the first time wondered if I *was* making a mistake here.

'Hope can't visit me on this ward. It would terrify her.'

'Agreed.'

Chloe's head jerked up in surprise.

'But in the hospital foyer there are several shops, a café and two fast-food outlets,' I said, itemising everything I'd noted on my quick reconnoitre before searching for the neurology ward. 'She *could* visit you there.'

The important part of winning any argument is to know when you should simply stop talking to let the other person take it all in. When I felt enough time had passed, I pressed on: 'You could sign yourself out of the ward and meet us down there tomorrow afternoon.'

I knew she was going to say yes even before she did. I could see it in the light that suddenly switched back on in her eyes as the idea found a place to settle and grow. 'Do they let you just sign out of a ward?'

'Hell, yeah,' I said with the cockiness of an old-time lag. 'I used to do it all the time.'

Once, a long time ago, I'd been within days of pledging my love and loyalty to a man who ultimately had heard those promises from another woman. What neither of us could ever have imagined was that a day would come when we would find ourselves working together to conceal something from him.

'Ryan will *never* say yes to this,' Chloe had said, slowly shaking her head.

'That's why we won't tell him, until *after* Hope's visit. Once he realises he was wrong, he'll understand why we did it.'

'And if *we're* wrong?'

'We're not.'

Chloe scrutinised my face carefully, feature by feature. 'Are you actively *trying* to get us divorced?'

'Now, there's a thought,' I said, giving her a fleeting flash of a grin.

The visiting session wasn't due to end for quite some time, but I felt as if *my* visit had reached its natural conclusion. I got to my feet and wound my long red cashmere scarf around my neck as I slipped on my coat.

'Thank you for bringing these,' Chloe said, finally looking inside the carrier bags which I'd filled with pampering products, cosmetics and all the things I remember longing visitors would bring me in hospital, rather than the ubiquitous bags of grapes. She pulled out a pack of velvet-soft loo roll, a set of razors, and a manicure kit. 'You know your stuff,' she admitted, fingering a box set of shower gel and body lotion in the fragrance I remembered she'd worn for years. 'They might not get used for a while, though. I'm not allowed to shower by myself, and the nurses have been too busy over the last few days to help me. And strangely, Ryan's not allowed in the ladies' bathroom!'

'They'll keep,' I said.

I'd got as far as saying goodbye. I was almost out of the bay when I stopped suddenly, hesitated for a moment and then pivoted on my heel. I strode back quickly to the bed before I changed my mind. 'Grab your toiletry bag.'

Chloe looked startled and then, as she realised my intention, slightly horrified. But I could hardly back out now. 'This is already the freakiest situation in the entire world, so we might as well go all the way. Come on. I'm going to help you shower.'

Chapter 18

Chloe

I don't make friends easily or quickly. I've known some of the mothers at the school for over three years, since Hope's first day in the nursery class, and I *still* wouldn't call them good friends. Ever since Sally and Bob had moved to France to run their holiday letting business in the Dordogne, I hadn't bothered filling the best friend vacancy in my life. You don't have to when you end up married to the perfect candidate for the role.

So I wasn't looking for a new friend, and if I was, the very last person I would have picked would have been Maddie. I still wasn't entirely sure I could trust her, which made agreeing to stand naked and vulnerable in front of her in a hospital bathroom even more remarkable. I've always been the kind of person who'd rather queue for ages for a cubicle than use a communal changing room. There's always been a shyness in me that only ever disappears completely when my clothes hit our bedroom floor, and Ryan reaches out for me with the light of desire burning like a flame in his eyes.

In the thousands of times he'd seen me naked, I'd never once compared my body to the woman he'd made love to before me. But I did that day. To be fair, Maddie had been remarkably professional and matter-of-fact about the whole thing. I suppose she'd been on the other side of the fence enough times for it not to feel so strange to her.

When a moment of sudden giddiness had had me clutching at the plastic shower curtain, Maddie had quickly grabbed a nearby stool and plonked it onto the shower tray. It felt weird to be sitting under the torrent falling onto my head, and then downright unsettling when I blinked the water from my eyes and saw Maddie pulling off her own jumper before reaching for the bottle of luxury shampoo she'd bought me.

'You're not coming in here, are you?' I asked, practically having to sit on my hands to stop them instinctively covering my nakedness.

She laughed, and I wondered what Ryan would say if he could see us both right this minute, before deciding I really didn't want to know the answer to that one.

'No, I just don't see how I'm going to be able to shampoo your hair without getting my sleeves wet,' she explained.

I hated being so weak that even lifting my arms above

my head was presently beyond me. 'You'll get stronger,' she assured me, as she worked the rich lather through my hair with remarkable gentleness. 'When I first woke up from the coma, I was as weak as a kitten.'

That evening, when Ryan bent down to kiss me, I saw his nose twitching appreciatively at the cocktail of aromas that clung to me like a cloud. 'Hmm, you smell good,' he murmured, bending down and gently nuzzling my neck. He leant back and looked at me curiously. 'Have you washed your hair?'

I nodded. *That* was the moment when I should have told him. But to do so would mean I'd have to reveal our plans for the following day.

'Yes, somebody on the ward helped me this afternoon.'

It wasn't a lie. Not a *real* one. But my words tasted bitter, like cyanide, as they passed my lips.

I brushed my hair slowly and carefully in front of the mirror Maddie had included in the bag of products she'd brought in. My brushstrokes became hesitant as they reached the part of my skull where I now knew the tumour lived. I could visualise it, lurking beneath the hair, the skin, and the bone, like one of those unexploded Second World War bombs you sometimes hear about on the news. It wasn't a bad analogy. It could lie there for years – perhaps it *had* been there for years, but once it was uncovered, once the deadly mechanisms were exposed ... well, there's a reason why the bomb-disposal people evacuate everyone from an area, isn't there?

I pulled the belt of my dressing gown more firmly around my waist, making sure it was secure. Before leaving the ward I picked up the final parting gift Maddie had left behind for me to borrow. Her soft cashmere scarf might look a little bizarre teamed with my fleecy robe, but it would effectively hide the ugly bruises from my daughter's eyes, and that was all that mattered.

I'd been on edge all day; had almost phoned Maddie at least half a dozen times to call off our plans. All I kept remembering was the terrified three-year-old who'd gone through an agonising spate of night terrors, and the words of the doctors and specialists who'd advised us to remove all sources of anxiety from her world. So we had . . . we'd removed Maddie, and Hope had got better, and that should have made everything all right. But although we never spoke of it, I knew that neither Ryan nor I had felt good about the lies we'd told our daughter.

And today there would be more lies, at least until this evening when I would tell Ryan the truth. It was little wonder my blood pressure readings were worryingly raised whenever they were taken that day. It had been quite a battle to convince the nurses that I was well enough to leave the ward for a short while.

'If I drop down dead in the foyer, I promise my husband won't sue the hospital.' I'd meant it as a joke, but the stony look the ward sister had given me told me she was taking my words seriously. I realised too late that no one around here found the notion of people dropping dead remotely amusing, and suddenly neither did I.

As arranged, Maddie texted me from the hospital car park: *We're here. Are you okay to make your own way down in the lift, or shall we come up and get you?*

No. I'll meet you in the foyer, I texted back, my fingers clumsily misspelling practically every word with nerves. *I don't want Hope anywhere near the ward.*

I shuffled in my sheepskin slippers to the lifts, staring back through the glass of the ward doors. One of the nurses was frowning as she watched me wait for the lift. It made me feel like a prisoner doing a very slow and controlled jailbreak.

The lift doors slid open at ground level, and I levered myself away from the support of the carriage wall. The foyer was busy, a hive of people, all dashing in different directions, powered by a frenetic purpose. I'd only been a patient for a little over a week, and already I felt I was no longer part of this world. My illness separated me from them – that and the fact that I was the only one among them wearing pyjamas.

My eyes scanned the sea of people. I heard her before I saw her. There was a cry like the screech of a barn owl, if barn owls were able to talk and could say the word *Mummy*.

A few heads turned, and then a shape separated from the throng of people and began to hurtle towards me. It was probably corny; it probably looked like a scene lifted straight out of a Lifetime movie, but I didn't care. I dropped to my knees and held out my arms and Hope flew into them with the force of a pulled magnet.

I've no idea if we were drawing a crowd of onlookers, for I kept my eyes tightly shut until I was certain they'd be perfectly dry when I opened them again. I once vowed she'd never see me cry, and my diagnosis had strengthened that resolve rather than weakened it.

'Mummy,' Hope exclaimed, several decibels above a normal conversational level. 'What are *you* doing here?'

I looked up at Maddie, who from my kneeling position appeared to be about eight foot tall. She held out a pale long-fingered hand, and I gratefully placed mine in it until I was once again standing upright.

Hope twisted in my arms and looked up at Maddie. 'You said we were going to the shops,' her small voice was almost an accusation.

There was an impish look on Maddie's face, one that I'd seen a hundred times before on her daughter's. 'There are shops here,' she said reasonably, nodding in their direction.

'And then we were going to have burgers.'

Maddie pointed her finger at a nearby franchise, with a familiar bright yellow logo. 'We certainly are.'

'This is the hospital where they're going to make me better, Pumpkin,' I explained to my clearly confused six-year-old. 'Upstairs is where all the patients sleep and get their medicine, and down here . . .'

Hope threw her arms back around my legs, like an

ardent tree-hugger in the face of a bulldozer. 'Down here is the place where you can see your mummy,' she completed happily.

Maddie's eyes met mine over the top of Hope's head. 'It sure is,' she agreed.

The time went far too quickly. I held Hope's hand in mine as we strolled around the small collection of shops, unwilling to let go of her for even one minute. I picked up a cute plush dog along with several comics from the racks, and a couple of packets of sweets which in normal circumstances I would have tried to talk her out of. My illness was going to be very bad for her teeth, I could already see that.

I was two customers away from the till before I realised my handbag and purse were securely shut away in the locker beside my bed.

'I'll get those,' said Maddie smoothly, passing the assistant her debit card as they called us up to the till. Suddenly the years fell away and I was back in the past, in a different hospital, in a different shop, buying sweets for Gladys before bumping into Ryan in the hallway. History was repeating itself, and for a moment I felt scared, as if we were stuck in an inescapable spiral in time. She was sick, and now I was; she had Ryan, but now he was mine. But even more frightening was how it had all ended, with Hope believing her mother had died. And this time . . . ? Was this what happened when you tempted fate by telling one too many lies?

*

'What would you like to eat?' I asked, putting my arm around Hope and cuddling her close as I studied the children's menu.

'Cheesy burger and fries,' she shot back. 'It's what Daddy bought me the other night.'

'I see. It's all coming out now,' I said with a laugh, thinking of the freezer full of healthy dinners that Ryan was obviously ignoring.

'I wish you had come with us, Maddie, like Daddy wanted.'

I lifted my head slowly and caught the slightly uncomfortable look on the porcelain-white face opposite me. *It really* was *all coming out now.*

'I couldn't, sweetie. I had a date,' she answered, a little too rapidly. Her cheeks flushed pink, but it was impossible to know if that was from a lie, or the memory of the man she'd spent her evening with. *Allegedly.*

Despite ordering far more food than she normally consumed in one sitting, Hope was insistent that she wanted a milkshake. I was about to steer her towards a healthier choice, when Maddie leant forward and grinned mischievously. 'That sounds yummy. Why don't we *all* have one?'

I didn't want one, but I also didn't want to be Boring Mummy, Healthy-Eating Mummy, or Saying-No Mummy. We ordered three milkshakes, and Hope manfully began to suck on the straw so hard her pale cheeks turned red.

Maddie shrugged her shoulders at me over the froth of

her strawberry shake. 'Oh well, I could do with putting on a few more pounds.'

I slid my chocolate milkshake towards me. 'Please don't make me hate you any more than I already do,' I said sweetly.

Her laughter drew several admiring male glances from the surrounding diners. I imagine it always did.

Maddie

'I owe you an apology, Maddie.'

I stared into his familiar blue eyes and wondered which particular transgression he was referring to. Not telling me I had a daughter; lying to that daughter and telling her I'd died; or not waiting for me to wake up from the coma, and marrying someone else. There were so many to choose from. But in fact, it was none of those.

'I was wrong trying to keep Hope from seeing her mother,' Ryan admitted. His voice was low, presumably weighed down by the guilt. And yet he didn't seem to realise how carelessly he'd hurt me all over again.

'Which particular mother are you talking about this time?'

Ryan didn't 'do' uncomfortable or blush – at least not like Mitch did – but today he did both.

'Touché. You're absolutely right. It appears to be a mistake I keep on making.' His eyes were deep and sincere as he focused on mine. 'I promise you, I won't do it again. Not to either of you.'

A part of me wanted to close the front door on him then. He'd come, he'd said his piece, and presumably the weight was already lifting off his chest. I could send him away ... only when it came down to it, I couldn't. I held the door open wider, despite a separate part of my brain warning me: *This is probably not a good idea.*

'Do you want to come in? I was just making coffee.'

I didn't wait to see if he was going to follow, as though that somehow absolved me of responsibility. I padded barefoot back down my hallway to the kitchen.

'Who's looking after Hope?' I asked, glancing at the kitchen clock and realising it was past her bedtime.

'Megan, the girl who usually sits for us,' Ryan answered, taking the mug I held out to him.

'It's only instant,' I apologised, remembering how he'd always been a bit of a coffee aficionado. It's funny how so many small things, things I thought I'd completely forgotten, kept popping up and catching me off guard. It was like walking through a minefield of memories, waiting for the next explosion. I wondered if he felt the same way.

I glanced up over the rim of my mug and caught him studying me. He was one millisecond too late in pulling down the shutters. So he *did* remember, every bit as clearly as I did.

'When do they think Chloe can come home?' I asked, aware we were in danger of straying off the paved surface if we weren't careful. Chloe's name brought us straight back onto the highway.

'Soon I hope, although probably not until after the weekend now.' He sighed and sounded so lost I almost wanted to get out of my chair and go and put my arms around him. *Almost.*

'At least, thanks to you, Hope will now visit her.' He smiled gently and his face took on that particular expression it only ever wore when he was thinking about our child. 'You should have seen her on the drive home, Maddie. She was so happy, and I have *you* to thank for that.'

I gave a small shrug, because I didn't want him to see how much his words meant to me.

'I mean it; I'd never have been brave enough to take her in. I was too worried it would remind her . . .' His words trailed away awkwardly. I nodded to let him know I understood. 'But somehow you just *knew* it was the right thing to do. Mother's instinct, I suppose.'

The effort to keep smiling and not burst into very loud and embarrassing sobs was excruciating. He slid the knife back out of the wound he'd made, not realising he'd stabbed me with his words.

The smile he gave me broke my heart in a thousand different ways. 'When did you get to be so damn smart?'

'It must have been while I was sleeping,' I replied softly.

'If anyone should ask, you and I are dating.'

The thing I liked about Mitch was that you could drop a huge bomb like that, right into his lap, and he wasn't the type to leap up and down and make a big fuss. He was far more likely to just look down at it curiously.

'Are we? That's nice. Although, I don't actually remember asking you out.'

Fifteen love. He got in the first blush. I pantomimed fanning my highly pink cheeks and he laughed.

'Good point. You didn't,' I answered.

His bushy eyebrows rose. *Take your time*, they said; *no hurry at all*, they assured me; *but I* would *like an explanation*.

It was Tuesday morning, and Mitch was going to make a start on the second bedroom. 'I know you probably haven't picked things out with Hope yet, but while I've got the time off work I'd like to make a start stripping the walls and getting the woodwork painted,' Mitch had explained over the phone.

He'd caught me at a weak moment, when I'd only just walked in through the door after a last-minute impromptu visit to my parents for the weekend. Perhaps it was seeing Hope rush into Chloe's arms at the hospital that had suddenly made me yearn to see my own mother again. It didn't matter whether or not she recognised me. The call to be with her was almost primal, and too strong to ignore.

It was quite the drive for someone who hadn't been on the road for such a long time, but I found the journey on the long grey stretch of motorway almost cathartic. My dad had been delighted to have me stay, and had immediately gone out and bought an inflatable mattress and a whole new set of bedding. 'Because now you've got your licence back, you can come any old time you want,' he'd said happily.

'Not quite at the drop of a hat,' I replied, giving his hand a warm squeeze. 'At the moment I'm still picking up Hope from school each day.' I looked down at my feet, so that his perceptive blue eyes couldn't see my face. 'Although I imagine that will come to an abrupt end as soon as Chloe gets out of hospital.'

His arm went around my shoulders. 'How are you finding that, love? Is it very hard?'

It was a good question, and one I didn't know how to answer. 'It's wonderful ... and awful, all at the same time. It's like catching a glimpse of something through a closing door, or having a taste of a meal only to have them whisk the plate away at the last minute.'

Having Hope so close, and yet not really having her at all, was an agony I was still trying to get used to. I looked up and saw in surprise that my dad's eyes were awash with unshed tears. My words could so easily describe the daily anguish he went through as he watched the woman he loved slip further away from him. We were both helpless to hold on to the people we loved, so we did the only thing that we could, we held on to each other instead.

'So, this relationship of ours, is it serious?'

I smiled and my lips twitched wickedly. 'No, I don't think so. I suspect you're only after my body.'

Fifteen all; although I hadn't played fair, because I *knew* he'd blush at that one.

'Sorry,' I apologised, realising that I might have taken

it one step too far. Mitch was such easy company that sometimes I forgot our friendship was a new fledgling thing, even though we'd known each other since before my accident.

'Chloe seemed to be uncomfortable about the amount of time I was spending with Ryan, so I thought it might be better for her recovery if she thought I was seeing someone else.' It was a martyr's answer, and I wasn't even sure if *I* believed it.

'I see,' said Mitch slowly, beginning to remove a selection of DIY equipment from his toolbox and laying it out on the floor of the second bedroom. 'So are we going to have to go out to dinner with them as a test? Am I going to have to learn a backstory about our relationship, or answer questions on how you take your tea?'

I laughed. 'Boy, if I didn't know better, I'd say you've been watching a few too many rom coms, my friend.'

'I *love* rom coms!' Mitch declared.

His enthusiastic reply practically made me rock on my heels. Just when I thought I had the measure of this man, he went and surprised me all over again. 'You do?' I asked incredulously.

'Absolutely. *Picture Perfect*, *The Wedding Date*, *Pretty Woman*,' he reeled off, revealing that if he ever went on *Mastermind*, this should *definitely* be his chosen subject. 'They're all about fake relationships that eventually become real ones.'

Suddenly it felt very hot in the small second bedroom.

449

'Well, I'm sure we won't have to go to those lengths. I only made it as a throwaway remark.'

'Fair enough,' Mitch said with a shrug, picking up the wallpaper steamer and plugging it in. 'Just wanted to get things straight.'

My hand was on the doorknob when he stopped me with one last comment.

'Extra milky with a half teaspoon of sugar,' he said. I looked back at him over my shoulder and smiled. 'It's how you like your tea,' he said, before disappearing like a magician behind a cloud of vapour from the steamer.

Chloe

'I just wish you'd asked me first, that's all.'

The last thing I wanted to do on my first night home after a fortnight in hospital was to have an argument. But I could feel myself teetering on the edge of one.

'I honestly didn't think it would be a problem.'

Maybe it wasn't, I thought reluctantly; maybe *I* was the one with the problem. I looked up at him from my position on the settee, propped up by virtually every cushion in the house. From the moment he'd brought me home, Ryan had been treating me as if I was a piece of spun glass wrapped around a ticking bomb. It was an interesting combination.

He crossed the room and perched on the settee by my feet. 'I only thought as Maddie has been collecting Hope from school for the last few weeks, it made sense to ask her if she could carry on. I don't want you to overdo things, and you're not going to be up to driving for a week or two.'

I tried to lift myself out of the moment to question if I was being unreasonable. Was my knee-jerk jealousy over how much time Maddie had spent with Hope clouding my judgement? Yes, it probably was, but that didn't seem a good enough reason to back down.

'I could have still have picked her up,' I maintained stubbornly. 'I could have got a cab there and back.' It wasn't a logical suggestion, but I was probably several stations past logical by that point. I seemed to have missed my stop.

'If you want, I'll phone her and tell her not to bother,' volunteered Ryan. He waited for me to reply, and when I said nothing he pulled the phone from his pocket.

I caved before the number had connected. 'No. Leave it. It's done now.'

Ryan looked at me for a long moment. There were deep lines of concern etched on his face that told a very different story about how he'd coped over the last two weeks to his carefully edited version.

'I think I've forgotten how to feel normal. All I want is to go back to the way things were before.' Interestingly he didn't ask me if I meant before I discovered I had a brain tumour, or before Maddie woke up. That was just as well, as I wasn't entirely sure I knew myself.

'Maybe what I need is for you to hold me,' I said. Ryan's arms were instantly there, tenderly encircling as he pulled me against his chest. I could feel his breath fanning my hair;

hear his heart beating steadily beneath my ear, taste the salt of a single tear from either his eyes or mine when he kissed my lips. My senses were full of him, and suddenly nothing else mattered. *This* was what was important, being home with him and Hope. Everything else was background trivia.

'Everything's going to be all right now,' Ryan said, kissing the top of my head gently. It was a promise he had no authority to make, but I chose to believe him anyway.

Those first few weeks were the worst, because I was hiding so much from so many people. Hiding from Ryan my dread that I might not be the woman who'd grow old and grey beside him, despite the promises I'd made. Hiding the fear that my family's future might not include me. I could picture every milestone that lay ahead, like photographs still to be taken in an album. I saw a taller Hope, swamped by an oversized blazer on her first day at secondary school; I saw her dressed in something Ryan would probably hate, about to go on her very first date; I saw my teenage daughter laughing jubilantly as she tore up her L plates. I saw all the things I might never get to see.

Who'd be standing beside her at her university graduation? Ryan would be there, older and distinguished, more grey than dark blond, with his arm around Hope, who'd be gowned in a robe and mortar board. But who was the person standing on the other side of her? And further down the road, on her wedding day, was there an empty space in the family photograph for the smiling mother-of-the-bride?

Probably not, for there were was already an excess of candidates for that position.

And yet when Ryan asked – which he did at least fifty times a day – how I was feeling, I gathered up every one of those fears, bundled them out of sight, and told him I was fine. So it felt perfectly natural to give Maddie exactly the same answer when she arrived at our door with Hope, on the day Ryan had eventually returned to work.

It had taken me longer than normal to answer the bell. I'd developed a habit of walking slowly, as though I was balancing a weighty book on my head, instead of a collection of metal implants inside it. It didn't help the tumour, but my deportment had most definitely improved.

'No, you're not fine,' answered Maddie with quiet certainty, after Hope had run past us, no doubt in search of her cat. I felt my hands tighten on the door jamb, which I was using for support. I stared into the face of the beautiful woman standing on my porch, and hated the fact that she saw beneath my mask so easily. She saw what my husband, my child, my consultant, and every other person who asked me, could not. When you stare death in the face, when you look deep into the red-hot coals of its eyes, it changes you somehow. It had changed me, and it had changed her. And I knew right then, on that very first day, that the relationship I had with this woman was about to alter in ways I'd never imagined or expected.

It took four days before I asked her in for tea. Four days before I stopped treating her like an unpaid chauffeur. I

453

was kind of hoping she'd say no, but of course she didn't. It was very different from the first time we'd invited her into our home. I didn't reach for the best crockery. I laid no fancy tea tray. I pulled out mismatched mugs and dropped builders' teabags into them. I could hear Hope through the open door of the kitchen, chattering away to Elsa, as she did each day. My ears pricked up instantly at her words about a nasty 'mean boy' in her class who'd made her cry.

My eyes went to Maddie's, instantly concerned. She leant forward on the tall stool she'd perched on. The narrow width of the breakfast bar put us so close together, she only had to whisper her explanation: 'Apparently some little shit told her that she and I both look like blood-sucking vampires.'

Immediately my thoughts went to every childcare book I'd read – and I'd read a lot – that advised how to deal with that kind of bullying. I began scrolling through my options: make an appointment with her class teacher, or should it be the head, or perhaps it would be best to have a quiet word with the parents?

'What did you say to her?'

'Nothing. But I might just have licked my lips when we walked past him in the playground.'

I groaned, and put my head in my hands, and for once it wasn't because of the mass growing inside it. 'You can't do things like that.'

'Clearly I have much to learn. Luckily Hope has a good cop and a bad cop for a mum.'

I looked at her for a very long moment. 'You're not at all how I always imagined you'd be.' Maddie looked puzzled. 'All those months, well years, really, when I visited you in the hospital, I created an idea in my head about the person I thought you'd be.' I looked slightly embarrassed by my admission. 'We became friends – in my imagination, anyway.'

Maddie took a mouthful of her tea before replacing her mug with care on the worktop. 'So how does the *real* me compare to the one you invented?'

'I'll have to get back to you on that one,' I said cautiously.

She shrugged and her face transformed into an enormous smile as our daughter ran into the room. 'That's good enough for now.'

Chapter 19

Four Months Later

Maddie

Spring is a horrible time of year to discover you have a life-threatening condition. When everything around you is coming back to life after the dark days of winter, it must seem doubly cruel to find yourself suddenly swimming against that tide.

The things that stood out most for me that spring were the discoveries I made. During the months when the days began to grow longer and warmer, I learnt that the only thing sweeter than your sleepy child's goodnight kiss is the early-morning cuddle you get when they leap into bed beside you.

I learnt that I was rubbish at haggling, after paying a thousand pounds too much for the second-hand car I bought. 'I could have gone with you,' Ryan had offered, when it was too late to be of help. I learnt to count to ten before smiling and saying politely that it didn't matter.

I learnt that Mitch was excellent at wallpapering but that I aced him at painting window frames, which meant I spent several weeks covered in paint splotches, working happily alongside him as we transformed the second bedroom in the flat.

I learnt I missed my physical therapy sessions when Heidi finally told me that we were 'done'. I also learnt that gym membership is only cost-effective if you actually go regularly, and that it's much harder to motivate yourself without a pocket-sized peroxide dynamo yelling in your ear.

I learnt how to use Tinder – not for me, but for Mitch, after he moaned about yet another disastrous first date he'd been on. I learnt I was far better at picking out potential girlfriends for him than he was. I also learnt to ignore the strange feeling it gave me when several weeks later he was *still* seeing the girl I'd found him on the site.

But the hardest lesson I learnt that spring was that I was nowhere near as smart or as astute as I'd once thought. I missed signs all over the place. I mistook a warrior for a pacifist, and a lion-heart for a weak one. I thought my job was to help Ryan and Chloe, I thought she needed my support to face her illness. But in fact Chloe Turner was the strongest person I'd ever met. It takes a very special kind of woman to devote whatever time she has left to train someone else to be her replacement. That was something else I learnt.

*

'Don't let Hope have her ears pierced until she's thirteen.'

We were sitting side by side on uncomfortable wooden seats in a draughty village hall. I was swivelled on my chair, staring at the group of excitable little girls in matching pink tutus lined up beside the low platform that was about to serve as an impromptu stage.

I turned back to look at Chloe, whose smile was wide as she found Hope's face searching for her among the assembled line of mothers.

'What?'

Chloe nodded and smiled at some unspoken question she'd read on Hope's face. She lifted up the small camcorder from her lap and gave her daughter a confident thumbs-up. She answered me without looking in my direction.

'Pierced ears. We struck a deal; it involved the eating of broccoli. Thirteen, don't forget,' she said.

The meaning of her words took their time to filter through to the appropriate part of my brain. I finally got it just as the ballet teacher slid the CD into the player, and the first strains of the opening song began to fill the hall.

'Chloe—' I said, unthinkingly reaching for her hand, which wasn't something I could ever remember doing before.

'Shhh,' she said. 'It's starting,' She nodded her head towards the stage where the line of ballerinas had begun to leap around exuberantly. But she held on to my hand for more seconds than I was expecting, and when I looked at her profile as her eyes followed Hope's every step, I saw the tears begin to slowly trickle down her cheek.

Chloe

You always remember where you were when you first hear devastating news: 9/11, the death of Princess Diana, those moments are forever seared into your memory. It was easy for me to recall where I'd been when I received my own dreadful news, for it was exactly the same place I'd been the first time, across a desk from Dr Higgins.

'I'm very sorry, Chloe, the latest MRI shows a worrying increase in the size of your tumour.'

I reached out blindly for Ryan's hand and it was already stretched out towards me, waiting. I focused on the bones of our fingers, on the feel of his skin, on the fusion of his grip on mine as the doctor's words thundered like a waterfall around us.

'I've passed on your results to the neurosurgical team. You'll be hearing from them very soon to discuss your options and how we should proceed from here.'

I don't remember getting out of my chair, or leaving the consultation room. I don't remember the walk back to the car, except that the sun felt warm on my back. There were birds calling from trees heavy with summer foliage, but they all fell silent at the sound of my sobs. It was almost as if they understood.

Strangely, I liked Mr Owen from the very first moment I met him. It was an unusual reaction to have on meeting the man who was going to cut into your skull. He was a straight talker.

'I don't want to do this surgery, Chloe.' The blue of his eyes was so pale, they were practically white. They were also extremely troubled. 'You're a very young woman, and a mother. And this is a very high-risk operation. If there was any alternative to surgery, anything at all, please know that I'd be recommending it to you right now.'

I swallowed noisily and glanced across at Ryan, who was sitting rigidly in the chair beside me. The hand that wasn't clenching mine was balled up in a fist on his thigh, as though he wanted to punch someone. I hoped it wasn't Mr Owen.

'What about radiotherapy?' I asked hesitantly. 'Could we try that first?'

Mr Owen shook his head regretfully, and gave no sign of the irritation I'm sure all medics must feel when patients try to recommend their own course of treatment. 'Because of the size of the tumour and its placement, I very much doubt I'm going to be able to remove it all. After the surgery, when you've recovered sufficiently, that will be the time to begin our radiotherapy campaign.'

Campaign. I liked that word. It made it sound like we were an army going into battle. In a way, I suppose we were. My smile was a little watery, probably diluted by all the tears I'd shed over the last few days. 'Well, it's nice to have something to look forward to.'

'When?' Ryan's voice had probably not sounded that croaky since he was an adolescent. He cleared his throat and tried again. 'When do you propose to do the surgery?'

Mr Owen sighed and looked back down at the array of

tests results spread across his desk. There were a great many of them. 'I think we should look at scheduling you in within the next few weeks at the most. I don't feel we should delay it any further than that.'

I breathed in and out slowly, thankful for the surgeon's honesty and yet terrified by the risks he'd so clearly outlined at the outset of our conversation.

'Worst-case scenario?' he'd echoed, with a look of obvious reluctance on his face. I guess all doctors must hate that question, it was probably right up there with *How long have I got, Doc?* in the list of things they never want a patient to ask.

I'd braced myself in my chair, like a skydiver who realises too late that they're frightened of heights. But when the doctor's strange pale eyes focused on mine he must have seen my resolve. No sugar coating, no euphemisms. I needed to *know*.

'My greatest concern is that we won't be able to control the bleeding on the table. The stents that have been managing your condition could now hamper us.'

'Which means?' I was probing, because the only power I had left was knowledge. If things were really as bad as the expression on the surgeon's face led me to believe, then I needed to know it all.

'You could bleed to death on the table. The operation could leave you severely incapacitated. You could end up paralysed, or in a severe vegetative state.'

'Like a coma,' said Ryan. He had a look of a man who was about to relive his very worst nightmare.

'Yes, like a coma,' said Mr Owen.

Maddie

'Maddie, can Sam and I watch another episode?'

Hope stood in my kitchen doorway, her school skirt crumpled and something which looked suspiciously like jam down the front of her logo'd sweatshirt. I *knew* the doughnuts had been a mistake, but it would have been rude to have said so to Mitch, particularly as he'd ended up consuming half the box himself. Too late, I remembered Chloe's rule about Hope changing out of her school uniform as soon as she got home.

'Okay with you?' I asked Mitch, who was sitting at the kitchen table cradling his third or fourth cup of tea.

'One more,' he said equably, 'then I will definitely have to get him back home to his mum.'

I pulled up the second chair at the small table, and tried very hard not to stare at the stray grains of sugar that were lodged in Mitch's beard. He saw me looking and grinned. 'Better add sugary doughnuts to the list of things I should never eat when out on a date,' he said, brushing the residue from his chin and reaching into the box for one more calorific treat. It was a measure of how comfortable we now were in each other's company that something that would have once turned him crimson now didn't register even pale pink. But then of course, *we* weren't on a date. This was a mercy mission, and I was unashamedly hijacking his evening with Sam in order to keep Hope distracted.

I didn't feel particularly proud of myself, trying to

hoodwink my own daughter, but until Ryan and Chloe were back from their appointment at the hospital, it was easier to avoid all questions that involved 'Mummy's bad head' or the word 'operation'.

'Does she always call you Maddie? Never Mummy?' Mitch asked, this time taking greater care to ensure his beard was unsullied by crumbs.

'Yes. I mean, she obviously knows that I *am* her mother. But Chloe was Mummy for six years before I came along, so naturally she has prior claim to the title.'

'You have a claim too,' Mitch said loyally.

'Now doesn't seem like the right time to push it.'

'No. Of course not.'

We were silent for several minutes, the only sound filling the flat was the high-pitched squeals of laughter from the programme our carefree offspring were watching in the other room. Although this was the first time Sam and Hope had met, they'd got on immediately in that weird instant-friendship way children seem to have. If only adults had that ability, if only they could see a person and know immediately they would make a connection. That thought took me, not surprisingly, to my all-too-successful attempt to find Mitch a female companion.

'So how are things going with Caitlin?'

For a moment Mitch looked slightly uncomfortable, before admitting. 'Very good, actually. You picked well.'

Yay. Go me, I thought, trying to fix a smile that looked halfway genuine onto my lips.

'You should give it a go,' he urged, nudging my arm heartily in a come-on-in-the-water's-fine kind of a way. I resisted the impulse to rub the spot on my arm which I was fairly certain would be sporting a bruise when I took off my jumper later.

'No thanks. I think I'm done for the time being. There's quite enough going on right now to think about. I don't need any more complications.'

Mitch nodded thoughtfully. 'Yeah. I get that. It's all about timing. To be honest, I wasn't at all sure about this online dating malarkey.'

'Do people still say "malarkey"?'

'Yeah, they brought it back while you were in your coma.'

That's what I liked about Mitch: his very dark and unexpected sense of humour. It caught me by surprise every single time.

'I've been in love twice in my life,' Mitch admitted, switching lanes in our conversation faster than an F1 driver. 'Perhaps it's greedy to be looking for it again.'

I looked at him curiously, wondering if I dared ask him who the second woman had been, if Colleen his wife had been the first. But then I heard the catchy theme tune of the programme the children were watching and realised we were about to be interrupted. That question would have to wait for another day. The hallway filled with the sound of two pairs of racing footsteps heading our way.

'Perhaps I need to improve my wooing skills,' said Mitch,

getting to his feet. 'And yes, they brought back "wooing" too, before you ask.'

I smiled.

'Do you think I should bring Caitlin some flowers on our next date?'

'Not sunflowers,' I said, almost as surprised as he was by the way the words had shot out of me. I glanced over at the kitchen window ledge where the bunch he'd brought me that afternoon was displayed in his grandmother's crystal vase.

'No. Not sunflowers,' he agreed.

'Any news yet?' asked my dad, strangely whispering down the phone, because that was what I was doing.

'Not yet,' I said, retreating to the darkness of my kitchen, to a spot where I could see Hope fast asleep in the second bedroom. 'Ryan phoned briefly and asked if Hope could stay here tonight. I think he and Chloe had a lot they wanted to talk about.'

My father gave a small grunt of understanding. He was very fond of Chloe, I knew that, and for the first time I wasn't upset by that realisation. 'Did he say if they were going to have to operate?'

I thought back to Ryan's voice, cracking with emotion, as he'd briefly summarised their appointment with the neuro-surgeon. 'It's not looking good,' he'd said. I suspected that he was crying by the time he'd hung up the phone. But what I really hadn't been expecting was that so was I.

'At least the doctors are pleased with you,' my father said, his voice heavy with relief. 'That's something to be thank-ful for.'

'They must be, if they don't want to see me so fre-quently now.'

'I just wish they knew . . . I just wish they could definitely say . . .' His voice trailed away over the ground we had cov-ered so many times before. Eventually, you had to stop asking the questions *Why?* and *What if?* when you realised no one had those answers.

'I guess there *are* no guarantees in life, are there?' said my father, sounding resigned.

I thought of a young blonde woman, facing an unknown and terrifying future and sighed sadly.

'No, Dad, there aren't. Life doesn't work like that.'

Chloe

I slid the top drawer of the chest to a close, watching the three white envelopes slowly disappear from sight. They stood out starkly against the muted shades of the clothes they were resting on. They would be easy to find. Not least because the envelopes were fat and bulky, crammed with what should have been a lifetime of words, condensed down to just a few sheets of paper.

I looked around the bedroom one last time; noticed an almost invisible rumple on the covers of our large double bed, and crossed the room to twitch it flat. Would I ever see this room again?

Ryan had already taken down my small bag. He was probably loading it in the car right now. There hadn't been much to pack. And anyway, in less than twenty-four hours my need for possessions could very well be at an end. Ryan refused to allow me to say things like that out loud, but he couldn't stop me *thinking* them.

I stopped in the hallway and looked through the door of Hope's bedroom. Elsa was curled up in a ball on the foot of her bed, but I couldn't summon up the energy to turf her off. The doors of the pumpkin doll's house were wide open, for Hope had been playing with it right up until the moment Ryan had taken her to school. I looked from the cat to the doll's house and tried to remember a time when worrying about whose gift had pleased Hope more was even remotely important.

I walked to the head of the bed and picked up Hope's pillow, burying my face in its depths and breathing in the smell of her. The cat looked at me curiously as the only sob I was going to allow myself that morning was muffled by goose down and feathers. I heard the sound of the front door closing, and knew it was time to go. I ran my hand lightly down the cat's back, hearing her immediate throaty purr in response. 'Take good care of her, Elsa,' I whispered. 'Make sure you're always there when she needs you.' My steps were heavy as I walked slowly from the room, hoping the cat would have more success with that task than I would.

Ryan was in full coping mode. He locked the back door,

put down cat food, and set the dishwasher going, as though this was just any other morning. Which of course was exactly how we'd played it with Hope. Obviously she *knew* I was going into hospital, but over the last six months that sadly was no longer an unusual event.

'Are you sleeping over?' she'd asked me, chasing the last spoonful of her Rice Krispies around the bowl.

I smiled at the expression that she'd only recently learnt after spending nights at Maddie's flat. Would she keep the flat on afterwards, I wondered. Maybe, for a while. Apparently she'd worked hard at making a lovely bedroom for Hope. I'd kept meaning to go and see it, but somehow I'd run out of time. But then I'd run out of time for so many other things too: to have a baby; to get my first grey hair; to celebrate a milestone anniversary. I shook my head. The list was too long and too sad to contemplate.

'I might be away for a few days,' was the answer I eventually decided to give Hope. And in a world where miracles really *do* happen, that might not be a lie. Patients following my kind of surgery were allowed home in what seemed like a ridiculously short amount of time. Or, alternatively, they never went home at all.

We didn't say much on the drive to the hospital. By that time everything had been said, and what was left over was written in the letter I'd left for him anyway. He drove the entire journey one-handed, the other firmly gripping mine. It was probably irresponsible and dangerous, but we made it to the hospital in one piece.

Saying goodbye to Hope as she ran off to the car, all gazelle-thin legs and flying ponytail, was hard. I'd held her in my arms a little too hard and a little too long, in much the same way that Ryan had held me through the night.

We'd made love, both of us trying to hide the inescapable truth that we could be doing so for the very last time. It had been slow, and sweet and tender; the kind of lovemaking that was worthy of remembering. Hours later, when Ryan had thought I was asleep, I'd felt him slip quietly from our bed. The door to our en-suite bathroom opened and then closed, but the wooden panel wasn't thick enough to mask the sound of his sobs. When eventually he'd come back to bed, he'd pulled me into the curve of his body, his arms locking tightly around me as though afraid someone would steal me away before morning. He whispered 'I love you' into my hair, not just once, but many times. I fell asleep to the words, as though they were a lullaby.

In the glare and bustle of the hospital it was hard to hold on to those moments of tenderness. They kept being pushed aside by an incoming tide of formalities which were required before major surgery. There were blood tests, a final MRI, and forms that had to be signed. My hand was shaking when I wrote my name, and the expression *signing your life away* had never felt more true as I passed the documents back to the nurse.

At lunchtime I sent Ryan down to the ground floor to buy us sandwiches that I knew neither of us would eat.

He returned with the cellophane-wrapped packages and a suggestion.

'Why don't I get Maddie to collect Hope from school?' That way I can stay with you all evening, or overnight if they let me.'

The way you've done so many times before, I thought sadly. But he'd been younger then, and there had been no daughter to be considered. Even so, it was harder than I expected to turn him down.

'No. You have to go.' I lifted one hand to gently cup his cheek. 'When I fall asleep tonight, I need to know that Hope is safely tucked up in her own bed, with all her own things around her, and that you're in our room beside her. If her whole world is about to change, I'd like to know that before it did she was in a place surrounded by happy memories of the three of us.'

'She'll always have those.' It was the closest he'd ever come to admitting that by this time tomorrow he might once again be a single parent. Except, of course . . . he never would be.

'I wish you could see things the way I do. I think it would help you,' I implored. Ryan shook his head, and I could sense his unspoken frustration. 'Everything happens for a reason,' I said quietly, wondering if he was any closer to accepting those words than he'd been a week ago, when I first voiced them.

Apparently not. 'No, it doesn't, Chloe. There isn't some big cosmic master plan. Fate hasn't orchestrated any of this. This is just random, unrelated shit, happening to the very best person in the whole world.'

I took his hand in mine and raised it to my lips, tenderly kissing his fingers. 'I think you may be biased.'

He almost smiled then, but at the last moment his eye caught the clock on the wall and his face dropped. We were almost out of time. But then, if what I believed was true, we'd been running out of time for the last six years. Nothing was random. There was a reason for everything. The place we now found ourselves was exactly where we were always destined to be.

'This isn't inevitable, Chloe. You didn't come into my life to fill a breach that was there because of Maddie. You weren't serving a purpose that's now over. You came into my life because we were meant to be together. We're *still* meant to be together. Please don't stop fighting to stay with us,' he begged, his mouth turning to kiss the hollow of my palm. 'Promise me that.'

'You know I won't,' I said brokenly, gathering him into my arms for one final goodbye, before gently pushing him away. 'Now go and collect our daughter from school. I'll phone you both later to say goodnight.'

Ryan nodded, blinking back tears. I wondered how far he would get before he allowed them to fall.

I doubt that he'd even reached the lift before my own started.

Mr Owen didn't look well. I could see that in the bright glare of early morning sunlight streaming through the window of my hospital room. His face looked drawn and

471

he was pale enough to be mistaken for one of Maddie's close relatives.

'Are you feeling all right?' I asked him ridiculously, as though our roles had suddenly been reversed. It felt like a reasonable question, as this was the man who would literally have my life in his hands that morning.

Mr Owen's smile was slow in forming. 'I have to admit, I didn't get much sleep last night.' That had to be one of the very last things you want to hear your neurosurgeon say. 'I was up half the night thinking about this surgery, to be perfectly frank.' Oh no, *that* was the last thing you wanted to hear.

He replaced the chart at the foot of my bed, but before leaving I saw his glance fall on the small framed photograph on my bedside locker. The surgeon's unusually pale eyes softened, and crinkled at the edges like the blades of a fan, as he looked at Hope, Ryan and me on a happier occasion.

'You have a lovely family,' he said warmly. 'Let's get you back to them as quickly as possible, shall we?'

Those were words I definitely liked, and I kept them firmly fixed in my head like a mantra as they wheeled me down to the operating theatre.

Maddie

The plastic carrier bags were heavy and were cutting into my fingers as I walked along the pavement in the sunshine. I'd had to park quite a distance from the house, but that was fine. At least I wouldn't be blocking the driveway in case he had to leave suddenly. In case there was an emergency.

I'd been nervous the very first time I had walked up the path to their front door, all those months ago, and I was nervous again. Same feeling, different reason.

Ryan looked dreadful, but no one wants to hear you say that, so I pretended the huge panda circles beneath his eyes were perfectly normal. He opened the door with his mobile phone in his hand, and for a moment I thought he was in the middle of a conversation, until I noticed that the screen was unlit. I wondered if he'd been holding the device all day, and imagined that he probably had.

'I don't want to intrude,' I began, crossing his threshold and doing exactly that, 'but I thought you might appreciate some company while you're waiting.'

His smile was the same, but different, to the one I remembered so well. 'Thank you, Maddie. That's kind of you.'

I lifted both arms high to show him the two plastic carriers. 'And I've brought you a couple of meals, in case you didn't feel like making anything.'

His eyes widened incredulously. 'You cooked a meal?' Some things about me he clearly remembered only too well.

'Well, *technically* Marks and Spencer cooked it. I'm more of a delivery girl here.'

The sound of his laughter seemed to surprise him almost as much as it did me. 'Thank you. That was really thoughtful. I think there's still some room in the fridge.'

I followed him to the kitchen and the large American-style

refrigerator, whose shelves were stacked high with foil-covered casseroles and ceramic dishes. 'Some of the school mums had the same idea,' Ryan said, coming to stand beside me as we surveyed the loaded shelves. 'I guess whatever happens, we're not going to starve.' Only someone who knew him well could hear his voice wasn't quite steady.

'Is there any news yet?'

Ryan shook his head, and a lock of blond hair fell across his eyes. It was still harder than it should be not to instinctively reach out and brush it back. Perhaps it always would be.

'No, it's too soon. The surgery started at nine, but they warned us it could take anything up to ten hours.'

We both looked towards the wall clock. Chloe's ordeal was only a quarter of the way over. It was going to be a very long day.

He made us coffee, so strong that the spoon could practically stand up unaided. I sipped the bitter brew without complaint.

'How was Hope this morning?'

The smile he kept exclusively for anything concerning our daughter crept back onto Ryan's face. 'She was fine. She spoke to Chloe, but she was anxious to get to school.'

'Are you *sure* she's mine?' I asked, teasing out a second unexpected laugh from him.

'It's her school sports day tomorrow, so apparently they spend all of today practising.'

'How hard can it be to balance an egg on a spoon?' I questioned.

'You'd be surprised. Although some of the parents take the whole thing way more seriously than the kids do,' Ryan said wryly. 'You *are* going tomorrow, aren't you?'

'Absolutely,' I assured him. 'Chloe made sure it was in my diary. She was certainly super-organised before she went into hospital.'

'She always is,' Ryan said, and the quiet pride and love in his voice was a small sharp stab, like the unexpected prick of a needle.

I finished my caffeine-heavy drink in silence and glanced at my watch, convinced much longer should have passed than the twenty minutes since the last time I checked. 'Waiting sucks, doesn't it?'

There was an expression on his face that made me realise, of all people, he knew that better than anyone. Which made what he had to say next all the more unexpected: 'I'm sorry, Maddie.' His voice was heavy with the weight of a thousand regrets.

'What for?'

'For *not* waiting.'

I was staring into the bottom of my empty cup, because all at once it seemed a safer place to look than into his eyes. 'You did wait,' I murmured.

'I didn't wait for long enough, did I? I broke my promise to you.'

I lifted my head at that, more shaken than I thought it was possible to be that he'd remembered that long-past conversation. 'Wherever you are, whatever happens, I will always be there for you.' Those words had haunted me in the months after I woke up. What I hadn't realised until that moment was that they'd also haunted him.

'It was a long time ago. We were two different people back then.'

Ryan shook his head sadly, not allowing himself to be let off the hook. 'I broke my word.' He'd also broken my heart, but he didn't need to hear that. Not today. Not ever, come to that. And now, unbelievably, he was living through a second nightmare, as another woman he loved fought to stay with him. How could that possibly be fair?

'I forgive you,' I said, knowing that was all I could say to lighten the load he'd been silently carrying since the night the hospital had phoned to tell him I'd come back. My hand reached across the breakfast bar and squeezed his, and for a moment the kitchen swirled with all the *what-ifs* and *what-might-have-beens*.

And then everything changed, as the phone he'd placed beside his cup juddered and began to ring. We both looked down at the screen, with twin expressions of shock. Two words glowed brightly above her photograph.

Chloe calling.

Chapter 20

Chloe

I lay on my hospital bed, smiling at my wiggling fingers, with all the fascination of a newborn baby. Everything still worked: my toes; my legs; everything. I got every question they asked me right. Admittedly, knowing my own name and what date it was didn't exactly qualify me as a Mensa candidate, but it seemed to please the medical team nevertheless.

A jubilant-looking Mr Owen visited my bedside shortly after I was brought back from Recovery. Even before he opened his mouth I could tell by his face that the operation had been a success. What I hadn't fully realised until he began to speak, was *how* amazingly well it had gone.

'To have been able to remove a tumour of that size so easily and speedily ... it's practically unheard of,' he declared, shaking his head slightly in disbelief. 'It goes beyond textbook perfect,' he said, looking like a man who'd won the surgical lottery. 'If it didn't sound so fanciful, I'd say it was practically a miracle – if you believe in such things.'

'I most definitely do,' I said, shivering slightly as I felt the fingers of serendipity graze lightly down my spine. 'I've always believed in miracles.'

They said it was the adrenalin pumping through me. They said that was why I was on such an incredible high and why I felt no pain. The nurses kept telling me to calm down, as though cheating death was something anyone could ever feel calm or nonchalant about. Maybe they were right. Maybe in a day or two it would hit me, and the pain and discomfort I'd been expecting from the surgery would track me down and catch up with me. But in the meantime all I could feel was euphoria.

Phoning Ryan, hearing his voice when I hadn't been certain I would ever do so again, had made me cry. But this time they were happy tears. While I waited for him to get to the hospital, I went through my phone directory, sending the same two-word message to practically everyone I knew: *Still here*. Some replies made me smile, others made me cry, but the one that touched me most deeply was unexpectedly the one from Maddie: *Thank God. Hurry home, miracle girl, we need you.*

*

'No. Absolutely not. No way.'

'I don't see why not. I feel amazing.'

'Mrs Turner ... Chloe, you had major surgery yesterday morning. I can't believe you are asking me if you can discharge yourself from hospital today.'

I blew out a long stream of air through my pursed lips. She was tough, this ward sister. I'd known I was going to meet with resistance, but it hadn't occurred to me anyone would be this unbending.

'Obviously I'm not asking to be *discharged*. I do appreciate how serious my operation was.'

I saw the sister begin to relax. 'Oh, I apologise. I must have misunderstood what Nurse Price was saying. I thought she meant you wanted to leave the hospital today.'

'I do,' I said, delighted we were all finally on the same page. 'But only for the afternoon. I promise to come back afterwards.'

The sister shook her head with a *now-I've-heard-it-all* expression on her face. She'd be telling this story for years to come, I realised. I knew I had to try a different tack.

'Do you have children, Sister?'

She looked surprised by the question. 'Yes I do, actually. A girl of ten, and a boy of seven.'

I nodded, feeling slightly more encouraged. 'Well, wouldn't you do just about anything you could to make them happy?'

'Yeeees,' replied the woman standing between me and freedom.

'Well, yesterday my little girl could have ended up without a mother. My operation could very easily have ended that way.'

479

The sister wasn't made of stone, for I thought I saw a small softening in her eyes. 'I know. You've been very fortunate. Which is all the *more* reason why you shouldn't even think about jeopardising your recovery by doing something as crazy as leaving the hospital for the afternoon.'

'I know you only want what's best for the patients on your ward. But you have to believe me that *this* is what is best for me. I need to see my daughter, and she needs to see me. Not in a hospital bed, not even downstairs in the foyer. She needs to look up, just like every other little kid in her class is going to do this afternoon, and see her mummy watching her from the edge of the sports field. Please don't say no to me. Don't make me break her heart.'

For a second I thought I glimpsed the glitter of a tear in the corner of the older woman's eye. She blinked rapidly, and it was gone. 'A neurosurgical ward isn't like a day spa. You can't just pop in and pop out at will, you know.' She was saying the words she had to say, but I could hear there was less conviction in them than before.

'I take total responsibility for my actions. I'll sign whatever disclaimer you need me to sign. But, please, let me go.'

She shook her head as though she couldn't believe anyone could act so irresponsibly, but she'd seen the determination in my eyes and heard the steel in my voice.

'It's always the mothers,' she muttered mysteriously under her breath, before looking up to meet my eyes. 'I'll see what I can do.'

Maddie

I stared at the two dresses, totally unable to decide between them. Which one said 'school sports day', I wondered: the blue one with the floaty skirt, or the red silk one with the deep V-neckline? The ringing of my phone on the dressing table offered a welcome delay in having to choose. Chloe of course would have had the perfect outfit already picked out, but then she was used to this kind of school event. Regardless how many times I'd stood at the school gates to collect Hope, I was still very much the outsider. In the pecking order I think I came in just above the au pairs.

I padded across the bedroom in my underwear to answer the phone, not bothering to read the display before pressing Accept. Hearing her voice threw me in that spooky kind of way, when the person you've been thinking about suddenly gets in touch. And then, when the enormity of everything she'd been through in the last twenty-four hours hit me, I was thrown all over again that she was well enough to make phone calls. I thought *that* was the biggest surprise of the day. I was wrong.

'How are you feeling?' I asked.

There was an undercurrent of urgency in her voice, as though she was anxious to quickly get through the opening pleasantries. 'Exceptionally well, thanks.'

'That's amazing, I would have thought—'

'Maddie,' Chloe interrupted, as though she had no further time to waste on inconsequential matters. 'It's Hope's school sports day today.'

I sat down on the padded velvet stool before me and saw the wry smile appear on my face in the dressing-table mirror. I should have known this wasn't a social call. She was checking up on me, making sure I hadn't forgotten that I had promised to attend.

'Yes, I know,' I assured her. 'In fact, I was just trying to decide—'

Once again she cut me off. It was very un-Chloe. 'Good. Well, I want to go.'

'I'm sure you do,' I said with understanding.

There was audible relief in her voice. 'I *knew* you'd be the right person to ask.'

I took a pause and wondered what I'd missed. 'Ask? Ask what?'

'The school sports day this afternoon. I want you to take me there.'

I played her words through my head a couple of times, trying to imagine an alternative interpretation that I simply hadn't grasped. There was none.

'You want me to take you to Hope's school this afternoon?' I said, pronouncing each word slowly and carefully, as though talking to a foreigner.

'Yes. That's why I'm calling.'

'Are you crazy?'

I heard her sigh of impatience all the way from her hospital bed. The hospital bed which I was pretty sure she shouldn't even be thinking of leaving.

'No. I'm deadly serious. Will you do it? Will you come and collect me?'

She was moving on to practicalities, but I was still stumbling with the whole stupid concept. 'Truly? Can you hear yourself? Do you know what you're asking?'

'I am making perfect sense,' said Chloe, a frisson of irritation icing her voice, making her tone much cooler than it had been at the start of the call.

'No you're not,' I refuted. 'When they were messing around in your head, did they put a few bits in backwards or something, because this has to be just about the most ridiculous thing I have ever heard.'

'I thought *you*, of all people, would understand.'

I saw immediately what she was trying to do with that slightly hurt tone. She was trying to appeal to my softer side. Clearly she hadn't yet realised that I didn't have one. Not about this, anyway.

'Why are you asking *me*, Chloe?' I said, suddenly knowing exactly why. 'Why aren't you asking Ryan, because obviously he's going to be going there today too?'

There was a long moment of silence at the other end of the line.

'You haven't told him, have you?' I pressed, feeling a bit like a prosecutor in a court of law. Albeit minus the funny wig and robes, and dressed only in a bra and briefs.

'Ryan wouldn't understand.'

'Well, he definitely wouldn't be alone there. *No one* in their right mind would understand.'

'And that's why I knew you were the right person to ask.'

'Wow. Your charm skills are going to need some work.

Calling me crazy isn't going to make me any more inclined to change my mind, you know.'

'No. That wasn't what I meant,' said Chloe quickly, sounding not at all apologetic that she might have offended me. 'What I meant was that, out of everyone, you would understand how important it is not to miss out on key moments in Hope's life. Today is a big deal at her school. I've been there every other year for this event.'

'You hadn't just had brain surgery on those other occasions,' I couldn't resist pointing out.

She went on smoothly, as though I hadn't spoken: 'Hope is a very smart little girl. Despite our best efforts at shielding her from the truth, she knows how sick I've been. She knows it was serious. To be there for her today would mean the world not just to me, but more importantly to her. Can you imagine her face the moment I walk in and she sees me?'

'I can't, actually. I'm too busy imagining Ryan's.'

'Let me worry about Ryan,' Chloe said, pulling rank as his wife. Which of course was her right.

'What does the hospital say?' I asked, after she'd left just enough time for me to begin to waver.

Afterwards I realised how neatly she skirted that question. 'They're happy for me to go if I sign a release. And I'll be going straight back afterwards.'

'This still sounds like a terrible idea. What if you collapse, or something?'

'I won't,' Chloe said with an unshakeable assurance she had no right to give.

Again there was a long pause. She was good at this, I had to admit. She knew I was dithering. To think, only five minutes earlier the biggest decision I'd had to make was which dress to wear.

'Look, Maddie. I'm not asking for your approval here. I'm not asking you to condone this as a great idea. But I *am* going to do it. I can phone for a taxi if I have to. But I'm going to do this, with or without you.' She paused before delivering, with superb timing, her closing thrust. 'But it would be an awful lot easier doing it *with* you.'

She was waiting for me. Sitting on the edge of her hospital bed, one eye fixed on the door, the other on the clock.

'I was worried you'd changed your mind,' was her greeting. I'd lost count of how many times I had done exactly that since our phone call a few hours earlier. And yet, despite all good sense, here I was, doing as she had asked.

'I got hijacked by the ward sister on my way in,' I explained, passing her the large carrier bag I had brought with me. 'Plus it took me longer than I expected to find everything in your bedroom.'

Chloe reached for the bag and peered inside. 'Is it all here?'

I nodded, still trying to shake off the memory of the disapproving expression on the ward sister's face as she stopped me on my way to Chloe's bedside. She hadn't needed to tell me how stupid she thought this plan was; her flaring nostrils and tightly locked lips had spoken very eloquently for her.

Chloe reached into the bag and began to shake the creases

from the pretty flower-patterned dress that I'd found exactly where she said it would be in her wardrobe. As someone whose own closet was always in a permanent state of chaos, I couldn't help but be impressed with Chloe's organised bedroom. I found everything on the list of items she'd asked me to bring to the hospital. As well as a couple of things I'm fairly certain she *hadn't* intended me to find.

'Would you mind drawing the curtains around the bed?' she asked, her fingers beginning to work on the knot of her robe. I pulled the brightly patterned drapes along the track until all that was left was a narrow gap in which I stood. Chloe had slipped the robe from her shoulders and was now fumbling blindly behind her back with the ties of the hospital gown. I hesitated for a second before stepping closer to the bed and twitching the curtain in place behind me.

'Move your hands. I'll do that,' I instructed, reaching for the ties.

She was playing Russian Roulette with this crazy scheme of hers and somehow, despite the fact I should have known better, I seemed to be committed to helping her load the gun.

Chloe might have been putting on an incredibly brave face, but she was weaker than she was willing to admit. After I'd zipped up her dress and fastened the sandals onto her feet, she had needed to take a breather in the chair beside the bed.

'Did you bring the straw hat?' she asked, slightly breathless. A fine film of perspiration was glazing her upper lip and her colour was closer to my own than usual.

'I did, but I think this might work better.' From my own bag I pulled a length of gossamer fine material, like a magician performing an illusion. I'd been intending to drape the delicate scarf around my bare shoulders, but when I noticed how well it matched the colours in Chloe's dress, I knew it could be put to a better purpose.

I hadn't been sure what to expect following Chloe's surgery. My imagination had conjured up images ranging from a heavily bandaged Egyptian mummy, to a neatly turbaned sultan. So the remarkably small wound dressing at the back of her head had taken me a bit by surprise.

'I think we could probably hide the entire dressing if we use this as a hairband,' I suggested.

There was something I couldn't quite read in Chloe's eyes as she obediently twisted in her chair and lifted the hair off the back of her neck. It was a vulnerable pose, exposing not just the edges of the stapled wound but also the neatly shaved section of her skull. I worked quickly but gently, anxious not to hurt her as I wound the scarf over the bandage and teased her hair in place to cover the bald patch. I knotted the scarf loosely at the side of her head and when I stood back to survey my handiwork, I had to admit it looked kind of cute.

She studied the finished effect in the small mirror I held out for her, her eyes a little misty as they lifted to mine before giving me a small nod.

'Thank you, Maddie. That looks great. Can we go now?'

*

She needed my arm for support all the way to the lift, and I was already worrying about how far away I'd parked the car, as well as the walk to the school playing field at the other end of our journey. Walking past the ward sister's office with its open door had been an uncomfortable ordeal. I was aware of her stopping whatever it was she'd been working on to watch our slow and careful progress down the length of the ward and out through its double doors. I glanced back once over my shoulder and saw her slowly shaking her head.

As we waited for the lift to respond to its summons, Chloe leant back against the wall, her eyes closed as she caught her breath, while I looked at my watch and tried to calculate if we would get there on time. If we didn't take too long getting back to the car, or get caught in traffic, we could still make it. Just. The lift bell pinged and once again I held out my arm to support Chloe, but before the aluminium doors slid open, we were stopped by a voice calling us from the direction of the ward.

'Wait!'

We both turned, wearing similar expressions of shock at the sight of the disapproving ward sister approaching us at a pace just short of a run. It's not easy to sprint when pushing a wheelchair, even if it's an empty one, but she was definitely giving it her best shot.

'Here,' she said, thrusting the wheelchair towards me. I grabbed hold of one handle. 'Make sure you bring back the chair and my patient in one piece,' she instructed. Her voice was terse and gruff, but the expression in her eyes told a different story.

Neither of us said a word as Chloe carefully lowered herself onto the chair as the lift carried us down to the ground floor. But we were both smiling.

I waited until I had negotiated my way out of the hospital's complicated labyrinth of roads before raising the subject which I knew had the potential to destroy the present truce between us.

'So, I read your letter.'

I took my eyes briefly off the road to look at her. Chloe's hands had tightened in her lap at my words, but her gaze remained fixed on the view through the windscreen. Her back had stiffened, and I knew from her immobility how much my words had shocked her.

'That was private,' she said eventually, her voice tight and controlled.

'It was addressed to me. How private could it be?'

Her head turned to look at me. 'You weren't meant to read it.'

'Why write it then?'

I heard her deeply indrawn breath, as though summoning up all of her strength not to get angry. 'You weren't meant to read it *yet*. I only wrote it in case—'

'I know why you wrote it.'

'Then you should have left it where it was. Did you open the other letters too?'

'No. Of course not,' I said, genuinely offended that she thought my scruples were entirely non-existent. 'Those weren't mine to read. I left them in the drawer.'

We travelled for almost another two miles before I spoke again.

'*I know the two of you were meant to be together. I know that when I'm gone everything will return to the way it was always meant to be. And that makes it easier to leave.*'

'You memorised the entire letter?'

'Only the truly ridiculous bits. Oh wait, that would be all of it.'

'None of it is ridiculous. It makes perfect sense.'

I gave a small humourless laugh. 'Ryan told me about this crazy notion of yours. That you'd come into his life because both he and Hope had needed someone after my accident, and that now I was back, your role was finished.'

'It's a theory.'

'No it's not. Well, not a valid or logical one. And even if it *was* right, you seem to have totally ignored one fairly inescapable truth.'

I glanced over and saw her eyebrows had risen, waiting for my words. 'I don't love Ryan any more, and just as importantly, he no longer loves me.'

'Yes he does,' said Chloe quietly, and there was such pain in those words that something cold took hold of my heart and froze it. 'He just doesn't realise that he still does, that's all.'

That statement took three miles of driving before I felt capable of responding.

'The woman I was at twenty-eight would have happily spent the rest of her life as Ryan's wife, but the woman I am now ... well, I'm different. And you seem to be forgetting something else ... I'm seeing someone.'

'Oh yes. Your landlord. Your *faux* boyfriend. I almost forgot about him.'

I swallowed guiltily; making sure the lie would come out smoothly. 'He is *not* a faux anything. Mitch and I are very close.' I always blush when I lie, it's what would make me absolutely terrible at poker, yet strangely this time I managed to control it.

'I understand why you've invented this relationship. Ryan might believe in it, but I don't.'

'It's not for you to believe or disbelieve. In fact it's none of your business, Chloe.'

'Whatever you say,' she replied, turning to look out of the side window, preventing me from reading her face. 'But I just can't see you with a man like that. A woman like you could have anyone she wants. What could a man like Mitch possibly give you?'

'Sunflowers,' I whispered, feeling the warmth of something I'd only just begun to realise flood through me.

Two sets of traffic lights and one roundabout later, I spoke again, knowing if we were going to get through the afternoon, we couldn't be sniping at each other. 'There were some nice bits in your letter too,' I admitted.

Chloe said nothing, but her face turned back from the side window.

'The things you said about me and my mum ... I liked that.' Chloe nodded slowly. 'And saying how you felt that Hope was lucky to have me ... well, that meant a lot.'

Chloe's smile was slow and knowing.

'But it still doesn't mean that Ryan and I would ever have got back together if—'

'—if I'd died?' Two women who'd both stared death in the face weren't afraid of using the words.

'Yeah. Even if you'd croaked it, we still wouldn't have ended up married.'

I took one hand off the wheel and gently shoved her upper arm. 'So don't do it.'

She turned towards me and then unexpectedly shoved me back, as if we were two children roughhousing in a playground, instead of two grown-up, perfectly sensible women.

'Not planning on it. Not anytime soon, anyway.'

'Good,' I declared, looking up to see the rows of colourful bunting strung across the entrance to the school car park. 'Because I've kind of got used to having you around.'

'Ditto,' said Chloe.

I turned off the car engine and we shared a single look that I knew I would remember for the rest of my life.

I hauled the collapsed wheelchair out of the boot of my car and stared at it helplessly for a moment, as though if I did that for long enough the thing would somehow miraculously assemble itself. Keeping one hand on the roof of the car for support, Chloe walked up to stand beside me.

492

Without a word she bent down and began locking clips into place, snapping on the footrests and fastening the seat with the speed and slick proficiency of a military expert assembling an assault rifle. Her hands flew over the chair, and when she was done, she looked up with a small expression of triumph. 'I used to volunteer in a hospital, remember?' Gathering the folds of her skirt in one hand, she lowered herself onto the chair. 'Besides, after you've done battle with a buggy, any mother worth her salt could put up a wheelchair with her eyes closed.' It was a tiny unthinking reminder of something I would never know.

I gripped hold of the wheelchair's handles and began to steer us towards the school, past the rows of parked cars, whose chrome work glinted dazzlingly in the July sunshine.

'Ryan's here,' Chloe observed quietly as we walked past a familiar vehicle. She drew in her lower lip and bit down on it nervously. At least it gave her face some much-needed colour.

'You could always tell him I abducted you,' I joked. She smiled weakly, but I could see she was genuinely worried.

I took one hand off the wheelchair to squeeze her shoulder reassuringly. 'He'll just be pleased to see you. Although not as much as I imagine Hope will be.' Chloe's smile told me I'd found exactly the right thing to say.

'There's a pathway down the side of the building,' she advised as we reached the edge of the playground. 'It'll bring us out at the back of the field, so hopefully we can sneak in without drawing too much attention.'

The event must already have begun, for over the top of the

building I could hear the vague strains of a woman's voice amplified by a microphone.

'That'll be the Head's speech,' Chloe said as we disappeared out of the afternoon sunshine and down a narrow track shadowed by trees. 'She gives the same one each year before the races begin; how it's not about winning, but about taking part.'

'Admirable,' I said, trying not to picture the shelf full of sporting trophies and shields my mother had once proudly displayed. Every school has one. The annoying kid who wins every single race, seemingly without trying that hard. That had been me, once, a very long time ago. Had Hope inherited my highly competitive streak? Was she the result of my nature or Chloe's nurture, or an intriguing combination of us both?

Luckily, July had been hot and dry and the ground beneath the wheels of the chair was baked biscuit hard, with fissure-like cracks running through the solid earth. I was glad of that, for tipping Chloe out of the chair before we even reached the field would have been an extremely unfortunate way for the afternoon to begin. We emerged unexpectedly from beneath the canopy of trees, and it took a few seconds for my eyes to adjust from the sepia of the dappled pathway to the verdant technicolour of the playing field.

On a small raised dais some distance away, the head teacher was giving her speech to an audience of parents sitting on rows of slightly-too-small-to-be-comfortable wooden chairs. At the edge of the field, too far away to make out individual faces, the children sat in rows, arms firmly folded over tiny chests, legs neatly crossed.

'Let's stay here until she's finished,' whispered Chloe, as I drew us to a stop beneath the overhanging branches of a tree.

There was no reason for anyone to know we were there. Our arrival had been silent, muffled by the thick springy turf beneath us, and yet less than a minute later a head in the second row of chairs slowly turned around. A fluttering, like a trapped butterfly, flickered unexpectedly at the base of my throat.

Ryan swivelled all the way around in his seat and I watched the kaleidoscope of emotions cross his handsome face. Shock came first; then a frowning disapproval, which was quickly pushed aside by something that was so familiar, it had the power to transport me back in time.

He began to smile, slowly at first, and then more broadly. I watched it creep upwards, not confined to lips and cheeks, but travelling all the way to his deep blue eyes. This was how we had begun. How it had all started, with a smile across a sea of heads. His eyes focused in my direction. I was transported back to that industry event, back to the moment when I'd glanced over my shoulder to check who he was smiling at . . . only to discover it had been me.

It's impossible not to return a smile as broad as that, and my features were already mirroring his in the July sunshine when I noticed the angle of his head and the direction of his gaze. The smile was coming straight towards me, but this time it *wasn't* for me. The sun was suddenly too warm, the day too sticky, the memories too painful. I took a single step back into the shadows, as Chloe claimed something else that had once been mine.

Ryan got to his feet, stepping over legs and bags and other obstacles, while never once breaking eye contact with Chloe. He reached the end of his row and a woman behind him glanced back, towards the spot where we stood. I recognised her as one of Chloe's school-mum friends from Hope's party. Her mouth dropped open prettily to form a huge O of amazement. She clutched at the arm of a woman sitting beside her, who turned and gave a small gasp. By the time Ryan was free of the rows of chairs, both women were on their feet. The first one was crying, and the second one didn't look too far behind her.

Like a Mexican Wave gone wrong, more and more heads began to turn our way. An increasing number of parents had got to their feet. The headteacher, unable to ignore the fact that she'd clearly lost her audience's attention, stumbled over her words, and lifted a hand to her eyes, using it as a visor to see who'd interrupted the smooth running of the afternoon's proceedings.

'Just sneak in at the back, huh?' I said, bending down and whispering into Chloe's ear.

The Head had finally made out the identity of the late arrival, and any hopes we'd had of making a low-key entrance were now a thing of the past. 'Mrs Turner,' she exclaimed, perhaps unaware that her microphone was still turned on.

'That's torn it,' I said, which was the last thing I think Chloe would have been able to hear because someone – I believe it was the woman who'd first spotted us – began to clap. The rhythm of her applause was slow and measured. A solo performance, until another pair of hands joined in, and then another, and another. The sound rose like a cresting wave.

My voice was husky when I spoke. 'Do they do this every time you turn up in the school playground?'

'Every damn time,' replied Chloe, tears streaming down her cheeks.

I missed the moment when Ryan swept Chloe into his arms, for I was distracted by an unfolding commotion happening on the far side of the field. I heard an adult's voice, raised in agitation, calling out an instruction. Whoever it was aimed at must have been taking very little notice, for the adult voice was growing louder and angrier. That's when I realised that it wasn't an instruction, but a name that was being called out. 'Hope'. Nineteen six-year-olds were still sitting crossed-legged on the grass, doing exactly what they'd been told to do, but number twenty had leapt to her feet on hearing the head teacher say her mother's name, and was heading across the field with the speed of a miniature twister.

She wove through the legs of adults and when they saw who she was, they stood back to clear a pathway. There were very few dry eyes among the parents – including the fathers – as Hope leapt into her mother's arms with such force that, without Ryan's steadying hand, the wheelchair would surely have toppled over.

Mother and daughter rocked silently backwards and forwards in an unbreakable embrace. I watched them for a moment, until it hurt too much to do so. I turned my face to Ryan's, and the sympathy in his eyes when he looked at me was almost my undoing. He knew me. He *still* knew me, and right at that moment I couldn't decide if that was a blessing or a curse.

Around us, as the applause finally began to peter away, our arrival continued to sabotage the afternoon. One by one Hope's classmates also got to their feet and scattered to join their parents. Children were running everywhere, and parents were scooping them into their arms and hugging them close, even though they'd probably only seen them hours earlier.

I glanced over towards the dais and saw the Head being approached by several members of her teaching staff, who looked at a loss as to how to restore order.

'Now look what we've done,' I said to Chloe, who'd finally lifted her face from Hope's neck.

There was a sudden ear-splitting squeal as the head teacher once again picked up her microphone. 'Ladies and gentlemen, children,' she began, and then stopped, looking around the school field at the unique and poignant reminder of the fragility of life, and the bond between a child and its parents. Whatever it was she'd had been intending to say was suddenly abandoned as her face transformed into a smile. 'Just for this year, I propose we break with our normal tradition and allow the children to sit beside their mums and dads for the rest of the afternoon. Please listen out for when your class's races will begin.'

She looked down at the teachers clustered around the dais and they all shrugged their shoulders, but not one of them could hide the fact that what had just happened on the field had affected them all.

Chloe

The good thing about having brain surgery, if there can be said to be *anything* good about it, is that you can do just about anything and no one is going to get really mad at you. When the teachers had clawed back some kind of order to the proceedings, and the older classes were beginning their races, Ryan's face took on a more serious expression.

'So whose crazy idea was this prison-break plan?'

'Maddie's,' I lied smoothly, giving Maddie a huge panto-mime wink which I made sure Ryan saw.

'It was more of a road trip than a prison-break,' Maddie mused, playing along.

'Yes,' I agreed, giving her a co-conspirator's smile. 'More of a *Thelma and Louise* sort of thing.'

'That didn't end so well, if you remember correctly,' Ryan said dryly.

'All I can promise is that I'll try not to blow up a tanker

on the drive back,' Maddie said with a sweet smile and a totally straight face.

Ryan's lips twitched, and for just a moment I wished that Maddie wasn't quite so funny, or so beautiful, or so ... so *here*. I pushed the thought back down but it had left a bitter taste on my tongue.

A little while later, when the teachers called for Hope's class to go to the track for their races, she was reluctant to leave my lap.

'Come on, Pumpkin. You know how much you love to run.'

Hope shook her head so violently that her plaits slapped me lightly across the cheek.

'Would you like me to walk you over there?' offered Maddie, holding out her long-fingered pale hand. I could sense the indecision running through my little girl's small body.

'Maddie could probably give you a few tips on running,' Ryan added cajolingly. 'She used to be a bit of a superstar on the running track.'

Maddie looked up, and I saw the surprise register on her face. 'I'm surprised you remembered that.'

His eyes were on hers and there was a softness in them that suddenly worried me. 'I've not forgotten anything.' He paused and suddenly seemed to snap out of whatever mood had descended upon him. 'Besides, your mother used to constantly brag about it.'

Hope was suddenly looking at Maddie with renewed curiosity. 'Were you good at races, Maddie?'

'I won a few,' she said, with something which I now suspected was false modesty. 'I'll tell you how I did it on the walk over.'

Hope slithered off my lap, and despite the heat of the day there was a cold and empty spot inside and outside of me as I watched her walk off with her hand firmly grasped in her mother's.

Hope won her race, came second in the egg-and-spoon, and third in the three-legged, probably because she was about a foot taller than the girl she'd been harnessed to. I was beginning to feel tired, and was actually looking forward to the idea of returning to the comparative calm of the hospital ward. But there would be no leaving until what some parents regarded as the most important event of the afternoon had taken place.

For the final time that day the head teacher picked up her microphone to make an announcement. 'Gentlemen, I'm sure you don't need me to tell you what's coming next. Will all those taking part please make their way to the start line.'

I saw Maddie looking around her in bemusement, in much the same way I had done three years earlier at my very first sports day. Men all around us were getting to their feet. Some were slipping out of their jackets and pulling off ties. Others were kicking off their smart shoes and replacing them with the trainers they'd brought in preparation for this moment. A couple of dads emerged from the school building wearing shorts and vests. I shook my head, still unable to grasp how competitively they all took this.

'What is all this?' asked Maddie.

'The Fathers' Race,' supplied Ryan, also getting to his feet. He'd taken his own jacket off earlier in the afternoon, but was now unbuttoning the cuffs of his shirt and rolling up the sleeves. I saw Maddie watching him with a fascinated expression on her face.

'You're racing?'

He nodded. Hope, who was sitting on the ground beside my wheelchair, looked up adoringly at her father. 'Daddy tries very hard, but he never wins,' she said with brutal honesty.

I smirked and shared a special look with Ryan.

'That's because taking part is more important than winning,' Ryan said, ruffling his daughter's hair before bending down to drop a kiss on my lips. 'Wish me luck.'

'Break a leg,' I said, laughing at the comical expression my words brought to his face. 'Only don't really do that, because we've only got one wheelchair.'

Maddie waited until he'd gone before turning to me, clearly bewildered by what was going on. 'They take it *that* seriously? It's not all done for laughs?'

'Far from it. I think some of the dads even train for a few weeks before the big day.'

Maddie shook her head, and I could hardly blame her for being surprised. Watching the collection of men at various levels of fitness thunder down the length of the field each year had always looked like a heart attack waiting to happen, as far as I could see.

'If you think this is bad, you should see the women in the mothers' race. Those two over there,' I said, subtly directing her attention towards two individuals who were already removing their high-heeled summer sandals and replacing them with high-performance running shoes. 'Between them they've won this race for the last ten years. No one else gets close.'

'What about you?' asked Maddie, idly plucking up random blades of grass from her position on the floor beside Hope as we spoke.

'I bring up the rear each year,' I told her with a laugh.

'Mummy's really good,' said Hope with touching, if misplaced, loyalty.

It felt strange to have three of us cheering Ryan on as the pack of around forty runners powered down the field as if it were a steeplechase. The race went much as expected. There were a few who fell; a few more who wisely dropped out without completing the course; and a handful who took it way too seriously. Luckily Ryan didn't fall into any of those categories.

'Fifth,' he said, returning to join us a few minutes later. 'I'll settle for that.'

I smiled and hid my look of amusement as grown men with grazed knees and grass-stained trousers slipped back to join their wives and children with slightly embarrassed expressions. A few were muttering 'never again', but I'd put good money on them putting in a repeat performance next year.

'And now mothers, please,' crackled the voice over the microphone.

Maddie

'Mummy, can you get out of the chair to run with the other mummies?'

I really felt for Chloe at the look of regret in her eyes as she gently touched her daughter's cheek. 'Not this time, my love. I'm not well enough this year.'

Hope looked disappointed, which showed more than anything how good a job we'd all done at not letting her know how sick Chloe was.

'Now I won't have anyone to cheer for,' Hope said sadly, and I suddenly understood why parents who weren't good at sports put themselves through this annual ritual, because everyone wanted to be a hero in their child's eyes, even if they were the one limping in last over the finishing line.

'Next year,' Chloe promised solemnly, tilting up Hope's chin so she could look into her eyes to pledge her promise. 'I'll run it next year.'

I kept my head down, staring at the grass I had steadily been plucking up blade by blade, while I waited for the inevitable question.

'Maddie? Would you run in the mummies' race?'

I bit my lip and slowly raised my head to meet my daughter's beseeching face.

'I don't think so, Pumpkin. The race is for the mummies and daddies from the school. No one here knows who I am.'

It was a lie, of course. Although I continued to garner curious looks every time I was seen with Hope, almost everyone knew our story.

'And it wouldn't be fair if you had a whole team of mummies to run in the race, while your other friends only had one,' I said, which I thought was a very reasonable argument. 'And then what if people started asking if the nannies or the au pairs could run instead of the mummies? Well, it would just get silly.'

'But you're not a nanny or a pair,' said Hope solemnly, which made all three of us smile. 'You *are* a mummy.'

There was a long moment of silence. Around me I could see mums of various ages heading down to the start line.

'She has a point,' said Ryan quietly. He glanced across at Chloe, and I could see he was asking for her approval.

'You should do it,' Chloe said, her words coming out in a rush, as though if she didn't get them out quickly she might possibly snatch them back at the last minute. She gave a small wry laugh. 'Hope might actually have a mother who stands a chance of getting placed if *you* run.'

Her eyes went over to the two women who between them clearly believed had the race sewn up. The one with the cropped red hair held out her hand, and the shorter blonde woman placed her own within it. Perhaps it was the quiet smug complacency of that handshake that decided me. Or perhaps it was because here, at last, was something that as a mother I could possibly do better than Chloe.

'I don't know. I haven't run in years.'

'It's like riding a bicycle,' Ryan said with a grin. 'Only without the frame and the wheels.'

'Very funny,' I said, but even though I hadn't yet said 'yes', my fingers were already unbuckling my sandals. I always preferred to run barefoot.

'You can do this, Ace,' Ryan said, and suddenly I really, really, wanted to.

I got to my feet.

'Yay! Maddie's going to run,' squealed Hope, leaping up beside her father.

'Last call, mothers,' came a summons from the field.

I turned to go, but before I could, Chloe reached out and grasped my hand, pulling me down towards her. 'Go win it for our girl,' she urged.

The redhead was looking daggers at me as I went up to speak to the teacher waiting at the start line. She was patently eavesdropping as I spoke to the young woman with the whistle looped around her neck. 'I'd like to run in Chloe's place this year,' I said quietly. From the look on the redhead's face, she'd heard me clearly enough. She reached out and grabbed the arm of the blonde woman, her only competition, or so she had thought. To be fair, her friend didn't seem to be fazed, and merely shrugged her shoulders in a nonchalant way.

'I don't see there's any problem with that,' said the teacher kindly. She glanced over to the edge of the field, where I saw Ryan had repositioned Chloe's chair to get a better view. Hope waved excitedly at me, and I waved back.

'Excuse me, but the rules of the race say that it should only be *mothers* who compete.'

I didn't know who this woman was. Her children were older than Hope, and she clearly wasn't one of Chloe's friends. I turned very slowly to face her. 'Would you like me to take a blood test?' Her blonde friend sniggered and several of the other mothers smiled back at me from their positions on the starting line.

'I just don't think it's very fair, changing things at the last minute.'

'Life isn't fair,' I said, glancing back at my three-man support team on the edge of the field. 'Get over it.'

The woman looked very much like she wanted to smack me, which would certainly have been an interesting way for the afternoon to end. To make sure that hers were the only toes I was stepping on, I turned to the other twenty or so women who had chosen to run in the race. 'Is everyone else okay about me running?'

I was greeted with a chorus of yesses and absolutelies and go for its.

I smiled sweetly at the redhead and took my place a couple of runners further down the starting line from her. I breathed in and out slowly as I waited for the race to begin. *You can do this legs*, I told my limbs silently. *Heidi made you strong again, all you have to do is remember how to move.* I smiled down at my bare feet on the grass. *And if you could just manage to move faster than the redhead can do, that'd be great.*

I took one last glance over at Chloe, Ryan, and Hope. They were all smiling. Chloe raised her thumb in the universal symbol of good luck.

'On your marks.'

I felt my heart quicken.

'Get set.'

My muscles tensed.

'Wait!' I cried, straightening from the position my body had automatically adopted in preparation for the spring forward.

'What is it?' enquired the teacher, whose arm was still poised above her head, waiting to start the race.

'This is wrong,' I said.

The redhead made some grumbling comment, but I ignored her.

'This isn't right,' I said, looking at the row of runners who were staring at me as though I might possibly have lost my mind. And maybe I had.

'Can you please give me a moment?' I asked.

'Oh really!' said a voice from my left. No prizes for guessing who that had been.

I broke away from the line of women and lightly jogged over to the edge of the field.

'What's wrong?' asked Ryan, his eyes clouding in concern. 'Are you not feeling up to it?'

'I feel fine,' I said, gently pushing him aside and taking the handles of the wheelchair out of his grip.

'What the f—' began Chloe, as I started to steer the chair onto the field.

'No swearing in front of our daughter, please,' I said primly. Behind me I heard Hope giggling.

'Are you totally crazy?' Chloe asked, as I continued to propel us to the start line.

'Not totally,' I said, my face splitting with a grin as I saw the smiles of approval of everyone we went past. 'Just enough to do this.'

'For Christ's sake, is this some sort of joke?' The redhead was staring at Chloe and me as if we were ruining her big moment.

'Not at all,' I said, with what I thought was admirable restraint. 'You should be very happy.' She raised one overplucked eyebrow at that. 'If it was just me running ... I'd have creamed you.'

Her blonde friend laughed, and earned herself her own look of disdain.

'Okay now?' asked the teacher at the start line.

I looked down at Chloe and then back up to the teacher. 'Yes. We're good.'

'On your marks. Get Set. Go.'

The redhead was gone like a tangerine greyhound, her blonde competitor tight on her heels. The tendons of my arms stood out like cords as I began to push the chair down the field. From the sidelines I could just about make out

Hope's cries of encouragement above an unexpectedly loud roar from the rest of the crowd.

I was aware of several runners at the periphery of my vision. They should all have been far ahead of us, and yet strangely they seemed to be running at exactly the same pace as I was pushing the wheelchair. I glanced back over my shoulder and saw at least four of the other mothers just standing on the track. One clearly had something in her eye, at least that's what seemed to have happened by the huge and exaggerated fuss she was making as she clapped her hand over it. No less than three other runners stopped and crowded around her, offering assistance. They were all grinning.

A woman who was running, and I use the term extremely loosely, beside me, suddenly dramatically slapped her hand to her side. 'Stitch,' she gasped out, coming to an abrupt halt. It was the first time I'd ever seen anyone suffer from that kind of injury while walking. Nevertheless two other mothers immediately came to her aid, narrowing down the field of runners yet again.

I passed a woman I recognised from the playground who was hopping around theatrically on one leg. She yanked off her trainer to shake out something invisible from within it. She gave me a shrug and retired to the edge of the field.

The cheers from the crowd were increasing with every runner who fell by the wayside, some quite literally. One of the kindergarten mothers could have got herself an Oscar for the way she dramatically staggered around crying 'Cramp, cramp,' in a way shot gangsters do in old movies. When she crumpled to the ground, people were literally cheering like maniacs. I glanced around and saw the entire field was littered with mothers who were now no longer in the race. Yet about three-quarters of the way up the track were the two women who between them had always had the race sewn-up.

'Third place work for you?' I asked, bending down and speaking into Chloe's ear.

'Go for it,' she urged.

'Hold on,' I warned, as for the first time since the race began I started to run. It wasn't fast, and it probably didn't look very elegant, but we were moving at a fairly rapid lick down the field, powered by the cries of encouragement from all around us.

I looked up and saw the two women ahead, still giving it their all. From where we were, it looked as if the redhead had it in the bag, which was a shame. But then, surprisingly, the blonde looked back over her shoulder at us and suddenly began to power ahead of her friend. They were neck-and-neck for a few seconds and then gradually she began to inch ahead.

I'm not sure who saw it happen. Maybe no one; maybe everyone. But I saw it all with perfect clarity. I saw the blonde swerve out of her own lane and deliberately veer into the path of the woman running beside her. Whether her foot *deliberately* came out to bring down her fellow runner was never really certain, but all I knew was that they both tumbled to the ground in the only genuine fall of the entire race. This was no pantomime, no play-acting, but as I pushed

511

the wheelchair past them, I thought I might possibly have glimpsed the blonde mother give me a very brief wink before returning to nurse her ankle.

Five metres ahead was the finishing line and all around us people were screaming out encouragement. Four metres, then three, then two. It was hard to keep pushing when you're laughing, but somehow I managed it.

The line was just ahead and in the second before I propelled us across it, I took one hand from the wheelchair and held it up, Chloe slapped it in a high-five, but instead of dropping away she gripped hold of my hand, her fingers tightly lacing with mine.

And that was how we crossed the line.

Together.

Chapter 21

Three Months Later

'999. What is your emergency?'

'It's my mummy. She won't wake up. Please can you hurry? Can you send a doctor to my house? It's 5 Mansfield Avenue.'

'What's your name, sweetheart?'

'My name is Hope.'

'Okay, Hope. Can you tell me what happened?'

'There was a loud crash and now they're both on the floor.'

'Who's on the floor, sweetheart?'

'They both are.'

'Okay, someone is on their way to you. You're being very brave.'

'Tell them she's got a pulse, but it's very weak.'

The operator gave a sharp intake of breath and there was relief in her voice. 'Is someone else there with you, Hope? A grown-up?'

'Yes, but she's on the floor, doing breathing into Mummy's mouth.'

'Who is it doing the breathing, Hope? Who's there with you?'

'My mummy.'

'Okay, Hope. I know this is all very scary. Just hang on. Help is on the way.'

Three Hours Earlier

Maddie

'They really need to get some better magazines in this place.'

'You say that every single day,' Chloe replied. 'Why don't you bring a book?'

'Then I couldn't do my daily rant about the out-of-date *Readers Digest* collection, could I?' I said with a smile. 'How did it go today?' I asked, noticing for the first time that Chloe looked exceptionally pale and wiped-out after her session.

'You'd think after four weeks I'd be getting used to it, but . . .'

'Only another two to go,' I said encouragingly.

I got to my feet and felt a momentary and totally unexpected head rush, which had me reaching out for the back of the chair for support.

'Are *you* okay?' Chloe asked.

I breathed in deeply and felt the room steady. 'Yeah. I'm fine. Just got up too quickly.'

'I wish I could do *anything* quickly,' Chloe said with a small sigh.

I reached for her arm and gave it a gentle squeeze. 'You will. Soon. In another two weeks you're going to be done with radiotherapy and all of this will fade away and become a distant memory.'

Chloe's face was worryingly pale, and there was a tremor in her hand which I don't remember having seen before as she anxiously tried to tug her hair in place to cover the new area of exposed skin on the back of her head.

'It'll grow,' I said sympathetically.

'I know,' she replied, looking troubled by far more than the loss of her hair, although it must have been hard to lose it again when it had only just started to grow back after her surgery.

'I will definitely *not* miss this place,' Chloe declared, falling into step beside me as we headed for the exit of the radiography department. 'Nor that bloody mask I have to wear.'

'Perhaps they'll let you take it home as a souvenir when you're done?' I said. 'You could have it as a Halloween costume. That'd keep the trick-or-treat kids away from your door.'

Chloe looked at me and shook her head. 'For a mother, you don't like children all that much, do you?'

'Only our one,' I said with a grin. We stepped out through the automatic doors and I immediately shivered in the chill of the October afternoon.

'God, it's cold out here.'

Chloe gave me a curious glance. 'Not really. Although the hospital is heated like a greenhouse, so maybe it's just the change in temperature you're feeling. Or maybe you're coming down with the bug that Hope had last week.'

'I hope not. I still have chauffeur duties for the next fortnight.' I smiled at her, but then the banter died on my lips as I noticed how much trouble Chloe was having keeping up with me as we crossed the car park to the place where I'd left my car. I tried to put it in the same spot each day, as it was the closest I could get to the entrance. Chloe was too proud to admit it, but even that short distance was becoming a real struggle for her now. Her weakness worried me, though we'd been warned to expect that her treatment might leave her exhausted. I resolved to have a quiet word with Ryan about it as soon as I had a chance.

Chloe

My hands were trembling as I attempted to buckle up the seat belt. I saw Maddie watching me; saw the frown lines marring the perfection of her brow, before she leant across and took the clasp from my fingers and clicked it into place.

'Are you sure you're okay? Do you want me to go back inside and get someone?'

I shook my head, and then instantly regretted it. I was getting a blinding headache. 'I just want to go home. I need to rest.'

For a moment I thought Maddie might put up an argument, but then she slipped the key into the ignition and started the engine. 'Why don't you close your eyes and try to have a nap on the drive back,' she suggested.

'That doesn't make me very good company,' I said, already feeling my eyelids fluttering to a close.

'Oh, you're rubbish company anyway,' said Maddie sassily. 'I don't know why I bother sometimes.'

She was joking, I knew that. I knew her well by now. Better than I once could ever have imagined or believed. She was nothing like the Maddie I'd invented all those years ago, when *she* was the one who was sick. This Maddie was funnier, quicker, and also a great deal kinder than I ever would have suspected. Although for Ryan to have loved her as much as he had, perhaps I should always have known that. She also swore a lot more, but I was used to that by now.

For some reason I suddenly felt the hot sharp sting of tears behind my closed eyelids. 'I can't thank you enough for doing this; for driving me here every day.'

'Not that again,' said Maddie with a huge long-suffering sigh, which didn't fool me at all.

'I mean it, Maddie,' I said, forcing the invisible lead weights off my eyes so that I could look at her when I spoke. 'You didn't have to give up your time to do this.'

She looked embarrassed, the way she always did whenever we had this conversation. 'Yeah, well that's what happens when you don't have a job, people take advantage of your good nature.' She took her eyes off the road and pulled a silly face so I could tell she was joking. But I'd known that anyway. 'And I was going to have to collect Hope from school every day until you got your licence back, so it made sense to do this too.'

She made it sound like giving up six weeks to help look after me was a small deal, but it wasn't. Not for me at least. It was a huge one. 'I just want you to know how grateful I am.'

She squirmed in the driver's seat, and I knew I should stop now or risk making her feel truly uncomfortable. 'You're a good friend,' I said, reaching out my hand to cover hers on the steering wheel.

I'd never called her that before. I'd always felt our extraordinary relationship defied all conventional labels, but for some unknown reason, today I felt a burning need to say the words out loud. To make sure she knew how I felt.

'And you're a pain in the arse,' she said. And it would have been a perfect way to have shot me down, if only her eyes hadn't been glinting brightly, or her deep red lips hadn't betrayed her with a tremble.

Maddie

'We're home,' I said, shaking Chloe gently. Beneath her jumper I could feel the bones of her shoulder. They seemed a little more pronounced to me than they'd once been. It was yet another concern to add to my growing list to discuss with Ryan.

Chloe's pale grey eyes swam for a moment before coming

into focus and realising we were now parked in her driveway. 'Sorry. I must have gone straight out. I didn't snore, did I?'

'All the way back,' I said, walking round to the passenger side in case she needed help walking up the path. Not that I'd be of much use to her today if she did, I thought, wishing I could shake off the vague head-full-of-cotton-wool feeling that had made concentrating throughout the familiar drive much harder than it should have been. It was probably just as well Chloe had been asleep, because she would certainly have complained about the heater which I'd had blasting out hot air throughout our return journey. Not that it had helped, for I still hadn't been able to banish the icy chills running through me. It looked as if Chloe might be right; I'd caught Hope's bug.

'Shall I make us some tea?' I asked after Chloe had located her key and let us into the house.

It had stopped feeling odd, opening up the kitchen cabinets and rummaging in the drawers of her domain, some time ago. I was used to working among other women's things, I thought, as I dropped teabags into the mugs and waited for the kettle to boil. Everything I ever used, every single thing, belonged to either Mitch's grandmother, or to Chloe. Nothing was really mine. Perhaps it was time to do something about that?

'Shall we take these into the lounge?' I asked, as though I was the host here instead of her. The fact that Chloe didn't appear to find that odd was further proof that she was struggling today.

I took her arm as we crossed the hallway, because it was easier to help her to the settee than worry about how I'd pick her up off the floor if she didn't make it there. Even so, I hadn't been expecting her to lean on me quite so heavily, and by the time I had settled her back on the couch, I could feel a slick film of perspiration drenching my body.

When Hope was dropped off by one of the other mothers some twenty minutes later, I could legitimately have left and gone back to my own flat. But there was something that was niggling me, a cautionary voice warning me not to leave until Ryan had returned.

'Do you mind if I stick around here for a while?' I asked nonchalantly, as though I had no other plans, and hadn't just rattled off a message to Mitch cancelling our arrangements for that evening. He'd understand; I knew that. And I wouldn't need to explain or justify which member of the Turner family needed me most: Hope or Chloe. Either way, Mitch would get it.

'I thought you had a *date*,' Chloe murmured.

Even without the finger gestures, I knew she'd put the word in inverted commas. To be honest, my relationship with Mitch was probably as much of a mystery to me as it was to her. It was more than friendship, of that I was certain, but it wasn't a romance. For a while I'd thought it might be, but we were like a train that had somehow found itself shunted into the sidings. It was as if we were waiting for something. But I had absolutely no idea what for.

'My date cancelled on me,' I lied.

'Then he's an idiot,' said Chloe with unexpectedly fierce loyalty. 'Any man who'd let you slip through his fingers is plain dumb.' She stopped suddenly and we shared a slightly uncomfortable moment, as we realised she'd just described the actions of her own husband.

After Hope left Chloe's side to play on the floor with her cat, Chloe got shakily to her feet. 'Do you know what, I think I *will* go and lie down for a while. Is that okay with both of you?'

Hope nodded happily.

'Do you need a hand getting upstairs?'

Chloe shook her head, her eyes going instantly to the little girl on the floor. One day, when she was old enough to understand, I promised myself I would tell Hope how courageously Chloe had fought against her illness, so that Hope's childhood could remain as unscathed as possible. One day she would know everything her mother had done. I would tell her.

I watched Chloe leave the room; saw the way she rested her hand on almost every piece of furniture as she passed, as if she needed them all for support. I switched on the television, but found it almost impossible to concentrate on the flickering images on the screen. I found myself listening out for the sound of Chloe's careful tread on the stairs, and then the sound of her footsteps in the upstairs hall.

A wave of concern swelled up within me for no reason whatsoever, and I sprang suddenly to my feet. For the second time that day I felt my head start to spin.

'I'm just going upstairs to check on your mum,' I said to the back of my daughter's head. She nodded, absorbed with whatever was happening on the television.

She didn't turn around.

Chloe

The weariness was all-consuming, trying to suck me under. Each foot felt as though it had weights strapped onto it, like astronaut shoes or those funny boots that divers wear. I paused, one hand already on my bedroom door, when Maddie said something from the hallway below. I turned around as she began to rapidly climb the stairs.

There was a moment when I didn't realise anything was wrong. Maddie stood before me, as she'd done countless times before. A glimpse into the future of how Hope would look one day: tall, slender and beautiful ... and pale. Always pale. And yet, this time even her lips seemed strangely bleached of colour. And then I noticed her hand on the wooden banister, not resting on it lightly for balance, but clawed like a bird's, almost gouging into the rail for support. She was looking at me, straight into my eyes ... and then suddenly she was gone, tumbling back with an almost slow-motion balletic grace down the stairs she had just run up.

There was a crash; a horrible, horrible, crash and then the lounge door was flung open and Hope hurtled through it. She saw Maddie, lying crumpled at the foot of the stairs and the cry she gave as she ran towards her echoed not just through the house but through my very soul.

'Mummy!'

It was the first time Hope had ever called her that, and Maddie never even heard it.

Chapter 22

Chloe

I saw Ryan before he saw me. I saw the expression on his face as Hope catapulted into him. I saw the look in his eyes before he found me behind the glass doors. It answered a thousand middle-of-the-night questions, which I knew I would never need to ask again.

Time passes differently in a hospital. When you're a patient, each day feels like a week. But when you're waiting for news of someone you care about, each minute feels like a lifetime.

I had no idea how long it had been since the paramedics had brought us here. The time Hope and I spent in the bleak impersonal waiting area might already have tumbled from minutes into hours, for all I knew. My priorities were split; but however anxious I was about Maddie, at least she had a team of people working on her. All Hope had was me. I rocked her in my arms, soothing her with words and promises that could all very well be lies. How could I tell her that *everything will be all right* after we'd both seen Maddie carried from our home on a stretcher? Those words should have no place in my vocabulary, not when the sound of the ambulance siren was still echoing in my ears.

I didn't attempt to phone Ryan when we first arrived at the hospital. A quick glance at the clock had told me he'd be driving on the motorway by then, which was neither the time nor the place to receive bad news. Although if there *was* a location where getting that kind of information was less devastating, I had yet to discover it.

Eventually, when Hope's sobs had settled to soft hiccups, I gently eased myself away from her. 'I'm just going to go in that room to phone Daddy,' I said, pointing to an adjacent office with a full-length glass door. 'You'll be able to see me all the time. But I need to go somewhere quiet so I won't disturb anyone.'

Thankfully, Hope didn't seem to notice that there was no one around who could possibly be disturbed by my call. There are things no child should ever see or hear. Watching one mother desperately trying to save the life of her other one was definitely high on that list. I had no intention of adding to the damage by letting her hear my call to Ryan.

Reception in the hospital was typically poor, and I could feel my agitation rising as I strode the perimeter of the room, my phone held out like a divining rod, searching for a signal.

When eventually I found some, my fingers were slow and clumsy on the keypad as I made the call.

Voicemail. I stared at the device as though it was deliberately trying to make a terrible day worse. There was an almost irresistible urge to hurl the useless piece of technology at the wall, but good sense won through and I chose to leave a message instead. But I was interrupted by a commotion from the corridor.

Even through the closed glass doors I could hear a loud pounding sound, like a jack-hammer on tarmac, or feet slapping heavily on a tiled surface. With the phone still pressed to my ear, my eyes went to Hope. I saw the moment when her look of uncertainty dissolved into one of indescribable relief. There was only one person in the world capable of producing that look, not just on her, but on me too.

I spun around and saw Ryan running at speed down the empty hospital corridor. He was moving so fast each foot barely seemed to make contact with the floor before it was leaping upwards, taking him forward. A man who could run that fast didn't deserve to come *fifth* in any race.

But more startling than the speed of his approach was the expression on his face. If that look had a name, it would have to be *apocalyptic*. For it was the look of a man facing the destruction of his very own world.

Hope was suddenly gone in a blur of arms and legs as she leapt from the seats to run towards her father. Ryan said something, which I couldn't quite catch through the door, but Hope's answer came through clearly enough.

'They took Mummy away in an ambulance.'

I saw her words rock him, even as he scooped her up into his arms. There was an agony on his face, the kind I hope I will never see again.

I flung open the door and the immediate relief in his eyes humbled me as I stumbled towards them both. Somehow he managed to free one arm to draw me fiercely against his side.

'I was just trying to call you,' I said, my voice muffled against the solid wall of his chest.

'I got home early. There was no there.'

I couldn't even begin to imagine the horror he must have lived through. 'Then one of the neighbours came out and said she'd seen an ambulance, and that a woman had been taken away. I thought ... I thought ...'

'It was Maddie,' I said, my voice cracking on her name.

He nodded, and his arm tightened around me as he said gruffly, 'I've been trying your phone and hers for the entire drive here. No one picked up. I didn't know who ...' He took a long breath, to steady himself. 'And then, just now, when Hope said it was Mummy ...'

Hope's face was awash with tears as she swivelled in her father's arms. Her eyes, Maddie's eyes, met mine.

'It *was* her mummy,' I said, reaching out and gently touching our child's cheek. 'Just not this one.'

After Ryan had lowered Hope back onto the plastic seats, I quickly explained what had happened.

'So she fell?' he asked, clearly struggling to imagine it. He was lucky. Somehow I didn't think I'd ever be able to erase the memory of it.

'Yes. But something was wrong before that. That was *why* she fell.'

'And the doctors haven't said anything yet?'

I shook my head.

'I should call Bill,' Ryan said. My glance went to Hope and he nodded. 'I'll go outside.' He turned to leave and then suddenly came back to press a single hard kiss on my mouth. The taste of fear still lingered on his lips. 'God forgive me for saying this,' his voice was a hoarse admission, 'but if it had to be anyone—'

It was an hour before anyone came to speak to us. Sixty minutes when the worry gradually fermented into the kind of anxiety that should carry its own health warning. By the time a vaguely familiar figure emerged through the double swing doors, I could practically taste a sick dread rising up from some unspeakable well within me. The memory of Maddie's still and unmoving mouth beneath mine, the frantic searching for a pulse under my inexperienced fingers was something that would haunt me forever, whatever happened next.

Ryan got to his feet and extended his hand to the doctor. There was recognition on both of their faces, and suddenly I realised why the doctor looked familiar. He'd been Maddie's physician. The fact that he'd been summoned to attend to her now should have calmed and reassured me. Instead it did the exact opposite.

Hope had thankfully fallen asleep, curled up in a ball on the vinyl chairs, allowing the doctor to speak frankly to us both. Even before he began to talk, I knew the news was bad. I recognised that look. I'd seen doctors and nurses employ it more times than I cared to remember when I'd worked on the geriatric ward. I'd seen it too at first-hand, when the doctors had taken me aside from my own mother's hospital bed.

'Obviously we will continue to do all that we can for Maddie, but—'

'I don't understand,' I said, my voice sounding almost angry. 'Was it the flu that made her fall? Is that what happened?'

There was a look of compassion on the doctor's face, and also one of regret. 'I don't believe Maddie has the flu.'

Ryan and I shared an equally confused look. I asked the question we were both thinking: 'Then what happened? Why did she collapse?'

In answer the doctor walked a few steps further away from our sleeping child and motioned towards a row of vinyl chairs, indicating that we should sit down.

'Maddie has been experiencing certain problems over the last month or so.'

My eyes went to Ryan, as if secrets had been kept from me. Secrets he knew about. But the shocked expression on his face told me he was as much in the dark as I was.

'What problems?'

The consultant appeared unfazed by our reaction. No doubt he had seen them all. Grief hits families in many different ways. And despite what anyone might say to the contrary, we *were,* most definitely, Maddie's family.

'We had reason to believe the after-effects of her coma were beginning to present themselves. She had developed symptoms that were causing us considerable concern.'

'So why didn't you do something about them?' Ryan's voice was a curious mixture of grief and anger.

'Because Maddie wouldn't allow us to. Not yet. She was adamant; she refused to come in for any of the tests until the end of October. She said whatever we had to do would have to wait until then.' The consultant looked genuinely pained that his hands had been tied. 'She never would explain what was so important that she had to delay her own treatment.'

I looked over at Hope. Fast asleep, dreaming of a happier day; a different day; one that wouldn't end with the destruction of her world.

'Me,' I said, my voice small but knowing. '*I* was the reason she was waiting. She wanted me to get better first. She put me—' I shook my head, because that wasn't right either. I looked at Ryan and then slowly back at Hope. My family. The most precious thing in my world. How could I not have seen that we were also the most precious thing in Maddie's too. 'She put us first,' I said sadly.

The room was quiet and although I had never set foot in it before, it was horribly familiar. Ryan had taken Hope down to the cafeteria to get something to eat, but I had refused to go.

'Someone should stay with her,' I said, my eyes locking on his as we travelled back to another time and place where we'd both said these words before.

'You've not been well,' Ryan protested, his eyes travelling over my face.

'I'm well enough to sit with her,' I insisted determinedly. 'I'm not leaving her until Bill gets here.' Ryan nodded slowly.

I was glad when he and Hope had left for the cafeteria. I stood at the edge of the room and was rocked by the feeling of déjà vu. 'Hello, Maddie. It's Chloe.' The old greeting tripped from my lips like liquid honey.

I pulled up a chair beside the bed and reached for her hand. It was cool and utterly immobile. With difficulty I wound our fingers around each other. I needed to make sure she could feel me. I had to believe that she still could.

'The thing is,' the consultant had said before leading us to the room where Maddie was lying, 'we never really understood what had happened to make her wake up a year ago. It never made sense – not medically. It was almost unheard of. But this regression; this slipping back into a coma . . . Well, I have to be honest, we have no idea what's caused that either. But this, or something like it, has always been our biggest fear. Maddie knew that, right from the very beginning. She always knew this could happen.'

I reached up a hand and smoothed a straying strand of Maddie's long dark hair back from her forehead. I would bring a hairbrush on my next visit. She looked as beautiful now as she had always done. Asleep or awake, Madeline

Chambers remained not just the most beautiful woman I had ever seen, but also the bravest and the kindest.

'And so, here we are again, my friend,' I said quietly to the woman who could no longer hear me. I squeezed her hand, desperate for even the smallest sign that she knew I was there beside her.

'I was wrong, wasn't I?' I asked the comatose woman in the hospital bed. It was surprisingly easy to fall back into the familiar habit of talking to her in this way. 'And yet I was also right too.'

Awake I knew she would have challenged me, but now I would have to talk for us both. 'I thought I'd come into Ryan and Hope's life to fulfil a purpose. I thought I was there to help them heal after you left them. And when you woke up, I thought I was no longer needed. My job was done. I thought that was why I got sick. But I was wrong, wasn't I?'

I gave her a moment in case she felt like jumping in, but although her chest rose and fell, she was somewhere else. Somewhere she had been once before.

'But one of us *did* come back because they were needed. One of us found a pathway out of the darkness to a place where her family were waiting.'

I lifted Maddie's hand to my lips and tenderly kissed the smooth white skin. 'I couldn't have got through the last few months without you. You know that, don't you? You've been the rock I needed to lean on. You've been there for me, and for Ryan, but most of all, you've been there for Hope.' I reached out and gently stroked her hair. 'I'm so glad she got the chance to know what an amazing and incredible woman her mother is. I'm glad *I* got to know.'

I leant over and kissed the porcelain perfection of one pale white cheek.

'Sleep well, my friend. For now. And when you're strong enough, make sure you find a way to come back to us again, Miracle Girl.'

Epilogue

Ten Years Later

Hope

There was a sudden break in the traffic and the cluster of pedestrians at the crossing surged like scurrying beetles into the road, leaving me standing alone at the kerb, the only one rigorously heeding the little red man's warning. The road was empty, I could see that, but I never took risks when crossing. And besides, it would be really bad form to get knocked down right outside of a hospital.

It was warm inside the building, and I knew I was going to regret the thick jumper I was wearing by the end of my visit. I climbed into the lift with a group of other visitors. Most of them were carrying something for the patients they were going to see: magazines, flowers, one or two of them were even holding the clichéd bunch of grapes. But my hands were empty.

I found my way to her room on autopilot, and knocked lightly on the door before slipping inside.

'Hello. It's Hope.' I crossed to the bed and bent to kiss her cheek. I shrugged out of my jacket and drew one of the chairs closer to the bed, before reaching for Maddie's hand and taking it in mine.

'So what's new with you?' I asked chirpily, and then paused just in case this would be the day when she chose to open her eyes and say: *Well, actually, Hope* ... I gave a small snigger, knowing I'd probably fall off my chair or have a heart attack, or maybe even both if that happened.

'Okay. Well, I'll go first then, shall I?' I launched into a detailed account of everything that had happened at school since my last visit three weeks earlier. 'And I got an A on that History test.' It was hard having a parent who didn't seem to care what score you got, good or bad. Sometimes it was the small silly things like that which hurt the most.

'Mum said she'll be coming to see you on Friday.' I leant closer to the bed, as though sharing a secret. 'She has a book she's going to read to you. I warn you, it sounds very dull.' I let that information sit with her for a minute. 'So I reckon now would be a good time to wake up, so you don't have to endure another boring historical saga.' I was always doing this, giving her small incentives to wake up. As though all she was waiting for was a good enough reason to finally open her eyes. So far, she'd managed to resist every single one of them.

But surely today I had the best reason of all. 'In case you'd forgotten or lost track of the date, I thought I should probably remind you that it's my sixteenth birthday next week.'

I glanced down at the woman who still looked so much like me that even *I* found it freaky. 'Obviously I know you won't have got me anything, so don't worry about that.'

I looked down at my mother's unmoving eyelids. She really did look as though she was sleeping. I mean, I like sleep as much as the next teenager, but my mother had taken it to a whole new level. Ten years – well sixteen, if you add the first coma in too. Surely enough was enough by now?

'I'm going to have a party,' I said, hoping to lure her back to us with something she wouldn't be able to turn down. Except of course she'd silently declined all offers to join me at my last nine birthday parties, so why should this one be any different?

I sighed and glanced around the room. Even though it was December there was an enormous vase of sunflowers on the window ledge. There always had been, for as long as I could remember. And it was always in exactly the same place, so that when she opened her eyes (he always said 'when', and never 'if') it would be the first thing that she saw.

I smiled. 'Do you want to know a secret?' I asked my silent mother. She said nothing, so I took that as a 'yes'. 'I've met a boy.'

This would be a good moment for her eyes to fly open in shock, I thought. But there was no flicker of awareness on her face. I looked down at my third parent, the one who never told me off, never told me to tidy my room, or got cross when I came home late. I laid my head down on the mattress, right beside her hand, making it easy for her to stroke my head ... just in case she wanted to. 'I always thought you'd come back in time to give me advice about boys and stuff,' I said sadly. 'I mean, I know I could ask Mum, but, between the two of us, I think you know more about that kind of thing than her.'

I lifted my head and looked at the beautiful woman whose voice I could no longer remember, not even in my dreams. 'Did you have a boyfriend when you were my age?' I sighed sadly. 'There's too many things I want to ask you; too many things that only you can tell me.'

I pulled my chair closer to the bed. 'Couldn't you just try to let me know that you can hear me?' I pleaded. 'You don't have to do much. Just move your hand ... or just one finger, if that's easier?' I focused my gaze on the long slim fingers resting on top of the white sheet. They didn't move, and I felt guilty for trying to bully her awake.

'I'm sorry. I know you'd come back if you could. I guess it's not time yet.'

When I bent down to kiss her goodbye our hair mingled on the pillow, making it impossible to see where hers ended and mine began. So much joined me to her, and yet so much separated us.

'I'll come back and see you on my birthday. We'll celebrate together. How would that be?' I whispered into her ear.

In my head she answered; in my head she said that she

was looking forward to it; in my head she said that she loved me.

'I love you too, Mum,' I said, a little embarrassed at the way my voice was breaking. 'I'll see you soon.'

The room was quiet after the girl left. Rain was beginning to lash against the windows, and daylight was fading, setting long mysterious shadows free to dance upon the walls. But in a room full of silence even a tiny sound is deafening. It was faint at first, practically indiscernible, but gradually it grew louder as the woman's index finger first twitched and then began to move backwards and forwards over the starched hospital sheet, not just once, but again, and again, and again . . .

Acknowledgements

Writing is a solitary profession, but producing a book requires the talents and skills of a whole army of people. When I look back over my shoulder, I'm incredibly thankful to see a small squadron who worked tirelessly to produce the book you've just read, and whose unofficial job description could well include 'making my dreams come true'. And guess what ... they've done it again.

A huge thank you to all the skilled professionals at Simon & Schuster, with special gratitude to my editor Jo Dickinson for her wisdom, patience and support. Thanks also to Emma Capron, Sara-Jade Virtue, Jessica Barratt and a whole host of talented individuals who make the magic happen. It's a very special family to be a part of, and I'm very happy to call it home.

Thanks also to my agent Kate Burke from Diane Banks Associates, who continues to safely navigate me (both figuratively and literally) through the world of publishing. I wouldn't want to do this without you, Kate.

To my friend and fellow author Kate Thompson, thank you for your enthusiasm when I first outlined this story to you, and your inspired suggestion (made over a salt beef bagel . . . long story) which took the end of the book down a different path – and made it all the better because of it.

A special thank you to Martin Ingram, who has been my optician for over thirty years. Not only did Martin provide me with invaluable information regarding Chloe's eye tests and allow me to borrow his name, he has also managed to stop me walking into objects for the last three decades! The blame for any mistakes or tweaked facts in those scenes is mine alone.

Writing about serious medical conditions is something to be undertaken with both respect and caution. Walking a tightrope between medical facts and telling a story that is purely fiction is a tricky balancing act, and I hope readers will forgive me for any liberties I may have taken in order to bring you the story of Maddie and Chloe.

One person who was instrumental in helping me to tell Chloe's tale (because largely it is *her own* story) is a woman I'm extremely proud to call my friend, Bev Leverton, to whom this book is dedicated. I could think of no better blue-print for Chloe than Bev, who I've known for over twenty years; who is the only woman I've ever entrusted to look after my own children; and who I have never once heard complain about her condition. Behind that enormous smile and generous heart is a true hero, and a totally lovely person. Thanks for all your help, Bev, for answering dozens of inane emailed questions, and for the three-hour-long phone call!

There's one group of people I would particularly like to thank, because without them, I simply wouldn't have a job. To the readers, bloggers and reviewers, thank you for parting with your money and buying a ticket into a world I've created. I hope you've enjoyed the journey, I hope you've met some interesting people on your travels and that before long you'll come back. You are always welcome.

And lastly, to the three people who are my world. No matter how many miles separate us, your love and support is always there, waiting, when I reach out for it. Ralph, Kimberley and Luke, thank you for telling me I could do this; *should* do this; and smiling on proudly when I finally did.

FIND OUT MORE ABOUT

DANI ATKINS

Dani Atkins novels are jam-packed with emotion and
family drama. You won't be able to put them down.

To find out more about her writing, visit
www.SimonandSchuster.co.uk or follow Dani
on twitter: @AtkinsDani

All of Dani's books are available to buy now
in print, eBook and eAudio

Dani Atkins
Our Song

He's the love of *her* life. He's *your* husband.

This is the story of Ally and Charlotte, whose paths
have intersected over the years though they've never really
been close friends. Charlotte married Ally's ex and first
true love, David. Fate is about to bring them together one
last, dramatic time and change their lives forever.

Full of Dani's signature warmth and emotion,
this is a gripping and emotional family drama. With
breathtaking plot twists, Dani explores themes of
serendipity, friendship and love. What would you do if
your husband was the love of somebody else's life? And
when faced with an agonising decision, could you
put the past behind you and do the right thing?

'Truly magnificent storytelling'
Veronica Henry

**SIMON &
SCHUSTER**

Dani Atkins
This Love

Sophie stopped believing in happy endings a
long time ago, but could this love change all of that?

Sophie Winter lives in a self-imposed cocoon – she's a
single, thirty-one-year-old translator who works from
home in her one bedroom flat. This isn't really the life she
dreamed of, but then Sophie stopped believing in happy
endings a very long time ago, when she was fifteen years
old and tragedy struck her family. Her grief has left her
scared of commitment and completely risk averse. Sophie
understands she has a problem, but recognising it and
knowing how to fix it are two entirely different things.

But one night a serious fire breaks out in the flat
below hers. Sophie is trapped in the burning building
until a passer-by, Ben, sees her and rescues her. Suddenly
her world is shattered – what will be the consequences
of this second life-changing event?

'Dani Atkins is the undisputed queen of fiction that
packs a huge emotional punch, and this captivating
story is another outstanding example' *heat*

SIMON &
SCHUSTER

booksandthecity.co.uk
the home of female fiction

BOOKS | NEWS & EVENTS | FEATURES | AUTHOR PODCASTS | COMPETITIONS

Follow us online to be the first to hear from
your favourite authors

booksandthecity.co.uk

books and the city

@TeamBATC

Join our mailing list for the latest news, events and
exclusive competitions

Sign up at
booksandthecity.co.uk